I0542136

Crestfield

This book is a work of fiction. Names, characters, places and incidents are products of the author's imagination or are used fictitiously. Any resemblance to actual events or locales or persons, living or dead, is entirely coincidental

Copyright © 2014 by jack

All rights reserved

ISBN 978-0-692-10179-7

Edited by Junior

Technical support by Randi

Crestfield

Crestfield is a small town. Matter of fact, it has always been a small town and I suppose it always will be. But to me it's as big as a town needs to be. Even though Crestfield is small, the slow rolling hills and the immense cornfields that surround us make our little fiefdom feel as big as the sky. When I was a boy, my grandpa once told me that at the far end of every cornfield lies a silver stairway to heaven. I knew that night I'd find me a stairway, if only in my dreams.

I believe there are few things in this world of ours more pleasurable than fresh air and a clear view of the point where the green earth and the blue sky convene. Here in horizon country we don't have skyscrapers sullying our view of the heavens. Tall buildings can crush a body's spirit and torment the soul. And if you're lookin' for fancy, chances are you won't find it in Crestfield, but you will find a lot of good, honest, hardworking people. And for my money there's not a whole lot else that really matters. Yes, from time to time Mother Nature can be tough on us, but there are two sides to every coin. And for every winter there's the renewed hope that blossoms bright in spring. And without fail, our steamy summers always lead us to the rich colors of fall. All in all, I'd say we've got it pretty darn good.

"Dad, who are you talking to?"

"Myself. I'm talking to myself. You got a problem with me talking to myself?"

"No, but can you be quiet for a while?"

That's my son, Jack. Family and friends call him Junior. Now and then when folks are in a pinch they address him as Officer McCool. He's smarter than I am; leastwise that's what my eldest daughter, Madison, says.

Junior is fair-haired, tall, and blue eyed, just like his mother, but muscular and barrel chested like my side of the family. He's kinda intimidating with his rigid, athletic way of moving, but he's actually a gentle soul. He has always been a whiz-kid, so it wasn't a big surprise when he returned from college with a couple of diplomas. He keeps them on the wall uptown in his office. His sisters and brother all admire and look up to him. I believe the folks in Crestfield would agree that, all things considered, Junior turned out to be a very nice young man.

"Dad! Please stop that. Maggie stay close to Dad - close, close, good girl."

Maggie rubbed her shoulder against me and then Miller yelled, "Over here!" At least it sounded like Miller to me.

I walked toward the voice, with Maggie of course, and then Junior told me to be quiet again. I was getting angrier by the second. Imagine my own son treating me like some child. Then we stopped.

"Junior, why are we stopping?"

"Hello Mill– oh good lord, she's been cut to ribbons. Mercy sakes, who would do something like this? Is this the way you found her? I mean, have you moved anything?"

"No Junior, I haven't moved a thing."

"Junior, who has been cut to ribbons and what is that smell?" I asked.

"Dad please, you have to move back. Maggie! Back, back, take Dad back. Good girl."

Maggie is my German shepherd guide dog. She's been with me for a little over a year now. I don't know how I ever got along without her. She means the world to me. Heck, I wouldn't–"

"Junior, what kind of god-forsaken monster would do something like this?" Miller asked.

"Miller, is that you?" I asked.

"Dad, please. Yes, it's Miller, but please don't talk right now. Miller, I'm so sorry, look, I don't know what to tell you. When was the last time you remember seeing her?"

"I saw her yesterday grazing out in the back pasture with the others. She wasn't there this mornin', so I set out lookin' and found her here. Junior, there's something else you better have a look at. Got a bunch of strange prints coming in from and going back out to 25. You ever seen anybody that wears rectangular shoes, cuz that's all there is, a bunch of prints that are about a foot long and maybe 6 inches wide," Miller said.

"What? Dad you stay here. Maggie, you stay, stay girl. Dad, stay here, we'll be right back."

"I want to go with you!" I demanded.

"No, stay here, we'll be right back. Come on Miller, show me the prints."

They walked away and left me standing there like some idiot. I thought of that old sign out on the road that leads to Miller's farm. You can't tell what the sign says now cuz it's been shot at so many times. I have to admit that during my youth I shot it a few times myself. It's a small black and white sign with a 25 in the middle. As far as I know, that old road runs all the way down thru Mizzeruh.

As they walked back, I heard Junior telling Miller that something rectangular was tied to their feet. Probably to disguise the size and type of shoe they were wearing. Why would anyone do that? I suppose so's they wouldn't get caught. All the same, it'd be difficult to walk with rectangles tied to your feet.

"Junior, what is going on? Tell me right now! Just cuz I can't see you doesn't mean you can't see me. I'm right here, dog-gonnit."

"Dad, can you just listen and be quiet for a little bit? Please."

"Junior, I'm no dummy, so don't you treat me like one. Miller, tell my son I used to be good at many things. Tell him, Miller, please."

Miller didn't say a word.

I've been friends with Miller Bartles since about second grade and he never did have a whole lot to say. Like most of the folks around these parts he's a hardworking, keep your nose to the grindstone kinda guy.

"Come on, Miller, say some–"

"Dad! It's ok, Miller. Dad, I know all about the things you could do, but you said you'd be quiet if I let you ride out here with me. Please, Dad, this is very serious."

I started to give 'em both a piece of my mind for ignoring me when I heard the radio in the police car squawk.

"Miller, I'd better get that, it's probably Tommy calling from the station. I've got to let him know what's going on here. I'll be right back. Maggie girl, you stay close to Dad. Close, close, good girl."

Tommy is my brother. Fact is, he's my oldest brother. He's the Chief of Police and a good'n. Least that's what I hear. I guess we look as much alike as most brothers do. Except he has black hair and I have brown. And Tommy is built kinda like a bear and I'm built more like a, you know I've never really thought about it, but I guess maybe I'm built like a monkey. I like monkeys. Anyhow, I knew when Junior left it might be my only chance to find out what was going on. So I asked.

3

"Miller, can you please explain what the heck is going on here?"

"Jack," he softly said. "Someone or some-thing has cut up one of my cows and left everything here on butcher paper. It's just plain sickening."

"You say there's butcher paper right out here in this field?"

"Yes, and that isn't the half of it. When I first got here, the poor cow was still alive."

"Miller, are you ok - you sure about that? How'd you know the cow was still alive?"

"I knew she was still alive because I heard her moo. Then when I got here, she looked up at me. She had big old tears running down her face, never seen anything like it. I had no idea an animal could cry. I could not bear to see her suffer any longer, so I went back in the house and got my rifle and put her out of her misery. Who would do such a despicable thing?"

"No, Miller, the question is why anyone would do such a thing. Aren't all of your cows Holstein's?"

"Yes, she would have been for milking."

I heard footsteps, but they were soft - like a girl's steps. Then Miller told his wife Becky to go back in the house. She must have seen what was layin' there because she began to ball. She didn't say hi, so I did.

"Becky, please go back inside, oh to hell with it. Come on sweetie, I'll walk you back."

I heard her cry some more, and hard.

"Oh Lord, what's next?" Miller asked as he and his wife slowly walked away.

I was standing there all alone, with Maggie of course. I could hear singing from the trees that surround Miller's fishing hole, which some dummies call a pond. Then it came to me, I had one of them great ideas that only come along once every blue moon. It had rained the night before and there was no mistaking the smell of the abundant rich soil all around me. I sat down and took off my shoes and socks. I dug my fingers and toes deep into the moist black earth and it felt so good I just had to tell someone. "Maggie girl, this is without question one of the best doggone feelings in the whole wide world."

4

She panted an 'I know' back to me and then licked me across the cheek. As I sat, I could see the raging red and orange leaves covering the old hackberry trees surrounding Miller's pond. Maggie and I were peaceful as all get-out. Then I looked deep down inside myself so I could remember what things looked like when I was a boy.

I saw dozens of Blue Jays up in the trees whispering to each other. They were gossiping about all the goings-on at the farm. They chucked and clicked and softly whirred a beautifully orchestrated song; they sounded like the milk falling on my rice crispies in the morning. Oh, how I wish I'd wake up some day and not have to imagine such things, but imagining is a lot better than doin' nothing. The Blue Jays weren't alone. Even though I couldn't see 'em I could hear a volery of Yellow-headed Blackbirds. They declared just like a garden full of rusty gates as they hopped over each other in their flurry to glean seeds off the ground. And from a distant mezzanine I saw a tiding of Black-billed Magpie's lingering on white fence posts. They were waiting for a chance at the ripening carrion that lay next to me. I'd just looked up at a Red-shouldered Hawk circling high in the cobalt sky when Junior walked back and started in on me.

"Dad! What the heck are you doing? Gosh! Come on, put your... oh wait a second 'til I go get a towel out of the car."

He walked away in a huff. He's good at huffing, but not near as good as he is at saying gosh. He ran back.

"Dad, here let me clean you off. Why would you go sticking your feet in the dirt? Gosh! Not your hands too. Stop laughing, this isn't funny. Ok, ok. Dad, please don't start crying, please don't cry. You go ahead and laugh if you want. What? Yes, there are too many wicked people in the world. Yes Dad, I will catch all of them. What? I'm gonna take you home right now. Ricky and Jake from the rendering plant are on their way out here. Ricky's gonna take some pictures and then Jake's gonna take her home. Yes, they'll be nice to the cow. Feel better now? Good. Dad, let me take a few more notes here and then we'll head home."

I stopped blubbering and listened to Junior write in his little notebook.

"Junior, why do you take so many notes?"

"I take notes because sometimes I can't see the forest for the trees."

"What the heck does that even mean?"

"It means there have been too many times when I re-read my notes and figure something out. It's usually something that was staring me right in the face when I first took the notes, but I just couldn't see it. The notes help me organize my thoughts."

"I get it. The notes help you keep your ducks in a row," I said.

"You know Dad, you slay me sometimes. Yes, they help keep my ducks in a row."

"You're a good son, what would I do without you?"

"Thanks, let's go home, Dad. Come on, girl - you too."

I heard Junior on the talkie thing-a-majig all the way home. The worry and strain in his voice made me very sad.

Crestfield Police Station   2

***Junior*/Nearly two weeks had come and gone** since the day I took Dad out to Miller's farm. Our local newspaper, the Crestfield Canon, ran an article about Miller's cow that covered the entire front page. That day the Canon set a record for the number of papers sold in a single day. There was a paper-boy and even a few paper-girls on every corner. Didn't matter whether you were a farmer or not, it was the talk of the town. As a police force, we did all we could to keep what we knew under our hats, but remember it is a small town.

Fingers were being pointed in all directions, it was infectious. And when an unknown vehicle or a stranger passed by, well, they had a finger pointed at them too. There had been enough rumor and innuendo to start a small riot. Thank goodness that never happened. The story received so much attention we were even mentioned on the national news stations. Farmers and the hard work they do are central to our character and way of life here in the Midwest. We're very proud of who we are. So, although the publicity we received wasn't what we considered to be positive, it was publicity none the less. And some folks ate it up. We found out right away from our coroner, Lloyd Brown, that an animal tranquilizer called Acepromazine had been used to calm the cow enough to lead her out to the road. But Lloyd said there was another drug used to paralyze the cow that he couldn't identify. So, he and the rest of us patiently waited for the toxicology report to come back from none other than the FBI. No question about it – it caused a stir, it was oddly stimulating.

Anticipation rose to a boil when one of our police officers called in to tell us he had just found a note placed under the windshield wiper on his police cruiser. He believed it was from the person that had cut up the cow.

"Ricky should be here in a few minutes. The note or letter he found was left on his roller," my Uncle Tommy softly said.

Roller is Ricky slang for police car.

Ricky Reed is and has been my best friend since we were - well, since I can remember. He's a tall, skinny, red-headed and freckled high energy guy, with a smile that can sure light up a room. There's not a person in town that doesn't know and like Ricky. Dad says I'm lucky to have someone like him working alongside me, and I believe Dad's right.

Dad told you we live in a small town. How small? Well, we only have four full-time and three part-time police officers in Crestfield. My Uncle Tommy is the Chief, Ricky is our number one patrol officer, and I am the town detective. Those are our official titles, but now and then we switch places. Not on purpose, it just happens that way.

Sometimes for the Fourth of July, a parade, or a high school football game we deputize our trusted part-time officers - Johnny Bose, better known as Shadow and our close family friend, Matt Healey, who is like a brother to all of us. We're comfortable with the two of them because they're dependable and adhere to the laws. Well, except for the fact that now and then they like to fight first and ask questions later.

We have a part-time meter maid named Rita Streams. Everybody knows Rita only works the middle of the day so a little less money goes in the meters during the morning and evening hours.

And finally, we have one full-time do-it-all dispatcher, my youngest sister, Randi. She wears a uniform just like ours and goes out on calls all the time. She looks a lot like me, but she's stouter and has an attitude about her that says, you're gonna mess with fire if you mess with me.

Randi's also the best marksman in the county, if not the entire state. People around these parts say she could part a fly's hair even if the fly was sitting on a moving cow three cornfields away. A bit of an embellishment, but then again from what I've seen, maybe not. Whoops, to be continued - Ricky just drove up.

Ricky came storming into the station. He has the darndest sideways way of walking. It's like he's walking a straight line, but he's turned talking to somebody. And that somebody is always on his right side. He was walking his walk, but with a renewed bounce in his step.

"Hey Ricky - how you doin'?"

"Hey pardner, I'm fine and dandy and have I got news for you."

"Yeah, so I heard. Tommy already told me, but I sure want to hear what you think about this letter you found. By the way, where is it?"

"I've got the doggone letter right here in my pocket." Ricky set his RC Cola and half-eaten Moon Pie down on his desk. As usual the bottom of the RC bottle was full of peanuts. "You know this guy has a lot of nerve apologizing for doing something like that. What a sick mother–"

"Ricky! Don't say it - Randi can hear you."

"So," he said.

"Sew buttons on your underwear. There's no need for talk like that. So let's try to keep it professional, ok? We gotta find this perp, and the sooner the better," I stressed.

While I was talking, Tommy quietly walked into the office behind Ricky and stood without saying a word. When he said hello, Ricky nearly jumped out of his skin.

"Doggone it Tommy, you know I hate it when you sneak up on me like that," Ricky scolded.

"Sorry Ricky, but Junior's right. We've gotta find this guy and in a hurry, but without rushing."

Ricky stood there with his mouth agape before he said, "Tommy, what did you just say? I know what a circle is and you just took me around one. How can we hurry without rushing?"

"Ricky, what Tommy means is if we rush we might miss something, but if we don't find this person, and soon, he might do it again," I explained.

"Oh no, says in the letter that he ain't gonna do it again," Ricky responded.

Tommy was running out of patience and raised his voice a little when he said, "Ricky, please explain how you found the note."

"Well, I was out on 34 and Charlotte waved me down as I drove by the Chicken Inn. She said Earl Jenkins had fallen asleep at the bar and they couldn't get him to wake up and go home. I went in and shook Earl real hard, she was right; he wasn't wakin' up for nothin'. Lester was there washing down the floors and I told him to go ahead and throw a bucketful of soapy water on Earl. Lester did and Earl woke up in a hurry and started swingin'. You know Earl's a great big guy and it took both Lester and me a long time to get him wrestled to the ground. We finally had him quiet–"

"Ricky! Gosh darn it. You can't just stand there and talk all day like that. Tommy and I have been here listening for long enough. Now when did you find the note and where is it?"

"Ok, ok, gee-whiz, when I walked outside with Earl I saw something flappin' in the wind on the passenger side of my windshield."

Tommy gave Ricky one of his looks.

"Tommy, you sure can give a guy the jumpin' willies lookin' like that," Ricky said followed by a shiver.

Tommy repeated the look and Ricky fast as can be reached in his pocket and pulled out a wadded-up piece of butcher paper. Tommy put on a pair of rubber gloves and unfolded the paper. There was a message typed on it. He flipped the paper over, front to back, and then front again. Then he spread the paper out on the desk and we all silently read.

Dear Crestfield Police,

I'm sorry you had to take the time to drive all the way out to Miller's farm to see my handiwork. It's not perfect, but heck a cow is an awfully big canvas to work with, maybe too big. I was just practicing, so no worries. Oh yeah, tell the farmers I won't be harming any more of their precious animals. You have a good day and thanks for all your hard work.

To Hell with the Devil, 4114

After we'd all read and re-read the letter several times, Tommy looked straight at Ricky for a moment before he spoke.

"Ricky, did you grab hold of the paper with your bare hands?" Tommy asked.

Ricky stuttered, "At, at first I did. How else was I supposed to pick it up? I mean I had no idea what it was. Then it hit me that this was from somebody that knows something about Miller's cow. I put my keys on it to hold it down. Then I ran around my roller and opened up the front door. I grabbed my gloves off the seat and put 'em on. I only touched the paper with my bare hands on a couple of corners or so."

Ricky had no sooner finished explaining when Randi walked in the room. She was acting just a little too cool and calm. It was plain to see there was something on her mind and it was something important. She hurried up and said, "That was Lloyd on the phone and he says the cow was drugged and drugged good. I mean knocked out, but at the same time awake."

As I said earlier, Lloyd Brown is the county coroner and the kind of guy that takes forever to get things done. Says it's necessary so that he can be thorough and not miss important stuff. According to him he's always shorthanded. Usually we have to call him so it was strange for him to call us. And I wanted to know why.

"What kind of drug are you talking about? Did Lloyd say what it was?" I asked.

Randi stood there for a moment without saying a word. She knew we were all dying to find out, but I guess she decided to make us beg. So the three of us stepped closer, turned an ear her way, and waited.

Finally, she looked down and pulled a folded piece of paper out of her back pocket.

"One of you guys is going to have to read it because I can't pronounce the word and I tried several times," Randi said.

Tommy calmly put his reading glasses back on and slowly read, "strychnos-curare."

We all just looked at each other and then Tommy said that he'd actually heard of the drug curare. He said he was pretty sure it was the black pasty drug that the Indians of the Amazon use to bring down monkeys and other animals. He said it renders them paralyzed, but not dead.

"I've read about the drug in crime novels. If you keep the victim breathing, you can cut off an arm or a leg. They'd know what you were doing, but because they're paralyzed they wouldn't be able to do a darn thing about it. It would be sheer torture. But in the books, it was always used on people, not animals. That must be what happened to poor Miller's cow," Tommy said with a grimace.

"Yes, Tommy, that's almost exactly what Lloyd told me," Randi agreed.

"Man, that sure is creepy. Strick-no-cuh what?" Ricky muttered. "How'd you say it Tommy?"

Still confused, we all looked at Tommy again. So he repeated the word three times.

"Curare, Cure-ar-ee, Curare."

Ricky blurted out, "Sounds like Ferrari, but with a c."

Tommy patted Ricky on the back and softly said, "You got it, Ricky."

"Ok, where do we go from here? I mean this guy's here in Crestfield not the Amazon," I said.

"Maybe the person we're looking for isn't a guy, maybe it's a girl?" Ricky offered.

"I don't believe so, Ricky. From what I know about mutilation and torture, the field is pretty much entirely male. There's something about the power and domination factor that men with fragile egos need. Anywho, that rules out most women. Well, except for those dominatrix gals. But in the end they are actually giving in to what the male wants and pays for. They're just doing it on their own terms. No, this is a male and a sick one. I think we need to have our guard up because this guy is not your average bear, and you can take that to the bank. This guy is not rehearsing to be a butcher either. Least not the kind of butcher we see at the neighborhood grocery. We need to find him and like I said, the sooner the better. Now getting past the gender question, one of the first things we need to do is figure out what forty-one fourteen means. Anyone have any ideas or thoughts on the matter?" I asked.

Everyone just kinda sat and stared at each other. Smoke was beginning to ease out of our ears when Ricky says, "Hey, maybe it has something to do with the bible. You know some passage with a hidden meaning."

"That's a good thought Ricky. And since you thought of it, I'm putting you in charge of asking the local heads of church what it might mean," I said.

Ricky nodded ok, but his eyes said no. He started to say something - I didn't let him.

"There's something there - we know that just from him signing to hell with the devil. Ok, Tommy, Ricky, Randi, do you think he's saying I don't like the devil or is he saying I'm going to hell to be with the devil?"

Again, nobody said a word which was not that unusual for Tommy, but for the other two it was something of a miracle. Finally, and at exactly the same time, Ricky and Randi both said, "It's his initials."

"You mean where the letters of his initials are in the alphabet?" I asked.

They both nodded yes.

I was thinking out loud at that point and said, "It's an idea that needs to be explored, but I have my doubts because not that many people have four names."

Then Tommy stood up. He does that when he wants what he says to be crystal clear.

"The letters could be any combination of the numbers that are here. Or maybe it's two people? Doesn't really matter, we catch one, we'll catch the other."

He was right, which gave us even more pause. He let us stew on it for only a half-a-minute or so before he meted out our duties.

"Ok, we know a lot more now than we did yesterday, and it's time to get out there and find this guy. But before we do anything, I'm going to warn the three of you that you cannot for any reason let anyone know what we know. This person has been quiet for a couple weeks now, and we want to keep him that way. He wrote us because he has a need to brag and we're going to let him. Psychologically speaking this person is not walking on the same side of the street that we are, but don't be fooled, he's very dangerous. For now here's what I want you guys to start with. Ricky, you didn't seem that excited about the forty-one fourteen thing so I'll check on that. You need to keep your eyes peeled and your ear to the ground. Junior, I want you to go down to Clarinda and see if there are any new releases. You might want to check in with the Sheriff too."

We looked at each other after the Sheriff was mentioned. Tommy and the Sheriff do not get along. I thought, *no wonder he asked me.* Tommy turned and looked at Randi.

"Randi, you need to stay by the phone. I've got a feeling this guy is going to get brave and give us a call. Ok, let's get out there and remember - not a word about any of this."

The very next morning the letter and the drug we discussed in private were plastered in big letters on the front page of the Canon. It read:

FBI *finds* **Curare,** *the knock out drug...*
  Killer apologizes and then brags...

Didn't take long for Tommy to walk over to the building where the paper is printed, it's next door. The person Tommy was looking for was sitting and waiting at his desk.

That person is Burt Silvers, owner, editor, and top reporter for the Crestfield Canon.

Dad says Burt is a shifty, loud-mouthed, bald headed baked potato. I admit it's an unbecoming description, but it is a fairly accurate one.

"Morning, Tommy, I've been expecting you," Burt said with false bravado. "And before you start in on me it was not one of your people that told us about the drug."

"Ok Burt, then who was it?"

"Now, Tommy, you know we can't reveal our sources. We have rights, we're protected."

"Burt, I'm not going to care about any rights you think you have if something you print sets our person off. If he harms another animal or worse yet a person, you have my word that I will walk over here and arrest you. That's after I throw you on the ground and handcuff you. Are we clear on that?"

"Tommy, just because your brother is the mayor, it doesn't give you the right to throw your weight around."

"Ajax has nothing to do with this, so you leave him out of it. I meant what I said about arresting you. Do you understand me, Burt?"

"Yeah, I understand this is not high school. You can't just go around throwing people on the ground, Tommy. There are laws."

"Yes, there are laws, and you're looking at them. Don't push me on this, Burt."

Tommy turned and slowly walked toward the front door to leave when Burt stood up and hollered, "Just because you're sober right now doesn't mean diddly-squat Tommy! I knew you when!"

Tommy immediately turned and watched Burt run into his bathroom and lock the door. Tommy had demons, but we were all comfortable in the feeling that the demons were behind him now. It wasn't something we ever talked about, it was just understood. When Tommy walked back in the station, I could see the humility and hurt written all over his face. I thought maybe it would be best if I left him alone.

"Tommy, I'm gonna take Dad down to Clarinda Cove." I gently posed. He didn't respond, acted as if he didn't hear a word I said.

"Dad hasn't seen Madison for a couple of weeks now and little by little it does seem to help. Think I'll do as you suggested and ask the doctors if there's anyone there that has a history of hurting animals or who might want to hurt animals and such. It's worth a try."

Tommy didn't say a word, he just gave me a nod yes. That day the Canon went on to break the record for the number of papers sold in a single day it had set just two weeks previous.

**Madison**/**Being the daughter** of a man like Jack McCool is not easy. And that is as kind as I can possibly be on the subject. I say that because if I was only his daughter that would be one thing, but I'm also his therapist. And that alone is extremely difficult, and I might add, quite unusual. According to most professionals, it's not just unusual, it's a bad idea. I understand that, but in fairness to both of us, there is no other option.

After Dad was in the accident, he received the best physical care and subsequent rehabilitation anyone could possibly hope for. But in terms of mental healthcare, which he sorely needed, well, he didn't have that kind of insurance. So there's only one-way Dad can receive the care he needs, and that's if it's free, enter me. Dad is still a complex person even though he suffers from a type of dementia that is worsening and has no equal. Trust me, I've read just about everything there is on the subject. At times, the things he says and does make perfect sense, but they're usually followed by thoughts of his that are fragmented and loosely connected. It's during these bizarre episodes when his behavior is tantamount to an unruly child.

In all fairness, he is not the person he would have been. Lately, due in part to his cognitive decline, he has been experiencing extremes. He's elated one second and then sad and quite depressed the next. Manic-depression is not that unusual, but having the episodes happen only moments apart is.

During our last few meetings we've been working on something in his head that he wants to see, but it just won't come to the surface. I've tried counseling, regression hypnosis, and drug therapy. But up to now there has been no significant progress. I've probably told you more than I should, but I figure it's for Dad. And now I'll have to let you go. Speak of the devil.

"Hi Dad, come here and give me a hug," I said.

Maggie walked Dad over to me and we hugged. It was one of Dad's short hugs, something was on his mind. Then Maggie let out a quick little bark that said, 'Hey, what about me?'

"Oh, you need a hug too don't you, Mags."

16

I knelt on one knee as Maggie walked over with her head down. After I hugged her, she gave me a lick or two on the face.

"Dad, I love this dog a little more each time I see her. It's amazing how much better off you are since she came into your life."

"Hey, you stay away from my girlfriend. I don't want you telling her things that aren't true."

Dad's humor is very subjective.

"Ok, Dad. Maggie girl go back to Dad. Close, close - good girl."

I noticed that Junior was pacing back and forth. He's a little edgy all the time, but this was at a fresher tempo than usual.

"Hi Junior, is there something on your mind?"

"Hi sis, no I'm fine. I'm going to take a walk down by that man-made pond you call a cove. I'm also going to talk to a few of your colleagues. I'll be back at eleven, is that ok with you?"

"Yes. Junior, be careful what you ask."

"I will. Dad, would it be ok if I take Maggie out for a walk?"

"Sure thing, the fresh air will be good for her. Maybe you can get her to chase a stick. She needs the exercise."

"You got it. Come on girl, Dads ok now - you can come with me."

Maggie didn't move a muscle 'til Dad said ok. Then she was off and running with Junior.

"Ok Dad, the last time you were here we talked our way through the accident and you said you had gained some peace with the whole thing. Do you still feel the same way?"

"I suppose so except I still don't understand why your mom couldn't wake up. Maddi, will you read the story to me?"

"Dad, please stay on task. I'll read you some of the story later. Ok, Dad, Dad! Please pay attention. Now you know we've been through this, many times. Mom had a couple drinks, and except for a little rum cake during the holidays, she never drank. Mom had every right - why does that still bother you? We need to move on to today and tomorrow. That's what really matters."

"I just - oh lord, please help me. I miss her something awful."

"Dad, come on, please don't cry. You know it hurts–"

He suddenly stopped crying, smiled, and said, "I feel like chasing a stick."

"What?"

"I'll bet you I could swim out and get a stick before you could. Come on, Maddi, you look like you could use some fresh air."

"Dad, I like it when you're happy like this, but–"

"Come on, Maddi, let's be happy."

"Ok Dad, now that you're happy and back in the now, why don't you tell me what it is you see, you know - right now."

And in his happy voice Dad sang, "I see trees of green - red roses too. I see 'em bloom - for me and you. And I think to myself - what a wonderful world - Yes, I think-to-my-self - what a wonderful world."

"Dad, that was very nice. I like it when you're happy."

"Oh yes, I'm much happier when I'm happy, but I'll be danged if I'm gonna let Junior treat me like some child. Maddi, how does the rest of the song go?"

"I'm not sure Dad, but I'll listen to the song when I get home and write it down. Would you like that?"

"Tell you what I'd like. I'd like to choke that guy that cut up Miller's cow. He had no right doing that. Next time I'm out here you can teach me the rest of the song and then I'll be happy, because right at this moment I feel so sad. Madison, can you tell me why that guy ran your mom and me off the road?"

"I don't know, but I wish I did. Dad, tell me what you saw, do you remember what color the car was?"

"It was the color of a peckerwood that's what color, a peckerwood that was sporting a slanted John Deere hat."

Dad had told me about the peckerwood with the slanted hat many times before. And the fact is, nearly every trucker and farmer in the Midwest wears their hats slanted to the left. It keeps the sun out of their eyes when they're driving. So I didn't ask anything more and of course, by this time, Dad had begun to cry. I decided to let him. Sometimes he just needs to get it out. He never cries for more than a half-a-minute or so. I think he forgets why he started crying in the first place. Right on cue he stopped crying.

"Madison, I hate all of this. I'm gonna move out west and live as a deaf-mute."

"Dad, that's something Holden says in the story. It's not real and you're not moving anywhere."

"I can move wherever I want to."

Then he reached up for me and started moving his hands all over my face.

"Come on, Dad, you know that bothers me?"

"I need to remember what you look like. I don't want to forget. Now read me the story."

"Dad, stop that, I look just like you."

"You have a mustache. How'd that happen?"

"No Dad, I don't have a mustache and how did what happen?"

"How'd you end up looking just like me and Junior came out looking just like his mother?"

I started to answer him, but I could tell he wasn't listening - he was thinking about mom. I often wondered myself why I looked almost nothing like her and sometimes grew tired of hearing how I looked just like my dad, as if I had no identity of my own. We bantered back and forth for another half-hour or so, but with little progress. At every curve in the road I ran into a roadblock named Dad. My patient was floating on a cloud, a thousand miles away. I was tired and decided to leave him there, wherever there is. Thank goodness Junior came back.

"Hey Dad, you feel like going for a short walk with Maggie, Maddi, and me?"

"The heck with walking - I feel like chasing a stick. And you have to run to do that."

Junior looked at me and I threw up my hands. Maggie had already sidled up next to Dad so we headed out to the cove. Maggie knows that Dad likes to walk pretty fast so she double timed it. Junior and I stayed behind and kinda strolled along at our own easy pace.

I could see that the wheels were still turning in Junior's head, so I decided to ask him why.

"Junior, it's been a month of Sundays since I've seen you so agitated. What's on your mind? I hope you didn't–"

"No, I didn't talk to any of your colleagues. Madison, do you remember clubfoot Billy, the rapist?"

"Yes, I remember Billy Thornton. You really should stop saying rapist. And how would you like being called clubfoot?"

"Ok, ok, I'm sorry. So you do remember him? Where is he? I mean, where'd he go after you guys were done with him?"

"Done with him? Junior - shame on you. I've never heard you talk like this. When Billy left here, he was a sad, broken down little man with a physical deformity that caused him more grief than I could ever explain. To answer your question, he went home to his parent's farm. They rolled a doublewide out in the trees on the eastern edge of their property, he lives there. Law says he can't leave without informing the local authorities. That's you. So, I'd say since you haven't heard from him, he's out there right now. Why do you want to know?"

"Maddi, I didn't mean to be mean, but the guy that cut up Miller's cow used Acepromazine to get the cow off the farm. And Billy used the exact same drug when he attempted to." Junior stopped and thought about his choice of words. "When he attempted to molest Jolene Meadows, and he would have succeeded if he hadn't been spooked by Ricky, which is a whole nother story. So, you see we have to explore every angle. I'm sorry sis, but this guy is going to strike again and we have to stop him."

"Ok Junior, apology accepted. If you go out to see Billy, you'd better be careful. He's awfully good with a knife, and he keeps one on his person at all times. You know yourself that he had time added to his prison term for cutting his cell-mate's ear off. That's after he had drugged the guy and tied him to his own bed. Billy could have killed him, but he said he just wanted the guy to know what it was like having a deformity. I guess the guy had called Billy clubfoot one too many times. Anyway, Billy made sure the roommate was watching when he flushed the ear down the toilet. By law I can't give you any specifics, but there were moments during our sessions when Billy revealed a loathing for humanity that I've not often seen or heard."

"Boy sis, you were just telling me not to say bad stuff about Billy and then you make him sound like Jekyll and Hide."

"All I'm saying is, make no mistake about it, he could turn on you without a moment's notice." I hesitated, wondering exactly how to get my point across. "I know you, Junior, and I know you're always overly trusting of others. Promise me you'll be careful."

"All right, I promise I'll be careful. Now, if it's ok with you, I'm gonna change the subject." Junior took a deep breath and then slowly exhaled. "What does Billy do? I mean how does he support himself? Do his parents take care of everything or what?"

"No, Billy studied in prison and became a saddler."

"A saddle maker?"

"Yes, I guess he's considered one of the best in the country. Junior, if you go out there, and I know you will, please don't threaten or spook him."

"Sis, I won't spook him. I just want to find out what I can. Ok, I'm going to take Dad home. He always needs a nap after coming out here." Junior softly said as he walked a few feet away from me and then bent over and picked up a stick.

He walked back to me with a smile on his face and said, "Look at Dad - he's so happy when he's outside with Maggie. Chase a stick - you have to admit he's pretty funny sometimes."

"Yes, he is Junior. I just hope he stays that way. I mean I don't want him getting any worse, but I'm afraid he will."

Junior/**I wasn't hungry** but Dad was. So I took him to his favorite haunt, the A & W Root Beer out by the highway. He seemed content and really happy, especially when he fed Maggie half his hotdog and fries. He knows that kind of food is bad for her, but he just loves to share. I got him home and watched him fall asleep in his recliner, right next to the radio. Said he wanted to hear the Louis Armstrong song – "What a Wonderful World". It never came on.

I keep some street clothes at Dad's and changed into them. I thought a police uniform might put Billy on edge. Before I left, I took Maggie's harness off and made sure she had plenty of food and water. Then I hugged her and, like always, told her to watch Dad and keep him out of trouble. A tall order, but I knew she would.

It took me about ten minutes to drive out to the Thornton farm. About five years ago Billy's dad, Jeb Thornton, had a very serious rollover accident while driving his tractor. After the accident, Jeb just couldn't do all the work around the farm that was necessary. So he leased the land to a conglomerate.

Farmers' leasing all or part of their land has become common in the Midwest. Heck, why not? Farming is nonstop, backbreaking work.

I pulled off of 25 and drove east for half-a-minute or so before I turned north up their gravel drive. Nel Thornton was in the garden wearing bib overalls, gloves, and a huge sun hat that covered her long blonde hair.

She stood erect like a statue as I drove up. And then I watched her shoulders relax a bit when she saw who it was. A big smile slowly spread across her face as she waved hello. Waving to someone when you greet them or when you're saying goodbye is a Midwest tradition that I hope never dies. I waved back to her as I got out of the car. I stopped next to the house in front of the detached garage. The place looked to be in great shape. Someone was spending a lot of time caring for the house and the huge lawn area.

"Hello, Mrs. Thornton, how you doin'?"

"Hello, Junior, I'm doin' just fine thanks and please call me Nel - Mrs. sounds so old," she said, still retaining a hint of her Scandinavian accent.

I stumbled a bit before I got the words out.

"Ok - Nel."

"Sure is nice to see you, Junior. Have you come all the way out here to look at my plump tomaters?" she said with a twinkle in her eye.

"No ma'am, but now that you mentioned it, Dad loves fresh tomatoes, so if it's ok, I'd like to buy a few. That is if you don't gouge me too much with the price, them being award winners and all."

Nel let out a good laugh.

"That's awful nice of you, Junior. And no, I won't gouge you too much - just a little."

She laughed again. I guess because it was so sincere, her laugh felt wonderful. I studied Nel real hard at that moment and realized she didn't have a stitch of makeup on yet she was, for a woman of her age, still quite beautiful. Her Norwegian blue eyes were as bright and clear as a summer sky. And her cheeks were the color of - well, I guess rosy would fit just fine. It was probably right after I said rosy, *to myself of course* - when I started feeling weird. Here I was staring at a woman that had to be at least twenty years my senior. When I came out of my little trance, I realized that she felt my stare and was beginning to blush. I needed to change the subject, and fast.

"How's Jeb been doing? Haven't seen him in town for quite some time now. I know that was a bad tumble he took off of that tractor. He's ok isn't he?"

"Oh, heck yes, why that old crow will probably live to be a hundred. He complains about his miseries, but I know most of the time it's just for attention. And of course, I give it to him, the attention that is."

She laughed again and so did I.

"Should I go inside and get Jeb? He's listening to the weather report."

"No, that's ok. Actually, I wanted to see Billy - if I could."

Nel's smile faded to a look of concern.

"Is this about Miller's cow? Billy isn't in any trouble is he?"

"No ma'am, I just wanted to see how he's getting along and all. Would it be ok if I wandered out to the trailer to see him?"

"Sure, but I wouldn't wander out there, it's way too far. You'd better drive your police car. Let me call Billy and tell him you're coming."

Nel went inside the kitchen and I heard her talking to Billy. It sounded like she was trying to calm him down. She looked out the window at me and waved me inside.

She was holding her hand over the receiver when I came in and whispered, "Billy said come on out, but don't bring no sidearm with you."

"No ma'am, I won't. I don't carry one."

She looked at my side for a gun, there wasn't one. Most policemen carry a revolver of some kind, but I never felt the need. However, I did have my Colt Cobra 38 in a holster under my left arm. I was going to tell her about it, but decided not to. I said to myself, *I'm not going out there unarmed.* While Nel continued to talk to Billy, I stepped over to look in the front room. Jeb was there sleeping in his recliner next to the radio. Reminded me of Dad.

"Ok Junior, Billy says to come on out. I'll put a half dozen tomaters and a sugar cookie or two in a bag for you. You can pick 'em up when you come back. Your dad still likes cookies, doesn't he?"

"Oh heck yes, if given the chance, he'd eat them day and night."

Nel giggled. We walked outside and Nel pointed east.

"Follow that path east for a bit then after that clump of trees you see in the distance, turn left and head north. From there his trailer is out another minute or so."

"Thanks for being so hospitable. I shouldn't be out there too long."

I jumped in the cruiser and headed east through row after row of tall corn and eventually came to a little tree shaded area where the cows used to gather to drink. There was an old water nozzle over a long rusted-out trough. Ten feet away there were a couple of dried up salt blocks. And another ten feet past them stood Billy.

Didn't say a word, he just stood staring at me. He had a rifle slung over his shoulder. He was the spitting image of a tiny, red-headed, wooden soldier.

Billy has always been what you would call undersized, but it's his childlike face in combination with his diminutive frame that leaves most people scratching their heads. Oh, and of course, his clubfoot and the way he walks. I wasn't sure what he was up to, so I slowly got out of the car and walked towards him, my hands away from my body.

"Hi Billy, wasn't expecting you to come meet me. I mean you didn't have to trouble yourself."

He stared at me for a long time, too long. Finally, he said, "Hello, Junior, it's no trouble. You can ride out to the shop in my truck. This road gets pretty rough in spots. Come on."

I followed him around a thick hedgerow and there shining in the sun was a vintage, midnight black, flatbed Ford truck.

"39?" I asked.

"Nope, it's a 38 - just like the gun you got hidden inside your jacket."

"Well, you sure got me there. How'd you know?" I asked as a coldness ran through me.

"I know because you're a detective and that's what they prefer. And I know you, Junior - you don't need a gun at your side to make people think you're a tough guy. Now Ricky, well, that's a whole nother story."

"Ok, well, if it's all right with you, I think I'll keep the gun right where it is."

"Ok by me. You ain't gonna need no gun with me, anyhow. And just so's you know, this rifle is registered to my dad. It's legal.

"Well, I know this is private property and all, but I don't think you're supposed to be carrying around a weapon. Billy, just make sure you leave the rifle in the truck. Ok?"

He nodded yes and I said, "Let's go."

Billy walked to his truck with that same old skip and a hop I remembered. I followed and got in the passenger side. The truck was like brand new on the inside too.

He started it up and it purred like a big cat as we drove north on a narrow path right through the middle of the corn fields.

"Must have set you back a pretty penny - you know getting this old truck running and looking this cherry. Not to mention the time and effort. Is that a new motor? Sure sounds like it."

"Yes and no. I rebuilt the old one from the engine block up. It's a brand new old motor. Sounds good, doesn't she?"

"She sure does. Where'd you learn how to work on motors?"

"At my home away from home; prison where else. I had a lot a years to learn as many ways to make a living as I could. Believe it or not I knew I belonged in prison. I also knew that someday I would get out, and I wanted to be sure I could provide for myself, and my parents. At first, I decided I was going to be an expert in the repair of motors. I worked hard at it until the warden called me in one day and set me straight on a few things. What he did was kinda cruel, but I'm glad he did it. Junior, can I ask you a question?"

"Shoot, I mean go ahead."

"If I had come back and opened up a garage, would you have brought your car in for me to work on?"

At first I didn't understand where he was going, that is telling me all about the warden and so on. But when he asked me the question, I understood in a hurry.

"I guess not, Billy, I guess not."

"Thanks for telling me the truth. So you understand that nobody else around these parts would have come to me either, especially the haters on the jury at my trial. So anyway, there I was with the warden and I wanted to slug him. I'd already spent a few years learning to work on automobiles. Then he smiled and said, 'Ok, I know you're upset, but I have an occupation that will make you more money than working on cars and you can do it in the comfort of your own home.' Next thing you know he walks me down to the work area and introduces me to a guy that had just been hired to teach inmates how to make saddles. He showed me the tools and a couple of saddles he'd made and I was beginning to like what I was hearing. But the clincher came when he told me how much people pay for a custom-made saddle. I was sold on the idea. The warden said thanks for listening and walked away. I started that day with the intention of becoming the best saddler in the world. End of story and here we are."

Crestfield

We drove by an old tree house and slowly pulled up to his carport. He stopped short of what appeared to be a fresh concrete driveway.

"I just finished the driveway a day ago. Need to let it cure for a couple days before I can park my truck on it."

"You did the work all by yourself?" I asked.

"For the most part I did, Mom helped level it. She held the other end of the metal straight edge. It's pitched about two inches from the north end down to the south."

"I helped my Uncle Ajax put in a slab for a shed out by their pond. Was harder work than I thought it'd be."

Just before I opened my door I reminded Billy about leaving his rifle in the truck. He gave me a look, but he didn't quarrel with me, not one little bit. I got out and while I stretched, I noticed that just like his parent's home everything was shipshape. We walked by shade trees surrounding the double-wide, and the leaves on the trees were turning to the bright colors of fall. It was a simple, single story manufactured home, but still quite handsome. Imagine an oasis of sorts hidden right in the middle of a cornfield. I followed him up the steps in front of his home and stopped on the porch. When I went inside, I stood and stared. It wasn't fancy, but it was certainly done with taste and at the same time it felt comfortable.

"Billy, you have really done a nice job with your home. I like it."

"Thanks, I do too. Only bad thing is being here alone. That's something I'm hoping to change and soon. I know a lady in Vietnam that says she would like to live in America. Knows all about me and says she's ok with everything. I've been working on the legalities of getting her here for quite some time now. I believe she's gonna come here early this next spring. I get real nervous just thinking about it."

"You know, Billy, that sounds great - I mean the lady not the nervous part."

"Thanks, enough of all that. Junior, you want something to drink? I got pop or I can make some Ovaltine or Postum if you want. Don't really drink the stuff myself."

"No thanks, Billy, I'm fine."

After I said I was fine, I looked over on his wall and there was a shotgun mounted above his Franklin stove.

"Billy, I don't think you're supposed to have a gun in your home."

"That's an old A H Fox twelve gauge that belonged to my grandpa Thornton. It don't work, the firing-pins have been removed."

I walked over to take a better look. The gun had a lot of fancy scrollwork all over it.

"It sure is a handsome gun."

"Thanks. That's why I keep it up there. It's just for looks. Come on, Junior, I want you to see my workshop."

"Ok, sure."

We walked out a side door and down some steps into a ten by twenty foot workshop that was neat and clean as a whistle. I stood there and stared at two saddles on saw horses. They were simply beautiful.

The workmanship was stunning. Billy's tools were all lined up over his work area and there was the beginning of a new saddle on the headless body of a wooden horse. I looked at Billy and he had a big smile on his face. He was proud of his work, and I believe he was happy that he could finally share it with someone.

"Well Junior - wha-da-ya think?"

"I think I'm impressed as all get out. This is simply amazing. Has anyone else seen your work? I mean anybody around these parts."

"No, not even my parents. I invite them, but they really don't want any part of me. It hurts a lot. Mom will talk to me because she pretty much has to, but Dad - well, he won't even look at me, let alone talk to me. I give them money every month for rent. And pay for the utilities and almost all the food they eat, but still nothing."

"I'm really sorry, Billy. Listen, I'm sure you know why I'm here. So I'm just gonna take a few notes, that ok with you?"

Billy shrugged his shoulders and stared at my notebook before he said, "Ok by me."

"Good deal and this shouldn't take very long. I'll leave you be if you can just tell me where you were the day Miller's cow was cut up. That was Tuesday, the 5th of September."

Billy nodded and then looked down at my notebook again as he spoke to me.

"Well, I can't leave the property without letting the authorities know. The last time I did leave was to see the shrink at the mental health facility in Clarinda Cove. So it's been months now since I left the farm."

Then he looked up at me and there was something in his eyes that said please listen.

"Junior, I have something I need to tell you."

I braced myself for the worst and then gave him my best ok go ahead look. He stammered a bit and then continued.

"What I wanted to say is - I never intended to harm Jolene, I just wanted to talk to her."

I didn't expect to hear what he'd just told me and was a bit confused, but I wasn't about to lie to him.

"Billy, come on now. Most people don't drug someone when they want to talk to them."

He shouted, "You do when you're born lookin' like me!"

He caught me off guard - that is raising his voice, but there was something there that told me he was telling the truth. There was also the information Madison had shared with me. And where it concerned Billy, I had the familiar devil on one shoulder and the angel on the other. I did my best to shield my inner thoughts, but he could see right through me. So I decided that an apology was in order.

"I'm sorry, alright, Billy, I'm all ears."

His breathing became pronounced and he stammered,

"Junior, it, it's no fun being called names your whole life. I just wanted Jolene to know it hurt when she called me clubfoot. And she did it a lot. I figured the only way I'd ever get her to listen was with a little help. Before Ricky walked up on us I hadn't t-touched her or well, you know done anything. And I wasn't going to either. You gotta believe me."

"Billy, I admit there's something in your voice that says you're telling me the truth, but I think you can understand why most people wouldn't believe that for even a minute."

He put his hand up in the universal stop position, and so I did.

"Junior, you're right - I know that, but I just had to tell someone. It's a guilt that is hard to live with. I just wanted to talk to her, that's all."

He sat down on the stool in front of his workbench. We didn't speak for a minute or two. It got real uncomfortable in the room. Felt like there was dead air floating around us. Finally, he opened up what looked like an appointment book and studied it for a bit.

"Listen, you know what Junior - I had a buyer here from Austin, Texas on Tuesday and Wednesday. His name is Hank Bodine and I've got his phone number right here. If you give him a call, I guarantee you he'll tell ya he was here and so was I."

"Well, that oughta do it for now. Thanks for cooperating, Billy. When I get back to the station, I'll give him a call. I've probably overstayed my welcome. So do you think you could give me a ride back to my car? I'd like to get back to town so I can check on my dad."

"You know, Junior, I heard about the accident when I was in the joint. I'm really sorry. Man that'd be tough going through a tragedy like that. You must miss your mom somethin' awful."

I put my notebook away.

"Yes, we all miss her, but thanks. And you're right - it has been tough to deal with. Say, Billy, what's out back of the workshop?"

"Not much, come on I'll show ya."

We walked out the back door. I tripped over the concrete rake he used on the new driveway. The bull-float, jitter bug, and metal straight edge were leaning up against a small dumpster. A pair of cement covered knee pads were hanging on the back wall. In the middle of the backyard there was a round table with a big shade umbrella; and one lonely chair.

"Spend much time out here?"

"Yeah, this is where I take my breaks. A soft breeze usually comes through in the afternoons. I have a bottle of pop and try to think positive thoughts. Works sometimes, you ready to go on back?" he said with a fractured smile.

"Yeah, I suppose so. Thanks for the tour."

Billy drove me back to my car and as I was getting out, he thanked me for listening.

"No problem, Billy. I'll talk at you again."

I headed back for his parent's house and when I got there, Nel was waiting with a bag in her hand and a smile on her face. As she walked up, I rolled my window down.

"Nel, what do I owe you for the tomatoes and cookies?"

"Heck Junior, you don't owe me anything. I was just havin' a little fun with you," she said as she leaned over and handed me the bag. I did my best not to stare.

"Dad's gonna love your tomatoes. Oh, and the cookies too. Thanks, bye now."

She was sweet as can be and waved a nice goodbye. I drove away feeling good about things. The good feelings were short lived. When I passed by the window on the side of the house, I sensed a presence all around me, like I was under a microscope. I looked over at the house and my eyes locked onto Jeb Thornton's. He didn't just stare at me, he looked right through me. I suddenly felt the overwhelming need to hurry and stepped hard on the accelerator.

<u>Dad</u>/I woke up after a cat-nap and headed for the kitchen. I was really thirsty so I began running through my mental list of things I have in the icebox to drink. I reached in and my hand went straight to a bottle of pop. I felt around a little bit and by the shape of the bottle I knew I'd picked up a Coke, my favorite. I popped the top off, I love that sound, and then I took a big drink. There's nothin' like an ice-cold bottle of pop to refresh a body. I started back for my chair, when I heard Maggie come in the house thru the back door. She spooks the neighbor, so Junior built a fence around a little more than half of the yard so she can go out and play if she wants. She ran up and rubbed the side of my leg to let me know she was there.

"Hi girl, have you been out lounging or have you been digging for that doggone gopher again? Well, no matter cuz I've got an ice-cold Coke and I'm gonna sit here and listen to the radio. I called this morning and asked the guy at the radio station to play my song. He said he would. Mags, you know where the music comes from? No, well, it comes all the way up from St. Joe. Hard to believe, but it's true."

I set my bottle on the end table and turned the radio up a bit. I waited and hoped they'd play my Louie Armstrong song. I heard Maggie give a short growl and head out the back door. Sometimes she can hear that little buzzard of a gopher digging. As she went out, she must have hit the back door with her big old tail cuz the door closed behind her. She does it all the time and it's no problem, I know the way over to the door by heart. I got comfy and reached for my bottle of Coke, it wasn't there. Then I heard someone take a big drink.

"Is that you Junior?"

"No Jack - I ain't Junior."

No doubt I was spooked when I heard the strange voice. My being spooked changed to anger in a hurry when Maggie started scratching like crazy on the door. She was frantically barking which only proved to increase my anxiety.

"Uh, why don't you be neighborly and let the dog in please," I requested.

"What! So you think you're funny, hah. Don't you worry, Benny will take care of your dog, that's for damn sure," he answered.

I tried to get up, but he pushed me back down in my chair.

"Don't you dare hurt that dog!"

"Shut up, I give the orders 'round here."

"You know, Mr., I don't have any money, but if there's something else you want, just go ahead and take it. I probably don't need it anyway."

"Keep talking and I'll have Benny gut you like a bluegill. Listen, I want you to tell those damn cops to stop. Tell 'em they ain't never gonna catch us. And the more they meddle, the more people gonna get hurt. And some of the people in this damn town deserve gettin' hurt."

"Wha-da-ya mean? Why Crestfield is full of a lot of nice people," I said.

I heard him walk to the front door and open then shut it real quick like. I thought it was a good time for me to hightail it to the back door and let Maggie in. I didn't make it even one step before he threw me back into my chair - and hard!

"Listen Mr. - uh, you know I don't even know your name. What is your name?"

"My name is Benny."

I wasn't sure what to think when I heard the voice. Benny was about a foot shorter than the other guy and had this irritating high-pitched nasal voice.

"Uh, you know, Benny, they can do wonders these days with adenoid problems."

He responded with a nerve-racking lengthy high pitched, "Shut up!"

"Ok, but you sound like a flit when you talk in that munchkin voice."

He hit me so hard across the jaw, spit flew out of my mouth. I put my hands up to protect myself, but it didn't do any good. He hit me again square in the mouth. One of my front teeth broke off and stuck in my throat. Then the big guy grabbed me by the arms. *I think it was the big guy.* He pulled me out of the chair and threw me across the floor. I coughed real hard and the tooth flew out and ricocheted off the wall. *This guy means to hurt me. Do something, Jack!*

I could smell the fireplace and reached for the poker. He stepped on my hand and I felt the bones grind against each other. He laughed right out loud and then jumped up and stomped down on my hand. I heard the bones crunch. I rolled over on my back and pulled my hand into my body. Maggie stopped scratching and he laughed harder.

"You ought to see what you look like, Jack. You're a mess."

Benny laughed real hard at me just before the big guy got down right next to me and said, "Ok, well, Junior will be coming home soon. So I guess we're done here."

Then he turned to Benny and said, "I'll take care of Jack, you go finish off that damn dog. Make sure she can't bother us again."

"Gotchya," Benny said with fervor.

"You leave her alone!" I hollered just before one of them turned the volume up on my radio.

A moment later the big guy picked me up by the neck and started dragging me backwards across the front room. His forearm was so tight across my throat I was choking. I reached up with my right hand and grabbed his wrist to keep him from crushing my windpipe. Lordy he was strong. That's when I noticed he was wearing extremely rough leather gloves and they smelled like raw hamburger. With all my might I tried to break free. He squeezed harder still. Before I could do much of anything, he had me in the kitchen. I heard him open one drawer and then the next. He was searching for something and getting more frustrated by the second. Then for some reason he let go of me. I said the first thing that popped into my head.

"You ever chased a stick?"

I think I felt my head split open, but I'm not sure. I was sure that Junior would come and get me.

Misery 6

***Junior*/I knew something was wrong** the moment I walked in Dad's house and Maggie didn't come greet me. I went in the front room and no Dad. For some reason I pulled my gun out of its holster and slid down the hall. I checked the bedrooms and the bathroom, still no Dad. I turned and ran back down the hallway and into the kitchen; Dad was there on the floor. I'm not sure if I hollered Dad or not, but I do know he didn't answer me. He was unconscious and curled up on his side. There was a disquieting amount of blood splattered across the cabinets and floor.

I knelt right next to him and could hear him breathing, which was a relief of sorts. I took out my handkerchief and pressed it hard to Dad's forehead. Then I felt around on the kitchen counter. The dish towel was there. I pressed it to the back of Dad's head. I sat and held the bandages for a few minutes before I reached up for the phone and called Randi at the station. I told her to send an ambulance to Dad's house. I guess I was screaming so loud she couldn't understand me, so she asked me who I was. I calmed down just enough to say, "It's me – Junior! I'm at Dad's, send an ambulance, do it now!"

I hung up and ran to check the backyard and tripped over Maggie. She was lying on the porch in a pool of vomit. Her eyes were fixed and dilated and she was unresponsive. It was clear to me she'd been poisoned. A rage boiled over in me and I ran like a crazy man out to the front of the house and into the street. I yelled with all my might - at nothing. There wasn't a car or a person in sight.

Tommy and Ricky got to the house before the ambulance. Tommy is not the kind of person to waste time with small talk. He walked straight into the kitchen and stopped. He looked down at Dad and then at me.

"Is he still alive?" he asked.

I nodded yes. And then he sat down next to the two of us, leaned over and spoke right into Dad's ear.

"Jack, you listen to me. You have to fight, you hear me - you've got to fight!"

Then he stood up and asked about Maggie. I pointed at the back door. Tommy picked up the phone and dialed the station, his eyes never leaving Dad.

"Randi, I want you to call Matt and Shadow right now and tell them to set up a roadblock out on 34. I want them to check every car. Yes, every car. Tell them to bring in anybody that looks or acts even the slightest bit strange. Yes, right now. You got it? Oh, and call the Sheriff's office, tell 'em what happened, they'll know what to do. Ok thanks, yeah, bye."

Tommy got off the phone and walked straight out the back door. I guess to see about Maggie. Ricky had been standing next to me, his head shaking back and forth. He got down on his knees next to Dad and held my makeshift bandages to Dad's head. As he did, his shoulders slumped forward, his chin fell to his chest, and tears rolled down his cheeks. I kept asking myself if this was a dream but got no answer. By that point I'd fallen into a hole in my soul, some might call it full-blown shock.

The guys in the ambulance came in and asked me to move a couple of times before they shoved me out of the way. That's when I came to for a moment, something had caught my attention. I listened as Dad's radio played his favorite song, "What a Wonderful World".

A broken heart   7

Madison/I was in the middle of what turned out to be a long session with the purple haired, knobby knuckled, Viola Custer. Viola is one of my many outpatients. Her mental illness is a common one, old age, which is, in the profession, usually referred to as senility. One day of each week I try to spend time with the elderly. Today I was near my house visiting the Prairie View assisted living facility. Viola was explaining to me why she believes she doesn't belong in Prairie View. She says that one of her neighbor friends, a Mr. Kincade, has been trying to date her so that he might steal her jewelry, *all of it costume jewelry.*

"So you see, Doctor McCool, I should move back home. It's the safest place for me."

"Viola, you know we've been through this before. You sold your house over ten years ago."

"I did? Well, I want it back."

"Now Viola, that wouldn't be very fair to the couple that bought the house, would it? There are three teenagers living in the home. Where would the family go if you moved back in?"

"Why, I suppose they could live with me. I don't take up much room. And then there'd be someone there to change the channels on the TV. Yes, that would be very nice indeed."

I was just about to use a technique that usually works with Viola and most of my older patients, change the subject. That's when one of the aides came running into the room.

"Doctor McCool, you have an urgent phone call from your sister!"

"Which sister?" I asked.

"I'm sorry, your sister Randi. She said something about your dad's dog being poisoned. She's on line two."

I picked up the phone and pressed two.

"Hello, Randi?"

"Yes, it's me. Maddi, I don't know exactly what's happened other than Dad was attacked by someone and Maggie was poisoned."

"What! Where is–"

"Madison, Tommy says for you to go to the vet. He says Dad is being taken care of at the hospital. He needs you to stay with Maggie so he can look for the person that did this."

"I don't understand."

"Madison, I don't understand either, please." The line suddenly went dead.

"Randi, Randi! are you there?"

All was quiet for a moment longer, then I heard a violent sob.

"Ok listen; I'm on my way to the vet. Please don't cry. I'll call you as soon as I can. Randi - are you ok?"

No answer.

"Randi, I'm not leaving 'til I know you're ok. Is anyone there with you? Randi, please answer me."

"Yes, Ricky's here. I'm ok, please Maddi, just go."

"I'm going right now. I'll call the first chance I get. Try not to worry, bye."

I immediately turned to the aide.

"Nancy, please take Viola to the cafeteria and get her some cake and milk and then help her to the TV room."

I didn't wait for an answer. I picked up the keys to my car and ran. I was in my car and racing towards Cromwell road when I realized that my dad was in the hospital and I was heading to a veterinarian to see about a dog. There was something very disturbing about the logic. Then as I drove into the parking lot, a car sped past me going out. My head jerked sideways to get a look at the driver. It was Henry Freeberg, the vet. I asked myself, *why isn't he taking care of Maggie?*

The confusion in my mind was building with every passing second. I ran into the building and didn't stop at the reception counter. I only stopped when I got to the surgical area. Maggie was there lying unconscious on an operating table, a large tube protruded from her clenched jaws. My hands involuntarily covered my mouth. And it was suddenly very difficult to breathe. The emotions that flooded through me were overwhelming.

I stood and stared at Maggie. I guess I was trying to understand how anyone could do something so terrible to an animal. My heart was pounding like a trip-hammer. I wanted to help her, but there was nothing I could do.

I felt so completely lost. I had just reached for a hanky when someone said, "Hello Madison."

I didn't need to see who had said hello because I knew it was Henry's son, Ray. He handed me a handkerchief and I wiped a tear or two away and did my best to compose myself.

"Hello Ray, thank you for the hanky. I'm sure you can understand my confusion. Why isn't your dad here? Please tell me what's going on."

"Maddi, I'm sorry about what's happened. To answer your question, my dad is going to your dad's house to try and find out what kind of poison was used. He'll be back as soon as he knows a little more about how and when things took place."

"Why would when matter so much? I mean it happened today, that's when."

"Once again I'm sorry. You see, Dad thinks Maggie was drugged before she was poisoned."

"That doesn't make much sense, but I'll just have to trust your dad. Now is there anything I can do for Maggie?"

"No, I'm afraid now we just have to wait and see. She's resting comfortably and her vital signs are good. Only time will tell. If there's something she needs or that will make things better, I'm sure Dad will do it. If I know Dad, he'll be back soon, then he can fill us both in on what he knows for sure. Now you'll have to excuse me, I have a very sick cat to attend to."

Ray walked out of the room and I stared at Maggie for a bit before I grabbed a stool and sat and stroked her brow. She looked so peaceful, and I felt as though my heart was going to burst. My mind began to stray and eventually I wandered all the way back to high school. Unfortunately, I had drudged up some random and unwanted thoughts.

You see Ray and I had dated towards the end of our senior year. Our relationship never really amounted to much. So I'm sure you can understand my confusion when just before he took off for college, he told me that he was pretty sure he loved me. What does that mean, pretty sure? What a gigantic commitment on his part. It's almost laughable. Although at the time I don't think I was laughing. Anyway, Ray went away to college and I stayed home. I stayed because someone had to take care of Dad.

After Junior graduated from college, a second time, he was hired by the Crestfield police department. And I finally got my chance at higher education. I made the best of things and eventually returned home. By the time I came home, Ray had married and started a family. He'd dated and then married my best friend, Jan Hughes. I didn't have a problem with them getting married. Except for the fact that I had been talking to Jan all those years I was away to college and she never mentioned Ray. Not even once. I've asked Jan but have never received an answer as to why she didn't tell me about her relationship with Ray. Maybe some things are better left unsaid?

Now Jan and I don't talk, and we rarely see each other. It's strange being strangers in a town as small as Crestfield. I had just given up worrying about water under the bridge when Henry came walking into the room. Henry is not the most talkative person on the planet, so he just gave me a Midwest wave before he started checking Maggie's vitals. I know what it's like when you're busy and can't talk so I said nothing. Eventually Henry turned to me as he pulled a plastic baggy out of his pocket, the contents of which looked like raw hamburger meat.

"Henry, is that hamburger meat?"

"Yes it is Madison, and I'd bet my bottom dollar there's more here than just meat. I don't know if Ray told you but from my initial examination of Maggie, I believe she was poisoned after she was drugged and put to sleep."

"Ray did tell me that, but you'll have to pardon my ignorance. I mean how in the world could a dog, or for that matter any animal, be poisoned when they're unconscious?"

Henry walked back out to the front desk and immediately came back carrying a bright yellow funnel with a long green rubber hose attached.

"This is how. The hose was forced down her throat and the poison was poured in. I could tell from the tearing in Maggie's upper esophagus that something had been hastily shoved down her throat. And when I test the vomitus I've collected, I'm sure I'll discover what the poison is. My first guess is ethylene glycol or your common automobile antifreeze, and a bit of arsenic. Fortunately for Maggie, the gag reflex works whether a person or for that matter a dog is awake or not. She vomited up the poison before it could work its way into her blood system and vital organs. Madison, this is an extremely cruel and calculating person we're dealing with."

"Henry, I understand all of what you've just told me, but I don't understand the why."

"Madison, I'm not sure I understand what you mean. What why?"

"Why would you poison a dog that is unconscious and therefore no longer a threat?"

"Oh, I see. Well, the dog may not be a threat to you at that moment, but when it wakes up, it certainly will be. Maggie will never, I repeat never, forget the smell of the monster that caused her, and I might add Jack, so much pain. Madison, I'm not a detective, but I'd say without hesitation that this person plans on returning. And when he returns, he does not want to deal with a 75-pound dog that doesn't like him and has big teeth. Madison, I know this is awful, but it could have been much worse. This person could easily have killed Maggie. I believe he just didn't have the time to finish the job."

"Henry, I almost wish you hadn't told me all of this. But I'd say you're right. Do you know how Maggie was put to sleep?"

"I'm sorry, Madison. I forgot to tell you that part. I found a puncture wound near Maggie's right hindquarter. I figure when Maggie didn't eat the hamburger, well, then the monster had no other choice but to dart her with what I believe is Atravet."

"I'm not familiar with Atravet."

"Atravet is more commonly referred to as Ace or Acepromazine."

"Oh lord, isn't that the same drug that was used on Miller's cow?"

"As a matter of fact it is."

"Henry, are you thinking what I'm thinking?"

"Yes, I believe I am. There can be little if any doubt that the crimes are connected. We have an absolute maniac among us."

"Henry, this is my last question. In your opinion is Maggie going to be ok?"

"It's hard to tell just yet. She was given enough of the drug to knock out a small horse. It could be hours or even days before we know if any, um, serious damage was done."

"Henry, you're keeping something from me. Please tell me everything."

"Madison, I really don't know everything, but you're right there is something else. There are some potential complications. Due to genetic mutations some dogs, herding dogs in particular, have had negative reactions to Atravet. Many have died from even small doses of the drug. Maggie is definitely a herding dog. If she makes it through this then our greatest fear will be a slight or possibly a complete loss of hearing."

"Please lord no - a blind man and a deaf dog. Henry, may I use one of your phones?"

"Why certainly. Use the one in my office; it's a little more private."

I called the police station and Randi answered on the first ring.

"Crestfield police, how can I help you?"

"Randi, it's me, where is everybody?"

"They're all out searching for whatever clues they can find. Junior's still at the hospital with Dad."

"Randi, are you ok?"

"Yes, I'm fine now. How's Maggie?"

"Only time will tell, but I - I think she's going to be ok, she has to be. Dad would be lost without her."

"Oh, that makes me happy."

"Randi, Dad's in the hospital and Maggie is unconscious and you're happy?"

"Yes, I'm happy because you wouldn't tell me how much Dad needs Maggie if you didn't believe in your heart that they were both going to be ok."

"Randi, I love your optimism and I hope you're right. I'm going over to the hospital, call if you have any news and I'll do the same. Love you, bye."

After I hung up, Randi probably sat and stared into space. Why would she do that? Because I can't remember the last time I told her that I love her.

Hard times   8

___Junior___/**I rode to the hospital** in the back of the ambulance with Dad. My mind was still in a haze, but I did manage to stay out of the way. When we arrived, I stepped out of the ambulance and helplessly watched as the guys rolled Dad toward Doc Mayland. He looked at Dad for only a moment and then at me. His eyes spoke volumes and the fury in me welled up like a violent storm. For the first time in my life I knew that I was capable of killing another human being. I shook with anger as I watched Dad being rolled away. At that point I don't really know why, but I walked to the curb where patients are dropped off and picked up. I sat down on the wooden bench and the anger in me slowly gave way to a crushing sadness.

I knew Madison had gone to check on Maggie. And I wasn't sure when she'd get to the hospital, but I knew she'd get here as soon as was possible. I didn't even hear her walk up. She just sat down and very slowly put her arms around my shoulders. She didn't just comfort me - she reassured me. Madison has always had a way of keeping things grounded and real. It may sound a bit callous, but I was happy to have someone there with me. Someone that is, to share my mounting fear and desperation with. We didn't speak. We just sat staring into space. I guess we were both anticipating the unknown. I finally came back down to earth and asked Madison about Maggie.

"Tommy got her to the vet just in time, I hope. She's still very sick and in danger, but–"

"But what?" I asked.

It felt like Madison was only telling me part of the story.

"Henry thinks she's going to make it. The next couple of days will tell."

"Thank goodness," I said.

A little bit of good news woke me up and there were things that I needed to do. So I decided there was no time like the present. I got up - walked inside - and called the station. I needed to check in and get an update from Randi. She told me that they were ok and that I should stay at the hospital with Dad.

"Is Madison there yet?" she asked.

"Yes, she's here."

"Good, ok Tommy and Ricky are busy canvassing the neighborhood looking for any leads. The biggest problem right now seems to be the location of Dad's house."

I knew exactly what she meant.

"Yeah Randi, being that Dad's house is near the north end of Sycamore. If someone came in from the north, and there are a couple ways of doing that, they would easily be able to get in and out without being seen, even in broad daylight."

She said, "Yep, that's the problem."

"You know, Randi; there are some snoopy people that live by Dad. We have to hope that someone saw or maybe heard something. Let's keep our fingers crossed. One little lead is about all we'll need. Have you been able to reach Dezi or Buck?"

"No, our little brother is out training right now with the army, and I'd like to be able to tell Dezi something positive about Dad's condition before phoning her," she softly said.

"Keep trying to reach them. They would want to be here. Ok, Randi, I'll let you go now. You hear anything, call the hospital and as soon as I know more about Dad, I'll call you, bye."

Madison and I waited and waited and then finally a nurse I didn't recognize came and told us Doc Mayland would like to see us in his office. Madison and I were anticipating the worst but hoping for the best as we ran to the doctor's office. Doc Mayland was sitting in silence behind his desk.

When I walked in, I read the name plate in front of him and said to myself, *that's strange - I didn't know his name was Martin.*

"Come in, please sit down," he said.

Doc Mayland has a very slow and deliberate way of talking so at times he can really test your patience.

"Your dad has been through quite a storm."

I found that to be a strange way of looking at nearly being beaten to death.

"He has some injuries that are going to take time to heal, but heal they will."

I was on edge and wanted to tell the doctor to hurry, but I held my tongue.

"And as you probably figured, it's the head injuries that are our main concern," he said.

I started to respond when Madison beat me to the punch.

"Doctor, with all due respect, please tell us what his injuries are, how you plan to treat them, and when we can see our dad."

"Madison, you always were one to get right to the point. Ok, as you wish."

It took him a good fifteen minutes to go through all the injuries, how he thought they had occurred, and what needed to be done. He was obviously tired and finished by saying Dad was in room thirty and that we could go see him. The following is fairly close to what we had been told.

'The person or persons that attacked Dad had fractured his jaw, and his right front tooth had been knocked out in the process. They hadn't yet taken any X-rays, but they were pretty sure that several bones in his left hand had been broken. And those were the less serious injuries."

He went on to say that the most serious injuries had probably occurred at the end of the beating. Dad had been hit on the back of the head with his own meat tenderizer, which is missing. The blow was delivered with such great force that it fractured his skull and left him with a six inch tear in his scalp. This led to what was probably the most serious injury. Dad's face had been catapulted forward and hit the edge of the countertop next to the sink. His nose was broken and he had a small fracture of the forehead just over his right eye. The frontal lobes along with the rest of his brain had been bruised and had begun to swell. Doc said they had done everything possible to relieve the swelling, short of opening his skull. And for safety measures, he was, at present, in an induced coma. It was going to be days if not weeks before they'd know if any permanent damage had been done. Finally, while he was unconscious and down on the kitchen floor, he'd been kicked so hard in the side that three ribs had been broken. So just breathing was causing him a great deal of pain. Doc finished by saying, "All things considered your dad is lucky to be alive."

I'd never considered being beaten a lucky thing. Madison and I walked at a fevered pace towards room thirty not knowing what to expect.

When we got to Dad's room, my heart sank. Dad's head and half of his face were covered in ice packs and bandages. The cheek and eye not bandaged were so swollen and discolored I could just barely recognize him. He had tubes running everywhere from his nose and mouth down to his ribs and arms. He had bandages covering his torso and a soft cast of sorts on his left hand. There was a little board that kept his fingers extended and separated. It looked more like a flipper than a hand.

Madison and I stood silently watching as a young nurse was doing her best to make Dad comfortable. She could probably feel our eyes on her back and turned ever so slowly and gently gazed at us before she softly spoke.

"Hello, my name is Jenny and I'll be taking care of your dad this evening. I think he's resting pretty well now. I'll check back in a half-an-hour or so. Just ring the bell if you think he needs something."

She quietly walked out and left us there in our fog. I looked at Madison and I know we were both thinking the same thing. Genevieve was our mother's name, but everyone called her Jenny. We didn't say it out loud, but I think for whatever reason we were both happy that this Jenny was watching over Dad.

Nobody likes being scolded 9

Junior/I sat gazing at Dad, silently wondering. Madison, on the other hand, was talking to Dad as if he was awake and answering her. I started to ask if she thought Dad could hear her, but she stopped me before I could say one word.

"Yes, I know he can hear me. He's almost in the same world right now that he's always in. Watch his eye flutter when I talk."

I watched for a few seconds and I'll be doggone if she wasn't right. Dad was responding to everything she said. I sat and watched and wondered. I was thinking that it wouldn't take much for Dad to go off the deep end. I tried to imagine what he'd be like with more mental damage. That was a difficult thing to approach let alone settle on. Dad was already in some people's minds a bit on the crazy side of the tracks. Any more damage and the cheese would probably slide clean off his cracker. I suddenly felt a specific type of heat that I remember experiencing as a kid. Madison wasn't talking anymore. I looked over and she was studying me. I knew immediately where the heat was coming from. She had one of her intense looks going on and then she just came right out with it.

"Junior, I know exactly how that little mind of yours works. If you give up on Dad for even one second I'll make your life a living hell."

I started to protest, but it was useless to even try.

"You hear me. Dad is going to be ok. And if he wasn't - well, how would anyone know. So, if someone asks - you tell them Dad's going to be ok. You understand me!"

"Gosh Mad, you don't have to get so darned angry about the whole thing."

"Yes! Yes I do have to get angry. I'm the one that has been working with him since the accident. So you keep your grubby little mitts off him. You hear me!"

"Gosh! Ok, I'll think positive and relay the same to anyone that asks. Is that what you want?"

"That's not what I want. It's what I demand, at least from you."

"Ok, ok. I'm going to walk over to the station and see what needs to be done. I haven't helped do anything and am not feeling too great about that. And now you come at me out of the clear blue and give me heck. Honestly Madison, sometimes I think you don't like me or something, gosh!"

I figured it was just the intensity of the moment that got Madison all riled up at me. Maybe she saw the desperation in my eyes. She is trained to do such things. Anyway, I told her I was heading to the station. She just stared harder at me.

I left room thirty with angry eyes on my back and soft eyes coming at me. Jenny was walking toward Dad's room, I guess to check on him. She smiled and told me there was a car waiting out front for me. I walked out the front of the hospital and watched Shadow as he got out of Ricky's roller. Shadow's simian side to side gait along with his deep set Neanderthalian eyes and beetle brow can at times be quite unsettling. In fact there are times when just one glimpse of Shadow can convince me that I've traveled back to the beginning of time. But for some reason today his Mr. Hyde features and dogged attitude were very reassuring. We both waved.

"Hey Shadow, how you doing?"

"Hey Junior, I'm fine, but right now I'm not what matters. How's your dad?"

"He's going to be ok, but thanks for asking," I said as he walked right by me into the hospital.

"Shadow, where are you going?"

"I'm goin' inside to stand watch in front of your dad's room. Nobody's gettin' in there without goin' through me first. And I guarantee you they'll be sorry if they try. They'll be lookin' down the barrel of a forty-five. See ya Junior."

I figured Tommy had made the decision not to leave Dad alone. Once again he was right. I bent down to look in the car and Ricky was there smiling back at me. He's such a great friend. The moment I opened the door he said, "Hey Junior, how you holdin' up?"

I started to answer, but he beat me to the punch.

"And how's your dad? Tell me he woke up and said something funny."

"No Ricky, he didn't. But I just know when he wakes up he will."

"I sure hope so. Junior, Tommy wants everyone to meet at the station in about an hour. So we have time to eat, are you hungry?"

"I hadn't thought about it, but I suppose I could eat. Where do you want to go?"

"How 'bout we go to Molly's? My treat."

"That'd be just fine. Molly's is usually pretty quiet and right now I need quiet."

Ricky parked his roller right in front of the open door so he could keep an eye on it. The moment we walked in, Molly smiled and waved a nice Midwest hello. Then she walked straight to me and gave me a warm motherly hug.

To me Molly Eagan is the comfort a child seeks after a nightmare. She is the helping hand for a neighbor in a time of need. She's the granite that will not yield in the eye of a storm. She is the earthy yet pretty girl next door that can beat you in Indian wrestling or a foot race and smile while she's doing it. She's the gal that loves to laugh at a good joke. To me Molly is the quintessential Midwestern woman.

"Junior, I hope you're doin' ok. If there's anything I can do to help out, please don't hesitate to ask. Not trying to pry or anything, but this is a small town. I've heard several different stories about your dad. How is he?"

I started to crumble, but I remembered the scolding Madison had given me. So I decided to tell Molly Dad was doing fine and was going to be ok. I don't think she bought what I was selling, but she politely listened.

"Thanks Molly. Dad's got a few scrapes and scratches, but I'm sure with time he'll be back to normal, whatever that is."

The three of us had a little chuckle after I said it, but we knew it was a friendly way of sharing something very sensitive. Molly sat the two of us at the end of the counter. I knew she'd make sure we were left alone. Ricky ordered his usual super, a well-done burger with fries. He says his mom told him a person can get the same diseases cows do if the meat isn't cooked for a long time. I think he's crazy, but I'm used to it and that's probably one reason my dad and I are crazy about him.

"You know, Ricky, sometimes I think you're crazy, but the fun kind of crazy - like Dad."

"Why thanks Junior, that's the very best compliment anyone has ever given me. You're worried aren't you?"

I didn't say anything. I didn't need to, Ricky knew me far too well. Just when the silence started to get uncomfortable,

Molly strolled down the other side of the counter and slid the plates right in front of us.

"Here you go, Ricky, just the way you like it, burnt to a crisp," she said with a smile.

Ricky smiled back a thank you. Not a word was spoken after we started eating and it wasn't because our mouths were full.

To wit   10

Benny - I'm raging again. I'm gonna hurt someone - and soon. Just cuz mom was bad doesn't mean I'm bad too, does it?"

High pitched voice "Maybe? Your mom was crazier than you. She stunk as a mother."

"You little creep. I've told you a thousand times not to talk about my mom like that."

"Sorry big guy - no can do. Did you forget that you're the one who brought her up, and for about the thousandth time."

"Shut up, you little jerk. If I wanted to, I could hurt you real bad."

"You go ahead and try. You're all talk. I may be small, but I'm mighty. You told me so yourself - a thousand times."

"Go to Hades."

"Sorry, you'll have to take that trip all by your lonesome. You hurt Jack real bad. Why'd you do that? He was supposed to be our messenger. If you kill someone, they can't deliver a message, that's for sure."

"Leave me alone about that. And besides Benny - you hurt him too."

"I hardly touched him."

"You little liar, you kicked him so hard it knocked the wind out of me."

"You big dummy - you did all the kicking - not me."

"I'm gonna crush your little head and then squeeze the yoke out."

"Can't you come up with something better than that? You know something original. I've heard you say you're gonna crush my little head a thousand times. It's getting old."

"Shut up before I crush... I've got to think for a bit so be quiet - you hear me?"

"Yeah, I hear you. You're gonna think. This I gotta see."

"Shut up Benny."

The big guy stood tall and adjusted his tie. *There was no tie*. He cleared his throat and began a much-practiced soliloquy.

"The level of nobility in a ground hog is not in step with a turkey. The ground hog can dig Tom turkey, but he can't

51

walk like Tom. A slippery slope so suddenly sour makes my day go by - hour by hour. I hold what is in my hand so my feet will stay flat when I stand. Jack be nimble Jack be quick. Jack couldn't jump so he chased a stick. Mommy, mommy, there's no food in my tummy. You can fix a flat or live in one. And you can be a foil or wrap it around some jelly, but you can't foil a foil when it's stuck in your belly. Daddy, you hurt mommy's tummy. The road to Hades is a one-way street. You can't walk back cuz you burnt your feet. The river Styx is long but not too wide, my mommy's screaming on the other side. Green is red, and red is green, but they make me blue when, when, when, Daddy, my head was in mommy - you hurt mommy."

"Jesus - man you can ramble on like no other schizoid I've ever heard."

"Shut up Benny. I told you a thous–"

"Are you gonna go see Jack or not?"

"No, I got other people to see first. I told you I'm raging and someone's gonna get hurt!"

Benny gestured with the middle and index fingers on both hands, "Did the voices tell you to say that?"

"Shut up! The voices are real. They're as real as you Benny. They're real!"

"Yeah right, you're an idiot."

Pieces of the puzzle   11

***Junior*/Ricky and I** got to the station with a few minutes to spare. I walked in the back door and looked through the window into Tommy's office. My Uncle Ajax was standing there with his shoulders slumped forward and a worried look written in capital letters across his face.

Uncle Ajax is the Mayor of Crestfield and has been for several terms now. He's good at the job. He's a short stout guy with an attitude due to his lack of altitude. He's got thick brown hair like a wolverine and a mustache to match. His eyes are green, but come off a bit muddy due to the distressed look he almost always wears on his face. Dad tells me that when Uncle Ajax was a kid he constantly moped around with his thumb in his mouth. And people would ask why he was so sad, even when he was happy. On the flip-side, although he doesn't look it, he's actually a pretty fun guy, to a point. Fact is, he's only quiet when he's asleep, and when he's wide awake. Well, he's unabashedly vociferous and witty, just ask him. He loves to be heard, remember he is a politician. He's usually a bit unkempt and he talks with his mouth full of food. Yet the ladies love him, I have no idea why. Oh, and there's one other thing, maybe two. Uncle Ajax always wears a holster and a gun. The holster is real, the gun is not. Yes, it is a bit strange. You might even say weird or eccentric, but he's been doing it, or I should say wearing it, for so long now that when people see the holster and gun, they don't bat an eye. Now you may remember I said maybe two. Well, the two is in my mind the scary part.

Uncle Ajax also has this soft floppy doll that he carries around with him at all times. The doll is either in his hand or hanging over his shoulder. Little Jax as he calls him is tall, slender, well dressed, and, as dolls go, quite handsome. I suppose little Jax is Uncle Ajax's alter ego or something to that effect. Oh yeah, little Jax also wears a holster and a six-shooter.

I left Ricky standing like a sentry in front of his desk and walked straight into Tommy's office. As usual Uncle Ajax immediately gave me a bear hug. And when he let go of me, I thought for sure he was going to cry, but he fought back the tears.

"Hey Junior - how you holdin' up?"

"I'm doing ok."

"Junior, I was just telling Tommy how sorry I am that I wasn't here to help. I hope you understand."

"Of course we understand. Nobody could have known something like this was going to happen. You're here now and that's what matters."

"Thanks for being so understanding. So tell me how your dad is doing."

"Dad's resting and I'm positive he's going to be ok. He's an ornery cuss and won't let this get the best of him. You should know that as well as anyone."

"Oh, there's no end to his orneriness. Yes, I could tell you some stories, but that'll have to wait for another time."

His eyes rolled up toward the heavens the way they frequently do and then he finished what he was saying, "Right now, I'm going to run over to the hospital and relieve Shadow."

"You know what, Uncle Ajax - I think Dad can hear you when you talk to him. Least that's what Madison tells me. Won't matter what's said, just talk - you're good at talking."

"Junior, I'm going to take that as a compliment. And yes, I'll talk to him. Tommy, keep me informed. And if that ass Burt writes any more stuff to incite this sicko, well, you'll have my backing when you arrest him. See you guys."

Tommy just nodded and I said bye. Uncle Ajax said, in a raised voice, "Ok, let's go, little Jax."

He ran out of the office, carrying little Jax like a football. Randi and Ricky waved goodbye, but I'm pretty sure it went unnoticed. Tommy waited 'til Matt got to the station before we all crowded into our conference room, Tommy's office. He didn't say a word. He just pulled the chalkboard out and started writing. And so did I. First, he wrote suspects in the top right corner. Then he turned and looked at us and said, "So far we have only one suspect."

He turned and ever so slowly wrote Ricky just below suspects. Ricky was instantly on the defensive. He looked around like a schoolboy. His eyes were blinking at the speed of light. He tried speaking but could only mumble. Then he stood up and it appeared he might run, and if not for the fact that Matt and Randi were in the way, he might have.

He finally, blurted out, "I wasn't anywhere near Miller's farm that day, and I would never hurt an animal."

We all stared at him.

"Come on you guys - you know me."

We continued to stare.

"Ok, once when I was a kid I shot Mrs. Campbell's cat in the ass with my BB gun. But he'd been eating the petals off of mom's flowers and he was burying his crap in her garden. What was I supposed to do? Come on you guys."

"Ricky, the only prints found on the butcher paper are yours," Tommy said with a simper.

Ricky just shook his head no 'til Tommy finally put his hand on Ricky's shoulder.

"Ricky, we all know you didn't do it. I was just havin' a little fun, sorry."

Ricky, still red from the embarrassment of his BB gun admission, slowly turned to us and smiled. We all chuckled together and I can't tell you how good it felt to let a little tension out. After a minute or so I guess Tommy figured we'd had enough fun. So he put that look back on his face we all know so well.

"Ok, that's enough fun for one day. Now we need to get as serious as we've ever been. I don't think I have to convince any of you that this person or persons is vicious and given the opportunity is going to strike again. And to make matters worse, we don't have even one suspect. Ok, before we get started, Randi did you call all the hotels and motels in the area?"

"Yes I did Tommy. And there's not one person registered that seems out of the ordinary, at least no more than the usual. I'll keep trying, but I don't think our crazy stays in hotels. That's just my opinion."

"Ok, thanks. Alright, I said there were no suspects, but I do have a new lead, and I believe this lead will eventually pan out."

I didn't know about the others, but I couldn't wait to hear about this new lead.

"Tommy, almost anything even close to a lead would be great news right now. So what is it you know that we don't?" I asked.

"When I drove past Andy's grocery yesterday, Flo waved me down. She said Andy has seen a car with Union County plates drive by twice in the last week. The second time he saw the car was right after Jack was attacked."

Matt beat everyone to the punch.

"What kinda car?"

"Flo said the color of the car is tan and that's all she knows. I didn't get to talk to Andy because he'd gone out to his brother's farm and wouldn't be back 'til tomorrow. So Junior, you get to go talk to him in the morning. Find out as much about this car as you can. Are you ok with that?" Tommy asked.

"Yes, of course I am. I'll run by right after breakfast."

Tommy turned to the chalkboard and put a line under Ricky's name. We all had one last small chuckle. Then to the left of suspects Tommy wrote clues and then below that he wrote 4114 and turned to us.

"I went to every church in town and got the same answer for the numbers 4114. They all said it can be found in Deuteronomy. It means - and I'm quoting, 'to overthrow' and in particular, the overthrow of Sodom and Gomorrah."

Nobody said a word. We looked at each other for a bit before Randi asked, "So do you think Crestfield is the Sodom and Gomorrah the creep is alluding to?"

"Randi, that's what I was thinking, but the truth is I just don't know," Tommy said.

Tommy turned and wrote overthrow next to the 4114. Then he wrote the letters DAAD and DKD just below 4114.

"Ok, we have to look at these numbers as maybe being a type of anagram. What I mean is they might spell something that reveals a group or a motive. Or they could simply be the letters in the name of our perp."

Then he turned back to the board and wrote butcher paper just below the letters and then once again turned to face us.

"Ok, now for what I think is the hard part. What is the significance of butcher paper? I mean why?"

I could see that Tommy really was perplexed. So I offered an opinion.

"You know Tommy, it could be any number of things, but maybe it's just that when we wrap or store meat it's usually in butcher paper. And it would be easy to acquire - that is without anyone thinking that you're nuts or going to commit a crime."

I could see the wheels turning in Tommy's head and for whatever reason he was bothered by the type of paper. Something made me answer his pause.

"Ok, it shouldn't be hard to find out who has been buying butcher paper - that is, that's not in the business. You know, not a butcher."

Tommy stood silent for a bit and then gave Ricky the job of finding out whom if anybody had bought butcher paper in the last month or so. It was a long shot, but we had to at least try to find out. Then Tommy wrote Jack under butcher paper, but he didn't stop there. He kept writing and when he was done the last few entries on the list were: Jack, Maggie, Acepromazine, and lastly, Miller's cow. Then he turned to us and said, "I wasn't sure at first, but there can be no doubt now that the crimes are connected. And as Henry said, 'We have a maniac among us.'

We all sat still and silent for a long time. I was about to voice my agreement with what Tommy had written on the board when the back door flew open and Shadow came bouncing into the station.

"Hey guys. I got here as soon as I could."

"How's my dad?" I asked.

"Jack is resting quietly and Ajax is watching over him 'til we're done here."

Nobody said a word.

"Have I missed somethin'? I mean is somethin' wrong?" Shadow asked.

Tommy immediately put any worries Shadow may have had to rest.

"No Shadow, nothing other than the obvious is wrong. We're all understandably a little on edge and frustrated. And what I have to tell everybody now is probably going to make matters worse."

In unison we all turned in our seats to hear the bad news.

"An officer named Dumbrowski from the state criminal investigations department called me late this afternoon and made it very clear that if we don't find this guy and soon, the state is going to take over the investigation."

I know I wasn't alone in my thoughts at that moment, I was angry. This is our town and it's our people that have suffered. The news about Dad was spreading and it was just a matter of time before fear, and the subsequent change in behavior that comes with fear, take hold. This is a small town where people don't lock their doors because they feel safe, at least they used to. Now, well, I just don't know. I had a million thoughts slamming my brain when Tommy jerked me, and I suppose the others, out of our reverie.

"Listen, we all have a job to do. Trust me; we're going to find this creep. Anything you guys want to say you'd better say it now."

I think everyone had plenty to say, but nobody spoke, that is nobody except Shadow.

"Tommy, there's something that happened out at the hospital I should tell you about. It may or may not play a part in all of this." We were all ears. "There was this big guy that came by asking whether or not Jack was going to make it, you know - live. He had a southern twang when he spoke. Anyway, the guy wanted to go in the room and say a prayer for Jack. The guy gave me the heebie-jeebies - so I asked him what his name was. I think he said Smith? He said he was a very concerned citizen."

Tommy immediately asked Shadow if he had let the guy go in Jack's room.

"Heck no - the guy was creepy. So I told him thanks for his concern, but nobody was allowed to go in the room. There was somethin' about this guy that worried me. I got the same feelin' from him I had as a kid when I saw that tornado headin' for town. Anyway, he walked away and then I realized I had unsnapped my holster and my hand was tight around the handle of my forty-five."

I started to ask Shadow a question when Tommy put his hand up in the stop position.

"Let Shadow finish. Go ahead Shadow; finish what you have to say. Don't leave anything out."

"Ok, well, as he walks away I relaxed my hand because I realized he was a patient in the hospital."

I wanted to ask Shadow why he suddenly thought the guy was a patient. And without being prompted Shadow says, "I knew he was a patient because he was wearin' a hospital gown and slippers. I mean people don't walk around town in their pajamas. At least not the people I know. I wanted to follow the guy, but I couldn't leave the room unguarded. When Ajax got there, I told him to keep an eye out for the guy. Then I went to every room in the hospital and he wasn't in any of them. So I asked Marjorie, she's the head nurse. Anyway, I asked her if she knew who this patient was. She said there was nobody by that description that had been admitted into the hospital. Man, was I confused after she said that."

"Ok Shadow, thanks for not letting the guy in the room. Can you describe the guy?" Tommy asked.

"Well, I'd say he was about six feet four inches tall and he weighed at least two hundred and fifty pounds. Couldn't see much of his hair cuz he was wearin' an old hat."

I stopped Shadow right there.

"Didn't it seem a bit strange to you that this guy was wearing a hat in the hospital?"

Everybody in the room turned and stared at me. I think they thought I was upset and they were right. But, I mean who wears a hat in a hospital? Shadow then turned and his deep set feral eyes bore a hole right through me.

"Junior, if you stood in the hallway at the hospital as long as I have, well, you'd be amazed at how many of the men around these parts always wear their hats, even when they're in a hospital. To be polite they take their hats off when they walk in, but then they put 'em right back on."

"I'm sorry Shadow, I was wrong to interrupt you. Please continue," I said.

"Ok, well, the guy has brown hair, but he's turnin' grey at the temples. He had some reading glasses hangin' on his nose so it was hard to see what color his eyes were, but I believe they were a pale blue."

Shadow stopped and put his hand over his expansive forehead and didn't say anything for a long time before he continued.

"The guy talks like somebody that grew up in the south or out in the country. You know like somebody that has been around the block, but is slow, maybe even retarded. Personally, I think he's nothing more than a hat wearin' simpleton."

We listened to Shadow, but the fact of the matter is we were all dead-dog tired. It was past midnight and time to go home. That's when Ricky started frantically waving his arm.

"I just thought of something, Tommy. If we find the drugs used on Miller's cow and Maggie, we'll have our bad guys. Right," Ricky said.

"At first I thought the same thing Ricky. Problem is I'm sure our bad guy or guys have thought of that too. By now the drugs have probably been disposed of or poured down some innocent drain. We'll just have to wait and see. Ok, the last thing on our list is the undeniable fact that these crimes are related. Just goes to show that even small towns at times can have big problems. Make no mistake about it, there is a connection between Miller's cow and what just happened to Jack. The opportunity for evil is ever-present, but the motivation to do so in these cases escapes me. And that worries me to no end," Tommy softly said as the lines on his brow deepened.

We all sat in silence for a little bit before Tommy stood up and said, "Go home and get some rest. I think we're all gonna need it."

Lonely is no fun   12

***Junior*/When I walked out of the station,** there was no doubt it smelled like rain. It was nearly October, which by the way, is one of my favorite months. I guess I like this time of the year because I know there are still a few warm days ahead. And I've always loved Halloween. It was the one night as a boy when it was ok to run crazy through the streets, and boy did I. It was no secret that the faster you ran the more candy you picked up. And I always came home with a couple of pillow cases filled to the brim.

Those are some great memories, but on this night they were being shoved to the back of the bus. I couldn't get the clues off of my mind. My head felt weighted down and so did my feet. To walk from the station down Maple Street to my apartment takes all of about one minute. I needed to think and decided to go around the whole block. I turned the corner from Mills onto Birch and then headed south for our main street, Adams Avenue. I stopped to think about things so many times I was dizzy. It was ridiculous. When I turned the corner heading west on Adams, I stopped again, but the sound of footsteps behind me continued for a moment.

I felt my whole body tense up. I stood for a bit, but heard nothing and said to myself, *you're imagining things*. I started walking again, but at a quickened pace. No footsteps behind me. *See, you're hearing things*. I continued walking and turned back onto Maple. I was nearly home when I heard the footsteps again. This time it sounded like two people, but I couldn't be sure. I'd had enough, and a flood of emotions ran roughshod through me. I pulled my gun out of the holster. I never touch my gun, yet I'd taken it from its holster twice in the last twenty-four hours.

I was tired of having my back to the problem and decided an offensive move might be the best defense. I didn't want to be the next victim, so I began slowly marching back towards the noise.

"Ok, who's out there?" I asked.

No answer.

"If I were you I'd stop right where you are. I'm warning you I'm going to shoot first and ask questions later."

Still no answer, so just to be sure I decided to go around the block again, but in the opposite direction.

By the time I was halfway, I felt so ill at ease my skin was crawling, I was on high alert. Then out of the corner of my eye I saw someone moving in the Brown's shoe store.

I made up my mind I was taking no prisoners. I wheeled, crouched, and aimed straight at my own reflection. I let out my breath, shook my head a couple of times, and babbled, to myself of course. I was so exhausted I couldn't think straight. I sat down on the curb and tried to relax and let my head clear. Then with my nervous system on overload I screamed, "Come out so I can see you!"

My voice echoing off the buildings and the rain that began to pound the sidewalk was the only answer I received. When you start hearing things, yelling at shadows, and waving a gun around, there's a good chance you're overtired and in need of a whole lot of sleep. And in order to get some sleep, I had to go home.

I got up and ran through the pouring rain all the way to my apartment. I climbed the stairs, rushed through to my bathroom, and grabbed a towel. I shook my head as I wiped the rain off my face. Then I trudged out and opened my refrigerator. I reached in for the bottle of milk and started to take a big drink. The milk was so sour there were lumps in my mouth. I jumped over to the sink and spit the soon-to-be cheese out. I stood there without a single thought in my head. I was mentally and physically paralyzed, completely numb to the world around me.

I stared into space for an indeterminate period of time before a small electric shock ran through me. I remembered that Ricky had brought some beer over just a couple of nights ago. I went back to the fridge and looked in for the beer, it was gone. Then a weary grin slowly spread across my face. I also remembered that Ricky says beer will go bad if it's not kept very cold. He says you have to keep your beer in the vegetable bin at the bottom of the fridge, cuz it's the coldest. I opened up the bin at the bottom of the fridge and there next to a brown, half-eaten head of lettuce was a bottle of Miller. I grabbed my opener and popped the cap off with a flurry. I tipped the beer up and took a long pull. I'm not sure if it tasted like champagne as advertised, but it sure did hit the spot. I walked over, turned the TV on, and slumped onto my old divan.

Crestfield

I was too tired to get up and change the channel, so I just stared at that weird-looking X thing that comes on when a station stops transmitting. The volume on the TV was up just enough so that all I could hear was that freaky buzz. I hated it, but couldn't get up and change it. The beer was history in less than five minutes. I know that because I heard the bottle clunk on the floor.

The bottle fell just before I fell into a deep sleep. I went into one of my mean dreams. I call them mean because I'm the one creating them and they're always about me not having a girlfriend - and why that is. Oh, it's amazing how many reasons I can come up with as to why there's no love in my life. I had a very pretty girlfriend in college, but she came home with me once and I saw in her eyes that this was not the kind of town she'd ever want to settle down in. She wasn't mean about it or anything. I guess she had dreams of becoming someone important and the little town of Crestfield and I didn't fit in her dreams. I should add that her meeting Dad didn't help matters. No question about it - she thought Dad was crazier than a loon.

I was at the exact same crossroads I'm always at in my dreams when Nel came wafting towards me; her long blonde hair flowing behind her like a cape. As I reached out to my new succubus, a noise woke me, and it wasn't the TV. I opened my eyes and immediately said to myself, *Junior, I'm beginning to worry about you. You've got to find a girlfriend - and fast.* I got up and turned the TV off and then sat back down in the dark. I was shaking my head when I noticed a shadow go by the bottom of my front door.

I strained trying to see in the dark as I reached for my gun, it wasn't there. I'd taken it off when I first came in and slung it over one of the kitchen chairs. Then the shadow came back and stopped. I heard what sounded like heavy breathing just before someone put their hand on the doorknob. I immediately jumped into the kitchen and grabbed my gun. By that time the doorknob had begun to turn. And to make matters worse, I couldn't remember if I had locked the door or not. I thought, *when was the last time I locked the door? Maybe never.* So I held the gun out with my right hand and quickly opened the door with my left, and in crashed a soaking wet Billy Thornton.

"Billy! What the heck are you doing? I was going to shoot you. Gosh! I feel like shooting you just for sneaking around. You scared the crap out of me. What are you doing sneaking around like this? Billy! Answer me."

"Ok, ok, gee-whiz give me a minute to wipe this rain off my face."

Billy started a wiping motion, one hand then the other. He looked exactly like a fly preening its bug-eyed little face.

"Junior, I'm sorry. I didn't mean to scare you, but I need your help."

"Have you ever heard of a telephone?"

"That's the whole point. I was going to call, but somebody cut the lines to my phone. I had to sneak in the dark all the way over to my parents. I checked on them, they were ok. So I locked all their doors and got their car out of the garage and drove over here. There was nobody at the station. Don't you guys have somebody on duty at night?"

"Was that you following me?"

"Yes, sorry Junior, but I didn't know where you lived so I had to follow you."

"Why didn't you just say, hi Junior, I sure could use your help."

"I didn't say hi because I'm not supposed to leave the farm without permission. So I thought if I could follow you home, we could talk in private without me being seen. Sorry."

"It's ok Billy, and you're right. It probably wouldn't have been a good idea for you to be seen walking around town, especially at night, what with all the stuff that's happened in the last twenty-four hours."

"What has happened in the last twenty-four hours?"

"My dad was nearly beaten to death by somebody or maybe I should say some-thing."

"Oh my, that's terrible. Wait a second. Doesn't your dad have a guard dog?"

"She's not a guard dog, she's a guide dog. She was poisoned, but Tommy got her to the vet just in time. Madison is probably with her as we speak. The dog's name is Maggie and we think she's going to be ok, but she's not out of the woods just yet. Wait a minute. Billy, why'd you ask about the dog and not Dad?"

"I, I asked because you said your dad was beaten, but he was still alive. And well, shoot, I just figured if there's a dog protecting him nobody would be foolish enough to mess with a dog. Didn't mean any disrespect, sorry Junior."

"Oh, that's ok. Guess I'm just a little on edge at the moment. Come on in and sit down. Here let me get the lights. Whoa, what happened to your eye? That looks like it must hurt something awful. You need to have that looked at."

"Yeah, maybe I should have it looked at, but not now. Somebody took a shot at me when I was hiding behind that big tree back of the house. A piece of bark broke off and hit me smack dab in the face. Bullet only missed me by a few inches. I coulda been dead. I was trying to get out to my truck, but whoever it was made sure to position themselves between my truck and me. They shot at me with my gun. Can you imagine getting shot at with your own gun? Whoever this person is must have known where to look for the rifle. Anyhow, now can you see why I come all the way into town to get you?"

"Yes Billy, I can and I'm sorry I yelled at you, but all the same you scared the bejesus out of me. Ok, I need to call your parents and make sure they're safe."

After urging me to make sure I didn't scare them, Billy gave me the number. Nel answered on the first ring.

"Mrs. Thornton, is that you?"

"Yes, this is Nel Thornton, who's this?"

"I'm sorry Nel, it's me, Junior McCool. I'm calling to make sure you and Jeb are ok?"

"We're fine, but somebody has stolen our car. The garage door is open, and the cars gone. I was just gonna call you."

I didn't want to scare them so I told them Billy had borrowed the car because his truck wouldn't start. She wasn't going for that story at all.

"Why would he need a vehicle? Junior, you're not a very convincing liar. Now Billy or Jeb, well, they can tell a whopper and keep a straight face doin' it. Junior, we're fine here so please tell me what the problem is. And this time I want the truth."

"Ok Nel, I'm sorry about that. Listen, somebody was sneaking around out at Billy's and he couldn't get to his truck. So he borrowed your car. I'll send him home in the morning with an officer. Make sure all of your doors and windows are locked. You're sure you're ok?"

"Yes, Junior, we're ok, but I'm not ok with that story. But for now it'll have to do. You take care of yourself and tell Billy we're fine. Goodbye."

I told Billy all about his mom not believing the story and why I didn't believe it either. He finally relented.

"Ok, I'll tell you what I believe to be the truth. I'm pretty sure that the person out at my place doing the shooting is my old cellmate, Benny Smith. Guess he's still pissed off about his ear."

"Billy, why do you think it's him?"

"I think it's him cuz he told me it was him just before he hollered at me to come out and take my medicine like a man. He said he'd numb up my ear so that it wouldn't hurt when he cut it off."

"Well, in a way you can't blame the guy. You know - an eye for an eye."

"Yes, that's true and all, but he didn't come all this way just to cut off my ear. He told me he was going to get out someday and that he was going to kill me when he did. Junior, he ain't gonna do any cuttin', but he is gonna do some killin', that's for damn sure. Oh, and he wasn't alone. There was some great big dude with him."

"How do you know that?"

"I know that cuz I could see the other guy. He stood up once and took hold of his face with both hands and cracked his neck. I think he was showing me what he was gonna do to me. The guy is big and scary."

"Can you describe him?"

"It was dark, but he's big and he was wearing a ball cap slanted to the side just like most of the other bumpkins around here."

"Ok, I understand it was dark. So tell me what Benny looks like."

"Ok, but remember I haven't seen him for a couple of years now. People can change an awful lot in that much time."

"Come on Billy, I'm tired and I need to get some sleep. What does he look like?"

"He's about my height, bushy brown hair, brown eyes - and he only has just the one ear."

"Which ear? I mean which one did you cut off?"

"That's the strange part, Junior. I don't remember cutting his ear off. So naturally I don't know which ear got cut."

"You know what, Billy - I'm beginning to not believe anything you tell me. Now for the last time - which ear got cut off?"

"His left, I think."

"Oh, the heck with it - shoot - I can't leave your parents out there with those two hanging around. I'm gonna call Shadow and Matt - have them go check it out."

I got out my handy little phone book and after two wrong numbers I had Shadow on the line.

"Hey Shadow, sorry to call at such a late hour, but–"

"No problem, I was up studyin' for my exam with the state police. Darn it, there's a lot of stuff I gotta know. Anyway, what's up?"

"Well, I need a big favor. I was wondering if you and Matt could take a drive out to the Thornton farm."

"That's no problem, Junior - when do you want us to go out there?"

"Uh - if you can - right now."

"Oh geez, this must be serious."

"Yes, it is very serious. There were a couple of guys out there shooting at Billy."

"Shootin' at Billy? You mean with real guns?"

"Yes Shadow, with real guns."

"Ok, I've got one of the squad cars here. I'll go pick up Matt right now, we can be out there within a half-hour or so. I'm leaving right after we hang up. Have you got any special instructions?"

"Yeah, don't get shot and if you see anybody sneaking around the farm, stay away and call me. So be careful, I don't want either of you guys getting hurt. We need you to be healthy and, most importantly, alive."

"You got it," Shadow said just before he hung up.

"Ok Billy, I need to get some rest. I'll have Ricky follow you home in the morning. You can sleep here on the divan, it's comfy enough for one night."

"Ok, but can someone else follow me back out to the farm? You know I'm not a big fan of Ricky's."

"Oh yeah, I forgot about that. All right, I'll follow you - ok?"

I got my one spare blanket and pillow out of the closet, handed them to Billy, and told him to please go to sleep.

Ricky makes the front page   13

***Junior*/The next morning I rolled over in bed** and slowly opened one eye to look at the clock and immediately jumped up. It was eight o'clock. I always get up at six. Felt like I'd only been sleeping for a few minutes. I was scratching my head and yawning when I hurried out to the front room to get Billy up. The problem was - there was no Billy. I looked out the window for his car before I realized I didn't know where he'd parked it in the first place. And to make matters worse, I had no idea what kind of car his parents owned. I trudged over to the phone and stood there for at least a half-a-minute. I guess I was going to call somebody, I just didn't know who.

I reached out and just stood there with my hand on the phone - it rang. Holding on to a phone when it rings, is for some reason, very unsettling. After being spooked for a moment, I picked up the phone and managed to say a weak hello.

"Mornin' Junior - how's everything?"

"I'm sorry, who is this?"

"What the heck? It's me, Shadow. Just thought I'd let you know that there weren't any bad guys out at the Thornton place. Leastwise, none we could see. And we covered every square mile of that farm, and that's a darn big piece of property. Anywho, Billy got here at about six and we looked around again, still nobody. So Matt and I headed back home. Junior, there's something very strange about all of this. Do you think Billy was telling you the truth? He seemed pretty sketchy about the whole thing. At least to me he did. Junior, are you there?"

"Yes, I'm here. I'm just a bit cloudy this morning. Didn't get to sleep 'til - you know I don't know what time it was. Ok, well, thanks, Shadow. As far as Billy goes, I'm not sure. He seemed sincere to me. Where are you now?"

"I'm home, dropped Matt off and came home to get a little shut-eye. Somethin' you want me to do?"

"No, get some rest. I'm gonna wash up and go over to the diner and have a bite to eat. Then I'm heading over to talk to Andy. Anyway, thanks again, Shadow, I'll talk at you later, bye."

"Junior, wait a second. Have you seen the paper today?"

"No I haven't - why?"

"It's not cool, Ricky's on the front page. I'll bet Tommy and Ajax are steamin' right about now. I think we have a leak."

"A leak, what do you mean? Ricky's on the front page?"

"Junior, I think you'd better see for yourself, but the long and the short of it is that Burt says Ricky is our main suspect in all of this."

"What!"

"Junior, just read the piece on Ricky. I'll see ya later, bye."

As soon as I got off the phone with Shadow, I called Ricky, no answer. So I showered and got dressed as fast as I could. I rushed out the door and by the time I got to the diner I was nearly running. I looked in the diner window and saw an empty table. And there on the table was the morning paper with Ricky's police academy picture on the front page. The headline read: **Main Suspect Sought in Cow Caper**

I went in and before I could sit down, Mary Hardwick - the owner of the diner with the ever-changing hair color, was in my face.

"Well, Junior - this is another fine mess the police have gotten us into. Have you arrested Ricky yet?"

"Morning Mary, gosh your hair looks nice that color. *Her hair looked like it was on fire.* No, we haven't arrested Ricky. He's not a suspect."

"That's not what the paper says. Burt wouldn't make something like that up."

Ricky and I went all through school with Mary and I can tell you from firsthand experience that she may be short and stout in stature, but she's long and tall when it comes to gossip. I suppose that's one of the perks that come with owning a diner. I knew I was in for a fight, a fight that I probably could not win.

"Mary, please listen to me. Ricky had nothing to do with this, the paper is wrong. But you'll have to trust me on that. I really am in a hurry so can I please have a cup of coffee and a raspberry Danish?"

"Yeah, I'll bet you're in a hurry. I'll be back in a minute, but this is not over."

70

I sighed in relief, but I knew she was going to reload and attack again. I decided on a defense. I picked the paper up and held it in front me while I read all about Ricky being the only name on a list of suspects. He was the main suspect because he was the only suspect. I heard someone huffing and puffing coming my way.

"Here's your coffee and Danish, we're out of raspberry, so marmalade will have to do. Junior, you can hold that paper up in front of you all day long, but I know you can hear me. Now where's Ricky?"

"Mary, I really don't know, but I do know he's not a suspect and that's all I know."

She mostly mumbled all the way back to the kitchen, but I did hear her say something about Ricky and me still acting like we were in high school. I wondered if she'd apologize after she found out Ricky wasn't a suspect. I finished eating in a hurry and left enough money on the table for what I'd ordered and a decent tip. I wasn't up to hearing any more from Mary. I jaywalked across the street and as I stepped up onto the sidewalk leading into the station, I heard Mary yell, "Junior! You're lucky I don't make a citizen's arrest."

I wasn't about to look back and when I stepped inside the station, Tommy greeted me with, "Morning, was that Mary yelling at you? What does she want?"

"Nothing, she just wanted to hassle me a little more," I said.

"A little more - is this about Ricky?"

"Yeah, so you heard."

"Yes, and I'm pretty sick and tired of it. But something good did come out of all this."

"Something good, how's that?"

"I found out how Burt has been getting the information. And when Ajax gets here, I'm going to go over and arrest Burt for breaking and entering."

"Oh man, I don't want to miss that, but I have to go talk to Andy right now."

"Junior, you have plenty of time. Ajax can't get here 'til noon. When he does, we're going to go next door. We're gonna arrest Burt right in the middle of his lunch."

"How'd you find out, I mean who is his source?"

"Rusty is his source."

"What the heck? I don't think Rusty would tell Burt anything. I know for sure that Rusty can't stand Burt."

"You're right and Rusty had no idea he was the source. You see, Rusty doesn't just clean up our building, he does the whole block. Well, somehow Burt stole the key to our back door and made a copy - would've been easy to do. Rusty's getting up there in age and forgets where he puts the keys all the time. Burt must have waited for a chance, grabbed the key, and then made himself a copy."

"Sounds about right, but what proof do you have?"

"Not much except for this Polaroid of Burt staring at Ricky's name written on the chalkboard, and I should add - at the camera."

Tommy reached into his shirt pocket and pulled out a picture of Burt writing something in a notebook. I had to look several times before I said, "Well, that's Burt alright, but I don't see how you can prove that he's in your office. I mean, there's nothing but windows in the picture."

That's when Tommy smiled real big and told me to look in the top right-hand corner of the picture, and there it was big as life. There hanging all by its lonesome was our grandpa's World War One picture, oval frame and all. Then I smiled real big.

"I guess we got him."

"I guess we do," Tommy agreed.

"Ok, well, that's great and all, but how'd you do it? I mean, what kind of camera is it?"

"It's a regular camera; it has a motion sensor attached. Once tripped, it's set to take a picture every fifteen seconds. I moved the chalkboard into my office after we all met last night. So the moment he walked in the office, it started clicking."

"How many pictures did it take?" I asked.

"There are six pictures, but this one is the best. And I'm only gonna need just the one."

"That's great. Listen, I'm heading over to Andy's house. I'll be back as soon as possible. Don't do anything 'til I get back. Oh yeah, where's Ricky?"

"I knew Ricky would be upset so when I went out to see him this morning, I told him to stay home. I promised I'd call him after I dealt with Burt. Junior, there's no hurry so find out everything you can from Andy."

72

I started out the door when Tommy said, "I forgot to tell you that Madison called this morning and said there has been no change with your dad or Maggie, but they're both resting comfortably."

"Oh man Tommy, I feel horrible. I forgot to call Madison. I was supposed to check in."

"No worries Junior. Shadow told her all about the Billy episode, Shadow's out guarding Jack's room as we speak."

"Oh, what a relief, you know that doggone Shadow deserves a raise. He's supposed to be home getting some sleep."

"I don't know about the raise - you'd have to talk to Ajax about that. But you know as well as I do that when it comes to money, Ajax is as tight as they come."

"He sure is. You know Tommy; I haven't had a raise in over two years now."

"He's tight alright. I've heard folks say Ajax is so tight he could back up to a building and pull a brick out with his rear-end."

"Oh, that's a good one. Yeah, you're right. Ok, well, I'll be back as soon as I know everything there is to know about the car and its driver. See ya."

I chuckled as I walked out the door.

Junior/I grabbed a roller and drove down the Irving Street hill to talk to Flo and Andy. It's all of a three-minute drive. Flo was outside working on the flower garden in front of the house. She waved a nice Midwest hello as I pulled up the gravel drive.

"Hello Flo. How's the flower business this morning?"

"Why you know I don't have any business going on here. They're just for looks."

"Yes ma'am, I know. I was just having a little fun."

"Yes you were - and at my expense."

Everybody knows that Flo sells her flowers and tomatoes all over the county. She grows some pretty ones too. You're supposed to pay for a license to sell flowers, fruits, and vegetables, but nobody does. It's just the way things are.

"Ok if I go talk to Andy now? You know about that car he's seen passing by."

"Oh sure, but you'd better let me come with you. Come on, Andy's out back in the crick."

I was gonna ask why he was in the crick, but as soon as we got around the side of the house and maybe fifty feet from him, I knew why.

The smell was so pungent and foul my eyes began to water. I shut my eyes for a moment and when I opened them, I looked over at Flo. She had a small towel wrapped around her face. I backed away, but Flo just kept moving towards her husband. I had moved away, but it smelled like I was only a couple of feet from the skunk himself. This was the first odor I'd ever come across that actually had volume, weight, and color. Then I looked down and realized I was standing on the shirt and overalls Andy had at some point taken off.

I hopped for a step or two before I ran all the way out to the street. I could still see Flo and I watched her throw a couple cups full of detergent or maybe lye into a bucket. She yelled out that she'd already scrubbed Andy with tomato juice. I kept backing up 'til I was on the other side of the street. I tried yelling at Andy, but there was just no use in trying to communicate from such a great distance. Then Flo turned and walked back to me, but she stayed on her side of the street.

"Junior, would it be ok if Andy told me the particulars and I wrote them down for you? Then if you have any questions, you can call back later and we'll fill in the holes."

"Flo, under the present circumstances, I think that's a great idea. Yes ma'am, that'd work out fine. Thank you."

I backed up again and then decided to just go wait in my car. And about ten minutes later Flo came walking out with an envelope in one hand and a plastic bag in the other.

"Andy says sorry about that. As you probably figured out, he and his brother Orin's dog got sprayed by a skunk. Last time this happened it was about a week before I could let Andy come back in the house. And it's gonna be at least that long this time too. Can you imagine a grown man letting himself get sprayed by a skunk, and more than once. Sometimes I think you men never will grow up. Sorry to vent like this, Junior, but there are times when it is just plain misery living with a man."

"I wouldn't know about that, Flo, but you're probably right."

"Uh – Junior, can you please do me a favor?"

My nose had a pretty good idea what that favor was going to be.

"Could you please dispose of Andy's clothes? I'm sorry to have to ask you, Junior, but–"

"That's no problem Flo," I said.

I lied. I knew she meant burn them.

"I'll have them burned. You probably wouldn't want them back anyway, would you?"

"No I wouldn't, and neither would Andy. Thanks so much."

I threw the bag in the back seat and made sure to say thanks. As I backed out of the driveway the smell was immediately wafting around me like a bad dream. I rolled down the windows and drove as fast as the car would go back to the station. I walked in the backdoor and the invisible enemy marched right along with me. Ricky was standing there in the dispatch room with Randi and as I said hello, they both gagged.

I explained but it did no good. I was immediately told to get the heck out of the station. I left the envelope and went out to the car and grabbed the bag full of Andy's clothes. Then I headed back home to shower, once again.

I didn't want to offend anybody on the street so I walked home through the alley the delivery trucks use. I ran up the stairs and into my apartment. As soon as I shut the door, I tore off my uniform. Thank goodness it was my old uniform. I stuffed my shirt and pants in a pillow case. Then I got a large plastic garbage bag and threw everything in. I tied the top of the bag very tight but could still smell that smell. I got in the shower and washed with a bar of lava hand soap 'til I thought my skin was coming off. Then I filled the bathtub with hot water and some bubble bath that was left behind by a former tenant. After soaking 'til I was shriveled up like an old prune, I got out of the bath and dried off.

I walked down the stairs from my apartment and out onto Maple Street. I looked for the first stream of smoke I could see. I got lucky. Somebody was burning leaves on the south side of town. So I went back in the apartment, shoved a broom handle through the knot on the plastic bag, balanced it on my shoulder like a hobo, and carried it down the steps. I hurried south down the street. The odor and a couple of dogs trailed behind me. I crossed the railroad tracks and headed straight towards the billowing smoke. As I walked up, I waved a Midwest hello to Clifford Anderson. And of course Clifford did the same, but along with his wave came one heck of a strange look.

"Hey Cliffy, listen I know this looks weird, but your uncle got sprayed by a doggone skunk. And some of the smell seems to have stuck to these clothes. Ok if I burn this stuff?"

"Yeah, I heard all about it. Sure, go ahead and throw the bag on the fire."

I threw the bag on the fire and within seconds it lit up in a brilliant multicolored blaze. As the stench went up in smoke, I stood there and stared. I was mesmerized by the fire. I've often wondered if cavemen felt the same way when they stared into a fire. I bet they did.

I stood there in a warm stupor as the fire continued to crackle, and then I remembered I had things to do.

"Listen Cliffy, I've got a bunch of things I need to get done so–"

"Junior, you don't have to explain. Say hello to the family. Oh, and I want you to know that we're all keeping your dad in our prayers."

76

"Thank you, that's awful nice of you. Ok, well, I'll see ya later and thanks again."

We both waved goodbye and before I knew it, I had walked all the way back to the station. I was pretty excited to see what information Flo had retrieved from Andy.

***Junior*/I ran into the station** hoping to hear about the car Andy had seen. No such luck. Tommy was ready to go next door.

"Ok Junior, I'm not going to take any chances, so I want you there as a witness. Do not help me and don't you dare help Burt."

"I wouldn't help Burt, well, I would, but not in this–"

"Junior, I'm just messing with you. Bring along your notebook and write down exactly what happens, ok? And if he runs, let him."

"You got it. Wait, you think he's going to run?"

Tommy just nodded yes.

"Hey, what about Ajax?"

"Ajax is already over there. Let's go."

As we were walking out, Tommy yelled, "Randi, open the cell door and wait there!"

She yelled back, "Ok, you got it!"

When we walked out our door, I started counting and got to exactly twenty-seven right when we walked up to Burt's desk. Burt stood up in a hurry and made sure to keep his chair between him and us.

"Hey guys, what can I do you for?"

I looked at Tommy and he put his hand up in the universal don't say a word position and said, "I'll handle this."

He had a real calm look on his face as he moved ever so slightly towards Burt.

"Burt, do you remember me saying I would come over here and arrest you if you wrote any more of that damaging stuff in your paper?"

Burt inched his chair backwards.

"Tommy, now I have excellent sources as to the validity of what I wrote about Ricky. And we've been all through how the law protects my sources. So there's no need to go over that again. Tommy, you wouldn't willingly break the law would you?"

"Of course not Burt, but if you broke the law then I would be compelled - you know, bound to uphold the law and arrest you. You understand, don't you, Burt?"

"Yes, I do understand, but I haven't broken any laws. Junior, you're a witness to all of this - right? You're a fair guy and don't let your emotions outweigh your intellect, right? You'd protect a citizen if he was being unfairly treated, wouldn't you?" I nodded yes. "Ok, then I guess it's settled, Tommy. I have the right to protect my sources. Junior is a witness."

Tommy inched forward and Burt moved backwards.

"Yes, Junior is a witness and you have rights when it comes to your sources Burt, but you have no rights when it comes to breaking and entering. You broke the law and there are consequences."

The look on Burt's face changed from casual concern to desperation in a matter of seconds.

"Burt Silvers, you're under arrest for the crime of breaking and entering. I have undeniable proof that you broke into the Crestfield Police Station - and in particular, my office."

Tommy reached and took the handcuffs off his belt. At the same time Burt ran like a frightened deer into his bathroom and slammed the door shut behind him. Burt immediately screamed, "Get that toy gun out of my face!"

Burt's pleading was closely followed by Ajax yelling, "Burt Silvers, this is not a toy gun!"

We clearly heard the thump when Ajax hit Burt across the forehead with the barrel of the gun.

"Ouch, that hurt. Ajax, you're not licensed to carry a real gun."

"Shut up Burt, and then put your hands up, you're under arrest. Now turn around and open the damn door."

"I can't open the door with my hands up."

Ajax laughed just a little before he said, "Ok Burt, do it this way. Open the door with your right hand and then reach for the sky."

Burt did as he was told and out they came, Burt's arms held high. Ajax was smiling from ear to ear. Burt wasn't.

"You know something, Tommy. I've wanted to say reach for the sky since I was a little kid. Thanks for deputizing me, this beats the heck out of all that mayorin' nonsense."

Tommy didn't waste any time with particulars.

"Burt, put your hands behind your back, you're under arrest."

The handcuffs were snapped onto Burt's wrists.

"Tommy thanks again for letting me in on this one. I think I'll leave the same way I came in, through the back door. A politician can never be too careful. You know, damage control. Thanks Junior, and take care of our naughty little paperboy."

Ajax slipped out the back and Burt was marched out the front. His secretary and two of the print operators watched every move with a keen eye. It's common knowledge that Burt is a tyrant as a boss. So, although their faces were pretty much devoid of any outward expression, I believe all three were smiling on the inside.

When we got to the station, Tommy walked Burt straight into the jail cell. Then he removed the handcuffs and told Burt to get comfortable because he was going to be in jail for quite a while. Tommy walked out and Randi smiled at Burt just before she slammed the door shut. It took Burt all of about ten seconds before he started screaming, "You can't do this to me. I want my attorney. I'm supposed to get to make one phone call. I want my phone call and I want it now!"

Tommy walked back to Burt and stood and looked at him for a long time before speaking.

"Burt, if you keep this up, I'm going to drag you by the collar down into the basement. We have a nice little closet that we put screamers in. After a couple hours of darkness, they usually shut up. So what's it gonna be?"

"Ok, I'll be quiet, but only if you give me your word that I can make that call, and soon."

"Burt, do you understand what you've done? Do you know how much you hurt Ricky? When folks read somethin' in the paper they tend to believe it's true. You printed a lie about him. You hurt Ricky more than you'll ever know. And so I'm not going to promise you anything 'til you shut up. That's for starters. Then when Ricky gets here, you're going to apologize to him. And if you don't, you're going in the closet. If you do apologize and it appears that you're sincere, then and only then will I consider letting you make a phone call. Do you understand?"

Burt stared at the floor and didn't say a word.

"Last chance, Burt. Ricky's name was put on the chalkboard by me as a joke. Do you understand, a joke?

And now the joke is on me. You hurt Ricky and I'm responsible. Ok, I'm done talking. I guess you can apologize to Ricky through the closet door because that's where you're going."

Tommy called Randi over and asked her to unlock the cell.

"Burt, I'm going to give you a couple of aspirin before we go downstairs. And you're going to take them or I will shove them down your throat."

"Why am I going to take aspirin? I don't want any aspirin."

"You're going to take the aspirin because the fall you're about to have going down the stairs is gonna hurt a whole bunch."

Then Tommy yelled, "Randi, can you go get me a couple of aspirin?"

"Sure thing - give me a minute."

Burt immediately said, "Ok Tommy, I'll do it, but first you have to tell me why you think I'm the one that saw Ricky's name on the chalkboard?"

"Sorry Burt, it doesn't work that way. You and your attorney will hear all about the evidence when you're in front of the judge. Now there's a couple of ways we can give you those aspirin."

Burt finally saw the light because he began to plead with Tommy.

"Ok, ok, please stop. Alright Tommy, you win. I'll apologize to Ricky and I'll put it in writing. And of course I'll be quiet."

"That's better. But know this, Burt. If you let me down, I promise I'll make the next several hours of your life a living hell."

Tommy and I walked back to his desk, and he picked up the envelope that Flo had given me. A foul odor drifted my way. I didn't want to miss a thing so I got my notebook out. Instead of telling me about it, Tommy just handed it to me. I opened it up and the first thing I noticed was how nice Flo's handwriting was. She'd written:

1: two door, hardtop, 57 Ford Fairlane

2: tan

3: 88, Union County plates

4: driver is so short he could barely see over the steering wheel, and he wears his hat slanted to the left
5: the first two numbers on the license plate are 3-4.
6: Andy says the driver looked like he was talking to somebody next to him, but he couldn't see the passenger. Call if you have any questions. Florence and Andy

"You know what Tommy; this is a lot more information than I expected."

"Yes, and it's a lot of what I believe to be reliable information. I've already called the state police and they're working on the description. That will take a lot of man-hours to search for that car and owner. The biggest problem is that there's just no way of knowing whether the plates are the plates that belong on that car. But like I said at our meeting last night, we know more today than we did yesterday. Junior, can you do me a favor?"

"Sure, what do you want me to do?"

"I want you to go over to Ricky's and get him to come to work. This morning I went over there to apologize, and I did, but he hadn't even seen the paper. So I explained as best I could and I promised him I'd get Burt. He was pretty upset."

"Yes, I imagine he was. That would really upset Ricky and for that matter - anybody. I'll head over right now. Anything in particular you want me to say or do?"

"No, just make sure that he knows we have Burt and that, once again, I'm sorry. Tell him that somehow I'll make it up to him. My car's the only one here, take it."

"Tommy, Ricky knows you'd never hurt him on purpose. Try to remember that and don't worry, ok?"

"Yeah, ok," he softly replied.

"Ok, well, I guess I'll head over there right now. I'll call you when I get there or I guess when I know something. You know whether or not Ricky's coming to work. I better just go. See ya Tommy, bye."

A friend in need 16

Junior/I got in the car and looked over, and there on the seat was the morning paper. Ricky was on the front page staring back at me. I looked away for a moment and then I looked in the mirror. I pounded my fist against the steering wheel and asked the same question I'd just asked the day before about Dad, why? I tried to imagine the pain that was going through Ricky. I asked myself several times what I'd do in the same situation. I couldn't come up with an answer because I just didn't know.

I pulled out of the station and started tooling west on Adams Avenue. Everything around me was a haze. I didn't see one car or even one person, but I knew they were there. I glanced at the speedometer, and I was barely going ten miles an hour. I picked it up to about thirty and before I knew it, I was heading south alongside McKinley Lake.

I still get an eerie feeling when I'm near the lake. Many years ago Dad was forced off the road by an unknown driver. He and mom tumbled nearly fifty feet down the steep slope at the south end of the lake. That night we lost mom and Dad lost his sight and maybe his mind.

Those were some dark days in my life and I don't really enjoy revisiting them, but I had no choice. I had to find Ricky and bring him back to the station. I know he would do the same for me. Ricky's cabin was only five minutes away. As I drove, I found myself hoping and maybe even praying that Ricky hadn't read the paper. I said over and over to myself, *maybe he didn't read it*, but I know Ricky and I know he read it. As I turned onto his gravel drive, I looked up and there was nobody on the porch, I thought he'd be there like usual. I got a little worried and became even more so when I went in the cabin and it was empty. I walked back out the front door and stood on the porch. I was thinking to myself, *where would he go?*

Then I looked down by the lake and saw a leg swing from his neighbor's boat dock. I started walking down the hill to ask if they'd seen Ricky. It didn't take long to realize I'd seen that skinny leg before, it belonged to Ricky. He was sitting and running his bare feet through the water. I thought for just a moment again and hoped he hadn't read the paper.

I said hello and when he turned to see who it was, that idea was dashed. His eyes were puffy and red as all get out.

"Hey Ricky."

He didn't answer.

"Ricky, please listen to me. As much as I'd like to I can't change what has happened, I just can't."

Still not a word, I was not used to this.

"Ok, just hear me out. Things are really looking up."

A cold stare came my way.

"That didn't come out right. Ok, Tommy and Ajax just got through arresting Burt."

His eyes said, 'I don't believe you.'

"Honest, I was there. I saw the whole thing. Anyway, Burt realizes he was wrong about you, dead wrong. And he's going to apologize as soon as we get you back to the station."

Ricky finally had something to say.

"Wait a minute. I've just been publicly accused of a horrific crime and you think if Burt apologizes everything will be ok."

"No Ricky, I don't think everything will be ok, but it's a step in the right direction. Listen, he's not just going to apologize, he's going to write a retraction in the paper. And for the record, I don't think anybody really believes you did any of this in the first place."

He didn't look convinced.

"Ricky, you and I have been through worse, a lot worse. Come on, I know you. And I know you're a bigger and better person than this. And the Ricky I know always forgives and forgets."

Although it was small, he did finally smile.

"There you go, now that's the Ricky everyone knows and loves."

He smiled even bigger.

"Now doesn't that feel better?"

"Yeah, it does."

"Ok, great. Listen Ricky, Tommy feels like he's responsible for the whole thing. So I'm hoping you can find a way to ease his mind a little."

"I told Tommy this morning that I knew he was just playing, but I'll tell him again when we get to the station. How's that sound?"

84

"That sounds great. Come on, let's go get this thing over with. Oh yeah, there's something else I wanted to tell you."

"Yeah, what's that?"

"You should have smiled."

"When?"

"When you took your academy picture, it looks like a mug shot of Howdy Doody. Made me wonder where Buffalo Bob was."

He laughed and then as he walked by, he slugged me on the arm. We've been doing that since we were kids. A slug to the arm is probably the best confirmation of friendship a guy can get. As I followed him off the boat dock, I happened to look down and there floating just below the surface of the water was the front page of the paper. A translucent Ricky was staring back at me.

We walked back up to the cabin so I could call Tommy and let him know we were coming in. I put my hand on the phone and it rang. Two times in one day? It was Madison.

"Hey Maddi, what's up?"

"Maggie is what's up. She stood up a little bit ago. She wants Dad."

"How do you know she–"

"I know because I've seen and heard her search for him before. She starts off by putting her nose to the air and then she moves her head from side to side. If she doesn't find him right away - well, then she whines. When she finds him, the whine is always followed by a sharp bark. There have been no barks up to now. She knows Dad's missing and she knows what her job is and she's trying to do it."

"Well, what do you think we ought to do?"

"We ought to do what I'm about to do. And that is take her to the hospital. It might serve two purposes. I think if Dad can hear her bark or maybe even whine, he just might wake up."

"I thought he was in an induced coma?"

"Not now he's not. That was for the short term. Doc Mayland would like Dad to be awake. He wants Dad to tell him what hurts. Once they find out the full extent of his injuries they can treat them in a more efficient manner. They already have a good idea what his injuries are, but...."

"But nothing, they want to know if he's brain damaged. That's what they want to know."

"Either way Junior, it's going to happen. I think the sooner the better. I mean, eventually we have to know. This is not going away. This is not one of the comic strips you usually had running through your head as a boy. You know, where the hero comes to the rescue."

"Ok sis, you can stop right there. And how do you know what I was running through my head? Have you forgotten that I was around before you?"

"No, I haven't forgotten anything. But one thing I clearly remember is you having long and involved conversations with Spider Man."

She laughed into the phone.

"Alright Madison, that's enough of that. Ok, Dad could use the company whether he knows it or not. And Maggie would love to be anywhere near Dad, that's for sure. Do you think the staff will let you bring a dog into the hospital?"

"I'd like to see them stop us."

"Ok then - geez, I'd hate to be the guy or gal that tries. Anyway, I'll see you at the hospital - let's say late afternoon."

"Junior, don't you dare try pulling that on me. You're going to give me an exact time."

"Ok, how about five - on the dot."

"Ok, I'll see you at five. Junior, don't you dare make me come and get you."

"Gosh, Madison, you're so... oh, never mind."

I started to say goodbye.

"Junior, don't hang up - what happened with Billy?"

"Well, so far nothing. I'll tell you about it this evening."

"Junior."

"Yeah."

"I'm so what?" she asked with attitude.

"Maddi, I'll see you at the hospital, bye."

I hung up in a hurry - I was afraid of what might happen if I told her the what.

Right under my nose   17

Junior/**While Ricky got dressed I called Tommy** and told him we were coming in.

"Junior, let me talk to Ricky," he asked.

"Ricky, Tommy wants to talk to you for a minute."

Ricky came out with no shoes on and his shirt out. He said hello and then didn't say another word until he was putting the phone back on the receiver.

"Gotchya, bye."

He went back into the bedroom and finished dressing. When he came back out he looked like a whole new person. He had that same old sideways bounce in his step. I looked at Ricky in my rearview mirror a couple of times on the way back to the station. I think he whistled the entire way. When we walked in, Randi came running. She stood in front of us wringing her hands together before letting Ricky know she was definitely worried and positively on his side.

"Oh Ricky, we've all been so worried about you. Nobody believes any of that crap Burt put in the paper. I'm so glad you came to work."

"Thanks Randi. You have no idea how nice it is - that is to know that I have friends that believe in me. Now all I have to do is get the people that don't know me to believe I'm not some monster. I think that's the part that bothers me more than anything."

"Ricky, you don't have to worry about those people. Wait a second, who doesn't know you? Anyway, what I meant was they're going to believe what they want no matter what you say. And Randi is right - the people that know you don't believe any of it."

The moment I was done talking I heard Burt yell something about a phone call. Of course Tommy coming out of his office was next.

"Hey Ricky, it's great to have you back here where you belong. You know we need your help in all of this. We don't function very well as a team when one of the team is missing. Come on, follow me, it's time for Burt to make good on his promise," Tommy said.

The three of us followed Tommy by Randi's station down the hall. When we got to the cell, Burt was shaking the bars just like some desperate guy you might see in a movie. Burt started to yell, but changed his mind when he saw Tommy.

"Something you wanted to tell me, Burt?" Tommy asked.

"Um, no I was just getting a bit hungry, and – oh, hello Ricky. Ok, can the three of you step back a bit so I can talk to Ricky - in private please? Thanks."

We stepped back and Ricky moved towards Burt. Ricky's hands were balled into tight fists, and he was breathing like a bull ready to charge. And before Burt could say a word, Ricky lit into him.

"Burt, you son of a bitch, I oughta kill you for the things you wrote in that damn paper of yours. Now everybody in town thinks I'm some kinda sicko or worse. You better have a damn good explanation, or I'm coming in there and pound the crap out of you. Why'd you do it, Burt? Tell me why!"

"I did it because I thought you were the suspect. I was just doing my job."

Tommy stepped up next to Ricky.

"Burt, I told you Ricky's name was on that chalkboard as a joke. You know that is the truth. And you know Ricky is not capable of doing something so horrendous. Now you said you would apologize and put it in writing. Are you going to keep your promise?"

"Well, Tommy - I did say I'd write an apology, but I didn't mean here. Not in a jail cell. I need to go sit down at my desk and have my attorney present while I write. You know, to make sure everything is done legally. You understand, don't you?"

"Yes Burt, I understand," Tommy said.

Burt's shoulder's relaxed a bit.

"I understand that something very bad is going to happen to you. And I believe it's going to happen right here in this cell - today!"

"Tommy please, I can't write under these conditions," Burt pleaded.

"Last chance Burt," Tommy warned.

Even though he had the chance, Burt didn't say a word. So Ricky immediately said, "Randi, where are the keys to the door?"

"The keys are next to the switchboard," she answered.

Ricky went to retrieve the keys and Tommy stepped up to the cell door.

"Burt, when was the last time you were - as Ricky so eloquently put it - pounded? Ok, well, if I were you I'd start talking and writing, and in a hurry. We're not going to stop Ricky when he comes back. In fact, we won't be anywhere near the cell when you try to break out."

"Wait a minute," I said in disbelief.

I couldn't let this happen and yelled, "Ricky, you don't really want to do this. You'd be putting your whole career in jeopardy - for Burt? Come on, this is crazy. Tommy, you can't let this happen."

I was pleading.

"Junior, I'm not letting anything happen, but if Ricky wants to exact a little payback, well, that's something I won't be around to see."

"Come on Tommy, please," I begged.

It was at this point that Burt once again pleaded with Tommy.

"Tommy, please listen to Junior. He hasn't let his emotions get the best of him. Please listen to the voice of reason."

We all heard the keys jingling just before Burt screamed, "Ricky I'm sorry! I mean it - I'm really sorry!"

Ricky walked up and put his hands around the bars the way you might grab a person just before strangling them.

"Not as sorry as you're gonna be."

I heard the keys jingle again, but Ricky wasn't holding them. Then in walked Uncle Ajax, with the key ring held tightly between his teeth. He was wearing a shiny new two gun holster, and so was little Jax.

Uncle Ajax had his plastic gun on his left hip and a revolver was in his right hand. He looked like some nut in a pirate movie.

"Hello Burt," he said like Humphrey Bogart.

Burt slowly moved several steps back.

"Somehow I knew you'd lie to get your ass out of jail. You never were gonna apologize to Ricky, were you?" he asked as much as said.

Ajax handed the keys to Randi and then pointed the gun through the bars.

"You know Burt, if you were fighting with – oh, let's say Randi. And well, you took her gun from her then somebody would have sound legal reason to shoot you, wouldn't they," Ajax inquired.

Burt just stared at the gun.

"So anyway, I think everybody except Randi and I are going to leave the station. I'll have no other choice but to shoot you. Least that's what the paper's going to say. Funny thing is, it won't be you writing the story, will it Burt. Maybe you'll live? Although most people that get shot in the head don't make it. Ok, everybody out - that is except for you Randi," Ajax ordered just before he shot a hole through the ceiling.

Burt jumped back several feet and started to whine as he manufactured some tears.

"Ricky, I'm sorry. I'm sorry a thousand times over. And yes, I know you're not really a suspect, but I've got to sell papers. You understand, don't you? Please say you understand."

Ricky didn't bat an eye let alone speak. It was at this point when Tommy repeated the demands.

"Burt, you're a sorry son of a... And I'm tired, so this is your last chance. What's it gonna be? The sincere written apology or the gun Ajax has pointed at you?"

I believe Burt was too frightened to speak.

"Ok Ajax, go ahead and shoot him."

Randi unlocked the cell door and Ajax walked straight to Burt. And I ran in behind Ajax. I was afraid to get in front of the gun Ajax was holding, but if I had to, I knew I would.

"This is insane. Gosh! What's the matter with you guys? Have you all gone crazy? Uncle Ajax, please put the gun down. There has to be a better way. Please!" I begged.

It was as if I wasn't even there. By this time Burt was huddled in the far corner, his hands wrapped around his head. And before I could get in the way, Ajax had the end of the gun barrel flat against Burt's forehead.

"Burt, this won't hurt at all. You'll hear a loud noise, then it'll all be over."

Ajax pulled the gun up, cocked it, and quickly put the end of the barrel back against Burt's forehead. I said to myself, *he wouldn't dare*. I felt helpless. Burt didn't even look up before he screamed, "Ok, give me a pen and paper, I'll write the damn apology."

I let my air out in relief as Tommy walked in the cell and stood next to Ajax.

"Ok Burt, if you're lying and you don't put pen to paper, then Ajax is gonna have to shoot you. Do you understand?"

"Yes Tommy, I understand. Now please get that maniac brother of yours out of here," Burt begged.

Burt's head was still buried in his arms when I saw Tommy and Ajax looking back at Ricky. All three of them had wry smiles on their faces. I had been duped right along with Burt. I said to myself, *oh man, I've been playing good cop - bad cop, and I didn't even know it.*

"Ok Randi, do you have a notepad and pen for our prisoner?" Tommy asked.

"Yes, of course I do," Randi answered.

She was back in a jiffy and for some reason she handed the notepad and pen to me. I walked over and handed them to Burt. He got up from the corner, sat down on his bunk, and then he took one last trampled look at Ricky. Burt wrote at a fevered pace. He started and stopped several times. It took all of about five minutes before he'd finished. He looked up at Tommy.

"Here you go Tommy, see what you think."

As Tommy read the apology, a tiny smile appeared across his face.

"Well Burt, I like most of what you've written, but you forgot something that's very important."

"What have I forgotten?" Burt asked.

"Burt, you know darn well what you've forgotten! You never said you were sorry. Now I'm only going to ask you one more time. Are you going to write an apology or not?"

"Uh, yes I am. Somehow I forgot to say I was sorry. I didn't do it on purpose. Here, give me the notepad."

Burt started writing again and when he was done, Tommy reread the whole thing.

"Ok Burt, that's much better. Except I'm not sure you should mention that the persons responsible are low down dirty cowards. What if they decide to come after you?"

"I thought about that, Tommy, and there's nothing to worry about. You see, I'm behind bars. And when I get out, I'll have the entire police department watching every move I make. Remember, I'm protected."

"Ok then, give me the notepad. I want this printed in tomorrow's paper. Who should I give it to?" Tommy asked.

"My secretary Helen will take care of everything. Now do I get to make that call?" Burt asked.

"Sure thing. Randi, take Burt into my office and let him make his call. Just make sure you dial for him. I still don't trust you, Burt. You understand - right?"

"Yeah, I understand. So let's make that call. I want out of here and the sooner the better."

Randi took Burt into Tommy's office and once inside she shut the door.

"Ok Burt, who would you like to call?" she asked.

"Call the Corbett law firm."

"Burt, you forgot the magic word."

"What? Oh yeah, please."

Randi dialed the number and then handed the phone to Burt.

"Hello Phyllis - this is Burt Silvers, may I speak with Carlton? Fishing! This is not my day. Ok then, let me talk to Stanley. Hello Stanley - Burt Silvers here. Ok, listen carefully. I'm in jail here in Crestfield. Yes, I'm in jail. I'll explain later. Right now I need you to come get me out. I know you've got a little drive ahead of you. Just make sure you start right now and don't dally. Ok then, one hour. Yes, bye."

After Randi walked out of the office with Burt, everyone else did the same. That is except for me. I didn't move an inch. I was pretty upset over the fact that I had been used in the little con game played on Burt. I started to move when Tommy walked out of his office and back to me.

"Listen Junior - I know you're probably upset about what just happened. But if we had told you ahead of time then you would have been acting. And that might have come off a bit phony. So if you think about it, we really had no choice. I'm sorry, but you have to admit it sure did the job."

"So you think I can't act?"

"No Junior, it's not that I think you can't act. It's just that I didn't want you to have to. There is some logic in there somewhere. Try to understand."

"I understand and I'll get over it. Just don't do that again, ok?"

"You got it."

"Ok - well, I'm heading out to see Dad. Oh yeah, and Maggie. She's up and moving about. Madison says Maggie might help in some small way to get Dad to wake up."

Tommy just nodded yes. I don't think he believes in stuff like that. I was heading to my office - when on the way I saw something that threw me for a loop. Ricky was hugging Randi, and it wasn't the kind of hug you give your mom. I thought to myself, *how many times can something happen right under your nose, Mr. Detective, before you wake up and smell the coffee?*

I think the two of them heard me so Ricky quickly walked away and then pretty much ran to his desk. I walked out to him and asked if he wanted to come with me to see Dad.

"Absolutely, yes I want to go see your dad, for sure."

"Ok, but I'm not letting you ride out there with me looking like that."

"Wha-da-ya mean? Looking like what?"

"I mean you're going to look pretty foolish out at the hospital with that lipstick on the side of your face."

Didn't take but a few seconds for the lipstick on his cheek to blend right in with the extreme red his face had turned.

"Ricky, why didn't you tell me? I thought I was your friend?"

"I didn't tell you because of rule number seven."

"What the heck? What rule number seven are you talking about?"

"If you'll read the policeman's manual, you'll see that it very clearly says that romantic involvement between employees is frowned upon and may be grounds for termination."

He had a point and with Ricky there is no bending of the rules. Well, at least he usually tried not to bend them too far.

"Ok, I guess I can understand that."

"Thanks for being so understanding."

"Wait just a minute there pardner. There's a limit to my understanding. When were you going to tell me? How long has this been goin' on?"

"Hey, that'd be a good title for a-"

"Ricky!"

"I don't know. We've been seeing each other since last spring. Randj said it would complicate things if I told you, so I didn't."

"Why I oughta. Did you just say Randj? Do you do everything - Randj tells you to do?"

"Lately, I mean yes, I guess I do."

"Ricky, you lily-livered sap sucker. You might as well be... Oh no, you're not."

"Well, now that you mentioned it. We were thinking on getting married, maybe this next spring. I was going to invite you."

"You were - were you? What a pal. Have you forgotten she's my sister and maybe, just maybe, she would have invited me herself?"

"Oh yeah, sorry."

"Sorry, that's all you have to say for yourself is sorry? So all of those times you told me you were going to go practice at the shooting range, you were actually going to see Randi?"

"Well, yes, but I was practicing my shooting too. She's a great teacher."

"Yeah, I'll bet she is. Gosh! Can you imagine my best friend and my own sister sneaking around behind my back?"

"I'm sorry, Junior. I, we, I didn't mean anything by it. Please, I'm sorry. And you're still my best friend, aren't you?"

"Yes Ricky, I suppose I am. And I will probably always be your best friend."

"Good, because I think I'm too old to go out and find a new best friend. And I wasn't just gonna invite you. I want you to be my best man."

"You do?"

"Well, sure I do, who else?"

"I don't know. I haven't had much time to think about the whole thing."

"So will you?"

"Yes Ricky, of course I will."

"Oh good, so now do you understand?"

"No Ricky, I don't, but eventually I probably will. And I guess there are worse things than... Oh geez, you're going to be my brother-in-law. Imagine that."

"Wow Junior, I hadn't thought of that."

"Yeah, that is a bit strange. Let's forget about this for a while, ok?"

"Yeah - let's."

We started walking over to the hospital. Not a word was spoken 'til we got right in front of that wooden bench out front.

"Ok Ricky, let's go see Dad. I wonder what he's going to say about you marrying his baby daughter."

"Oh Junior, you didn't have to put it that way. Heck, your dad and I go way back. We're good buddies."

"So you go way back, huh. How far back do you think he and Randi go?"

"Junior, I don't care what your dad says as long as he says something."

"Gosh, you're right, Ricky. I'm sorry - there really is nothing I'd rather hear right now. Let's go see Dad."

"Yeah - let's."

Madison/I told Maggie we were going to go see Dad and she nearly broke my front door down. She was weak, but the desire to do her job and, of course, see Dad was still very strong. I thought to myself, _Maggie, your loyalty and desire to please are beyond my comprehension. If only humans could be so deftly loving, loyal, true, and honest with one another._ I immediately wiped that thought out of my head.

It took us less than five minutes to get to the hospital. I don't think Maggie had ever been there, but when we got out of the car it seemed to me that she knew exactly where Dad was. Why did I think that? I thought that because she dragged me across the parking lot and through the front doors. When we got to the nurse's station, Marjorie jumped up and hollered, "Stop right there. Madison, you can't bring that dog in here without prior approval and I might add - a state license."

"Marjorie, she has a state license and you know it. And as far as prior approval goes, well, I'm here to get that right now."

Marjorie started to say something.

"Stop right there, Marjorie. If you want to keep the dog from coming in – well, I guess you're free to try, but don't blame me when she bites your hand or leg off. And trust me; to get to Dad she might do both."

I looked at Maggie and said, "Dad's here and this lady is in the way. Do you want to see Dad?"

Maggie immediately growled then barked at Marjorie. Feral doesn't do justice or come close to describing the look Maggie gave the lady standing between her and Dad. Marjorie got out of the way, but she just couldn't let things be.

"I'm gonna call the police on you and that damned dog."

"I think calling the police would be a great idea. Can you say hello for me, you bitch!"

"Why I never, Madison, you've gone too far."

"You think this is too far, huh? Listen carefully. The next time you try to get between my father and me, I'm gonna bite you myself. Now get out of my way."

96

Maggie accented what I'd just said to Marjorie with a sharp bark. And it took maybe a few seconds before I smiled real big. I didn't smile because she had barked. I smiled because I realized that Maggie could hear everything I said. And that was fabulous.

"Come on girl - do you want to go see Dad?"

She nearly yanked my arms off as she pulled me towards Dad's room. I have no idea how she or, for that matter, any dog can do things like that, but there was no question about it, she knew exactly where Dad's room was. She dragged me down the hall and we ran right past Matt, he was guarding the room. Matt and I managed to wave a short hello to each other before Maggie dragged me into Dad's room.

Once inside the room we both came to a screeching halt. Jenny was there bathing Dad. I was a bit uncomfortable. However, I don't think Maggie gave a hoot. The moment we got into the room she barked and jerked away from me. She had her paws up on the side of Dad's bed before I could say hello.

"Hello Jenny - I'm sorry, I hope Maggie's not bothering you. I guess she's anxious to find out how Dad's doing."

"Hello and no - she's not bothering me. Oh, I think she's simply wonderful."

Jenny stopped what she was doing and stroked the side of Maggie's head. Before that day I had never seen Maggie let a stranger do that. It was an odd thing to witness. Then Jenny bent a little at the waist and looked deep into Maggie's eyes.

"Hello young lady, we've been expecting you. Jack is better today, and I think that soon he'll be up for a nice walk, with you of course. Would you like that?"

Maggie let out a bark that anyone would recognize as a yes. Then Jenny turned to me.

"Your dad is much better today, but last night was extremely difficult for him. I believe he's in a dream world that at times gets a bit dicey. He was calling out names for several hours last night; he's very fond of you girls. He called out for the three of you many times."

I don't know how she knew that there were three of us, but it didn't really matter. Dad was better today and so was Maggie.

"Listen Jenny, I'm going to leave Maggie here with you and Dad if that's ok. I think I'll wait outside 'til you're done bathing him. Do you mind if the dog stays? I'd hate to try and make her leave right now."

"No of course not, I'd like to talk to Maggie for a bit, you know privately. That is if it's ok with you?"

"Um, yes I guess that'd be fine with both of us."

I walked out into the hallway and Matt stood up and offered me his chair.

"Here Madison, have a seat."

"Are you sure?"

"Sure, I'm sure. I need to stretch a bit anyway. I get kinda sore in the shoulders and back sitting here. Madison - ok with you if I go get a cup of coffee?"

"Sure - I'll stand guard. Between Maggie and me nobody is getting in this room, that is - nobody we don't want in."

"Ok, well, thanks. I'll only be gone five minutes or so. Maggie's ok in there by herself?" he asked.

"She's not alone, Jenny's in there giving Dad a sponge bath."

"What? I must be slipping. I didn't see anybody go into the room. Who's Jenny?"

"She's the nurse that's been caring for Dad."

"Wow, I better get two cups. Ok, thanks. I'll be back in a few."

I sat and listened, but I didn't hear even one word being spoken. Maybe Jenny was thinking about what you say to a dog. I sat very still for a long time and still nothing was said, leastwise nothing that I could hear. And like most women I have some pretty darn good ears when it comes to listening to other people talk.

I guess I had dozed off when Uncle Ajax came up and clapped his hands together, right next to my ear.

"What's up doc?"

I nearly jumped out of the chair.

"Gosh darn it, you scared me, Uncle Ajax! You know what?"

"What?" he asked.

"Chicken... Oh never mind what, it's good to see you."

Then, as usual, he gave me a bear hug.

"It's good to see you too, Maddi. Well, except for the fact that your Uncle Tommy and I got an awful lecture from

Marjorie about rules and regulations and such. By the way, where is Maggie?"

"She's inside with Dad and Jenny. Dad was getting a sponge bath so I thought I'd wait outside for a while. Worked out just fine, I think Matt needed a break."

"Oh yeah, he sure did. Marjorie gave him hell too. I guess she ordered him to come and arrest you for bringing the dog in here. Anyway, Matt wasn't about to arrest you so he called Tommy. Then Tommy calls me and we decided we needed to get here in a hurry. You sure did stir up a hornet's nest bringing Maggie."

"Yeah, well, there's gonna be hell to pay if Marjorie messes with me again. I'll give her a–"

"Madison, it's ok. We fixed everything with the big boss. Then he fixed everything with Marjorie."

"Who is the big boss?"

"Why little Jax of course, who else. You see, the mayor approves all the hiring for the hospital, and the firing. So if Marjorie wanted to keep her job - she was gonna have to keep her mouth shut, at least when it comes to Maggie. In her defense she does a good job running the hospital."

"You know Uncle Ajax, I think it'd be a good idea if you came down to my office someday," I said with reservation.

"Ok, but why?" he asked.

"So that we could talk," I softly said

"About what?" he derisively asked.

"About little Jax," I calmly said.

"How 'bout I bring little Jax and you can have a talk with him," he said with a sneer.

"I'm serious," I said with conviction.

"So am I," he said with more conviction.

"So that's how it's gonna be." I said

"That's exactly how it's gonna be," he said with a stern look on his face.

"Madison, please listen to me. I've just taken care of a volatile situation for you. I don't think we'll have any more problems with Marjorie so if it's ok with you, I'd like to move forward from here. Your dad is what matters now," he said with a fractured smile.

"Ok - you're right and thank you, but I'm still awfully darned mad at Marjorie. She got pretty cross with me - and for nothing."

"Uh, she told us you were pretty cross with her too. Madison, did you really call her a bitch?"

"Sure did, and if she pulls something like that again, I might add hog onto the end of bitch."

He nearly fell over laughing.

"Uncle Ajax, stop that, I'm serious."

"I know. That's what makes it so funny."

"You know Uncle Ajax; you don't always have to be a smartass."

He laughed even harder. I was about to tell him to stop laughing when Tommy rounded the corner and came walking towards us. He put on a nice Midwestern smile and waved hello.

"Hello Madison, I see you've got Ajax in good spirits. How'd you accomplish that? A few minutes ago he was giving Marjorie heck and now he's laughing. This sure can be a strange world at times."

"Hello to you too Uncle Tommy, I'm sure glad you're here. I'm not sure what made him laugh and I don't want to go back there. Um, where's Matt?"

"I sent him and Shadow back out to Billy Thornton's place. Don't know if you heard about what's going on, but I don't like it at all. I've got a bad feeling about Billy."

"Oh geez, Junior said the same thing."

"Yeah, well, when there's this much going on and so little to work with, you've got to follow your gut. And my gut says there's more than one nut causing all of this tragedy and turmoil. And every nut is a suspect from here on out."

"Uncle Tommy, I've never heard you say as much in one day, let alone in a matter of minutes," I said.

"Madison, I'm sorry I bent your ear, but knowing that my brother is in that room struggling for his life makes me sick. I want the persons responsible caught and punished, whatever that means. Ok, enough of that - I've got some good news. Buck called from Fort Ord and said he's waiting for Dezi. I guess he finally found her somewhere in San Francisco. They'll be here on the twelve o'clock eastbound train."

"Oh, Uncle Tommy, that's fabulous news, Dad will wake up for sure. Thank you, oh and of course you too, Mr. Mayor."

"Well, I was an afterthought, but a thought nonetheless. And you're welcome, Maddi. Now let's go in and see Jack," Ajax said.

The three of us walked into Dad's room and just had to stop and smile. Maggie was up on Dad's bed, lying right next to his feet. They were both sound asleep. Maggie knew we were in the room, but she was with Dad and that's all she cared about. I looked around and realized that Jenny was gone. She must have left when I fell asleep. The three of us looked around for a chair, but there was only one. Uncle Ajax grabbed the chair before I could get to it. He started to sit down and then gave me one of his devilish little boy smiles.

"Here Maddi, you didn't really think I'd take the only chair, did you?"

"Well, to be honest, I had my doubts. You and Dad are a couple of jokers."

He gave me his mischievous little boy look before he said, "We're not jokers all the time, but you're right. We are jokers some of the time."

Then he gave me his happy little boy smile. I sat without speaking for quite some time before I heard Ricky and Junior walking up the hallway. Then the three of us clearly heard Ricky say, "Junior, you shouldn't have let Marjorie talk to you like that."

"Oh yeah, what was I supposed to do Ricky, slug her? And if you're so darned brave why didn't you defend me?"

"Uh, I didn't want to interfere and because I know you can fight your own battles."

"Yeah right, you were scared. What do you think she was talking about anyway?"

They walked in the room and immediately saw Maggie up on Dad's bed. Ricky pointed at Maggie and said, "I guess that's what Marjorie was talking about."

I got a hug from Junior and Ricky and the chair hunt started all over again. Finally, Uncle Tommy walked out of the room and picked up the chair I'd been sitting on and brought it back into the room. The guys all stared at each other, but nobody moved a muscle. I thought to myself, *guys are so classically predictable. And I don't think I can sit here with this many strained male egos.*

So I said, "I'll go find some chairs so that everyone can sit down. Now while I'm away somebody sit in these stupid chairs."

Nobody moved.

"Geez, it's like talking to a room full of pee-pants, ornery Cub Scouts," I said.

I guess my comment got to Junior and Ajax. And they reluctantly volunteered to help me find some chairs. We walked out into the hallway and I looked to my right, no chairs.

"You guys go that way," I said as I pointed to the right.

I turned left and walked back towards the front desk. I didn't want to deal with Marjorie again, but if necessary I would. When I walked by the nurses' station there was nobody behind the counter and no extra chairs. So I continued towards the back entrance of the hospital. That's when I stopped dead in my tracks. I believe that humans have senses that are not yet fully developed. And right at that moment my senses were buzzing. There was no doubt whatsoever, at least in my mind - that I was being watched. I slowly walked around another corner and there, sitting by the elevator door, was a chair. I was just about to pick it up when someone tapped me on the shoulder.

I must have jumped halfway across the hallway. I crouched in a defensive posture, turned, and looked up. And there, standing by himself with a shocked look on his face, was my soft-spoken cousin, Wallace Ramsbottom.

"Wally! You scared the crap out of me."

"I'm sorry Madison - I didn't mean to. You know as well as I do I've always had this same face," he said with a laugh.

I didn't laugh.

"I'm sorry, you really are frightened. I was just going to help you with the chair," he said.

"Where were you? Wally, why did you sneak up on me like that?" I asked with a little attitude.

"Madison, I didn't sneak up at all. I was right there in the supply closet."

"Oh geez, I'm so sorry, Wally. It's just that I felt as though someone was watching me. Have you seen anybody around here in the last five minutes or so?"

"Well, now that you mention it, one of the patients was sitting in the chair you were going to pick up. But he left a while ago."

"What'd he look like? I mean, can you describe him?"

"I suppose so. He had on a hospital gown and slippers. And he was a pretty good-sized man. Why, is it important?"

"Yes, very. Was he wearing a hat?"

"As a matter of fact, he was. He had it slanted to the side like most of the men around here."

"Where'd he go?"

"I don't know, Madison. I have been very busy today."

"Ok Wally, thanks. Oh wait a second. Have you seen this man before today?"

"I believe so, but I can't be sure. We have so many people that come and go."

"Well, ok then, Wally. Can you help me find a few chairs to put in Dad's room?"

"Sure thing, but they can't stay there permanently. There has to be room for the doctors and nurses to move about. And Marjorie is madder than a hornet today. I don't know what got her so riled up?"

"Uh Wally, I'll take this chair back to Dad's room. Can you rustle up a couple more?"

"Madison, first I have to clean up a spill of some kind. Then I'll be there with as many folding chairs as you need."

I carried the chair back to Dad's room. I looked in and the guys were all still standing there. I guess Junior and Ajax hadn't found any chairs. I walked in the room and set the chair down next to Dad's bed so I could stroke Maggie's brow. The moment I set the chair down Maggie raised her head up and began to growl. She wasn't growling at me, but it sure felt like it. She jumped down from Dad's bed and circled the chair several times, the growl was non-stop. I was just about to ask her what was wrong when Junior beat me to it.

"What's wrong, Maggie girl? What is it? Is it this chair?"

Junior put his hand on the chair and Maggie barked loud enough to wake every patient in the hospital.

"Ok girl, do you want me to take the chair outside?"

"Uh Junior, she's a smart dog and all, but I'm pretty sure she doesn't understand what you just said," Ricky confidently said.

"Oh yeah, watch this."

Junior picked up the chair and walked out to the hall and set it down. When he walked back into the room Maggie jumped back onto Dad's bed.

Junior bent down to let Maggie lick him on the face, but Maggie looked past Junior and started barking real loud again. We all turned to see what she was barking at. There standing in the doorway was Marjorie. She pointed her finger at Tommy before she started talking.

"I told you Tommy. That damn dog has no business in this hospital. If she wakes up one of the patient's, I'm gonna call the Sheriff on you. Now I don't want to hear that dog bark again. You hear me," Marjorie said as she walked away.

I walked over and yelled, "Go do your damn job Marjorie, and stay away from this room!" Then I slammed the door shut.

We all heard Marjorie scream as she huffed away. As soon as she was gone, Tommy asked the question that was probably playing in everyone's head.

"Madison, where'd you get that chair?"

Before I could answer Tommy, the door to Dad's room flew open and in came Wally.

"Oh hi guys (he waved of course.) Don't you need the chair that's sitting outside in the hallway?" he asked.

He got a roomful of no's.

"Ok, sorry. Well, can one of you help me with the other chairs?"

The guys finally jumped to and helped poor confused Wally with the chairs. Then with Wally's help I explained what had happened out in the hallway. When I was done explaining, every guy in the room headed out the door. That is every guy except Wally. There was no doubt that they were going to find this guy if it took all night.

Long story short - it was nearly midnight when Junior came back to the room and told me they didn't even get a sniff of this unknown person. He finished by telling me that they were all going home, but he said he'd wait for me by the front doors. He looked extremely tired. There were plum colored circles under his red rimmed eyes. The tough part of the night for me had only just begun. I had to coax, wheedle, and cajole Maggie with all of my womanly abilities to get her to leave Dad and come home with me. After about twenty minutes, I finally won out. Maggie and I slowly walked past Matt, who was once again sitting and guarding Dad's room.

"Hi Matt, when'd you get here? I mean I didn't hear a thing."

"You and Maggie were out cold when I got here so I decided not to wake you. Something I can do for you?"

"No thanks, but thanks for watching over Dad. I know you guys must get tired and all. Did they tell you we think the guy that hurt Dad might be hanging around the hospital?"

"Yes, I'm supposed to call Tommy at home if I see or hear anything out of the ordinary."

"Ok, well, thanks again and goodnight."

"Night."

Maggie and I slowly walked out to the front doors of the hospital. I would have left Maggie in the room with Dad, but the thought of her biting someone, Marjorie in particular, and then dealing with the consequences was not an option I wanted to deal with. I was just not going to take that chance. It was spooky dark when we walked out to meet Junior. He was sitting on the wooden bench with his hands folded in his lap, sound asleep.

"Junior, come on, it's time to go home."

He didn't move.

"Junior, get up, it's time to go home."

He still didn't move. I walked over and touched his shoulder to wake him and he suddenly grabbed for his gun and hollered, "Stop! I'll shoot."

Junior had a look in his eye that I'd not seen before.

"Junior, what are you doing, it's me Madison."

Maggie started a throaty growl, but stopped when Junior said, "I'm sorry, geez I'm so tired and I was having some wicked dreams. Maddi, I can walk, but I was hoping you'd drop me off."

"Of course, come on and get in the car. You need some sleep."

Just before we got in my car, I looked up for a moment and then I looked at Maggie and she was doing the same. Even though it was pitch dark out I just knew there was at least one pair of eyes on me.

"Maggie, do you feel what I feel?"

She was tired too, but gave me a look that said yes and maybe we should get the heck out of there. Or maybe I was speaking for the both of us, doesn't really matter. I dropped Junior off across the street from his apartment. He hesitantly stroked Maggie's brow before he got out. And as he walked across the street, he waved a short goodbye.

"Bye girl, see ya Mad," he softly said.

"Bye," I said back.

I had the creeps all the way home. Thank goodness Maggie was with me.

To wit   19

Spoken from an alcove on the roof of the Crestfield hospital.

"**Benny**, if I ever have to spy on someone again and then hide, I think I'm gonna kill myself. I'm not afraid of them, why am I hiding?"

High pitched voice, "You're hiding because deep down inside you're a big coward. You're, without question, the biggest sissy I've ever come across. As a matter of fact, I think you should be wearing a dress. You have a few, why don't you put one on?"

"Benny, you stinking little jerk, I could throw you off this roof right now and nobody would give a hoot. You better leave me alone. I've told you a thousand times that I'll smash you and not blink an eye doin' it. What da-ya-think about that?"

"I think you're a sicko, and one of these days you're gonna fall off this ride you're on. I mean, you do know that you're insane, don't you?"

"Shut up, Benny. Just because you say it's so, don't make it so. I told you that a thou–"

"You shut up, you big idiot. We need to get the heck out of here and right now. We can't come back here anymore. We've been seen by too many people. Come on, I don't want to get caught. And I especially don't want to get caught with you. They'll call me a loser just for being on the same roof with a moron like you."

"I'm not going anywhere 'til I get Jack and that damn dog. If you had done your job, Benny, they'd both be outta my hair, but no. Benny, that dog bite on your hand is infected, look at it."

"If that snoopy old lady next door hadn't yelled at me, I wouldn't have got bit, so shut up."

"Benny, you coulda used a knife."

"You know I don't carry a knife with me all the time. And besides, you're afraid of knives. Hell, just the site of a knife can make you cry like a little baby. You big uh - baby."

"You leave me alone about that, Benny. Don't make me crush your little head."

"You don't scare me. You know big guy, there's so many things wrong with you that if a psychiatrist was to talk to you for even five minutes, he'd have to see a psychiatrist himself. Why do I waste my time talking to you? Alright, that's enough about that. You can stop pouting now. Come on you big idiot, we gotta get off this roof. I got a great idea - let's go spy on Matt."

"No, not Matt, it's that stoop shouldered, ape-faced Shadow that I want. And it's just a matter of time before I get him."

"Yeah right, you're all talk."

"Be quiet - I can't think when you're talking. Now shut up for a minute so I can think."

"Oh not again, you could float a balloon with all the hot air in that big head of yours. Of all the idiotic things – imagine you trying to think."

"For the last time, Benny, shut up! I can't concentrate with you yelling at me like that."

"Oh to hell with it, if it makes you feel better, go ahead and think."

"Once upon a time there was a little boy blue. He wanted his mommy to like him so they could live in a shoe. Daddy got mad and he stuck mommy with a dagger. Daddy tried to pick mommy up, but he couldn't so he had to drag'er. Ricker-racker-firecracker, I only like that part. If I get half-a-chance, I'm gonna tear someone apart. Yer thinkin' about Billy, but you had better watch your step, because I'm the passionate one and he's such a stupid git. Ricker-racker-firecracker, sis-boom-bah, Mommy, Daddy, Mommy, Daddy, rah-rah-rah."

"You know what big guy, I don't think I like you anymore. You're nuts. So do the voices tell you what to say or is it the other way around?"

"Face it Benny - you're nobody without me, nobody!"

Crestfield

A busy day   20

Junior/I had another fitful night of bad, bad dreams. A couple of the episodes were ok. I can't tell you about those, but for the most part the dreams sucked. I woke up sweating like a horse and looked at the clock; it was four in the morning. I knew I'd never be able to go back to sleep, so I put my slippers on and walked in the bathroom. When I looked in the mirror, I realized I hadn't shaved since the day I had gone out to see Billy.

Sometimes one realization triggers another. Leastwise, that's the way it usually works for me, and it did. I sprinted back into the bedroom and grabbed my notebook off of the nightstand and turned it to the Billy interview. *Yep*, I said to myself, you're not following up on your leads, which means you're not doing your job. I walked out to the kitchen and dialed long distance. A man answered on about the fifth ring.

The person on the other end said, "This better be good cuz I ain't just gonna hang up. I'm gonna find out where y'all live and then I'm gonna come shoot yer ass. Who is this?" he demanded.

"I'm sorry to wake you so early, but–"

"But nothing, who the hell are you?"

"This is Officer Jack McCool Junior with the Crestfield police, you know Crestfield–"

"Oh hell, why didn't ya say so in the first place? Shit howdy y'all got me pissed off. Do you know what time it is? Billy told me you'd be callin', but that was days ago. And he didn't tell me you'd be callin' at four in the got-damn mornin'."

"I'm sorry to have to call you so early in the morning Mr. Bodine, but there have been some tragic events happen here in the last forty-eight hours. Long and the short of it, somebody attacked my dad and nearly killed him. So I hope you can understand why this phone call is important."

"I'm truly sorry to hear that young man. Listen, could ya do me a favor and please call me Hank? Mr. Bodine is just a little too formal for my blood. Now what is it I can do you for?"

"Well Hank, I just need to know if you were here in Crestfield two weeks ago like Billy says you were."

"Actually young man, I was there for three days. I stayed in a little motel. I spent most of my time at that pretty little go'f course of yours. Nice course. I shot an 88, which is a damn good score, at least for me it is."

"Uh, that is a good score. So you came to buy a saddle, did you?"

"Why yes, of course I did. In fact, I bought two saddles. Certainly wasn't there for the night life. Gee willikers, that's a sleepy little town y'all got there."

"If you don't mind, I just have one more question. Did Billy come to you, or did you drive out to the farm?"

"Hell yes, I drove out there. I didn't just want to see his work. I wanted to see where and how he works. He's a damn good saddler. Got a couple buddies lined up to buy some saddles. Billy's gonna give 'em a discount, you know cheaper buy the dozen. Get it, b-yuu-whah. That's one of them double entendres."

"Yes, yes it is. Ok, well Hank, I think that'll just about do it. Again, I'm sorry for calling you so early."

I was ready to hang up.

"Listen Junior - have you got a minute?" he asked.

"Sure, how can I help you?"

"Well, when I was playin' go'f, I saw one of the damndest things on yer go'f course."

"Yeah, what'd you see?"

"Well, I was standin' by the ball-washer. Don't remember which hole. Anywho, there was this feller standin' right next to me waitin' to wash his ba– go'f balls. So I look down and this nut is wearin' a holster and in it he had what looked like a damn cap-gun, right there on his hip. I've never seen anything like it. Do you know this person?"

Thank goodness, he didn't give me time to answer.

"Just thought I oughta let y'all know that you got a nut on yer hands. Hell, we don't even carry a gun when we play go'f in Texas."

"No, you probably don't," I agreed.

I wanted to hang up. I knew what was next.

"Don't hang up Junior, it gets better. This nut-job also has a doll of some sorts slung over his shoulder. I mean I took a damn double take, twice. So I back away from the ball-washer, and this nut steps up and says something about playin' jacks. I think he was talking to the damn doll.

Then he puts a ball in the washer and while he's pushin' down and pullin' up on the handle he says, 'Washy, washy, washy, in the new Blue Cheer, rinsy, rinsy, rinsy, and the water so clear. Put it to your nose and it smells like a... He stopped for a second and then starts all over again and I'll be damned if he didn't just fall over laughin'. I felt like I was in some dag-gum weirdo movie in California. Isn't that the craziest thing you ever heard?"

"Um, yes Hank, that is pretty crazy."

"I got the hell away from him and in a flat hurry. Just thought y'all oughta know so's you can keep an eye out for the nut. Ok, well, call back again if ya need to. Bye, bye."

"Yes, ok, bye."

I hung up the phone before he could ask anything more about the 'nut.' Well, so much for not leaving any stone unturned. Billy had told me the truth, and I pretty much had to believe that he told me the truth about everything else. Maybe even Jolene Meadows. And that was hard to stomach. Was Billy sent to prison for something he really did not intend to do? If that was the truth, then it would be just as he said, 'hard to live with.'

I shaved and got myself dressed and whistled a soft tune all the way to the diner. And after eating a big breakfast, I started feeling a little better. Mary didn't apologize for the things she said about Ricky. I suppose I really didn't expect her to, but it would have been nice. I was just about to get up when Ricky came waltzing in with his sideways walk and said, "Hello Mary, how you been? Your hair sure looks nice today. *Her hair was the color of an eggplant.* Mary, did you read the paper yesterday?"

Mary shook her head no while she fidgeted.

"I was on the front page. I was accused of some pretty rotten stuff. Randi tells me that I shouldn't worry about spilt-milk because just about the whole town is in my corner. That sure does make a fellow feel good. You know, to have friends that will back him up when he needs 'em. Well, you ready to go to work, pardner?" he asked.

"As a matter of fact Ricky, yes I am. Let's get-er-done," I answered.

I got up and once again left enough money for my meal and a decent tip. Mary had quietly walked over to a corner table and was re-arranging the silverware. I think she was embarrassed for not telling Ricky the truth about how she reacted to him being in the paper. When we got outside, Ricky said, "Watch this."

Ricky went back and opened up the door to the diner and yelled across the room.

"Remember Mary, Randi didn't say the whole town, she said just about the whole town. She also said there was one turncoat. Mary, do you know who that turncoat might be? Well, my mom always told me to forgive and forget. But my grandma told me that paybacks are a bitch. So you'd better be on your toes Mary, because you're gonna get what's coming to you, that's for sure, you just don't know when."

Ricky closed the door on Mary, but we could clearly hear her yelling that she was sorry. And after we walked across the street, she ran out the door and over-and-over yelled how sorry she was.

I said to myself, *sorry is right*. "Ricky, I thought sure as heck you were going to do something crazy, you know like spill some ketchup on her or break a plate."

"I did what my grandma taught me. That is, make 'em worry about when they're gonna get it. She said it's the best payback because it lasts the longest."

"You know what Ricky? I think your grandma was right. Grandmas sure can be clever at times. I guess it's built in, you know - part of their DNA."

"Well, I don't know what DNA is Junior, but I believe you're right."

"Gosh you're funny sometimes, Ricky. I mean the best kind of funny. You know why?"

"No. Why?"

"You're funny because you're not even trying to be funny. Come on, let's go make Tommy laugh."

We went in the station through the back door. I said good morning and waved to Randi. Ricky one-upped me and gave her a wave and a wink. This was a side of Ricky I'd never seen before, and it was definitely going to take some getting used to. When we walked by Tommy's office, I think we both realized that we were probably not going to make him laugh, at least not on that day. He was sitting at his desk in the dark. He was slumped over and his head was hanging down. He was swearing something fierce under his breath.

112

I'd never heard Tommy swear, at least not like that. So it was a bit disconcerting to say the least. I looked at Ricky and he gave me the universal sign for, no way I'm going in there. I knew somebody had to and that somebody was probably going to have to be me. The door was open so I just walked in and asked if something was wrong.

"You're darn right something's wrong. Burt's what's wrong and I want to go over and break his neck, but I can't. At least that's what deputy district attorney Wallace told me."

"Marcia was in here this morning?"

"Yes, and she informed me that they're not going forward with the B & E charges against Burt."

"What? Why not? I thought with the picture the charges were good as gold?"

"I did too, but Burt's attorney says that the picture is not date coded. And so the picture could have been taken at any time. For all they know Burt could have been invited into my office. Marcia says I'm lucky they don't bring charges against me for forcing him to write the apology without his attorney present. In the end I only have myself to blame."

"Geez Tommy, you can't think that way. It was a good bust and if anybody deserves to be punished, its Burt. Have you talked to Ajax? I mean, what'd he say?"

"He says his hands are tied. I guess he owes a couple of favors to the people that run our legal system. He told me to forget about it. Said if we were patient, Burt would screw up again and then we'd get him. Fat chance of that happening."

"Listen Tommy, something really good did come out of all this. I read the paper this morning and people are gonna think twice about believing much of anything Burt writes from here on out. And we might not have to catch Burt. The perp might do it for us. Don't think he's going to enjoy the things Burt said about him in the paper."

"To be honest with you Junior, that's what bothers me most of all. If something happens to Burt, it's going to be my fault. I'm the one that made him write that stuff. I should have stopped him from saying anything about the guy. That's been our direction from day one. That is - not to antagonize or incite the creep. Geez, I don't usually make mistakes like this. Sorry Junior."

"Now wait just a minute. You don't have to apologize to me or, for that matter, anyone else. This police department and this town wouldn't be what it is if not for you. You'll see - things are going to work out."

"Thanks Junior, I hope you're right."

I left Tommy there in his office, but on the way out I turned on the lights. He didn't object. When I got out to Ricky's desk, he wasn't there. I didn't have to look very far for him because he was with Randi. They were holding hands. I don't know exactly why, but it's a strange feeling to see your best friend holding your baby sister's hand.

I decided it was a good time to give Madison a call. You know, see how she and Maggie were getting along. I called her office and she answered on the second ring.

"Hello, Page county mental health facility. How can I help you?"

"Hello Madison, where's Nancy?"

"Hi Junior, she took the day off. And at the present time the county can't afford to pay replacements. Guess what?"

"Madison, if you say chicken butt I'm not going to laugh. You got me on that one enough times when we were kids. Ok, what?"

"Chicken butt that's what, I got you again."

"Well Maddi, you're sure chipper this morning. What's got you in such a good mood?"

"You're such a typical guy. Did you already forget that Dezi and Buck are coming in on the noon train?"

"Oh yeah, I mean no I didn't forget, I just have been busy this morning."

"Busy doing what? Oh never mind, listen can you pick them up? I can meet you at the hospital during my lunch break. Let's say a quarter after noon or so."

"Madison, do you remember giving me heck for not being specific about what time I was going to be someplace? Well, the tables have been turned. So tell me exactly when you'll get to the hospital?"

"Ok Junior, I'll be there at twelve-thirty on the dot."

"That's better, see you then. Oh, wait a second. You're bringing Maggie with you right?"

"No I'm not, because she's already there. Took her early this morning and she jumped up next to Dad. Shadow says it's no problem."

"What about Marjorie?"

"She didn't come in to work today. I guess our encounter yesterday must have put a little starch in her panties."

"Gosh, you gals sure can be mean to each other. All right, I'll see you later, bye."

When I was finished talking with Madison, I felt a little better about things. Why, I don't know. I guess because she was happy and although I hadn't said much about it, I was really looking forward to seeing Dezi and Buck. The last month had been the month from hell. And I didn't ever want to go through another like it. So, some new blood in town would probably make for a fun time. And when Dezi or Buck come home, it's always who is going to laugh the hardest. I couldn't wait.

I walked into my little office and it seemed like weeks since I'd actually sat down at my desk. I straightened things up a bit and then without thinking my hand went straight into my jacket pocket and out came my notebook. I put my thinking cap on and really gave it heck. I read and then reread every word. I felt good about the effort, but not so good about the results.

There was definitely something wrong, but for the life of me I could not figure out what it was. As Dad would so eloquently say, I just could not get my ducks in a row. Thinking about Dad made me look up at the clock. The train was going to be here in ten minutes. I immediately jumped up and ran out to Randi.

"Randi, I gotta go pick up Dezi and Buck. Do you want me to bring them by here before I take them to the hospital?"

"No, Ricky's going to come by and get me. We'll meet you guys at the hospital."

"Uh, yeah that'd work out just fine. Ok then, I'll see ya later. Um, Randi, is there anything special you wanted to tell me?"

"No, there's nothing I can think of - about what?"

"Oh, never mind, it can wait. I'll see you guy's later, bye."

She gave me a strange look as I walked out the door. I walked out looking back at Randi and nearly ran over Burt.

"Whoa, sorry Burt, did you want something?"

"No, I just came by to thank you for trying to help me when Ricky and those uncles of yours had me believing they were going to kill me. Junior, do you think they might have really done it?"

I hesitated a little. I needed to think this one through, and fast.

"Yep, I'm pretty sure they were going to kill you Burt. They thought you had it coming. If I were you, I'd make myself scarce, you know hide somewhere."

"That's what I intend to do. Ok, well, thanks again, Junior. I'll talk to you later."

I jumped in the roller and flew the entire block and a half to the train station. I stopped at the far end of the parking lot. I had a surprise for Dezi and Buck. I sat and I sat, but no train. Finally, I got restless and walked into the depot. I walked over and tapped Riggs Stratton on the shoulder. He was busy sweeping the floor.

Riggs is his first name, but I haven't heard him called Riggs since maybe grade school. Like me - everybody calls him Junior.

"Hello Junior, how you doin' today?" I asked.

He just waved and maybe said I'm fine, but I really couldn't be sure. Junior is one of them low volume talkers - that is if he talks at all.

"Listen, I'm supposed to pick up my brother and sister, but I don't see a train anywhere. Is the train late today?"

"No sir, matter of fact it was early. It come into the depot about twenty minutes ago."

"Well, did you happen to see a tiny little gal and a tall young man hangin' around?"

"I believe I did, you say you know 'em?"

"Well, yes, I was supposed to pick 'em up. Did you see which way they went?"

"Nope - can't say as I did. Was you gonna arrest 'em?"

"No Junior, like I said they're my brother and sister."

"Oh, that's right you did. Well, they looked awful hungry to me. So I'd say your best bet would be the diner, but that's only a guess."

"Thanks for your help Junior, see ya."

I waved bye and somewhere between that little foldout dustpan and his broom I think he waved too.

116

I hightailed it across the parking lot to the roller and drove as fast as was safe back to the station. I jumped out of the car and ran through the station and out the front door. I kept on going across the street and flew into the diner, no Dezi or Buck. I asked Mary if she'd seen them, and she said no. *Her hair was the color of a dandelion.* I looked at the clock and the panic started to set in. It was twenty minutes past twelve. I was late and there was nothing I could do about it. I thought, *Madison is gonna kill me.* So I started running out of the diner, didn't make it two feet. Randi was standing right in front of me.

"Junior, if you hadn't run through the station like some nut, I could'a told you that Dezi and Buck went on ahead over to the hospital."

"What? Why'd they - oh heck with it. Ok, are you coming with me this time?"

"No, you're coming with us. Ricky's waiting for us at the station, let's go."

"How'd they get to the hospital, I mean who took 'em?"

"George took 'em."

"They took a cab?"

"Yep, now stop fretting about it. I'm tired of listening to you."

"Randi, why would you talk to your big brother like that?"

"Because I can - that's why."

I wasn't sure how to answer that response. And when we got to Ricky's roller, he must have instinctively known what was going on. So he gave me the universal choking sign, which meant shut up while you're ahead. Randi and I jumped in and Ricky smiled at me in the rearview mirror - and then drove as fast as he thought was safe to the hospital.

What Ricky thinks is safe is about twice as fast as what I think is safe. So we were going about three times the speed limit. We were there in nothing flat. For whatever reason I started getting antsy about meeting my brother and sister in our dad's hospital room. With all that has gone on in the last few days, I'd lost track of the fact that our dad had nearly been killed and was still unconscious. I guess I was hoping to give them a hug in a less stressful environment.

When Ricky and I were approaching the room, another reality became crystal clear. Dezi and Buck had not seen Dad in his present state. As we got closer to the room we could hear a wheezing of sorts followed by a little voice yelling, "Dad, wake up!"

I think you could put me on a boat in the middle of a storm, and I'd still know that the voice I heard was Dezi's. I walked in the room behind Randi and nearly collapsed out of sheer grief. Dezi was standing there next to Dad - shaking and crying. I looked over at Buck and he started a salute that almost became a wave and then he must have thought heck with it because he just reached out to me and we hugged each other. My chest was heaving.

I suppose Dezi could hear us behind her and she turned and ran to me. She's usually the happiest little thing in the world. But right at that moment she wore the look of a person trapped in some netherworld. Not a word was spoken as Randi joined the hug followed by Madison and an uncertain Buck. We stood there hugging one another for an awfully long time before Madison must have decided some communication would probably help.

"Dezi, please listen to me. Dad is resting comfortably and most importantly he's still alive. You've got to try and think good thoughts. I guarantee you he is going to wake up and when he does, he's going to get better," Madison assured.

"But I want him to wake up right now," Dezi demanded.

Then Dezi turned and violently slammed her fists on Dad's bed and screamed at the top of her lungs, "Dad - wake up!"

Immediately after Dezi pounded on the bed Dad's arms and legs flew straight up in the air, his hands looked like they were reaching out to Dezi. Dezi screamed again, "Dad, I'm right here. Dad - wake up!"

Dad moaned as he turned from his back to his left side. I think at that very moment we all believed that he was going to wake up. He was quiet for maybe ten more seconds before he mumbled what sounded like a few words. We looked at each other, but none of us could understand what he had said. We all stood hoping that soon his eyes would open, it didn't happen. I think we had all forgotten that Maggie was lying on the bed next to Dad's feet. But we were reminded of her presence in a big way. After Dad rolled over and mumbled, she lifted her head up and let out a crisp bark. The bark was followed by a slow whine. She'd mimicked Dad's response to Dezi's urging. At that point I felt a renewed optimism in everyone, especially Dezi.

"Madison, what just happened?" Dezi asked.

"Well, I'm not sure, but when babies react like that, it's called the Moro or mother reflex. It's considered a healthy and normal response to being startled. Dad's no baby, but I'd have to say his reaction to the stimuli was far too normal to be taken for granted. There is definitely somebody in there. And I believe it's the Dad that we all know." Upon hearing what Madison had just told us Ricky simply could not contain his delight and hollered, "I don't know about the normal part, but one thing I do know is Jack's gonna wake up. And that makes me wanna scream yahoo." And he did.

I don't think I was alone in my thinking at that point.

"Ricky, you certainly have a way with words," I said with a smile.

Everyone chuckled a bit and it just plain felt great. Our chuckle was followed by one of Dezi's little giggles and everyone laughed even harder.

The feeling in the room had changed from gloom to a measured joy in a matter of seconds. I for one had definitely reached the point where even a little joy was hugely appreciated.

A boat-load of tension had left the room and everyone was able to let their shoulders hang down a little. I took a close look at my younger brother and sister and suddenly noticed that they were changing. I guess the term most widely used is growing up. I wanted to know how things were going with both of them and with the change in mood it felt like a good time to ask.

"Well, how's my little hippie sister doing? Better yet, what have you been doing?" I asked.

She rubbed her hands together the way Randi does when she's got strong feelings rolling through her heart. And then of course she giggled before she answered me.

"I was doing great - un-until I found out about Dad. My apartment is right next to the Golden Gate Park. The neighborhoods there are so full of beautiful people. It's a groovy place to live. This last summer is now being called the summer of love. And to know I was there in the middle of it, well, that's just plain bitchen."

"Bitchen, Dezi, when did you start swearing? What the heck does bitchen mean?" I asked.

"I'm not swearing. And it means the same thing as any other word you might use to describe something that is cool or the best."

"Oh," was the only response I could come up with at the time?

"And I'm taking classes at the junior college. But the best thing of all is the music being played in the bay area. And of course the musicians that play the music."

Buck had been quiet, but must have felt the need to keep his sister out of harm's way.

"Dezi, you know how Dad feels about musicians. He says they're useless and should all join the circus. To quote Dad, 'musicians are predictably arrogant, self-serving, and worst of all - lazy.' And of course he had a few other descriptive words that I don't want to say out loud, but I'm sure you understand. The point is, Dezi, that I worry about you when you tell me about hanging out with, um - hippies and musicians."

Dezi giggled again and then she walked over to Buck and hugged him before she said, "Buck, thanks for caring about my welfare and all, but I'm fine. I make ok money tending bar - it's just part-time right now. And school and my friends are the best. They keep me safe and as far as musicians go, well, they're my friends. You wouldn't want me to neglect or abandon my friends, would you?"

"No Dezi, I didn't mean that at all. Ok, what I meant was–"

Before he finished what he wanted to say, he stopped and held his fingers to his forehead, just like Dad does.

"Dezi, please be careful, ok? If you tell me you'll be careful, then I think we'll all sleep a little better at night," Buck said with a smile.

A very strange thing happened as soon as Buck finished talking. Both of Dezi's sisters put their arms around her and pretty much shielded her from the entire world. They had become a fortress of three very strong, but different sisters. I thought Madison would be the one to tell us to bug off, but it was Randi that came to the rescue.

"You guys can lay off now. Whatever Dezi wants to do or become is her business. Stay out of her way. And if you insist on worrying about somebody, then you can worry about Dad. But don't you ever pretend to tell us girls how to live our lives."

Then Madison acknowledged Randi and, of course the boys in the room, by saying, "Bravo Randi, now do you testosterone machines get the picture?"

Buck, Ricky, and I were left slack-jawed.

"Ok, we get the picture and we don't want to fight or tell anyone how to live their lives. Ok, peace," I said as I flashed them the peace sign.

Things might have continued to worsen if not for our little flower child sister, Dezi. She giggled one of her really good giggles and told us she understood our concern but that she was fine and loving life. That was definitely good enough for the guys in the room. After our little misunderstanding, we all just stood and stared at Dad. That is, everyone, except for Madison. We could not help noticing her looking around the room and then she stared out the door. She had a very confused look on her face.

"Madison, is something wrong?" I asked.

"No, nothing is wrong - it's just that Jenny was right here before you guys walked in the room. She must have slipped out. I wish she could have been here to see Dad's reactions and the hope we all shared."

Everyone shook their heads yes in agreement until Ricky said, "Who is Jenny?"

"She's the young nurse that has been caring for Dad. You didn't see her?" I asked.

"No, did you?" he responded.

"Of course I did, I just said so."

"Yeah, I guess you did at that," he said.

We shook our heads a bit and then once again laughed with Ricky. It was the perfect time for me to ask if Dezi and Buck had eaten and, of course, where they were going to stay. Everyone agreed that Molly's was a good place to eat. As far as sleeping arrangements, we'd decide that over a hot meal. Randi and Dezi rode with Madison, and Buck jumped in the roller with Ricky and me. We were just about to cross the railroad tracks when the CB radio squawked.

"Junior here, who is this?"

"Well, let me see. You and Ricky and Randi all went out to the hospital. So I guess this would have to be–"

"Hi Tommy, After all the excitement that's been going on I forgot. How can I help you?"

"I think you'd better keep what I'm about to tell you under your hat. Marjorie's neighbor called me and says that Marjorie's car is parked sideways in her driveway. Says she hasn't seen Marjorie since she left for the hospital over a day and a half ago. The neighbor walked over and checked Marjorie's house and nothing has been disturbed. So she checked the car and the keys are in it, but her purse is gone. The neighbor says women always take their purse with them no matter where they go. She thinks Marjorie is either with her sister Grace or she's with her sister's boyfriend, Joe." Tommy blew out some air before he said, "I can't make stuff like that up. Anyway, the neighbor also says Marjorie has done this before and will probably show up any minute now. I still think I'd better go have a look. By the way, where are you guys?"

"We're stopped at the tracks right now. We're heading over to Molly's."

"Ok, you go ahead. I'll drive over to Cromwell and see about Marjorie. Did you say something, Junior?"

"No, that was Ricky. He said, 'Here comes, there goes the Burlington Zephyr.'"

"You know Junior, that was fun the first fifty times I heard it, but now. Ok listen, you guys go have fun and say hello for me."

"Will do, I hope everything turns out ok with Marjorie. Give us a call at Molly's if you need something. See you in the movies, bye."

To wit   21

"What? I can't understand you. Here let me take that rag out of your mouth. But you have to promise me you won't yell, promise? Ok, that's better. Now listen, if you yell, I'll have Benny hit you harder than the last time. Alright now don't yell–"

The moment the rag was removed Marjorie let loose with a blood curdling scream.

"Help me! You sick son of a bitch. You untie me right now. Help me! Somebody Help! Hell–"

The big guy cupped his hand over her nose and mouth as her head violently wrenched from side to side. She struggled for just one more breath of air and the scream that would follow before the ghoul could shove the rag back in her mouth. Her eyes permanently bulged with the realization that on this night she might not be going home.

"Marjorie, you promised you wouldn't yell. Benny, take her down to the water. You shouldn't've let that damn dog in the hospital, now Benny and I can't go there anymore."

High pitched voice, "You dumb bitch. If you had just kept your mouth shut, he was gonna let you go; now I've got a bad, bad feeling."

He began pulling her towards the water.

"Stop kicking. Ouch that hurts. Don't make me smack you again."

"Benny, stop messing around and get her down to the water. You want somebody to hear her. No Benny, the weights go on her ankle not her neck. That's good, yeah right there."

"She won't hold still. Help me," Benny said.

"Oh alright, yes that'll do just fine. Now Marjorie, you gotta listen - I'm gonna give you some instructions that will help you. Please don't yell or Benny's gonna have to hit you again. You don't want that now do you? Good, yes, shake your head yes again. Ok, good. Now I'm gonna take the rag out of your mouth. Please don't scream. Ok, here we go."

"I can't swim! Help! Somebody help me!–"

Benny swung the meat tenderizer he was holding down at his side and hit Marjorie square in the forehead. Her head flew back and she lay there on the soft moist earth as still and quiet as a porcelain doll.

"Benny, I think you killed her."

"No, she's ok - she's still breathing."

"Oh good, now you listen to me Marjorie, cuz this is very important. If you can swim across the pond, you get to live. But if you don't try with all yer might, you'll sink. You have some pretty heavy weights attached to your ankle. She's not listening. Are you sure you didn't kill her?"

"No, I didn't kill her. And besides, you hit her twice as hard as I did. Look how big you are."

"Oh shut up, Benny. You're making me sick. Take that rag out of her mouth before you put her in the water."

"Why?"

"What do you mean why? So she can breathe if she makes it to the other side of the pond."

"Are you crazy? She's never gonna make it. Ok, the rag is out of her mouth. Should I let her go now?"

"Just a minute, I have to give her more instructions. Marjorie, listen to me. If you hold your breath, you might be able to walk across the bottom and get out. Ok Benny, put her in. Yes, that's good. Look, she's floating. Oh no. Where'd she go?"

"She went straight to the bottom you big idiot. Is there something wrong with you? Walk out. Get me outta here! You're so stupid you're dangerous."

"Shut up, Benny. I'm smarter than you - so what do you think about that."

"I think we better get out of here, and now. That's what I think about that."

"Don't you want to wait and see if she makes it?"

"If she makes it? Jesus, you are insane. Get in the car or you're walking back."

"Don't tell me what to do, Benny. Remember, I'm the boss and you're the hired help."

"Yeah, whatever - let's go."

"Ok, but first I have to think."

"Think! Get in the car. You can think on the way back."

"Yes I can. Ok, here goes nothing."

He got in the car, sat up straight, and adjusted his tie.

"Once there was a miller who was poor, but he had a pretty daughter. Daddy said, get in that room, but Mommy never did what Daddy said she oughter. Adams rib is one for the ages. I can read, but I just can't turn the pages. That dog's in heat and she's got mean things all on her mind. Once I saw a rainbow over Mommy's head, but we ran and left it far behind. You better think twice cuz–"

"Oh, will you shut up! I can't take any more of your thinking - you're insane."

Junior/**We were all tired** and understandably beyond sad. So getting together for a meal was, in my opinion, going to be very therapeutic. At first little was said, probably due to the earlier exchange between the guys and gals. Thankfully once everyone began eating, any tension that remained was slowly swallowed up.

Somewhere in the middle of the quiet that comes with people doing a lot of soul searching and at the same time eating, it was decided that Buck would stay with me and Dezi would stay with Madison. We always start out like that, but eventually the visitor or visitors end up moving from one person to another. That way we all get to converse on our own terms.

We walked out to the parking lot, a cold wind had begun to blow. It certainly felt like winter was slowly creeping back into our lives. A reality that Midwesterners don't relish but live with just the same. Ricky kissed Randi good night right in front of everyone. The girls didn't bat an eye. They've probably known about the two of them from the very beginning. Now Buck and I, well, that was definitely a horse of a different color.

We did our best to act like nothing out of the ordinary had happened. We probably weren't very convincing. I thought, *oh well*. After the kissing couple was done, everyone else joined in. There were hugs and goodnights all around. Ricky dropped Buck and me off in front of my apartment. I asked him to come in for a beer, but I think he had other plans.

"Junior, Buck, thanks for the invite, but I'm pretty tired. And besides Junior, I know you never buy any beer. And since I only left the one hidden in the bottom of the fridge, you and Buck wouldn't have nothin' to drink," Ricky said with a smirk on his face.

"Just as well, I think we're all in for a busy day tomorrow. Tell Randi we said goodnight," I said with a smirk on my face.

Ricky didn't know that I had actually gone and bought a six pack of Budweiser, my favorite. Buck wasn't of legal age, but he assured me he wouldn't go out and do anything crazy, at least not on that night. I opened a bottle for each of us and we settled down to watch a little late night T.V. Johnny was on the tube and in rare form. I laughed my way through a beer and got up and went to the fridge for another. When I came back, Buck had stretched out on the divan. He was sound asleep.

I threw a blanket on him and then I sat on the floor and drank my beer. The T.V. was still on, but I wasn't really paying attention. The rhythmic breathing going on next to me acted like a giant sleeping pill. Somehow, I managed to shuffle my way through the apartment and into my bed. I immediately started in on what I thought was going to be another one of my mean dreams. The tables were turned, and in a hurry. I was being held by a pair of huge hands. I struggled to free myself, but there was no escaping. Suddenly I was hurled at breakneck speed through a tunnel of silver, blue, and gold lights. It was startling, but not scary. I finally came to a screeching halt and tried to run, but my feet failed me. As I struggled to get away, I heard someone in my dream softly telling me not to be afraid.

I had to find out who was talking to me and inched towards the voice. I slowly emerged from a dense fog and there, floating over a small body of water, was Nel. She was dressed in a silken black robe. Her yellow hair was wafting across her face. She pointed at a bright white light in the distance and said, "Don't be afraid - go to the light. Don't be afraid, go to the light." I turned and stared into the light. And without a thought or a decision on my part, I found myself gradually moving towards the light. I moved closer and closer. And then without a warning, the light went out. I turned several times in the dark hoping for a light to come on, any light. I asked Nel to tell me which way to go. She didn't answer. A phone rang and the light came on. That is, the light in my bedroom came on.

"Junior, Junior, the phone."

"Buck is that you?"

"Yes, of course it's me. What the heck is the matter with you? Why didn't you answer the phone?" he asked.

I thought I had my eyes open, but I was wrong. It took a lot of extreme effort and concentration before I could get my eyes to open. When I did it felt like my ceiling light was an inch over my face. I guess Buck had turned it on.

He sat down on the other end of the bed and stared at me like I was an alien in a Sci-Fi movie. And then he said, "Well, why didn't you answer it?"

"I didn't answer the phone because I was asleep. And also because I couldn't get myself outta the doggone dream I was having. Whoa, that was a weird one. Anyway, I guess whoever it was will call back. What time is it?"

I looked at the clock, it was only a little after seven in the morning. I said, "Who in the world would call at this hour?"

"Randi would call that's who. Don't worry, I answered the phone. She said for you to call her at the station as soon as you get up."

"Ok, thanks for getting the phone for me. Gosh, that was a doozy of a dream," I said as I tried to shake loose the cobwebs.

I got up outta bed and slowly walked to the kitchen. Buck was right behind me. I called the station and Randi answered on the second ring.

"Hello, Crestfield police - how can I help you?"

"Morning Randi, it's me, what's up?"

"Junior, you better get in here ASAP. I got a couple of phone calls this morning. Tommy was right," she said.

"Tommy was right about what?"

"Do you remember when he said that the guy responsible for Miller's cow would call? Well, he did."

"What? Did he threaten you?"

"No. Matter of fact he sounded like he was scared. Said for us to leave him alone and if we did, then he'd leave us alone."

"What in the world. Did he say anything else?" I asked.

"Yep, he said something that threw me for a loop, made me want to kill him," she coldly said.

"What did he say?" she wouldn't answer. Randi! What did he say?"

"He said they didn't mean to hurt Jack."

I stood there in the kitchen and my heart started pounding like a jackhammer. Then I went back in my mind to the day Dad was taken to the hospital. That's the day I realized that I could kill somebody. I knew how Randi felt. Then the light came on, again.

"Randi, did you say that he said, they."

"Took you long enough Junior, I sure did say that he said, they."

"Oh man, this is huge. Randi, what else did the sicko say?"

"He asked if I was mad at him and I said, yes! And then I said I'm gonna find you. And when I do, I'm gonna kill you."

"Oh Randi, I know how you feel, but we're not supposed to threaten or spook the guy," I said as a chill ran down my spine.

"Junior, I don't give a damn about any of that. When he mentioned Dad, I couldn't control my anger. I really do want to kill the guy. And if I get even half a chance, I'm gonna, that's for damn sure," she said, her voice quivering.

"Ok, I know how you feel. I feel the same way, but we have to stay calm. Ok, please."

"Yes, I will," she said in defeat.

"Oh, one more thing, do you remember Shadow said the big guy at the hospital had a southern twang when he spoke?" she asked.

"Yeah, Shadow did say that. Why?" I asked.

"This guy had a southern twang when he talked. Has to be the same guy," she said.

"Yeah, must be the same guy. Randi, you said you got two phone calls. Who else called?"

"Mrs. Cunningham, that old lady that's visiting from California - next door to Dad."

"You mean Walter's mom?"

"Yep, she's the one that called. Said she heard somebody talking in Dad's back yard. It was the day Dad was attacked."

"Whoa, that's huge. Wonder why she never said anything before today."

"That's the part that is kinda confusing. Anyway, I told Tommy when he got into the station this morning. He's over there talking to Mrs. Cunningham right now. Maybe he'll get things straightened out."

"Yes maybe, I hope. Randi, thanks for calling. I'm gonna get dressed and head over to Dad's. Maybe Tommy will still be there. I'll talk at you later. Wait a second. Are you there alone?"

"No, Ricky just drove up. We're ok. Junior?" she said in the manner of a soft question.

"Yeah, what is it?"

"Thanks for being such a great big brother."

"Why heck Randi, I ain't that big," I said with a smile on my face.

"That's funny. You know what kinda big I meant."

"Yes, I do. Thanks, and I'll talk to you later," I said with a lump in my throat.

I turned around when I got off the phone and Buck was sound asleep again. It was awful early and I didn't want to wake him, so I jumped in the shower. When I got out, Buck was up again talking on the phone. I heard him say, "Ok Uncle Tommy, I'll let him know."

"What's Uncle Tommy want?" I asked.

Buck jumped across the kitchen floor.

"Gee-whiz Junior, don't sneak up on me like that," his voice quivering as he said it.

"Sorry, but I wasn't sneaking. Anyway, what did Tommy want?" I said with a smile.

"That's not funny. He wants you to get over to Dad's right now, says it's important."

"Ok, I guess you can come with me if you want, but you have to promise you'll stay out of the way."

"Yes, I'll stay out of the way. Geez, it's like you're talking to some little boy or something."

"I'm sorry, Buck. It's just that when I took Dad out to Miller's place, he wouldn't leave well enough alone. He just kept interrupting me while I was trying to do my job. You know how Dad can be," I said with regret.

"Junior, please don't talk about Dad like that when I'm around. I like Dad just the way he is, or at least the way he was."

He stood with a gigantic pout on his face before he screamed at the top of his lungs.

"There's nothing wrong with Dad. You hear me!"

I didn't say a word. I'd never in my life seen Buck react like that. He took his duffle bag and went in the bathroom. He came out wearing his camouflage fatigues, boots and all. I still didn't say a word because I didn't know what to say.

"I didn't want to ride around in a cop car looking like Joe preppy, so let's just go," he said with a snort.

"You got it. And I understand. I mean, I understand about Dad," I said as he gave me the stare from hell.

Not a word was spoken on the way over to Dad's. It's all of five minutes, so not a big deal, I thought. When we got in front of Dad's house, Buck told me that he wasn't going to come in. Said he didn't want to get in the way.

"Buck, come on. This is not the way we get along with each other."

His body language said he didn't want to because he couldn't.

"Please Buck, you may see something that helps stop this misery from happening again," I said not knowing where this would all end.

"Junior, I don't want to go in there without Dad being there. Why'd this have to happen?" he asked.

"Buck, I don't know why. I've asked myself the same question more times than you could ever believe. And I still haven't come up with an answer. You couldn't know this, but I haven't been here since it happened either. Just didn't want to face it."

"You haven't?" he asked.

"No, I haven't."

I could see his body relax. And slowly the muscles in his jawed stopped their steadfast clinch. And when his balled fists opened up, mine did the same. He let out his breath and opened the passenger door and started walking up the short driveway, I followed. When we got close to the front door, we could hear music playing; Dad almost always had the radio on. That part felt familiar and somehow warm. When Buck opened the front door, I for one expected to hear Maggie give me one of her hello barks. No such luck. Buck and I looked over towards Dad's chair at the same time and there sat Uncle Tommy, sleeping. He was almost a carbon copy of Dad. He must have felt our presence and slowly opened his eyes.

"Hey you guys. Have you been here long?" he quietly asked.

"No, just walked in the door," I answered.

"Good. I talked to Mrs. Cunningham and she confirmed what I was thinking might have happened. Said she heard a couple of voices in Jack's back yard and asked, 'Jack is that you?' She didn't receive an answer and shouted, 'what's going on over there?' Then she heard footsteps running along the side of the house out towards the street."

131

"Did she see anybody?" I asked, hoping that maybe she had gotten a glimpse of our perp.

"She said by the time she got herself out onto the porch, they were gone."

"Is she here visiting Mrs. Streams?" I asked.

"Yes, Junior. Anyway, she and Mrs. Streams were out picking wild berries and both of them got into some poison oak or ivy, or maybe both. Looked like her whole body was covered and she said she had blisters in 'private places.' Told me she's having a heck of a time getting around. Long story short she was soaking in the bathtub when I came by that day. By the time she got herself up and dressed, Ricky and I were long gone."

"Tommy, where was Mrs. Streams?" I asked.

"She was uptown at the drugstore buying some lotion. It's just a matter of plain old bad timing. However, she has no doubt that she heard two distinctly different voices and that's a positive we can work with."

"Yes, it is," I said with a little hope beginning to surface. "At least we know for sure now that there are two guys that we're looking for. It removes a little bit of doubt. But we've only heard about some big guy. Haven't heard a thing about..." I stopped right there and thought back to my conversation with Billy the night he followed me home.

"What is it, Junior?" Buck asked.

"When Billy was at my apartment that night, he said he knew his old cellmate from prison was one of the guys out at his place. Says his name is Benny Smith. Why didn't I think of that? Geez, I'm slipping. Why didn't I put two and two together? Sure, Benny must be the guy with the big guy. We find out who Benny Smith is, and we probably find out who the big guy is."

"I know about all of that Junior, but it's not possible," Tommy said with conviction.

"Why isn't it possible?" I asked.

"After I sent Matt and Shadow out to Billy's the second time, I gave Billy a call. I wanted the truth. So I told him not to cut any corners and tell me who his old cellmate is. Billy hesitated. I knew he was going to lie. So I warned him of the consequences. He told me that Benny is actually Perry Benjamin Smith. Ring a bell?" he asked.

"We had a guy that grew up right here in Crestfield named Perry Smith. Don't tell me they're the same guy," I said as the light came on.

"Yep, one in the same and it gets more interesting. I talked at length with the warden at Fort Madison. Perry Smith wasn't released from prison until a week after Miller's cow was cut up. Now unless this big guy works on his own, and I don't believe he does, Benny or Perry is not our guy," Tommy said with more conviction.

"Gosh, it looks like we're back to square one," I said.

"Not necessarily. Junior, knowing there are two guys is critical. I believe in the end it will not only solve the who's who, but it will stop all of this violence for good. I also asked the warden about our unknown big guy, and he doesn't believe that Perry had any friends while he was at Fort Madison that fit that description. So the warden is going to check with the prisons in the neighboring states. Maybe he'll get lucky. For now there is one other thing we need to consider."

"What's that?" I asked.

"There could be a third party. You know - someone else that works with the big guy. It's not likely, but what if there are two Bennys," he said with a shake of the head.

"You know that happened when I was in the fifth grade. There were four guys named Joe. Man, that was confusing," Buck added.

"Yeah, that would be. So I've decided that we need to run down Perry or Benny or whatever his name is and encourage him to tell us who the big guy is," Tommy said with a sparkle in his eye.

"Uncle Tommy, do you know something that we don't," Buck asked.

"Yes, I do. Let's call him Perry for the time being, since that's his given name. Anyway, Perry has crossed over into Illinois several times to see a girlfriend. It's a parole violation for him to cross state lines. I know we're going to find him and when we do we, tell him we'll let the crossing state lines info slide if he'll tell us the big guy's name. And of course, he has to tell us where the big guy is. It's worth a try. Now all we have to do is find Perry," Tommy affirmed with even more sparkle in his eyes.

"Ok, you got me. What else do you know, Uncle Tommy," Buck asked.

"Our buddy Perry ran a couple of red lights in Osceola this morning. Like three-thirty this morning. Guess he was flat-out hammered. Arresting officer said Perry couldn't talk or walk let alone pass any kind of sobriety test. They've got him in their jail right now. So I guess you can drive, Junior. We're heading over to Osceola. Buck, you can go, but please sit in the back and stay out of sight as much as possible ok? Most people will think Junior and I have got a prisoner or something like that. You don't mind being a criminal for a little bit do you?" Tommy asked with a smile.

"Heck no, this is great. If I'm not gonna be with Dad I'd like to be with you guys. I'm ready. Are you gonna handcuff me?" Buck asked with a sparkle in his eye.

The three of us chuckled a little bit as we headed for the roller. When we got in, Tommy said, "Junior, can you go up to the station for a minute? I want to ask Randi something about that phone call she received from our bad guy." We got to the station in a hurry and when we walked in, Ricky was manning the phones.

"Hey, you guys, what's goin' on." he said with his usual enthusiasm.

We all said hello and at just about the same time asked where Randi was.

"Well, Tommy, I didn't think you'd mind if I let her spend a little time with Dezi and Madison. The three of them haven't been together for over a year now," Ricky said with a smile.

"Yeah, it's ok, Ricky. Did Randi say anything about the phone company calling? I really want to know where this guy was when he made the call to the station," Tommy said.

"Yes, some gal from the phone company named Cheri called. Said she's still working on it. She thinks it may have come from a pay phone, which makes sense. I mean if I was a bad guy, I'd use a pay phone just like they do in the movies. Heck, if I called from my house, there'd be cops surrounding me before I could whistle Dixie," Ricky said as he started whistling Dixie.

"Ok Ricky, we get the idea. Gosh you're funny," I said with a smile.

He kept whistling.

"Ok, well, I'll call the station later. I mean on the telephone. We've had trouble with calls from the car when we get as far away as Osceola," Tommy said as the three of us waved goodbye to Ricky.

Junior/**The three of us got in the car**. Tommy sat in the front passenger seat and Buck was slouched down in the back. We headed south to the highway and the vibe was much better than a day ago, maybe better than even one short hour ago. When we jumped onto 34 heading east, Tommy began giving Buck a little history on the things we were seeing and passing. Every farm and how long it's been there. Every sign that he'd shot at some point in his youth. And of course, every little town he'd visited and every tavern he'd frequented during his dark days, as he calls them.

Buck knew about most of the stuff Tommy talked about but pretended not to. Said he was too sheltered and young to remember. That was a nice gesture as to his respect for his Uncle Tommy. He's such a great younger brother. We'd only traveled a couple of miles when the sky unleashed a torrential downpour. One of those biggies that make people say things like, it's raining cats and dogs. What does that mean? I like it and all, but it is a bit silly. Now, "it's a gully washer" makes sense. At least it makes sense to me.

Anyway, we made very good time as the windshield wipers beat a steady rhythm all the way into Clarke County. Then as it frequently does all over the Midwest, the rain suddenly stopped and the sun broke through the clouds. I think Tommy realized he'd put the two of us in a bit of an awkward position, that is talking about his dark days. So as he often does, he segued into a different subject with the grace and art of an experienced and sensitive orator.

"Buck, having never been in the military, I'm a bit green on the subject and was hoping you could fill me on what a day is like in the army," Tommy asked.

I looked in the rearview mirror and watched a smile slowly appear on Buck's face. When I saw him smile I realized that I should have asked the same question a long time ago.

"Well, let me see," Buck said before he thought out his response. "We get up before the sun crawls over the mountains east of the base. Then my unit does an hour or sometimes two of physical training. Usually we stay on base and go through our obstacle course. That part I don't like so much. Other times we head out into the hills with a pack on our back and a rifle over our shoulder. We always do something different on our pack days. That part I like ok. Then we head back for morning chow. The food's not the best, but I think it's a little better than what you've probably heard. After we eat, we get a little R&R before we go to our classrooms. We study everything from math to military history and strategies. I really like the classroom stuff because it's going to lead me into what it is I really want to do," he said with a smile that suggested we ask him what it is that he really wanted to do. So I asked.

"Buck, what is it you really want to do?"

He rubbed his hands together the way you might if you were really hungry and said, "I want to fly helicopters. The army has a new chopper that they just started using in the war, it's fabulous. It's a twin-engine Huey-Cobra. The Huey model it's replacing has been a mainstay for a long time, but in the military, as in civilian life, nothing lasts forever. So after lunch we all have classroom work. That's my favorite part of the day because I get to learn the how's, when's, and what's there are to flying choppers. We learn everything from reading the instruments, load- bearing ranges, maintenance, missile operation, and of course how to fly 'em. And we're also learning how to ditch a chopper."

I don't know about Tommy, but hearing about ditching a chopper got me a little concerned, maybe a lot concerned.

"Buck, are you sure about this? I mean, it seems like nearly every other day in the news we see or hear about a helicopter being shot down. Looks like a dangerous thing to want to do," I said as I watched Buck's smile dissipate.

"Junior, we all make choices in our lives and this is the choice I've made, it's what I want to do. I know I have a long way to go and a whole lot to learn. But try and understand how lucky I am just to be in this program. If not for this, I'd be in Nam right now. Would you rather I be out there marching through some jungle with guys I can't see shooting at me? I mean, what's worse? At least this way I learn a skill I can use after the war is over. And from what I understand, our government is negotiating a ceasefire as we speak. Heck, the war might end any day now," he said with little conviction.

"Junior, Buck has made some valid points in what he just told you. And the two of us really have no room to speak when it comes to dangerous occupations. I know we're policemen in a small town, but there are still many things that we face daily that could go wrong, terribly wrong."

I felt very small after Tommy finished what he was saying. He was right about everything, and I knew it.

"Buck, as usual, Uncle Tommy is right. I want you to know that I'm with you one hundred percent in everything you choose to do, that is everything that's legal. So, if you're going to fly helicopters, then do all you can to be the best doggone pilot there is," I said as a smile re-appeared on Buck's face.

I eased off highway 34 and took Main Street north to the Old Town Line Road. The moment we walked into the Osceola Police and Sheriff's station, we were met by the Chief of Police, Clete Duffus. The Chief is a really big man and carries himself with a power and grace that can't be ignored. To me he looks like he could've been an All Pro pulling guard for the Chicago Bears.

The Chief waved just before he said, "Hey Tommy, Junior, I see you decided to bring the army with you. Things can't be that bad, can they?" he said with a smile.

The three of us said hello back to him and of course gave him a little wave. Buck's wave began with a half salute, habit I guess. I looked at Tommy and decided I'd let him do the talking.

"Hello Clete - this army guy is my nephew, Buck."

Buck and Clete exchanged hellos and a handshake before Tommy continued.

"So Clete, how the heck you been?" Tommy said with a smile.

"I was doin' just fine 'til this character in my jail caused me to have to get up at four in the damn morning. Some people just never can figure out that you're supposed to go home when the taverns close. I haven't seen anyone that drunk since the night I picked you up, Tommy. Boy, you were a sight to see," Clete said with a smile that didn't last very long.

"Ok Tommy, I didn't mean anything by that and I wouldn't have said it if I didn't think you could take it. I mean, you've been sober for a long time now, right?" he asked more than said.

"Cletis, if that comment had come from anyone but you, I might have gotten a little bit angry. But the truth is it happened, and I have to live with the things I've done in the past. And if that was the only drunken incident in my life, I'd be doing great. Problem is there were others. You know like the time you and I were picked up in Winterset and thrown in jail for being drunk in public. And thanks to you, we were also charged with disorderly conduct and resisting arrest. You remember starting that fight with the cop that arrested us don't you, Chief," Tommy said with a smile.

"Touché, guilty as charged. Except the way I remember it Tommy, it was you that started the fight," Clete said.

Tommy just stared back at Chief Duffus.

"Ok, enough of that, let's go have a look at Mr. Winkle," the Chief said.

"Who's Mr. Winkle?" Buck asked.

"Buck, I think Chief Duffus is talking about the prisoner - Perry Smith," I said.

"Oh yeah, now I get it. That's a good one," Buck said as he shook his head.

We walked to the back of the station which, by the way, was almost identical to our police station. We all looked in the cell and could only see a mass of brown hair attached to a snoring, disheveled little man. Chief Duffus asked a young officer to open the cell. The moment the door came open, the sleeping man leaped up and started swinging, at air.

"Ok, Mr. Winkle, you can stop with all the nonsense. Nobody's gonna hurt you, so just relax," the Chief said with enough intensity to cause the prisoner to stop and think for a minute before he sat back down.

"What the hell do ya want? Can't you just leave me be so I can get some sleep," the prisoner, Perry Smith demanded.

"Don't worry, you'll have plenty of time to sleep, but first these officers from Crestfield have some important questions for you."

"I don't have to talk to nobody and you know it," he said as he looked at Buck. "And why the fuck is the tin soldier here?" Perry asked with attitude.

Tommy wasn't about to let anybody talk that way about family and neither was I. We both moved towards Perry and then Tommy put his hand in front of me and asked me to let him talk.

"Hello Perry, you remember me?" Tommy asked.

"The name is Benny, so stop calling me Perry," he said.

"Sorry, but I only know you as Perry. I know it's been a long time ago, but we met once," Tommy said with purpose.

Perry stood up and took a good long look at Tommy. We watched the recognition happen in his eyes.

"Yeah, I remember you. Got the jump on me that day otherwise I'd'a kicked your ass. But hell, you ain't here about that. You know last time I heard, you was a drunk. Crestfield so dang desperate they gotta hire drunks for policemen?" Perry asked with a venomous smile.

"Listen, do you want to talk about twenty years ago or about going back to prison for probation violations? What's it gonna be, Perry?" Tommy asked.

"What violations are you talking about?" Perry quickly responded.

"Well, I'm sure there've been a bunch, but we'll just concentrate on you crossing state lines. You know that's a parole violation," Tommy said with conviction.

"I never crossed any state lines. You can't prove that," Perry said with a twitch.

"Yes, we can. We've already spoken to your girlfriend." Tommy lied. Nobody had spoken to the girlfriend. "She doesn't want any trouble, so she's agreed to tell us everything. Perry, I'm sure you already know that she doesn't want anything to do with you. That's probably why you got drunk in the first place. I know all about it, happened to me more times than I'd like to admit. The girl I'd be dating would get tired of being around a drunk and then she'd leave me, which always gave me one more reason to go get drunk. Well, your girlfriend feels the same way all of mine did," Tommy said.

I could see that deep down it hurt Tommy to have to tell the truth. And so could Perry.

"That loudmouth bitch. Man, you just can't trust any of them goddamned women. Ok, what is it you want to know? Make it fast because I'm getting real tired of looking at you assholes," Perry said just before he spit on the floor.

"All we want to know is the name of the big guy you hang out with," I said.

140

"Who the fuck said you could ask me anything. Who the hell are you? I didn't know they let boy scouts be policemen," Perry said with a dagger in one eye.

"I'm detective Jack McCool and if you don't like me asking you questions, then we'll leave you here and come back next week. Maybe you'll want to talk to us then," I said not sure of how he'd respond.

"Chief Doofus, you can't keep me here for another week," Perry hollered.

"For the last time, doofus is not my name. And yes, I can keep you here as long as I damn well please. So you better start getting real respectful and answer this officer's questions, all of them!" the Chief hollered.

"Yeah, and winkle ain't my last name you dick," Perry screamed with a vengeance.

Police Chief Duffus ran towards Perry and tackled him to the concrete floor. Perry hit the floor with a loud thump. The Chief immediately had Perry in a chokehold that made it hard for me to swallow. I think Perry was asking us to get the Chief off of him, but it was difficult to tell what he was saying, not really. Then the Chief picked Perry up and threw him back on the bed. Perry Smith's eyes bugged out, but he didn't move a muscle.

"Now, you little prick, are you gonna answer the officer's questions or am I gonna have to choke the answers out of you?" Chief Duffus hollered.

"Ok, ok, what the hell is it you wanna know?" Perry said in compliance.

"All I want to know is the name of the big guy that you hang out with. You know, the guy you took out to Billy Thornton's place," I said.

"I've never been to Billy's!" he screamed.

He looked at me and then he stared at Chief Duffus but didn't say another word.

"Ok, I'm sorry Junior, but it looks like you're just gonna have to leave the prisoner here. You can give me a call next week and we'll make arrangements to try this again," the Chief said with what sounded like sincere regret.

"Oh to hell with all of ya, his name is David. Now go away and leave me alone," Perry said.

"Not so fast, Mr. Smith. We need his full name, that means first, middle and last, please," I said.

"Oh, so you think if you say please I'm gonna jump to. Well, screw you ass–"

Chief Duffus hit Perry Smith square in the face and a stream of blood instantly ran down from his nose and over his upper lip. The Chief didn't stop there and threw Perry on the floor again. It looked as though he was gonna kick the crap out of him. So Tommy and I both grabbed hold of Chief Duffus and pulled him back. The Chief didn't say a word. I hoped he was just playing a game with the prisoner.

Perry looked up at us, his eyes trying to focus, his mind obviously ajar. His hair was hanging back towards the floor and for the first time I noticed the missing left ear.

He quickly dragged his hand through his hair and covered up the missing appendage.

"Ok," he said through the blood. "His name is David - David Daniels. And before you go hitting me again, I don't know his middle name. Now that's what you wanted, and I done give it to you. So leave me alone!" he screamed.

"Not so fast, Perry. You're also gonna tell us where he is. And you're going to do it now or I'm gonna finish what Chief Duffus started," Tommy said, fury dripping from every word.

"I don't know where he is," Perry said.

Tommy started walking towards the downed prisoner.

"Ok, I think he's in jail in Peoria and that's all I know. Now get the hell out of my face!" he screamed at the top of his lungs.

"Gladly," Chief Duffus said as the four of us walked out of the cell.

I heard the cell door slam shut, but I didn't look back. We had what we came for and I didn't ever want to see that guy again. We walked outside of the station with Chief Duffus and milled around for a bit. We had skipped lunch and somewhere during the milling we decided we'd just stay and eat in Osceola. We were hungry and tired and quickly decided on pizza.

After getting directions to the new pizza place in town we said our goodbyes. I was starving, and Buck told me he was so hungry he was ready to pass out. We had to drive all of about three minutes - when we walked in, the place was nearly empty. I kinda like empty places when we're wearing our uniforms outta town and have the army with us. We don't get stared at as much. We ordered one cheese and one pepperoni pizza, both large. When the pizza came, Buck just about inhaled the first two or three pieces. It was kinda like watching some strange but true show on TV. Best part was he didn't even know I was watching. Tommy was doing more thinking than eating. I knew he was getting ready to ask a question, and he did.

"Junior, did you take notes while we were in the station?" he asked.

"Didn't have time to, but I'm gonna right now. I figure any details I missed the two of you can help me with."

"Well, I think you oughta start with David Daniels and maybe finish with Peoria."

"What do you mean - finish with?" I asked.

"Don't think there's anything to gain by writing down the extracurricular stuff that went on," he said with a get my meaning behind it.

"Oh, I understand. I wasn't gonna write that stuff down. Gosh Tommy - what kinda nut do you think I am?" I asked in jest.

"I think you're the honest kind of nut. And that is a quality that is rare in this profession. But right now we need to stick to the basics. And I believe we got a little more information than we'd hoped for."

"You mean David Daniels and the D and D in relation to the 4114," I asked.

"Yes. Only problem is it was just too darned easy. Something's not right. And when he said he'd never been to Billy's. Well, if I was a betting man, I'd say he was telling the truth. And that part bothers me most of all," Tommy said in a tone I don't think I've ever heard, at least not from him.

"Yeah, I know what you mean Tommy, that bothered me too," I agreed.

I don't think Buck heard a word we said, but he can be clever like that. You know listening but acting like he's not. I decided to find out.

"So Buck, what do you think about all of this?"

"I think I'm hungry and I think we're gonna need more pizza. This is definitely not enough for four people," Buck said as he pointed out the front window.

Tommy and I turned and watched Chief Duffus get out of his car. He flicked the cigarette he was smoking halfway across the parking lot and then slowly walked in.

"You get hungry, Chief?" Tommy asked.

"No, but if you don't mind I'll take a slice of pepperoni," he answered before grabbing a slice of pizza. "Listen Tommy, I just had some elderly woman lives down in Leon come to the station. She went on and on about how a woman has got to have her purse with her when she goes out. Says it's just not proper and ladylike to do so. So I agreed with her. I usually don't try to make my job any tougher than I have to. Well, she stops talking for a minute and catches her breath and says, 'Can you wait here for a minute young man?' Well, of course I'm not going anywhere, so I say yes. Then she runs outside, for her age it was running. Anyway, she comes walking back in with a purse. I take a look inside and it's full of pictures, a wallet, ID, perfume, makeup, lipstick, Kleenex, and other feminine stuff."

"Clete, we understand the purse was full. So can you get on with what it is you were gonna tell us. I mean we haven't got all night," Tommy said with a more restless than curious tone.

"Gee whiz Tommy, you're sure getting crabby in your old age," the Chief said with a pair of intense eyes staring back at him. "Ok, ok. Do you guys know a Marjorie Lynn Jessen?"

When he finished saying Marjorie's full name, the air slid right out of me. And I think the same kinda thing happened to Tommy. Buck stared at the two of us and immediately felt the dread that coursed through our veins. He didn't speak.

"By that response, I'd say the answer is yes. So who is she?" the Chief asked in earnest.

"Clete, she's the head nurse at the hospital. She's been missing for a couple of days now. Found her car parked sideways in her driveway, keys still in it. When I checked out her house, nothing seemed to be missing and there was no sign of a struggle of any kind. Her neighbor told me Marjorie leaves for a day or two now and then and they don't think twice about it. Problem is, she was supposed to work the next day. And missing work is something she doesn't normally do. Man, what a mess. Clete, if the woman lives in Leon, why'd she bring the purse here? I mean, couldn't she have given it to Micah?" Tommy asked.

"I asked her the same question, Tommy. She said she rides up here with a friend every couple of weeks to shop. I guess they just continued on their way."

"Well, we've definitely got a missing person on our hands. And it looks like there could be foul play of some sort. Christ, I hope Marjorie's ok," Tommy said with a worried tone.

"Tommy, look, I'm really sorry to hear that. Anything you need me to do, just say the word. Any damn thing at all," the Chief said.

"Thanks, I appreciate that. Clete, can we have a look at that purse?" Tommy asked.

"Absolutely, you can take it if you want. I've got it out in the patrol car. I've already called Micah. He's expecting you to come down some time this evening. Hope you didn't mind me calling ahead for you," the Chief said in apology.

"Certainly, I don't mind. In fact, I appreciate the help. We're gonna need all the help we can get with this one. I have to tell you I have a bad, bad feeling about this. I suppose you've heard what's been going on in Crestfield lately," Tommy said as Chief Duffus nodded his head.

"Well, there's no question in my mind that Marjorie missing is connected to the other stuff. Don't know how or why, but my gut tells me it is. I guess we'd better head on down to Leon and have ourselves a look-see. Gonna be pitch black by the time we get there. Ok - are you two ready to roll?" he asked as we nodded our heads.

We walked out of the restaurant into a strong wind and a slight mist. The Chief got the purse out of his car, and handed it to Tommy and said, "Tommy, I meant what I said about helping. And I'm sorry I didn't say anything about your brother, I apologize for that. It's just that I figured you'd heard enough. Anything you need just give me a call."

Tommy told the Chief he understood, thanked him for his help, and said goodbye. The three of us slid into our car. Tommy was behind the wheel. And in no time at all we were speeding south down old highway 69. I looked out the passenger side window for just a moment, and it felt like we were slicing through time like a bright beam of light. And as the world raced by me in a confusing blue blur, a disturbing thought came to mind. *How will Madison react when she hears that Marjorie is missing or, heaven forbid, worse?*

**Junior**/**Not a word was spoken** as we crossed into Decatur County. I looked down for a second at Marjorie's purse and wondered why she would have come down here.

"Tommy, can you think of a reason why Marjorie would want to come down to Leon?" I asked.

Tommy didn't even look at me - he just shook his head no. I stared into the starless night for what seemed like hours before I saw the sign that said Leon next exit. We'd made the twenty-one-mile drive in just over ten minutes. I don't know why, but it felt to me as though we were late for a funeral. Tommy turned off the highway and headed straight to the tiny Leon police station.

When we pulled up, Chief Micah Walker was out in front of the station with a small, bright eyed, blue haired, elderly woman standing at his side. I couldn't help but notice that Chief Walker looked an awful lot like Abe Lincoln, but of course without the signature top hat. We got out of the car and one by one stretched and said hello. There wasn't a smile to be found.

"Hello Tommy, Junior. I see you decided to bring the army with you," Chief Walker said.

We'd already heard that twice today and I guess Tommy felt like that was enough. He just shrugged his shoulders.

"Micah, this is my nephew, Buck. He decided he'd like to ride along today. We had no idea the day would become so long," Tommy said in a weary voice.

"Yes, I understand. Look, I'm really sorry you're here under the present circumstances, but... When Clete called and told me you were coming down here, I thought it'd be a good idea if Mrs. Reed was here to show you exactly where she found the purse. Elizabeth, this is Chief McCool and his nephews Junior and Buck."

"Hello, it's nice to meet you young men. I'm so very sorry for your troubles and misery. Whenever you're ready, I'll show you where I found the purse. I think I should tell you that a woman doesn't go anywhere without her purse. Just don't make sense. Gives me a dreadful feeling deep down in my stomach," she said.

"Tommy, you can you follow me. We're only gonna go north a mile or so - back the way you came into town. I'll take Elizabeth in my car," the Chief said.

"Ok, I'll follow you," Tommy answered.

"Tommy, can you guys call me Micah from here on out? No need for formalities," Micah said as he helped Mrs. Reed get into his patrol car.

Micah didn't exaggerate when he said it was only a mile or so. We watched his brake lights come on and then he pulled to the shoulder and continued for only about ten more feet. It was dark when we came into town, but now there was nothing but complete and absolute blackness. I reached for my flashlight and hoped I'd changed the batteries. After a shake or two it came on and was working like it should. I sighed in relief and then shivered, why I don't know. It was cold out, but not that cold.

Tommy opened the trunk and was removing some of our orange plastic cones. We've had way too many of our police cars hit when they were parked on the side of these little two-lane highways. And it usually happens on misty nights like this one. Mrs. Reed slowly walked to the front of Micah's car. His headlights were on and pointing at a small cross in the ground that was only about five feet or so off the pavement. She pointed and said, "A young boy was hit and killed here many years ago. The purse was hanging on his cross. If that woman has been hurt, and I believe she has, there is a depraved and evil person out there somewhere. Can you imagine treating the lord and that little boy with such utter impudence - makes my skin crawl."

The emotion flowing from the woman was genuine and frightening. And if what she said was true, we were all in for much more than we had reckoned. I couldn't see in the darkness and realized that it'd be pointless to venture out.

"Ma'am, do you know this area?" I asked.

I shined my light on Mrs. Reed and she turned and stared at me with the eyes of a tortured animal.

"Of course I know the area. My family has owned this property for over a hundred years. That was my little boy that was run over and killed by a stupid, stupid..."

She turned and wept as she walked back to Micah's car. And in my mind I had been turned to stone. I looked over at

147

Tommy and he just shook his head. I started towards Mrs. Reed when Micah held his hand up.

"Junior, you're not the first person to catch hell from Elizabeth. She has been damning anyone and everyone since the day that boy was killed. You couldn't have known, and you have every right to ask questions and find out where your Miss Jessen is," Micah said with heart.

While Micah was speaking, Buck had walked up and put his hand on my shoulder.

"Micah's right, we have to find Marjorie. This isn't your fault, Junior," Buck softly said.

"Micah, what happened to Mrs. Reed's boy?" Tommy asked.

"Look, I'm not trying to be mean, but the boy was a bit on the special side. Luke was his name. One morning he hid behind a row of corn from the school bus driver. The driver called out for Luke and honked his horn several times, but the boy didn't come out from his hiding place. After waiting for a long time, the driver decided he needed to get the other kids to school. Those were the rules. When the driver pulled away from the side of the road, Luke jumped out in front of the bus. He was pronounced dead right there where the cross is stuck in the ground."

"Oh my, can you imagine the guilt and remorse that poor driver must have gone through," I said.

"Junior, the driver was Elizabeth's husband, Luke's dad. He was a hard-working farmer just trying to make an extra dollar or two for his family," Micah said as he looked at the cross for a moment. "Luke senior died a year later. I believe he died from the hell and torment she put him through. Elizabeth shut the world out and the place down after he died. Sold all the animals, stopped planting, and let the ponds on the property either dry up or become fouled. If you walk into the property a ways, you'll see what I mean. I'm sorry about all of this and I will help you men in any way I can, but for now I need to get her back home. You can't see the porch light she leaves on at night, but her house is about a half a mile straight east through the property. I don't think you could find anything out here right now. Maybe you oughta go on home and drive back down in the morning. Just a thought, but you do what you think you need to. Tommy, you have my number?"

Tommy nodded yes.

"Ok, well, you be sure to give me a call in the morning, goodnight."

Micah walked back to his car and helped Elizabeth Reed into the front seat. They drove by us heading north for maybe a hundred yards and then turned east. I looked towards Tommy and then Buck and realized there was no point. We were only three feet apart and we still couldn't see each other.

I turned my flashlight back on and then turned the light towards Tommy. He did the same to me.

"Junior, I'm not going home 'til I know for sure that Marjorie is not here somewhere. You and Buck can take the car. I'll walk back to town when I'm done searching the area. I know where Micah lives and I can stay there with him 'til you come get me tomorrow."

I started to tell Tommy that I wasn't going anywhere, but Buck beat me to it.

"Uncle Tommy, is this some effort of yours to give us little boys a break? Well, the hell with you. I'm not going anywhere if you don't. And that's that!" Buck yelled.

"Yeah, Tommy, what the heck is going on? I'm not leaving here without you. So if we're going to look for Marjorie, let's get to it," I said, genuinely pissed.

"Ok, that's what I was hoping to hear. Let's go find Marjorie. Buck, there's another flashlight in the trunk of the car. We're going to need all the light we can muster. Are you two ready?" Tommy asked.

"As soon as I get that flashlight out of the trunk, I think we'll be ready to go," Buck said in affirmation.

The three of us headed east into the freshening wind and mist, our lights shining on the ground in front of us. We each fanned our flashlight around in front of us the way a person with a metal detector might do. There was an old winding road that we followed for a long ways, but it led to nothing. We walked at least the length of a football field or so and still nothing. Not a footprint or a tire track. And the wind was beginning to howl all around us.

"Tommy, sometimes we do maneuvers at night. And when we feel like we're lost we're, taught to stop, crouch, listen, and smell. I've done it many times and it works. If there's something here that we need to know about, we'll feel it. Just trust me this one time, ok?" Buck requested.

I think Tommy and I were frustrated and not wanting to admit that we were pretty much lost. So I said, "Tommy, I don't think it can hurt to give what Buck told us a try."

Tommy didn't answer me.

"Tommy, what do you think?" I asked.

"Junior, I think that's a good idea, but it won't work unless you shut up and get down here with your brother and me."

I shined my light down at the ground around my feet and there they were, crouched like a couple of Indians around a campfire. I started to say something but decided to take Tommy's advice and shut up. I crouched down and turned my light off.

After I sat down, I put my hand right in front of my face and wiggled my fingers. I couldn't see a darn thing. I stopped trying to see and concentrated on listening to what was around me. I heard the wind crying, but I couldn't understand what she was saying. The three of us had been crouched for a long time when Buck broke the silence and said, "Do you guys smell that?"

I thought he was playing with us, but before I could say anything, Tommy says, "Yeah, I do smell it. It smells like dead fish or... yep, it's fish alright. Is that what you guys smell?"

I wasn't sure, but Buck was and said, "Yes Tommy, that's exactly what I smell. Ok, I'm tired of crouching so let's go check it out."

Our flashlights came back on almost at exactly the same time. And Tommy said, "I don't know about the two of you, but my knees couldn't have taken another minute of crouching. Let's go."

We continued walking in the same direction, felt like straight east to me. The wind picked up again and with every step, the smell of something rancid became stronger. Then suddenly the three of us stopped.

"Did you hear that?" I asked.

"I sure did," Buck answered.

"Sounds like waves of water lapping against a boat or something," Tommy said.

We continued walking when suddenly Tommy yelled, "Stop! Hold up right there. Look around you."

Buck and I both pointed our flashlights at the ground around us. We didn't see anything at first.

"Tommy, I don't see anything. What is it we're supposed to see?" I asked.

"There's a bunch of tire tracks, could've been made by Marjorie's car." Tommy said just before he shined his flashlight back and forth at our feet. "We could be destroying a crime scene. Junior, I want you to get off this little path we're on and take about ten steps to your left." I did. "Ok, Buck and I are going to stay right here. You're off the path now so keep going 'til you get to the water that we hear. Don't fall in," he said.

I continued walking and I could hear water bouncing off of something. I walked over a small knoll and shined my light out in front of me and there it was. The exact same body of water I had seen in my dream the night before. Nel wasn't there, but it was eerily the same.

I continued down the small hill with my flashlight constantly searching the ground around me. Then I saw what the water was lapping against. It was what was left of a very small boat dock. I continued walking and there next to the water's edge were a couple of corroded barbell weights. They had yellowed twine wrapped around them. I walked around the weights and eased my right foot out over the water and onto the dock. It held my weight. I took another step and another and still the dock held my weight. I stood dead still near the end of the dock moving my light back and forth when it flicked off of something white. I took a few more steps, the dock held firm. When I got to the white object, I took out my handkerchief, bent down, and picked it up. I thought I knew what it was but had to be sure. I folded the edges of the handkerchief back and shined my light on it. It was a name tag with two lines of print.

On the top line written in crisp red letters was *Crestfield Community Hospital*. And written on the bottom line in bold black letters was *Marjorie L Jessen R.N.* The cold hard reality of what I'd just found took my breath away. I closed my eyes as an ice-cold shiver shot through my bones. I suddenly felt the need to get off of that little dock and back to Tommy and Buck.

I carefully shifted my weight and started to turn around when Tommy yelled, "Junior, are you ok?"

He startled me just enough to where I must have twitched and my left foot broke through the old dock. My leg crashed downward and my foot slid along the bottom of the pond. I struggled to regain my balance and eventually pulled my wet shoe and pant leg out of the water. I wanted to let Tommy know I was ok, but first I had to make sure I secured the name tag. Before I wrapped it up, I took one last look. I didn't want to believe it was hers, but there could be no doubt. I suppose I was wishing that Marjorie was there with me. I wrapped up the name tag, put it in my shirt pocket, and started to head back. Tommy yelled again, but this time with much more intensity. I hollered back, "I'm ok. Stay there, I'll be right back."

Just before heading back, I turned and looked east one more time and there, plain as day, was the light that I'd seen in my dream. I remembered Nel saying over and over, 'Don't be afraid, go to the light.' I didn't go to the light but instead eased my way back off the dock. And with my heart stuck in my throat, I raced back to Tommy and Buck. When I got to them, Tommy shined his light in my face and said, "Junior, have you been crying?"

"No, I don't think so?"

I didn't say another word. I just pulled the name tag out of my pocket and handed it to Tommy. He shined his light on it and said nothing. I could see Buck shining his light over Tommy's shoulder. He didn't say a word either as he stared at the name tag. I'm really not sure why, but I crouched down the way we had done earlier. My mind was numb to the world around me. At that point I think I wanted to stay numb for a while, quite a while, but Tommy was not going to let that happen.

"Junior! Junior, come on we have to get back to the car. We need to let Micah know we probably have a crime scene here," he said.

I stood up and blurted out, "No Tommy, we have to go to the light."

"Junior, are you ok? What light?" he asked.

"Yes, I'm fine. At least I think I am. Please, I've been here before. I know it might sound crazy, but I had a dream last night and, in the dream, Nel told me to go to the light."

"Nel Thornton?" Tommy asked.

"Yes, Nel Thornton," I said back.

"Junior, it doesn't sound crazy - it is crazy," Buck added.

I thought to myself, *it does sound crazy.*

"Please, you have to trust me. Just follow me," I said.

I turned and started walking straight east. I was going to go to the light with them or without them. I really didn't care. At that point they thought I was crazy and were going to follow me just to appease me or they were family and trusted me. I was walking at a pretty good pace heading straight to the light I had seen in my dream. Tommy and Buck were right behind me. I walked straight east and after a few steps I thought, *Nel, please don't fail me now.*

I heard their footsteps matching mine, our lights shining into the blackness. We traveled maybe another fifty feet when Buck yelled, "I see the light. Tommy, do you see the light?"

I looked up and sure enough there was the light. I said to myself, *see I'm not crazy.*

"Yes, I see the light. Junior, keep going," Tommy said in a tone that told me he believed me.

We walked with a purpose that at the time none of us understood. Why we were walking towards it was still a mystery, but we continued. Then, without a warning I tripped and fell flat on my face. My flashlight tumbled out of my hand lighting up the ground ahead of us. Buck turned his light down right in my face and said, "Junior, is there something wrong with you? Get up and keep going. I think we're onto something."

"We don't need to go any further," Tommy said as he shined his light in my face. "What we're onto is what Junior just tripped over," he said as he moved his light back to the ground.

There lying still as a mannequin on the ground next to me was Marjorie. Without any conscious thought I scooted away from her. Tommy moved his light from her torso down to her feet and then slowly back up to her head. Within moments all three of us had our lights shining on what was left of her face. I shook my head and yelled, "No, no!" as Tommy slowly crouched down and touched her clothing.

She still had her nurse's uniform and coat on. Tommy put his right index and middle finger to the side of her throat and softly said, "She's soaking wet and cold as ice. I'd say she's been dead for at least a day or so. Don't know for sure, but I'd say she was in that pond at some point, very strange." He hesitated for a few moments. "She's been shot at least two times that I can see, maybe more. We need to leave and make sure we don't disturb anything. Try not to walk over any of the existing footprints. Hopefully we haven't already done so. We'll come back out here at first light. Let's go."

I moved my light towards Marjorie's face one last time. I winced and my head recoiled. I was sure that what I'd just seen would be forever carved into my brain. I turned away and followed Buck and Tommy. The three of us trudged back to our car trying to stay as far away as possible from the path we'd come in on. When we got to the car, Buck asked Tommy if it would be ok if he went back and put a blanket over Marjorie.

"Buck the same thought crossed my mind. But we can't take the chance of disturbing the crime scene any more than we already have. Please try to understand that she doesn't feel the cold anymore. Buck, I'm sorry," Tommy said.

Buck got in the back seat and hung his head. He knew that Tommy was speaking from experience and had told him the truth. But it hurt just the same. In the meantime, I had crawled into an imaginary hole in the universe. And I only came out when I felt the car move.

Tommy knew he had to deliver the bad news to Micah as he put the car in drive. We moved only ten feet or so when he braked and threw the transmission back into park. He just sat there, probably agonizing over what to do next. And then he turned to us and said, "Wait here, I'll be right back."

He got out of the car, walked back and opened the trunk for a moment, and then slammed it shut. I could see his flashlight shining on the cones he'd set out when we first got there. One by one he picked them up and then turned and walked away. Buck and I sat there hoping, but not knowing. Tommy was only gone for maybe ten minutes before he came back. He got in the car, put it in drive, and we slowly drove back into the little town of Leon.

154

Crestfield

I know Tommy was right about not disturbing the crime scene and all, but I hated the thought of leaving Marjorie out there all alone in the cold black night.

Marjorie was still steaming from her exchange with Madison when she drove up her driveway. And although she valiantly fought her attackers she was soon overpowered. Only semiconscious when she was pulled from the trunk of her own car, she knew that she'd traveled a fair distance. Blindfolded and bleeding she was led to softer ground where she could smell the decay of dead fish and water that was fouled in some unknown way.

The man that had hastily dropped Marjorie gagged and weighted into the cold water had no idea that she would actually follow his instructions and walk to the edge of the pond or lake in which she'd been harshly deposited. While struggling at the water's edge she felt strong hands lifting her from certain death. Once out of the water and gasping for air she managed to scrape and drag her face back and forth against the moist soil and remove her blindfold. She then sat on her rump and watched the assailants drive away in her car. All was quiet while she wrangled her way out of the twine that secured her hands. The weights that had been tied to her ankle were then removed.

She sat thinking about how lucky she was to be alive while desperately peering through the blackness for the hands that had removed her from this watery grave. Maybe, just maybe, she'd imagined the helping hands. She violently shivered. Not because she was cold, but at the thought of the beasts that had held her captive and what might have been.

Slowly regaining her faculties, she stood up and headed towards the nearest light in the sky, which she soon realized was a farmhouse. Hope running on high, Marjorie slowly walked maybe fifty feet before she felt the first red-hot poker sizzle and crash through her lower jaw. Her mind, once again clouded, she involuntarily lifted both hands to her mouth to feel and taste the blood rushing from her body. Marjorie never felt the next blistering dagger. It came and went in the wink of an eye. Now free from the struggle and pain life had thrown her way, she slipped into endless sleep. Marjorie heard the whippoorwill sing long before the rooster could crow.

Out of our hands   26

***Junior*/When I woke the next morning,** I jumped off the cot Micah's wife had made for me the night before. I looked across the room and there on a rollaway bed was Buck, he was still fast asleep. Worried that I might be left behind I ran out to the kitchen. Micah was there waiting for me.

"Junior, I'd say good morning to you, but I see nothing good about this morning. As soon as you can get dressed, we'll head out to the Reed property."

I ran back to the cot and threw my pants, shirt, and shoes on. I made just enough noise to make sure I woke Buck up. He raised his head and looked at me and said, "I'll be ready to go in five minutes."

When we walked back out to the kitchen, Micah had set out a bowl of cereal and a cup of Postum for each of us.

"Sorry boys, I hope you don't mind, I ran out of coffee."

"I'm not hungry, Micah. We need to get going." I looked around again and blurted out, "Where's Tommy?"

"Tommy was gone before the sun came up. Junior, I know you would probably run all the way out there if you had to, but the fact is there's just no point in hurrying. We're probably going to be out there for a long time today so please eat a little bit."

"Micah, I'm just not hungry and Tommy's going to need our help."

"Junior, he's not alone. The Sheriff and one of his deputies are already there with him. You need to understand that even though Marjorie was from Crestfield, it's now a Decatur County matter."

The reality of what Micah had just told me took a few seconds to sink in. I reluctantly sat down and so did Buck. I took a sip of the Postum and shook my head. I hate Postum. Buck did the same. I was just going to start in on the cereal when Micah's grizzled and lanky wife, Tilly, walked into the kitchen. She gave us a short wave of the hand.

"Morning boys - good gravy Micah, they're going to need more than a bowl of cereal. Why didn't you come out back and get me? Honestly, sometimes I think I married a child." Micah had a look on his face that told me he'd heard the same little speech before.

"You boys give me a few minutes and I'll have more ham and eggs ready to eat than you can shake a stick at."

Buck and I both said thank you at the same time, but what I really wanted to say was no thanks we're in a hurry. She had a hot plate of fresh ham and eggs in front of us before... Well, in a hurry. I ate a little faster than usual, which according to most people is still a bit on the slow side. That said, my little human vacuum cleaner brother was eating at a fevered pitch.

"My, this one can sure do some eating," Tilly said as she stared at Buck in genuine surprise. "I want you boys to know that I just feel terrible about what has happened to that poor woman out there. If you ask me, that Reed farm is a wicked place."

"Nobody asked you, Matilda," Micah said with a deftly seasoned tone.

She seared a hole thru Micah with her eyes just before she said, "I'll be in the livin' room if you boys need anything. Please be careful out there today. Bye, bye."

Micah finally stood up and motioned for us to follow him. We stepped outside to a cold gray day. As Micah put on his hat, he said, "Looks like we're in for some weather."

Neither of us said a word. We got in the car and Micah drove at about twenty miles an hour to the exact same spot we'd been to last night.

I was tired of the slow pace and tired of waiting. I jumped out of Micah's car and was walking as fast as I could down the path we'd been on the night before when someone yelled, "Stop!"

I looked over to my right and there was the Sheriff's deputy. He looked like he could have been Ricky's twin. I did as he'd said and stood still 'til he walked over to me.

"Didn't mean to alarm you or anything, it's just that Sheriff Muir told me to make sure nobody walked around here. He doesn't want there to be any chance that somebody might walk over existing footprints. Only problem is there aren't any footprints. There are a lot of tire prints, but they're probably from the lady's car. By the way I'm Cyrus, nice to meet you."

"Nice to meet you too, I'm Junior."

We shook hands as Buck walked up and stood behind me.

"This is my brother, Buck."

Buck started a salute and then waved and Cyrus did the same.

"There are no footprints at all?" I asked.

"Nope, there's nary a footprint that matters," he said with conviction.

"What do you mean, that matters? What footprints did you find?" I asked.

"What I mean is the only footprints we found are the ones you guys must have made last night. Heck of a thing you fellows walked into. I've never actually seen a dead body, least not in a situation like this. It must have been a spooky experience for you."

I was straining to see if I could find Tommy, but he was nowhere in sight.

"Uh, yeah, it was an awful experience." I said hoping he'd stop with the questions.

"Did you know her?" he asked.

"Yes, she's one of the nurses at the hospital in Crestfield. She didn't show up for work a few days ago."

After I finished explaining who Marjorie was, I heard Tommy yell for me to come on down. I walked towards his voice. I'd forgotten that there was a slight hill to climb between Tommy and me. I walked for maybe thirty steps or so and there he was.

"Junior, come on down, we're gonna fan out and search the area for shell casings or footprints or well, just about anything we can find. So far we've got a whole lot of nothing to go on," he said in a tired voice.

Buck and I walked to Tommy in what seemed like a much shorter distance than it did last night. As we got closer, we saw that there was a blanket covering the body. I stood next to Tommy and could see that someone had painted a couple of orange circles on the ground right next to the body. Inside the circles there was blood and what looked like human tissue and teeth? Then I took another look through the gray and could see somebody sweeping the area with a metal detector.

"Tommy, shouldn't there be a coroner here?" I asked.

"Yes, there should be and there is," Tommy said.

"Where is he?" I asked.

"The Decatur County Coroner is right over there walking around with the Sheriff," Tommy answered.

"Micah is the county coroner?" I asked.

"Yes, and in cases like this he depends on a doctor to do the medical examinations. So, we're waiting for the Wayne County Medical Examiner to get here. He should be here any minute. I think he's going to look at the position of the body and try to figure out where the shooter was standing. Marjorie was heading east, that much we know. And she was hit in back of the left lower jaw with what I believe was the first shot. The bullet went through and out the front of her mouth, took some teeth with it. Then she must have turned in shock and staggered toward the direction the bullet had come from, which is due north. The second, and I believe final, bullet hit her almost directly over her right eye hurling her straight south and on her back where she lies now. The hard part to understand is the pond. There's twine on the ground next to the dock that must have been used to tie her hands. There are also two twenty-five-pound weights that were tied to one leg. If they were going to drown her, why would they get her out and then shoot her? It doesn't make any sense, unless, of course, these people just wanted to torture her for a bit before they killed her. We may never find out. That guy you see wearing the brown trench coat next to Micah is Sheriff Muir. I guess searching for stuff with a metal detector is a hobby of his. After looking at the body, he felt like there had to be at least one slug that passed through her. He thinks he can find it. I don't know about that, there's an awful lot of property to search, but you never know. Ok, let's go take a look and see if we can't find out where the shooter was standing. You two remember how dark it was last night," Tommy said more than asked.

"Uh yeah, you do remember me tripping don't you," I said more than asked.

"Well, whoever shot Marjorie has to have used a night scope. Either that or they shot her in broad daylight. And I seriously doubt that. This person has had a lot of experience with firearms and must be an expert with a rifle. That much I'm sure of. Ok you guys - let's go find a footprint or two," Tommy said in a simulated rah, rah, voice.

We started walking straight north with maybe ten feet between us. I was in the middle and Buck was to my left.

As we walked, we each noticed the exact same thing, barren soil.

"Tommy, don't you think we ought to call the station and let them know what's going on?" I asked.

"Last night I sat next to the phone in Micah's kitchen for a long time. I was trying to decide whether or not it was a good idea to call at such a late hour. Well, I decided that there was no need to have them sleep on such bad news. So I called Ajax this morning and told him what has happened. He's the only person I trust not to go blabbing the news all over town. He's gonna wait 'til Marjorie's sister, Grace, is informed before he says a word to anybody. Then I called the station and talked with Matt for a bit. I guess the girls were out late last night, so he was covering for Randi. He said all was quiet. I told him we'd be home sometime today. Things are quiet now, but I'm afraid that once the news gets out about what has happened, Crestfield is going to be set on its ear. Micah is going to tell Marjorie's sister himself. I told him I'd tell her, but he said it's the coroner's responsibility to notify the next of kin. Micah makes a little extra money being the coroner. That's money I could do without. Anyway, I don't know if there is a right or wrong or best way to go about any of this; I really don't," Tommy said as he stared at the ground below him.

When Tommy stopped talking, I kept walking and shook my head in confusion. My mind was in a state of complete turmoil. I went back and forth trying to understand how and especially why this happened. When we reached a point maybe four hundred yards out, Tommy said, "Ok, I don't think anyone could make those two shots from any further out than this. We should move west maybe fifty feet and then continue to search for prints as we head back."

I slowly turned around and when I looked up, I saw the Wayne County Medical Examiner's van in the distance. It was parked on the side of the road - right next to the little cross. The three of us continued our search all the way back to where we'd started and silently watched two assistants put Marjorie in a black body bag.

"You must be the medical examiner," Tommy said.

"Yes, I'm Robert Hornell. And you must be the gentlemen that found the body," he answered.

Tommy said yes and Buck and I just nodded our heads. Hornell slowly took off the rubber glove he was wearing and shook our hands.

"Well, I can only guess that you're trying to figure out where the shooter was standing," he asked waiting for another nod of our heads. "After looking at the position of the body, I'd say you need to search in a more westerly direction. I'm sorry, northwesterly would be more accurate. And that brings the highway into play. The shooter could have made the shots from his or her car. The victim was hit twice as you may already know. Fragments from her incisors and cuspids sprayed in a southeasterly direction. Think of it in terms of the shots being fired from Washington State down towards Florida. One other thing, if I were you, I'd look for a knee print on the ground. The shots were made at a slightly upward angle from a kneeling or possibly a seated position."

"Can you tell me if the second shot was a thru and–"

"Yes, it was. I'd say the weapon used was a common deer rifle. And if Sheriff Muir finds a slug, I'd say it's going to be in the range of a thirty aught six or a thirty-thirty," he said.

"Do you think she was in that pond?" I asked.

"I can say with an amount of certainty that she was in that pond. I found what was left of a decayed bluegill in the left pocket of her coat. Gentlemen, I wish we could have met under different circumstances, but this is in fact the way I usually meet people. So if you'll excuse me, I must perform an autopsy and render a rather detailed report, comes with the job. Bye," he said as he walked away without waving.

"I think I detected a Boston accent," Buck said.

"Really, how would you know a Boston accent from a New York accent?" I asked.

"I know because my friend Vincent Gaglio is from New York and he doesn't sound anything like that guy," Buck said with confidence.

"Sounded like a Harvard grad to me, but it doesn't matter where he's from," Tommy said as he walked away from us. "Come on, we're going up to the road and see if we can't find out where the shooter was," he said with renewed vigor.

Buck and I followed Tommy as he walked straight west towards the highway. As we walked we watched the Medical Examiner's van turn around and head south. Then the three of us watched Micah put the handheld back in his car just before he got out. He walked straight back to us.

"Tommy, our dispatcher just got a call from an officer Healey. He said that the call you've been wondering about came from a phone booth in Keokuk," Micah said with a puzzled look on his face.

"Keokuk, I would never have expected that. I thought for sure the perp was calling from someplace close to Crestfield. Keokuk is on the other end of the state, doesn't make any sense. That is unless... Still doesn't make any sense," Tommy said.

"What call are we talking about?" Micah asked.

"The guy that claims he's responsible for all the havoc called our dispatcher a day ago and said for us to leave him alone, among other things," Tommy said as he looked down and once again shook his head.

"So I guess Keokuk confuses things a bit," Micah said waiting for Tommy to answer.

"Yes, it does," Tommy answered.

"Listen Tommy, sorry I had to give you such confusing information, but I gotta believe that eventually it will all make sense. For now the Sheriff and I are done searching the area. We found six slugs and no two of them look like they came from the same gun. One does look pretty fresh. It could be a thirty-thirty. We'll have all of them tested for the usual, but I can't promise anything more than that. I'm sorry. You've sure been through a lot of misery lately and it looks like there's gonna be more to come," Micah said.

"Yes, I'm afraid so. Micah, can you call Osceola from your car?" Tommy asked.

"No, but I can have my dispatcher call. What is it you want to know?" Micah asked.

"I want to make sure Chief Duffus still has Perry Smith in custody. Right now he's our only lead," Tommy said.

"Is he the guy you told me about last night? Micah asked.

"Yes he is. The only problem is he's known for breaking and entering and other small-time crimes, but he's not known as a murderer. I just don't think he fits. But we have to cover all the bases," Tommy said.

"I'm gonna go back to the station. We should have an answer from Chief Duffus by the time you're done searching for prints. I probably won't be there, I'm going to drive up and tell Marjorie's sister. See you guys," Micah said.

Tommy said thanks as he turned away. He started walking north along the highway, head down. I don't know if he was actually looking at the ground or not. I looked at Micah and the two of us just nodded before we turned away from each other. There was a dismal feeling in the air. I slowly started walking up the highway. Buck was walking at what I would call a military pace and was soon far ahead of Tommy and me. When we got to about the same distance out we'd gone earlier that morning, we all just stopped.

"Doesn't look good guys, we're well past four hundred yards and not a darn thing. You know, while I was walking, I started thinking about why someone would walk along this stretch of the highway. And I couldn't come up with one reason. In fact, the only reason you'd be here in the first place is if your car broke down. And if that was the case, you wouldn't go north, there's twenty miles of absolutely nothing in that direction. So obviously you'd go south and back into town. I'm sorry guys, but we're not gonna find any footprints out here," Tommy said.

"Tommy, we're not looking for just anybody's footprints. We're looking for somebody that had a reason to stop. They stopped because they were gonna shoot somebody," I said with attitude.

"Thanks Junior, that's exactly what I was hoping you'd say. The only footprints we would have found would have been from the person that shot Marjorie. And that person isn't going to just walk away and leave prints on the ground. They're evil but they're not stupid. They've been covering their tracks from day one. Junior, you saw the rectangular prints out at Miller's place. Do you think these people would make the mistake of leaving footprints? Well, I don't. What I do think is that we're wasting our time looking and I'm sick and tired of this... I want to find this guy and..." Tommy kicked at the ground below him in frustration and then said, "Let's go home and get some rest. We can get a fresh start in the morning."

"Um, Uncle Tommy - I wanna go home too. But, did you say rectangular prints?" Buck asked.

As Tommy walked away he said, "Yes, I did. Junior, you saw 'em up close and personal. Tell Buck about them."

"Buck, there were a couple dozen rectangular prints leading into and out of Miller's farm. And I'm almost positive they're connected to all of this. What Tommy is saying is that they don't want us to see their real footprints, pretty clever if you think about it. If you leave prints, you tell those looking for you what size and style of shoe you wear. And more importantly you tell them how many of you there are. I mean we believe there are two, but now I'm not so sure. It seems like we've got several people working at this. And the frightening part is they're working together."

When I was done explaining, Tommy and I started walking back to the car. Buck didn't move and I for one didn't care.

We continued walking when Buck yelled, "Do you two wanna see the print I found or not?"

I turned around, but Tommy didn't. Head down he just kept walking towards the car. "Buck what in the heck are you talking about? We've been up and down this highway and haven't seen a doggone thing. There are no prints, leastwise there's none that I've seen."

"I'm not talking about here on the road. I'm talking about right next to where Marjorie's body was laying. There's a print there," Buck said.

Tommy turned in his tracks and walked back to Buck.

"Buck, why didn't you tell us about the print this morning?"

"I didn't tell you because I was looking for footprints not rectangles. So get off my back gosh darn it!" Buck hollered in tired frustration.

"Ok, let's start over again. Buck, just take us to the print or the square or... Just take us," I said in frustration.

We trudged back to where we had found Marjorie's body the night before. When we got there, Buck walked about ten feet northwest of where the cones still sat. He pointed at the ground. "There's a square-like print here somewhere. I know I saw it. His eyes fanned the ground before he yelled, "There it is. I watched that guy with the Boston accent step on one corner of it, but you can still see it plain as day."

Tommy and I slogged back towards Buck and hovered over the rectangular print. It was exactly as Buck had said Hornell's footprint and all. And directly behind the rectangle on the ground was the imprint of where someone sat and waited to make the shot.

"Well guys, the Medical Examiner was right about the direction of the shot, but he was dead wrong about the distance. Now I can see it clear as a bell. The shooter just sat here and waited for Marjorie to walk by. He probably couldn't see two feet in front of him, but he didn't have to. When Marjorie's head passed through the light from Mrs. Reed's house, he fired. And even from close range, he almost missed. After being shot, Marjorie staggered and turned back toward the shooter and he fired again, didn't miss the second time. So Hornell and I were both wrong. The shot wasn't made from the highway and this guy isn't the expert with a rifle that I thought he was. Buck, thanks for paying attention. You know Junior, it's kinda spooky that Nel told you to go to the light. I mean, Marjorie went to the light and it got her killed," Tommy said as he stared me down.

I closed my eyes, *Tommy's right, it is spooky. How'd she even know there was a light?*

"Junior - Junior!" Tommy yelled.

"Yeah," I said as I tumbled out of my reverie.

"Can you take a couple of pictures? I need to get in touch with Micah. I think we're going to have to drive back up to Osceola."

I snapped a few pictures before I walked back to our car. I had just gotten in when Micah drove up and stopped his car right next to ours. Tommy was still standing by the side of the road, deep in thought. Micah leaned over and rolled down his passenger side window.

"Tommy, I don't have good news for you. Chief Duffus let Perry Smith out this morning. He said they really couldn't hold him any longer. There a little bit of good news though. They impounded Perry's vehicle and it's still in their yard. So he can't have gone too far. Sorry, I wish I had better news. I'm on my way up to Corning. Need to give Marjorie's sister the bad news. Are you going back up to Osceola?" Micah asked.

"Yep, there's a couple things I have to find out. Thanks for your help, Micah. I hope it goes smoothly for you. Not something a lawman looks forward to," Tommy said.

Micah waved goodbye as he drove away. Tommy immediately said, "All right guys - we're on our way back to Osceola."

We pulled away from the cross on the side of the road heading north. I looked back at Buck and he squint his eyes and shook his head. I know he was wondering the same thing I was. *Why are we going back to Osceola?*

**Madison**/**Dezi, Randi, Maggie, and I** sat with Dad for the entire day. We knew the guys had driven over to Osceola and might be gone for a long time. But we had no idea what they would find once they got there. During our stay with Dad a nurse came in and gently put a cast on his broken hand. It was frustrating watching him while the cast was applied. He mumbled on and on as though he was talking to somebody, but he was obviously in a faraway place. He was peaceful and all, but still he did not wake up. Every time I looked over at Dezi, it appeared to me that she was on the verge of tears.

"Madison, what caused Dad to go blind in the first place," Dezi asked while she fought back the tears.

"It's called cortical blindness. It's caused by oxygen deprivation to the occipital cortex," I said as my sisters both looked at me like I was crazy. "In lay terms Dad hit the back of his head really hard in the accident and that caused blockage to the posterior cerebral arteries." They stared at me again. "Dad had a severe loss of blood to the back of his brain," I said.

At that point I should have told them the damage was irreversible, but I just couldn't.

"Madison, why does Dad still think he can see?" Dezi asked.

"It's a condition called confabulation. Dad remembers what things look like so, sometimes he would swear that he could still see them. He doesn't do that as often now, he's come to terms with the blindness. I mean he knows he's blind and he's chosen to live with it," I said.

"Will he ever get better?" Dezi asked.

I hesitated for only a moment and Dezi began to cry. Seeing her cry reminded me so much of Dad I could not hold back the tears. It hurt me deep down inside. I guess Randi could feel the pain and then she began to cry. I tried to be strong for the three of us and not cry, but I failed. I looked over at Dad wondering where he was and bellowed, "To hell with it!"

The three of us held each other and cried for a long time. And the tears would have continued if not for Maggie. She must have felt the despair and sadness in the room and one by one came to us. She would put her paw on our leg and then wait for us to pet her. I believe dogs have a power to heal that cannot be measured or explained, at least not by human beings.

"Thank goodness for Maggie," I said.

Randi and Dezi must have agreed because the crying came to a halt. And after a few minutes, the three of us were once again in control of our emotions. I think Randi was the first to feel a bit uncomfortable with the silence in the room and said, "Listen, I really should get back to the station and help out for a while. Do you want to get together later for supper?"

And Dezi said, "Ok, but where? I don't think I can take any more hospital food. Maddi, do you think Dad's hungry? I don't think he gets enough to eat through that tube."

"I don't think he's hungry, Dezi. He'd probably make one of those faces he's so famous for," I said.

The three of us smiled at the thought of seeing Dad make one of his faces.

"Dezi, is there something you eat on the west coast that we don't have here?" I asked.

"Yes, if you can take me by the Super Value on the way home, I could get what I need. Are you and Randi ready to try my surprise supper?" Dezi asked followed by a giggle or two.

Randi and I looked at each other and I said, "I'm game if Randi is."

"Sure, why not? How about I meet you two at your house Maddi, is six o'clock ok?" Randi said.

Dezi and I looked at each other and nodded our heads in agreement.

"That'd be fine. Gives us a couple of hours to get supper ready," I said.

Randi waved and said goodbye. Dezi and I gathered up our things and, of course, Maggie and then headed to the store. When we got to the store, Dezi made a strange request.

"Madison, can you wait here in the car? I want supper to be a complete surprise."

"Ok, can you get some dry dog food for Maggie while you're in there?"

"Yep, I'll only be a few minutes. Oh, do you prefer chicken or beef?"

"Actually, I prefer vegetables, but I'll eat whatever you make," I said.

"Oh that's good, makes it easier for me. Wait, what about Randi? Do you know what she prefers?" Dezi asked.

"Randi will eat whatever you put in front of her. She and Buck are voracious eaters. Just be sure you make enough."

"Gotchya," Dezi said with a smile as she ran into the store.

I sat petting Maggie for only a minute or so when someone knocked on my window. I nearly jumped right out of my seat. And when I looked up, I realized it was Jan, my best friend from high school. We hadn't spoken to each other in years. After she married my ex-boyfriend Ray Freeberg, we went our separate ways.

I rolled my window down.

"Hello Madison. Listen, I know this is unexpected and I won't keep you. It's just that I heard about your dad and I wanted to tell you how sorry I am."

She had caught me so off guard I wasn't sure what to say, but somehow I managed to eke out a thank you.

"How is your dad? I hope he's going to be ok. He was always so nice to me - I just..."

"Thanks again for caring, Jan. I believe he's going to be just fine," I said with reserve.

"Oh that's so good to hear. I won't keep you any longer."

She hesitated and I could see that there was something else on her mind.

"Madison, would it be ok if we talked sometime, you know maybe after your dad gets better. There's something I need to tell you, but now is not the right time."

"Sure, I'd like that. My number's in the book, you can call me whenever you want. And thanks for stopping."

Jan didn't say another word, she just waved goodbye and mouthed a thank you, which for some reason at the moment felt right. I couldn't help but believe that she wanted to talk about Ray, and of course me. My mind had just begun to wander when Dezi opened the passenger side door with a huff.

"Gosh this dog food is heavy," she said as she looked in and smiled at me.

"Why didn't you say something? I would have helped you."

"I know, but I wanted to see if I could carry it myself. It was kind of a test of strength or something," she said as she giggled to herself.

"Ok, well, I think you passed the test. Now get in, we're running a little bit late."

We drove to my house which is on the west end of town. My house isn't big, or for that matter fancy, but it's close to the lake and the picnic grounds and that's pretty special to me. The moment we walked in Dezi had my liquor cabinet open and was busy making me a special drink of hers. She called it a Blue Cheer, said it would make me forget all the troubles of the day.

And I have to tell you it wasn't long before I was feeling pretty cheerful. Midway through my second drink Randi came waltzing through the front door. She took one look at me and said, "Ok Dezi, I want what Madison is having."

"It's a Blue Cheer and I'll have one for you in a minute," Dezi said with a smile.

By the time supper was ready, the three of us were feeling no pain. And I thought to myself, *good thing I don't have to work tomorrow.* When Dezi brought out our plates from the kitchen, the smell was fabulous, I was hungry. My plate was filled with a Chinese vegetable mix over rice. Dezi and Randi had the same, but with what Dezi said was sweet and sour chicken added. The meal was so good. I was amazed that my sister had somehow become such a great cook.

"Dezi, where did you learn to cook like this? This is one of the best meals I've had in a long time. It tastes so familiar. I feel like I've eaten this before, but I guess that's not really possible, is it?" I asked.

Then Randi said, "I'm sure I've had this before, but I can't really say when or where."

By this time Dezi was giggling up a storm. She seemed so happy that we liked supper. Then she walked into the kitchen and came back out with the secret to the meal. She was smiling from ear to ear.

"Dezi, you little trickster, I should have known better."

She was holding up a big can of Chun King.

"Wait a minute, where are the dried noodles that go with the meal?" I asked.

"They're in a paper bag. I keep the bag in my purse and nibble on them during the day," she said with a smile.

"What about the chicken?" Randi asked.

"The chicken and the rice are my little secrets. They're easy to prepare and fool everyone almost every time. Pretty neat huh," Dezi said with an even bigger smile.

As she held out her plate, Randi said, "I don't know about Madison, but I'd like some more."

"There's a lot more," Dezi said just before she laughed up a storm. "I made two cans of Dezi's Chun King surprise. Here, give me your plates," she said as she took our plates and walked back into the kitchen.

We ate every bit of the supper Dezi had made. Afterwards I nibbled on some of the dried noodles while I became even more cheerful. Through our inebriation we decided we'd eat at the diner in the morning and then go see Dad.

The world was a little less ugly that evening and somehow I knew I'd wake up the next morning with a smile on my face. When I crawled out of bed the next day, all was quiet around the house, too quiet. When I walked out to the front room, I found the note that had been left for me.

Good Morning Sleepyhead,

I decided to take the girls out for a walk. Ricky's going to meet us and then we're gonna sniff our way around the entire lake. It's ten now so we should be home by noon.

Love, Maggie

I couldn't believe how late I had slept and in spite of the pounding that was going on in my head a smile spread across my face. I rushed into the bedroom and got myself dressed. I took off running and then I realized there was no point so I walked at a leisurely pace. When I got to the lake I decided to go counter clockwise. I was hoping to meet them halfway. No such luck. They were nowhere in sight. So I just kept going 'til I got all the way around to Ricky's cabin. The girls were with Maggie on the porch. I thought they'd smile when they saw me, but that was not the case at all.

"Thanks for leaving me the note, Maggie. I thought you were going to go around the lake," I said waiting for a response.

Then I took a little better look and realized something was wrong, very wrong.

"Madison, we were going to go around the lake, but Ricky got an awful phone call just as we started to leave the cabin. Madison, I think you'd better sit down," Randi suggested.

"Is it Dad? Oh Randi, please don't tell me it's Dad," I begged.

"No it's not Dad, it's Marjorie. She's dead. The guys found her body on a broken-down farm just outside of Leon," Randi softly said.

"What!" I screamed. "What, I mean how did this happen?" I asked in desperation.

Just then Ricky walked out his front door.

"Maddi, we don't know what happened. All Ajax told me was that Marjorie is dead. Well, there is something else," he said before he sat down hard on the edge of the porch.

"What else? Please tell me!" I shouted.

"It appears that Marjorie was murdered. That's all I know," Ricky said as his head shook from side to side.

I looked over at Dezi and Randi and they had the strangest blank looks on their faces. Then it hit me like a ton of bricks. And Ricky and the girls watched it happen.

"Oh my - the way I spoke to Marjorie the last time I saw her. Oh my," was all I could say.

"Madison, this has nothing to do with you and I won't let you sit there and blame yourself. Do you understand me?" Randi said.

I put my hands over my face and cried the strangest cry. It was strange because I didn't know if I was crying for Marjorie or for me, probably the latter. I fell into a shell of some kind and the next thing I knew Ricky was driving the girls, Maggie, and me home. I went straight to my bedroom, flopped onto my bed, and cried myself to sleep.

Junior/ The drive north back up to Osceola was just long enough for me to make some changes to my notes. After I thought about it for a few minutes, I figured that we needed to go back to Osceola because Perry Benjamin Smith was now a murder suspect. And I had to add his buddy David Daniels to the list. After having written all of this down, I also realized that Perry was gone and we might be hunting for him for another day or so. This half-day excursion could possibly end up being several days before it's over.

"Buck, when do you have to be back? I mean, the army doesn't let guys take off for as long as they want, do they?" I asked.

"No, they don't. My sergeant told me to call if I was going to be more than a week. So, we've still got a few days. It's just that I'd really like to be with Dad for a while before I go. No, that's not the whole the truth. What I really want is for Dad to wake up before I leave Crestfield. Yeah, that's what I want more than anything," Buck said with a sad shrug of his shoulders.

"Buck, that's what we all want. So no matter what I'll get you back to Crestfield today," Tommy said.

"Oh, thanks Uncle Tommy. I didn't want to bother you with my problems. AI know all of what we've been doing is really important, but..."

"Don't think twice about it. We'll get everything done we need to," Tommy said as we headed into Osceola for the second time in what had become two very long days.

"Tommy, you don't seem that concerned with finding Perry, is there something you're not telling me?" I asked.

"No Junior, there isn't anything I haven't told you. It's just that for me Perry doesn't fit. I can't put a finger on it, but I just don't think he's good for this murder. Or for that matter any other murder. But we have to check it out. I haven't said anything, but I want to see what Perry was driving. That might tell us more than he would. Just a hunch," Tommy said.

When we got to the old town line road, Chief Duffus was there waiting for us. He eased out of his car and walked straight over to ours.

"Tommy, this little road trip of yours has certainly turned sour," he said with a frown.

"Yes it has. Listen Clete, the reason I came back up here is–"

"I know why you came back up here. You want to see what Perry was driving. Well, he was in his dad's pickup, it's a sixty Chevy. Anyway, one of my officers and I just went through the truck from top to bottom and there's nothing there. No tickets, no receipts, no ammo, no guns, no nothin'. And from what I know about all of this, Perry couldn't have committed the crime. Just wasn't enough time or enough people. He couldn't have driven two cars at once and his buddy, Mr. Daniels, has been in jail now for over a week. I'm sorry Tommy, but nothing works," Chief Duffus said.

"Yeah, you're right, Clete. I feel the same way you do, but I had to check. Ok, well, I guess we'll be heading back home. Not gonna be fun at all," Tommy said with a frown. "Wait, Clete, there's one more thing you can help me with."

"Anything, what is it?" Chief Duffus asked.

"I'm looking for a tan, 57 Ford Fairlane. Seen any of those around lately?" Tommy asked.

"Well, there's a kid here that drives a 57 Fairlane, but it's a blue convertible. It was his dad's car. You wanna go see it?" Chief Duffus asked.

"No, I appreciate the offer Clete, but no thanks, the car doesn't fit. Alright, I've taken up enough of your time. I guess I'll talk at you later. Clete, if you do see Perry, tell him to stay away from Crestfield. Tell him - if he comes into town and I see him, I'm gonna arrest him on the spot," Tommy said with a frown.

"You got it," Chief Duffus said.

Tommy gave a halfhearted wave and then pulled away from the curb. I turned around in my seat just in time to see the Chief wave a gloomy goodbye.

Junior/We were approaching the east end of town on highway 34 when we saw a Leon police cruiser with all its lights flashing on the other side of the highway. Tommy crossed over the median and pulled up behind Micah's car. Micah got out of the car, the lights strobing against his face. He walked over to the passenger side of our car and I rolled my window down.

"Hey Junior, Buck, Tommy, I just talked to Chief Duffus, and he said you'd be coming in pretty soon. Tommy, the mayor went out to the sister's house with me, said he felt obligated."

"Ajax went with you?" Tommy asked.

"Yes, and I'm sure glad he did. The news did not go over very well. You probably know Marjorie's sister, Grace, better than I do. Anyway, after I gave her the bad news, she got crazy angry. Said she and her boyfriend were gonna find the persons responsible and kill 'em. Now I've had people respond like this before, but she says she knows who done it. Says she heard and I'm quoting her. Says she heard that the ex-con, Perry Smith, was out to Billy's place with some big guy and that Perry tried to kill Billy. She says when Joe gets back into town, they're gonna find Perry and kill him. Joe's her boyfriend. Anywho, she was madder than a hornet and that's where Ajax sure came in handy. He talked Grace back down to earth and then when the reality of the whole situation hit her, she broke down. Oh lord she cried hard - cried like a little girl. Listen Tommy, I thanked Ajax, but I'd like you to let him know I couldn't have done it without him. Would you tell him that for me?" Micah asked.

"Sure I will, Micah. I'm probably going to see him this evening. We need to have a plan for the reaction we're going to get when people find out what's happened. I will also have a talk with Joe," Tommy said.

Micah stood by the car for a long time without saying a word. We could all tell there was something else on his mind.

"Micah, is there something else you wanted to tell us?" I asked.

176

"Well, no, but there is something I wanted to ask you." He hesitated for a little bit. "Did you know that Ajax has taken off his holster and gun?"

We just looked at each other.

"I guess you couldn't have known. Ajax said that when Tommy told him about Marjorie he was so depressed that the gun wasn't fun anymore. Said he put little Jax up on the mantel over his fireplace too. Says that's where he's gonna stay. I mean a toy gun and a doll are a little crazy, but everyone is used to seeing him like that. It was always funnier than the dickens when he'd blame the damn doll for him missing a putt. And the looks he got from strangers on the golf course. Well, those looks were priceless. I know I'm rambling on here, but I guess I was hoping you could talk him into putting the gun and the doll back on. I know it's a strange request I'm making, but Ajax is just not Ajax without the crazy stuff. You know what I mean don't you?" he asked.

"Yes, I know exactly what you mean, and I'll speak to him about it. It's just that he's kinda funny about little Jax. Micah, all I can promise you is that I'll do my best," Tommy said.

"Thanks, that's all I could hope for. Ok, well, you hear anything or need something done just let me know. And I'll do the same. We've gotta catch this guy," Micah said as he waved goodbye and walked back to his car.

After Micah pulled away, we sat there for a long time. Buck and I could see that Tommy was going through some kind of internal hell that he wasn't going to share with us. So we waited. And then without a word being said Tommy pulled back across the highway and drove at an alarming speed all the way to the police station. We got out of the car and Tommy said he had things to do and that we should go home and get some rest. Then he sped out of the parking lot. Buck and I stood looking at each other for a bit and then we walked into the station.

"Hey Matt, you the only one here?" I asked.

"Yeah, Shadow's out at the hospital. He's keeping an eye on your dad. This news about Marjorie has the whole town in a funk. From what I understand your sisters are all at Madison's house. She took the news pretty hard. Ricky's on his way over to see Ajax about something. And I guess you know Tommy just left the parking lot going about a hundred miles an hour. What's up with him?" Matt asked.

"I don't know exactly, but I'd say he's upset due to the fact that we haven't found the person responsible. And to be honest, we really are stumped as to the who's and why's and so on. This really is a terrible situation we're in."

I realized that I was talking and Matt was trying to listen, but he was visibly tuckered out. I felt awful for what I was about to say.

"I'm sorry for bending your ear, Matt. Listen, Buck and I need to go home and change clothes. Anybody needs me just tell 'em to give me a call. Ok, thanks for working overtime, Matt. I guess we'll talk at you later," I said as Matt gave us a short goodbye wave.

We walked back to my place and I immediately jumped in the shower. After I got out, Buck did the same. I hurried and put on a fresh uniform and then I called Madison's house, but nobody answered. So I called the hospital and they patched me through to Dad's room. Jenny answered the phone after just one ring.

"Hello Junior, how are you?" she asked.

"Hi Jenny, under the present circumstances I guess I'm ok. How'd you know it was me?"

"Oh, I suppose it was just a guess," she said.

"Listen, are the girls there?" I asked.

"No, they're not here yet. There's just your dad, me, and a couple of men working on the heating system. I guess they're making sure everything's in good working order for this coming winter. If you call back in about ten minutes, I'm sure the girls will be here," she said.

"Ok, well, nice talking to you and I'll call back a little later, bye."

"Wait Junior, make sure you call back. I know the girls want to speak with you. Ok bye," she said as she hung up the phone.

I sat in the kitchen with a million things running through my head. Then Buck walked in. He'd changed back into his street clothes.

"I'd better call the base and talk with my sergeant. He's gonna want to know what's going on and when I'll be returning," he said.

"Ok, but first let me call the hospital one more time. Jenny said the girls would be there pretty soon," I said.

"How'd she know that?" Buck asked.

"You know what; I don't know how she knew. They must have called her and told her they were coming out. Anyway, I'm gonna call right now."

I dialed directly to Dad's room this time and a man answered the phone on the first ring.

"Hello, room thirty."

"Hi," I said as I hesitated for a few seconds. "Um, can I speak with Nurse Jenny please?"

"She's not here, left a couple minutes ago."

The man said, she's not here in a manner that was very familiar, but I couldn't put a name or a face to the voice.

"Who am I speaking to?" I asked.

"Who am I speaking to?" he asked.

"This is Junior, what's your name?" I asked.

"My name is Puddintane, ask me again and I'll tell you the same," he said with a laugh.

"Dad! Dad! Is that you? Dad, answer me," I hollered.

"Why of course it's me, Junior. Who else did you expect? This is my room."

Buck looked at me while he shook his head in confusion.

"Junior, is that Dad on the phone!" Buck finally hollered as I stood dumbfounded.

"Junior, who are you talking to? You know it's rude to carry on a conversation with two people at the same time," Dad said in a joking manner.

"Dad, I'm talking to Buck. He's here in Crestfield. He came to see you. Dad, when did you wake up? What's going on? Please tell me. And why are you talking with a lisp?" I asked.

"I was gonna ask you some of the same questions. I guess I'm talking this way because one of my front teeth is missing. Who took my damn tooth? Geez, I take a nap and someone steals my tooth. Why am I here?" he asked.

Before I could say another word, I heard Dezi screaming, "Dad, Dad, you woke up. Dad!"

"Well, of course I woke up. Just took a short nap is all. Geez, you don't have to make a federal case out of it. Dizzy, what are you doing here? Last time we talked you were in

San Francisco. Randi, is that you I hear? And why am I in this room? I want to go home. And where's Madison and Maggie? I wanna go home," he said in a childlike manner.

Then I heard Maggie barking and the barking became louder with each passing second. Then Dad erupted in utter joy.

"Maggie, Maggie, oh I could see you in my dreams, but you were so sick. Oh girl, I missed you so much, you're so beautiful," Dad said over and over.

"Hey what about us?" Randi asked in jest.

"Yes, all my girls are beautiful," Dad said just before he started to cry.

And even over the phone I could tell that this cry was for real. Then Madison was on the phone.

"Junior, is that you?" she asked.

"Yes, it's me. Don't go anywhere. Buck and I will be there as fast as our little feet will carry us," I said just before I hooted like a big ol' owl.

"Come on Buck, we got to get to the hospital. And I mean right now," I said as we both jumped for joy.

"Madison, we'll be there soon. Don't let Dad go to sleep again," I said.

"No, I won't let him go to sleep. Just get here as soon as you can. We'll be waiting, ok bye," she said.

Buck and I ran out of my apartment and I just said, "Follow me."

We made it to the police station in nothing flat. I ran in and yelled to Matt that my dad was awake and that I was taking a car to the hospital. And he hollered, "I know, Shadow just called and gave me the good news. Be careful," he said.

I drove over to the hospital at Ricky speed. I think I jumped out of the car before it had completely stopped. Buck and I ran into the hospital and down the hallway towards room thirty. The closer we got the louder the commotion in the room became. Buck and I ran in the room and straight to Dad's bed. He was sitting up and telling the girls and Maggie how much he missed them. Then all five of us were hugging Dad. It was so fabulous. Eventually I took a load off and sat down.

180

I watched the excitement all around me and thought to myself, *I may never experience a day like this again, ever.* Then Dad went into this story that sounded very familiar.

"And there I was lost in this dream world with no way out. Madison, you were Dorothy and all through the dream you talked to me. Randi and Dizzy, you were there too. I think you were good witches."

Dezi objected and said, "Dad, we are good witches."

"I know that, but no matter how hard you good witches tried to help me I couldn't get out of the dream world. Maggie was there, but she was very sick. Junior, you were the Tin Man and Ricky was the Scarecrow. Ajax was the Mayor of Munchkin land. He was perfect for the part. And Tommy was the Cowardly Lion. Buck was there too. He was the soldier that gave Madison the bad witch's broom stick."

"Wait a second. Dad, are you making this story up for our entertainment? I mean I like it and all, but..." I stopped talking when I realized that everyone was giving me dirty looks.

"Ok, I know it sounds like the Wizard of Oz, and maybe it is. But I was there, and it really happened, everything, the tornado and even the flying monkeys. The wicked witch wore a silky black robe and a pointy hat. She looked a lot like the other witches, but she was mean as all get out. She had two goons with her all the time. One was really big and the other was very small. They never stopped trying to hurt us, but Jenny wouldn't let them. Finally, Jenny told me to say there's no place like home. I didn't click my heels, but I said there's no place like home over and over. And then Jenny put her hand on my shoulder and I woke up. Junior, she told me you were gonna call me. How'd she know that? She said she wouldn't be gone for very long. Where's Jenny? I want to thank her, I want Jenny," Dad said in a weary voice.

Before any of us had a chance to answer Dad, Doc Mayland walked in the room.

"Well, I guess the news is true. Jack, it's nice of you to have come back to Crestfield where you belong, but we can't have you getting overly excited. Now I'm going to have to ask all of you to please leave the room while I give the patient a once over. Madison, I may need your help, so if it's ok with you, I'd like you to stay."

Then he turned to the rest of us. "Please excuse us, we shouldn't be too long. Maggie, you can stay too," he said in a reassuring voice.

We all walked out and milled around in the hallway. I asked Shadow how long he'd been watching over the room and when he told me he'd been there all night, I felt just awful.

"Gosh Shadow, I had no idea you'd been here that long. I'll take over, you go on home. I'm sure Ricky will be here as soon as he can, and we'll be able to take turns watching Dad's room for the next day or so," I said. Shadow didn't move. "Come on, you need a break," I urged.

"Ok, I am kinda tired, but if you need somethin', make sure you call me. Junior, I just want to tell you how happy I am that your dad woke up. And from what I heard, it sounds like the old Jack is back. And that's a darn good thing. All right, make sure you call if you need somethin'," he said with a yawn.

Shadow stretched both arms high over his head, *he looked like an Orangutan.* And then he shook his massive shoulders for a bit and waved as he slowly walked away. "See ya," he said.

Randi sat down on the chair that Shadow had occupied for so long. Buck stood at attention and I fidgeted. I'm sure we were all wondering what was going on in Dad's room. Dezi must have been way too excited to stand around outside of Dad's room.

"I'm going out to the little courtyard and smoke a clove. Come get me when Doc Mayland and Madison are done with Dad?" Dezi asked.

"Is a clove legal?" I asked as Dezi gave me a frustrated look. Ok, yes, I'll come and get you. I hope they're not in there too long."

I couldn't hear any talking going on in Dad's room, but now and then Maggie would bark. I felt like that was a good sign. I poked my head in the door. There was something I had to get off of my chest.

"I'm sorry to bother you two, but Madison could you come out here for just a minute?" I asked.

She looked a little irritated that I'd bothered them, but she came out anyway.

"We want to see if Dad's cognitive abilities have been damaged," she said as I fidgeted.

"Ok, what is it, Junior?" she asked with an attitude.

"I was wondering if you could ask what he remembers about the guys that put him in the hospital," I said.

"Junior, of course we're going to ask him, but in due time. I know it's difficult for you, but for once try a little patience. Ok," she said as she walked back in the room.

"Gee-whiz Junior - can you just stand still for a minute. You're making me nervous," Buck said as he and Randi both stared at me.

They were right - I couldn't stand still. So I walked down the hall and looked out the window at the courtyard. Dezi was sitting all by herself, but it looked to me like she was carrying on a conversation with somebody. I stood watching and I thought, *When I've got a lot on my mind sometimes I do the same thing. That is, I talk to myself.*

I was lost in thought when somebody tapped me on the shoulder. I really don't know why but I jumped a couple of feet.

"Hey pardner, how you doin'?" Ricky asked.

"Gosh Ricky, don't do that. I'm so jumpy right now I might have turned around and slugged you."

"Wouldn't be the first time," he said as he laughed. "Ok, sorry about that. Listen, I was wondering if you could fill me in on Marjorie, and what you think happened at the Reed farm."

I went through the story from beginning to end and Ricky never interrupted me, not once. When I was done, Ricky paused for a moment before he said, "Did you know that the lady who owns that farm is my aunt?"

"What? Are you serious?" I asked.

"Yep, I'm very serious. Don't you remember when we were in the fifth grade and I missed the first week of school?" he said.

I didn't answer him because I couldn't remember, at least not at first.

"Well, I missed because my mom and I were driving back and forth to Aunt Elizabeth's farm every day. That little boy that was run over by the bus was my cousin, Luke. He was a good little guy and funny as all get out. I remember mom saying that Luke was kinda special. I didn't know what that meant at the time, but eventually I figured it out. Strange thing is we were a lot alike. The funeral was on a Sundee and when I came back to school on Mondee you asked me if I had been sick or something. Well, I really didn't want to talk about losing my cousin, so I told you that I had been fishing in Florida. Do you remember now?" he asked.

"Yeah, I remember. I knew then that you weren't really fishing, but my mom and dad told me you had been through an awful experience of some kind and that I should let it be. Gosh Ricky, I'm really sorry. This must bring up some bad memories for you. I had no idea that the little boy that died was your cousin."

"Yeah, I guess I'm gonna be gone for a few days again. Mom says Aunt Elizabeth was hurt something awful when she heard about Marjorie, put yourself in her shoes. So we're gonna go stay with her for a while. Look, your dad waking up is the best news I've had in a long time, but... Well, it's just a bit strange having such a horrible thing happen to Marjorie and then something happen that is so great. You know what I mean, don't you, Junior?" he asked.

"Yes, I know exactly what you mean. Out of respect for Marjorie and her family it just doesn't seem right for us to be celebrating," I said.

"Exactly, thanks, Junior. Well, there's more to this problem. You remember the argument between Madison and Marjorie just a few days ago. Well, I did my best and so did Randi and Dezi to try and make Madison understand that she had nothing to do with what happened to Marjorie. But Madison did not take the news well at all. In fact, I've never seen her so upset -ever," Ricky said.

"Ricky, that bothered me too. More than I can explain. When I get a chance, I'll talk to her about it, but you know Madison. And so you know she'll probably just tough it out. You know, grin and bear it. I think talking to her about it and letting her know that you care was probably the best thing you could have done. I'm gonna do the same and I know Dezi and Randi will too. Say, you said you were gonna spend a few days in Leon. When are you going?" I asked.

"That's kinda what I was getting to. I gotta go right now. I wanted to talk to your dad first, but your dad's door is locked. Can you please tell your dad that I'll come see him every day and that I'll take him and Maggie fishin' as soon

184

as he feels up to it, or maybe even before he feels up to it. Tell him I said that Junior, he'll get a kick out of it. Would you please?" he asked.

"Ricky, of course I'll tell him. And you're right; he will get a kick out of it. Ok, say hi to your mom. Well, I guess good luck and I'll see ya," I said.

"Thanks pardner, I knew I could count on you," he said as he waved goodbye.

He walked down the hall and around the corner and then he ran back.

"Junior, I forgot to tell you that Tommy wants you to meet him at the station tonight, right after supper. Says Matt, Shadow, and Randi will be there too. He's got something important to talk about. I asked him what it was, but he was pretty short with me. You know there's something really bothering Tommy, but he's not letting on what it is. Maybe that doggone Burt is up to something again," he said.

"No, I don't think it's Burt. But I know what you mean about something bothering Tommy. Ok, thanks for telling me. I'll be there. You go ahead on and remember to say hi to your mom."

After Ricky ran off, I just stood there staring into space for a long time before I took another look out the window. Dezi was still talking to herself. So I decided to walk back to the room and see if doc and Madison were done with Dad. When I walked up, Doc Mayland and Madison were just coming out of Dad's room.

"Ok, what's the good news?" I asked.

Nobody said a word, they just stared at me. That is until I asked the question again.

"Junior, let's wait 'til Dezi gets here so everyone can hear," Madison said.

"Ok, I'll go get her," I said.

"You don't have to, she's right behind you."

I turned just in time to see Dezi smile really big before she said to Doc Mayland, "What's up Doc?"

"**Dezi, what's up** is that your dad's wounds are healing quite nicely. As far as his cognitive abilities go - well, that part's a mystery and really can't be explained," Doc Mayland said as he looked at the floor and suddenly stopped talking.

"What can't be explained?" I asked.

"I think Madison should probably go over that with you," he said.

"Can we go in and see him?" I asked.

"You can go in and see your dad as soon as the nurse is done bathing him. Now if you'll excuse me I have another patient to attend to. Goodbye," he said as he walked down the hall.

Then the four of us turned and stared at Madison.

"What can't be explained?" I asked again.

"What can't be explained is that for some unknown reason it appears that Dad's memory and possibly his overall mental health have improved," she said just before the rest of us cheered.

"I understand your being happy, I'm happy too. But I believe it's far too premature to have a party. This sudden wellness Dad is experiencing could dissipate without even a moment's notice. And then all of our joy would become extremely soured. We need to take this one day at a time," she cautioned.

"Madison, just tell us what makes you think Dad has improved," Randi demanded.

"Maddi, please tell us," Dezi urged.

"Ok, I'm going to tell you, but you need to promise me that what I tell you does not leave this hospital," Madison said as she stared down the four of us.

In unison we all promised.

"Ok, Dad said something that caught me completely off guard."

Then it looked to me as though Madison had decided she wasn't going to say anymore.

"Come on, Madison, tell us, we have a right to know," I demanded.

"Ok, Dad has regained a visual of the night he and mom were in the accident. He says that earlier in the evening he talked to the guy that ran them off the road. Said the guy is big and has a slight southern accent. Dad explained to me that that's why he's always called the guy a peckerwood," she said before she stopped talking again.

"Madison, this is getting ridiculous. Finish what you were saying," Buck demanded.

"Ok. Dad says that if the guy was from around these parts, he would have called him a bumpkin or a hayseed. And it makes sense if you think about it. We, meaning folks in the Midwest, don't normally call men that are from the country peckerwoods. We almost always refer to them as either a bumpkin or a hayseed. Now I don't know if Dad is reasoning this out or he really did see the guy at some point that night. Either way Dad is thrilled that he can remember. The scary part is that now Dad's convinced we're going to catch the guy. And that bothers me," Madison said.

"Why would that bother you?" I asked.

"It bothers me because I don't want Dad to foster any false hope. It's been well over ten years now since the accident. We need to be realistic about this. I mean, what are the chances of finding this person now?" she asked.

None of us said a word.

"That's right, because the chances of finding this person after all these years are somewhere between slim and none," she said.

"Did Dad say anything else about that night?" I asked.

"Yes, he said that the guy was driving a new Ford Fairlane.

"He did? Madison, this is really important. Did Dad say what color the car was?" I asked.

"Dad said the car was black, why?" she asked.

"Oh shoot - I was hoping you were going to say the car was tan," I said.

"Why?" Madison asked.

"Why? Because Albert Anderson said he saw a Ford Fairlane drive by the day Dad was attacked. The problem is, the car he saw was tan," I said.

"Maybe the car has been painted," Dezi interjected.

"You know what Dizzy, you could be right," I said.

"Hey, Dad's the only person that gets to call me Dizzy," she said.

"Sorry about that. I just got excited," I said.

"It's ok, I understand," she said back.

"You know what, Dezi? I'll bet the car was painted to cover up the body damage. He did hit Dad's truck with a lot of force. Yep, that's gotta be it. Madison, I know I might be expecting too much, but did Dad say anything about who attacked him?"

"No Junior, he didn't, and I didn't ask him," she said as she pounded her right fist into her left hand. "It's just too early, and we need to be very careful right now. Even the slightest bit of trauma could cause a setback. And come hell or high water I'm going to do everything I can to make sure that doesn't happen. One thing you should all know by now is that Dad has always done things on his terms and only his terms. So when he's damn good and ready to talk about it, he'll let us know," she said with a bunch of attitude.

"Madison, you don't have to get mad at us, we agree with you. Please try to remember that we're all in this together. We're on Dad's side and that means we're on your side too," Dezi said.

"Oh Dezi - you're right and I'm sorry. It's just that..." Madison said and then stopped.

"What?" Dezi asked.

"It's just that it doesn't seem right that I should be so happy about Dad after what has happened to Marjorie. I still feel..." Madison said before she abruptly stopped again.

"Maddi, you're not alone in your thoughts. Ricky said the same thing only minutes ago. I think we all feel the same way. But try to remember we're only human," I said.

Madison didn't respond and all was quiet. That is until we heard Dad yell, "Doggonit, give me that washcloth, I can do this myself, I'm not some little boy. Hey, I said stop that."

We all stood a little stiff wondering what Dad was going to say next. But before he said another word, the door to his room flew open and a nurse with raging eyes came storming out into the hallway. And then Dad yelled even louder, "Where's Jenny? I want Jenny."

"Is that your dad in there?" the nurse asked.

We all nodded our heads which was followed by a couple of sheepish yes's.

"Well, then I feel sorry for all of you," she said before she huffed away.

Of course, we all immediately crowded into the room. And almost as soon as we were in the room the girls were running back out. Dad was naked and trying to wash himself.

"Dad, what the heck are you doing?" I asked.

"What does it look like I'm doing? I'm washing myself so I can go home. Tell 'em Maggie," he said just before Maggie barked. "Good girl. I knew somebody was on my side."

"Oh Dad, come on, you know we're all on your side. Here, let me get you dressed. Give me the washcloth," Buck calmly said.

"Well, at least one of my kids is willing to help me. Buck, get me dressed, I gotta get home. I've got things to do," Dad said with attitude.

"Dad, you big nut, we're all on your side. But you can't go home yet. Doc Mayland has to make sure you're completely healed up. Then I'm sure he'll release you," I said.

"I am healed. There's not a darn thing wrong with me," Dad said.

"Ok Dad, you're squeaky clean," Buck said.

"Thanks, now I'm ready to go home," Dad said.

"You can't go home in your pajamas. Why, you'd look like a knucklehead for sure," Buck said with a laugh.

"Put my clothes back on me!" Dad yelled.

"Dad you don't have any clothes here. Listen, I'll go to the house and get you some clothes. Then after the doc says it's ok, I'll take you home," I said.

"Junior, you promise you'll take me home?" Dad asked.

"Yes Dad, I promise," I said in relief.

"Dad's dressed now!" Buck yelled to the girls.

The girls flooded back into the room and begged Dad to tell them about the dream. I had my doubts about the dream and for that matter Dad, but he was alive and seemingly well. And that alone made me very happy. It didn't take long for Dad to talk himself into a deep sleep. And right after he started to snore, Tommy and Ajax came flying into the room.

"Is it true?" Ajax asked.

"Is what true?" I asked.

"Did Jack wake up?" Tommy asked.

"Yes, he did. You just missed him, but he'll be back before you know it. I'm sure he's gonna want to talk to both of you. He says he had a dream that we were all in. And according to Dad the two of you played major roles.

"He has always been a dreamer. Some of the stuff he has come up with over the years is just plain bizarre. Jack is a strange one," Ajax said.

"You're one to talk, Ajax, you big nut. I mean, talk about the pot calling the kettle black," Madison said with a boatload of sarcasm.

"Is that your trained opinion?" Ajax asked.

Madison realized that her uncle was questioning her lack of professionalism. But she was not about to back down and said, "No, that was just a learned opinion."

Rancor immediately hung in the air and before Uncle Ajax could respond, Tommy said, "There's no room for that stuff right now. So can the two of you please try to stay out of each other's way?"

"Thanks, Uncle Tommy. There's too much to be happy about. Right now all we need is love," Dezi said.

Dezi was right and we all knew it. And I think Uncle Ajax probably agreed, but he'd had his feelings hurt. So he walked out and sat on the chair in front of Dad's room

"Should I go get him?" Madison asked.

"No, let him sulk for a little bit. He'll get over it. Uncle Ajax enjoys sulking, it recharges his batteries," Tommy said.

All was very quiet, but only for a few moments before Ajax yelled, "It's called colorful."

Madison couldn't resist and just had to yell back, "What's colorful?"

"I am. I'm not a nut, I'm colorful."

I don't believe there's anything Uncle Ajax enjoys more than cracking himself up, so of course he was laughing pretty hard. And upon hearing Ajax laugh, everyone else joined in.

There was just no way any of us could keep a straight face. And at that moment, I believe we all received exactly what Dezi said we needed - and love was in the air.

The majesty of it all   31

***Randi*/You know,** I don't think the nurse that was washin' dad is coming back. And since dad seems so much happier when Jenny's taking care of him, I'm gonna go find her," Randi said as we all nodded our heads in agreement.

Before Randi took two steps, Dezi said, "I was just talking to Jenny in the courtyard. There were two people with her. A pretty young lady named Traci and a man wearing glasses that Jenny introduced to me as Uncle Tommy. They were both really nice and they told me some wonderful stories. I wish you guys could have been there."

When I heard Dezi say she'd been talking to these people, the confusion in my mind was a bit overwhelming.

"Dezi, where were you when you were talking to these people? I asked.

"Remember, I said I was going out to the courtyard. Well, that's where I talked to them. Why?" she asked.

"Why? Because I saw you out there, but there wasn't anybody with you. How could I have missed Jenny and these other people?" I asked.

Dezi looked at me with childlike eyes.

"Dezi, are you sure that's where you were talking to them?" I asked again.

Now everyone was paying close attention to our conversation. And before Dezi could tell me where she'd talked to the strangers, Uncle Ajax snuck back into the room.

"Dezi, I couldn't help but hear about you talking to these people. I had an uncle named Tommy that wore glasses and I had a niece named Traci. But they've been gone for a long time now," Uncle Ajax said.

"I told this Uncle Tommy that I also had an Uncle Tommy and he said, 'I know, and he's a nice young man. I have been with him many, many times.' I started to ask how he could have been with him, but somehow he knew what I was going to ask and he said, 'I've been with him his entire life. And sweetheart I've been with you too. In fact, Traci and I have been with all of you, maybe not in body, but always in spirit.' "When he spoke to me, it was as if everything he said was the truth. I didn't question anything he said because there was no reason to. I just felt at ease and well, kind of wonderful. There was more love around me than I could ever hope for," Dezi said with a glow on her face that radiated throughout the room.

When Dezi first started telling us about the people she'd met, I was confused and wanted to dispute her recollection, but within a short time I just couldn't. I couldn't because everything she was telling us immediately became the truth and there was no other truth. I felt the warm glow slowly but steadily spread from Dezi and in my heart I knew that the others felt it too.

"Dezi, what about the young lady named Traci? Did she say anything?" Uncle Ajax asked with wide eyes.

"Yes, she did. And when she was speaking, I felt the same warmth I did when Uncle Tommy spoke. Traci wanted all of us to know that Marjorie is now in devoted and loving hands and is experiencing a magnificence and splendor beyond our understanding. She said all the heartache and sorrow we've been feeling is born of earthly concerns and that these feelings shall pass."

"Is Jenny coming back?" Randi asked.

"Jenny told me she was needed elsewhere and that she had to leave. When she said she had to leave, I thought about dad asking for her and I started feeling sad again. Then Jenny looked over at Traci and Traci just said, 'Dezi, please trust in the majesty of it all.'

"At the time I didn't understand what she meant, but I think I'm beginning to," Dezi said as she gazed across the room.

Dezi stopped talking and none of us asked any more questions. I think there was just too much revelation and awe in the air. I walked out of the room and down the hallway to look out at the courtyard one more time. Why? I don't know. After staring at the courtyard, I turned around and headed for the nurses' station. When I got there, the new head nurse was checking something on her clipboard - so I waited 'til she looked up.

"Hi, I'm Junior. My dad's the patient in room thirty."

"Yes, I know, I'm Lucie Clayton and I guess you know I've taken over for Marjorie, such a sad, sad situation. I was just heading over to see how your dad's doing. I understand his mind has been working a little overtime. If you're worried about him sleeping, it's ok. There's a fatigue factor

192

that comes with a coma. Is that why you're here?" she politely asked.

"Well, no it's not, but thanks for telling me. I was a little concerned. I'm here because I wanted to find out about Nurse Jenny. I was wondering if you know where she's gone. Has she been transferred to another hospital or something?" I asked.

"Nurse Jenny? I don't know of any nurse in this hospital named Jenny," she said.

"What? Are you sure, she's been taking care of Dad since the day he was admitted," I said as I shook my head in confusion.

"Yes, I'm very sure. However, it is possible that Marjorie brought her in from another hospital. But according to my records we have nobody by the name of Jenny working at this hospital. Would you like me to check with payroll?" she asked.

I really didn't know what to say and just stood there dumbfounded.

"Officer McCool - are you ok?" she asked.

"Um yes - I'm fine. Listen; if it wouldn't be too much trouble, I'd like it if you could find out where she is and more importantly who she is. Dad and, for that matter, the rest of us are crazy about Jenny. She did a wonderful job with Dad and I'd like to thank her," I said.

She looked at me with a concerned eye before she said she would try to find Jenny. I said thanks and walked out the front door of the hospital and once again sat down on the wooden bench. I sat and tried my best to figure out what was happening, but I couldn't come up with one reasonable answer. I was so lost in thought that I didn't hear Tommy sit down on the bench.

"Junior, are you ok?" he asked.

"Um, yes I'm ok, it's just that..."

"I think I understand. You're trying to figure out what has happened, but right now there's no way of doing that. Trust me, eventually all the questions will be answered."

I didn't respond, and I don't think Tommy expected me to. He just got up and said, "I'll see you about five at the station, ok."

I still didn't say anything 'til he asked me a second time.

"Ok?" he repeated.

"Yeah, ok Tommy. I'll see you at the station."

He walked away and I got up, dusted myself off and went back in the hospital to sit with my family - and of course, Dad.

Madison/I'd been spending so much time with Dad, Buck, Junior, and my sisters that I'd neglected some of my patients at Clarinda Cove. So the day after Dad woke up, I did too. I got back to work and the structure did me a world of good. I was leaving for lunch on my second day back when someone knocked on the door to my office. I usually greet my patients out in the waiting area so it was a bit unusual to hear a knock on my door. I got up thinking it was probably one of my colleagues. I was very surprised when I opened the door.

"Hello Grace." I waited for her to return the hello, but she said nothing. "Please come in, here have a seat," I said as I pointed to the chair in front of my desk.

She sat down and slowly put both of her hands up to her face. Her shoulders trembled. She was obviously on the verge of tears. I grabbed a couple of tissues and handed them to her, still not a word.

"Grace please, is there something I can do?" I asked.

She finally managed to say, "No thank you, but there is something that I want to do."

I had been standing next to her and decided maybe she needed some space. So I walked around my desk and sat down. The moment I sat she said, "Madison, I came here because I want to apologize for the things I said to your Uncle Tommy when he came out to see Joe and me."

"I don't understand? If you said these things to Tommy, then why aren't you apologizing to him?" I asked.

"Because I said them to him about you," she answered.

"Oh - I see. Well, what did you say?" I asked.

"I said so many bad things about you I can't remember them all - and I don't want to. You see a nurse friend of Marjorie's had come by the day after she went missing and told me all about the argument the two of you had at the hospital. Well, at first I thought maybe Marjorie had just gone away to blow off some steam. But then I started thinking that you had done something to her. So when Ajax and the gentleman from Leon came to my house, I was furious. I was looking for someone to blame for her death and you were very convenient. I'm so sorry. Madison, I hope you can find the room in your heart to forgive me."

"Grace, I went through all the same feelings myself. I felt guilty and then I was angry which led to an overwhelming sadness. But I was never angry at you; I had no reason to be. So in my mind there's nothing for you to forgive. Grace, I'm sorry too and I hope you can forgive me."

The moment I finished talking I saw her shoulders relax and then I felt mine do the same. Then Grace smiled at me and softly said, "Thank you so much for understanding and I hope you can make it to the funeral."

"Well, of course I can make it. In fact, I believe that there will be people there from several counties. I know this is a sensitive time for you, but when is the funeral?" I asked.

"The coroner said her body will be delivered to Coen's sometime today. It's right there on Montgomery, you could surely walk there from your house," she said.

I absolutely hate funerals, but I did my best to appear grateful for the information. I knew all the information would be in the paper, probably by Wednesday.

"The funeral is going to be held out at the First Christian Church on east Townline St. Madison, I know you probably had things to do, so thanks for hearing me out. And like I said, I hope you can make it to the funeral."

"Grace, you're always welcome and I hope you find some way to get through this tragedy. If you ever need to talk, please come by or give me a call. Say - you didn't tell me what day the funeral is."

"I guess I got in a bit of a hurry. It's going to be either Saturday or Sunday. Just depends on how much work Ed and John must do to get Marjorie presentable. That's a part of all this that I'm not prepared to deal with, but I guess somehow, I will. Madison, before I forget, could you tell Tommy that Joe and I are grateful for him taking the time to come to the house and explain things the way he did. He couldn't give us much in the way of details, but he gave me his word that you and Perry Smith had nothing to do with Marjorie's death. And eventually it did set my mind at ease."

"Yes, I'll certainly tell Tommy for you," I said.

Grace walked out and I looked inside, of myself that is. I do that sometimes when I'm looking for answers that have not yet surfaced.

Atonement   33

Madison/**After we read in the Canon** that the funeral would be held on Saturday, Dezi and Buck decided to leave on Sunday. Dad was released from the hospital on Friday. Due to the situation at hand it was a sober occasion but an occasion nonetheless. We took Dad home and he was so happy it was hard not to fall in step and be happy with him. We decided not to tell Dad about Marjorie or, her funeral. After all he'd been through, it just didn't seem right to throw something so depressing at him.

On Saturday morning, I sat with the entire family at Dad's house and wondered if things would ever return to normal. Ricky had come back from his aunt's and volunteered to stay with Dad while the rest of us attended the funeral. Ricky said he'd seen enough misery and of course Dad was thrilled to have his company.

Junior drove us out to the church in one of the police cruisers. I couldn't begin to explain how strange the ride out there felt. Not because of where we were going, but because I once again had the unyielding feeling that we were being watched.

Once the doors were opened, the church filled up in a matter of minutes. I think every person from several counties that could walk and some that couldn't were there. The First Christian has always been known for its uplifting music and for its joyous array of shows. However, on this day a celebration would have been out of line. Pastor Leaf did all she could to bring to light the healing power of God in her sermon, but the mood remained excessively somber. Many people got up and said kind words for Marjorie, but the tribute that Grace had written for her sister was without question the crowning moment that day. When it came time to read, Grace slowly moved to the lectern, but try as she might she couldn't even get through the first sentence. We all watched as she tried several times to fight back the crippling emotions and read, but it was not to be. As she struggled, Joe moved in close and put an arm around her and for a few moments softly spoke to Grace. And although her hands trembled, she managed to nod and then gently hand the tear stained paper to Joe.

A truck driver by trade and usually a very quiet man, no one was aware of any special speaking abilities that Joe possessed. I guess Joe was a little closer to Marjorie than anyone had realized. And it was this concealed love that must have led to the powerful and heartfelt oration he delivered.

When he began speaking, his voice was lilting and peaceful. He read from the paper in front of him with purpose and skill and then at times I believe he read with his own broken heart. He spoke of God's forgiveness, but at the same time encouraged atonement. But as he spoke, we could all plainly see the inferno mounting deep in his soul. And with each passing word the passion grew and finally Joe erupted with all the fire and brimstone that exists in hell. His great fists pounded the lectern as the heat raged and then he furiously attacked 'the demon' that had taken Marjorie's life. He spoke with the ferocity of a seasoned cleric about eternal damnation and the ultimate fate that awaits the unfaithful. And when the fury in him reached its zenith, he raised his hands high over his head and shouted, 'I can't live with this hate in my heart. Hate tears at the flesh and ultimately consumes the soul. There is no room in rapture for hate and it must be purged.' At this point the church became deathly quiet and you could have heard a pin drop.

Joe took two steps back, dropped his arms to his sides, and gazed at the people in front of him. And as he gathered himself, a sense of peace spread throughout the church. Obviously near the end of what had become a sermon, Joe turned to hug Grace. They cuddled and quietly spoke to one another, and after they shared a tear or two, Joe slowly walked all the way to the center of the church. He surveyed the room and then softly said, 'I once heard a wise man say that we all deal with burdens in our lives. And at times the resulting misery flows like a raging river. But without enduring these times of great sorrow and woe, how could we truly appreciate the brightness of a new day. Marjorie is now in the midst of a magnificence and grandeur beyond description. Do not worry for Marjorie, but for one another.' Joe paused and then ever so slowly walked back to Grace and whispered in her ear. She turned to us and softly said, "Thank you for being here and god bless."

The moment Joe finished speaking I felt a resounding hallelujah pass through the entire church. And when as a community we walked out into the afternoon sun that day the healing process had already begun.

"Benny, why do people go to church?"

"I guess they go because, unlike you, they have a soul. They believe in God and each other. So they go to church to rejoice with their neighbors."

"Yeah, well, that may be true, but right now I don't care about you or them. So you can just do us both a favor and shut up."

"You're such a jerk. Have you once again forgotten that you asked me to answer a question? Man, for such a big guy you sure do have a little brain."

"You know Benny, one of these days I'm gonna crush your tiny head. What do you think about that?"

"I don't think you have the guts. We need to get out of here and right now. You can see with your own eyes that they're all coming out of the church. And if someone sees us, you'll be forced to run away screaming for your mommy. But nobody will care because they'll see you as the little chicken you really are."

"You leave my mommy out of this. Hey look, there's Madison. Someday I'm gonna surprise her with a visit."

"You better leave her alone. I'll tell you one thing right now. If you go visit her, I'm not going with you. Have you forgotten about that damn dog? Mark my words that dog is gonna get you yet."

"Shut up Benny, I have to think."

"Yeah, well you can think as I drive because we're outta here."

"Don't drive too fast. You know Benny, for some reason Joe and Grace scare me."

"You're scared of everybody, you big baby."

"I've got to think so just drive and leave me alone. And away we go. A leprechaun has a pot of gold and he clutches it to his chest. But his pursuers' hearts are filled with greed and they won't let him rest. A mountain top calls my name, but when I try to climb my legs are lame. There's a church full of children singing praise to a giant god. I want to be there too, but the children all know I'm a fraud. I have a list and I won't stop 'til I've crossed off each name. In the beginning there was a jury of twelve, but a few have left the game."

"You know what, big guy?"
"No, I don't. So shut up and drive!"

Junior/**All was quiet at Dad's house** the next morning. That is until Dad decided he was going to go with Buck and join the army. Dezi laughed 'til she nearly cried at Dad's antics. I think maybe she actually did cry a little. Dad finally stopped with his ridiculous notion when Madison reminded him that if he joined the army, he'd have to leave Maggie behind. He wasn't going for that at all. Sometimes I think he loves Maggie as much as his own children, maybe more. Randi stood silently at Ricky's side the entire morning. There's no doubt that being separated from her brother and sister depresses her more than the rest of us. Why? I'm not sure, but I think it's because she hates facing the moment when the train starts carrying them away.

We ate at the diner that morning and hardly a word was spoken. As we ate, it was decided that we'd walk to the train station. Maggie skillfully pulled Dad and he only complained once or twice. I carried Buck's duffle bag and Ricky carried Dezi's pink suitcase with the peace sign on it. He smiled the whole way there. And just before my little brother and sister boarded the train, the tears began to flow.

Sometimes I wonder why humans were given the great and unequaled ability to care about one another. Wouldn't it be easier if we were devoid of any emotional or psychological attachments? I like asking questions about stuff like that and then of course answering them. The answers help make that horrible feeling in my stomach go away. Sometimes it's not possible to find an answer, but I think it's healthy to try. After all the hugs and well-wishes, the train pulled away from the station. We all waved furiously and shouted I love you's, but the horrible feeling in my gut remained. Then as Buck's long arm waved, Dezi stuck her head out and shouted, "Find Jenny, Dad needs Jenny."

I think at that moment we all needed Jenny. None of us moved an inch until the train was completely out of sight. And as we slowly walked back towards the center of town, each of us kept our thoughts private and deep inside, they were not meant to be disturbed. Ricky, Randi, and I went back to the police station. And Madison drove Dad and Maggie back to his house. I suppose she went to work that day, but I'm not sure.

Ricky and I sat at our desks and Randi took over the phones which Matt had been tending to. Tommy and Shadow were out on a mission which none of us knew anything about. I went over my notes, but as before nothing popped out. That was the longest day in history; at least it was for me. The earth seemed to stand still as October rolled in with nothing more than a quiet promise that winter was just around the corner. This feeling of nothingness went on for a week, maybe two. I'd lost count. The only saving grace during this time was the fact that Dad had the cast removed from his hand and the stitches plucked from his head. He didn't complain and he never spoke of the monsters that had nearly killed him. I for one desperately wanted to find those responsible. We'd been told that Dad had regained some of his memory. If so he sure didn't act like it, at least not around me.

It was near the end of the month when we had a small gathering at Dad's for Madison's birthday. Dad prepared his famous chili that he calls 'the answer.' We ate and then sang a fun version of happy birthday. After we devoured the birthday cake, Madison opened her presents. Then we all relaxed and sat down to watch some television. Watching T.V. with Dad is a rough experience. We're only allowed to watch reruns or shows that Dad likes. And if we tell him what's happening during the show, he gets angry. He gets angry because he swears he can still see. And sometimes I think that maybe he can. It was getting late and I could tell that Madison was tired. Ricky and I gathered her presents and toted all of them out to her car. While we were saying goodbye, I heard the phone ring a few times and then stop. I figured whoever it was would call back. When I walked back in Dad had the phone up to his ear, and I heard him say, "Ok, I'll tell him, yeah, see ya, bye."

I walked through the front room and into the kitchen as Dad hung up the phone.

"Dad, who were you talking to?" I asked.

"That was Shadow. He said for you to call him ASAP. And I asked him why he would want you to call him ASAP when you know his name is Shadow. He didn't laugh even a little, so I think maybe you oughta call him right now," Dad said in a seldom used serious tone.

Ricky was standing next to me listening to everything that was said.

"Ok, I'll call him. Did he give you a number or is he in his police car?" I asked.

"He's in his car," Dad said.

I ran out to my police cruiser and patched through. Shadow immediately picked up.

"Hey Junior, I think you'd better get out here as soon as you can. We gotta bad one here," he said in a spooky tone.

"You got a bad one at your house?" I asked.

"No Junior, I'm at Burt Silvers' house. Listen, just get here as soon as you can," he urged.

"Yeah, ok, bye," I said as Ricky tapped me on the shoulder.

"What's going on, Junior? Why are you talking in such a strange voice?" Ricky asked.

"I don't know Ricky, I just am. Come on, we gotta get out to Burt's house and now."

"Why - everybody knows that ain't Burt's house. That house belongs to his mom. Burt just lives there," he said like a know it all.

"Gosh darn it Ricky, I know that. Just get in the car. No Ricky, not in the passenger side. You go ahead and drive," I said.

"Whoa, this is a first. You hate my driving," he said.

"Please Ricky, just go," I pleaded.

We took off screaming up Sycamore Street. I didn't want Ricky to run anybody over, so I turned on the flashers and the siren. Before I knew it, we were flying west on Adams heading for the hills just above the lake.

Ricky swerved once as we passed a car. As we drove by, I realized it was Madison. We made a hard left off of Adams and when we turned south up the hill I thought for sure we were gonna tip over, but somehow Ricky managed to keep the car upright. We came to a screeching halt and I noticed there were no lights on in the house.

"Grab a flashlight," I said as I ran towards the house.

Shadow was standing by the front door with his forty-five in his hand. I ran right by him and when I got inside the house, I yelled for Tommy.

"I'm up here in the first bedroom to your right," he said.

I bolted up the stairs and when I ran into the room, Tommy was kneeling, looking under a very large bed. I could see the soles of a pair of super white bare feet next to him. I involuntarily stuck both of my hands out to stop Ricky from running me over.

"Tommy, are those Burt's feet?" I asked.

"I don't know for sure," was all he said.

"What? Why don't you know?" I asked.

"I don't know because that's all there is here. Just the feet," he said with a grimace.

Ricky and I leaned over Tommy's shoulder and shined our lights under the bed. The only thing there was the feet. They'd been cut off just above the ankles. Ricky immediately gagged and puked into his hands.

"Damnit! Junior, get Ricky out of here!" Tommy roared.

I grabbed Ricky by the shirt and pulled him back out into the hallway.

"Listen Ricky - Dad always says when you feel nauseous you should breathe deep through your nose."

Ricky didn't say anything, he just stared into space. So, I helped him sit down in the corner facing the stairwell.

"You gonna be ok?" I asked.

He didn't say anything, but he did lift his hand up and wave it side to side. I took that as a yes.

"Junior! Come on, we gotta search every room in this house. We've gotta find Burt or at least what's left of him," Tommy said as he walked by me.

We checked every room upstairs and found absolutely nothing. Then we went down the stairs and slowly walked through the living room. We shined our lights over every inch, behind the chairs and couch, and still nothing. Then Tommy took off through the kitchen and opened up the basement door and disappeared.

I started down the steps when all the lights in the house came on. Tommy ran back up the stairs and said, "Follow me."

We searched the entire downstairs of the house and nothing. Then we walked out onto the back porch. It was clean as a whistle. We continued out to the backyard and slowly went in the garage. Burt's car was there, but his mother's car was gone. And once again there was no sign of a struggle. Tommy said, "Wait here." And he ran back into the house. He was back within a minute.

"I saw the car keys hanging on a ring in the kitchen pantry. We need to open the trunk to Burt's car," was all he said.

I don't really know why, but when he mentioned the trunk, I took a couple of steps back. Tommy turned the key and the trunk of the car popped open and once again nothing. Tommy walked around and looked in through the windows, but the car was empty. Then he said, "It's just as I originally thought. Come on Junior, we gotta wake Lloyd up." *Lloyd Brown is the Liberty County Coroner.*

Tommy started walking back to the house, so I followed.

"Tommy, what is as you originally thought?" I asked.

"Whatever happened didn't happen here," was all he said.

"Yeah, that's what I was thinking," I said as we walked back into the kitchen.

Tommy picked up the phone and immediately had a scowl on his face.

"Gosh darn it, the phone's dead. Junior, I'm gonna go next door and use Mrs. Taylor's phone."

We both started walking, but only made it to the living room when we heard Shadow yell, "Hey Junior, Tommy, Mrs. Taylor's here. She wants to talk to you. Can she come in?" he asked.

Tommy didn't say a word so I yelled, "No, hang on. We'll be right there."

We walked out onto the front porch and Mrs. Taylor was standing there with a scowl on her face that matched the one Tommy had on his. She had her arms folded in front of her like some Indian chief. For whatever reason she turned to me and said, "You listen to me, young man. I'm Burt and Lodema Silvers' next-door neighbor and I demand to know what is going on in there."

I started to answer her when Tommy said, "Mrs. Taylor, as far as we can see, there's nothing going on."

"If that's the case, then why are you here?" she asked.

"We're here because we received two calls from people that said they were worried because all the lights were out in the Silvers' house. Alice, were you one of the callers?" Tommy asked.

206

Mrs. Taylor turned a pale shade of red before she said, "Well, yes I did call, but that doesn't mean you can't tell me what's going on in that house. I saw Lodema drive away at three-thirty this morning. Burt wasn't with her. So why didn't Burt turn the lights on tonight?" she asked.

"Alice, are you positive you saw Mrs. Silvers drive her car this morning?" Tommy asked.

"Absolutely, we watch out for one another. She backed out the drive and waved to me just as she always does," Mrs. Taylor said.

"What were you doing up at three-thirty in the morning?" Tommy asked.

"I'm an early riser," she said.

Tommy let out his breath and then he said, "May I use your phone, Alice? I have to make a call."

""Oh my, something is wrong. Why don't you use the phone in Lodema's house?" she asked.

"Because her phone is dead, now can I use your phone or not?" Tommy asked as the scowl grew.

Tommy didn't wait for Mrs. Taylor to answer. He started walking next door to use the phone when Ricky yelled, "Hey, you guys better get up here!"

I'd forgotten about Ricky and I think Tommy had too. The two of us ran back inside and flew up the stairs. And while we were running, Tommy yelled, "Shadow, don't you dare let anybody in this house. And that's an order!"

Shadow hollered back, "You got it."

When we got to the top of the stairs, Ricky was standing there with a towel in his hand.

"I went into the bathroom to wash my face and hands and when I was in there, I heard someone crying," Ricky said.

"Where did you hear them?" I asked.

"Right there in the master bedroom," he said as he pointed down the hall.

Tommy and I had our guns out and then Ricky followed suit. We slowly walked to the bedroom and Tommy put his left index finger to his mouth and then he motioned for us to stay where we were. He pointed his gun around the corner before walking into the room. I watched him go into the bathroom as he'd done earlier. Then he came out and opened the doors to the armoire and then he checked under the bed, still nothing. He tiptoed to the center of the room and said, "This is the police. Don't be afraid, we're here to help you."

And then we heard a small voice say, "I'm in here. Please don't hurt me."

The voice came from the immigrant's chest at the foot of the bed. Tommy walked over and lifted the top open and just stood there.

"Mrs. Silvers, it's safe to come out now. Please come out," he said.

Tommy picked up a large hand-sewn quilt and threw it onto the bed. Then he reached in and helped a bald-headed Lodema Silvers out of her hiding place.

She whimpered, "Thank you. Oh dear god, I thought I was never going to get out of that smelly old trunk. Is Bertrand ok?" she asked.

"We don't know, ma'am. We were hoping you might be able to tell us where he is," Tommy said.

"Have you checked his room?" she asked.

I hurried up and said, "Yes, Mrs. Silvers, we have and he's not there."

I did my best to change the subject.

"Mrs. Silvers, your neighbor Mrs. Taylor is downstairs, and she says she saw you drive away early this morning. Did you go somewhere in your car last night?" I asked.

"She's such a nosy woman. No, I did not go anywhere in my car last night or this morning. I have been in the trunk. Bertrand came to my room about midnight and said he heard voices out back. He told me to hide in the trunk and not to come out. So I did, but eventually I fell asleep. If you have any more questions, they'll have to wait because I've got to use the restroom and right now," she said as she hurried into her bathroom and slammed the door.

Tommy quietly said, "Junior, when she comes out, lead her downstairs. Do not let her go in Burt's room. If she sees those doggone feet, there's no telling what she'll do."

I nodded and Tommy took off down the stairs. Ricky and I stood there for quite some time. I guess she really had to go. When I heard the toilet flush, a panic ran through me. I thought to myself, *how am I going to keep her from going in a bedroom in her own home?* She came out and walked right past Ricky and me straight to her son's room. She walked in, looked around for a minute, and shook her head.

"This is a mystery. Where could Bertrand have gone?" she asked.

"I don't know ma'am. Would you like to go down and talk to your neighbor?" I asked in desperation.

"I never like talking to that woman, she infuriates me. But I would like to know who she thinks she saw driving my car," Mrs. Silvers said as she opened a drawer and searched for a moment before she lifted a bawdy blue wig up and placed it sideways on her head. Then she walked right past me and down the stairs.

When she was at the bottom of the stairs, I looked in Burt's room. The feet were gone. I hurried down the stairs and walked over to Tommy. He was telling Shadow to keep the crowd away from the house. When Tommy said crowd, I looked and much to my surprise the entire neighborhood was standing right there in the middle of the street. I pulled Tommy aside.

"Tommy, where are the feet?" I asked.

"They're in the closet," he said back.

"You moved them?" I asked.

"Well, they certainly didn't walk there," he said.

At that point I couldn't continue. In my lifetime I had heard Tommy laugh many times and tell a few jokes. But I had never heard him joke about something as serious as what we were facing, and in particular, the feet.

"Tommy, you may have altered a murder scene," I said with a righteous attitude.

"No Junior - I haven't! I haven't because a murder did not take place in that room. I moved the feet to save Burt's mother from the shock she would have gone through had she seen them. Junior, there's only one person in the world that could have identified those feet as Burt Silvers' feet. And that person is his mother. And trust me she would have. A mother knows. And there is no question in my mind that those are Burt's feet. And there is no getting around the fact that I'm the reason Burt was attacked and is probably dead."

"What? Tommy, that's crazy. Why would you say you're at fault? I mean, there are dozens of people that hate Burt," I said.

"Junior," Tommy said in a real soft tone. "Thanks for trying to stick up for me, but the fact is - if I hadn't made Burt write the apology to Ricky, this would never have happened."

"You stood up for Ricky and that's a good thing," I said.

"Junior - do you remember when I said at our first meeting that no one was to say or do anything to anger or set off the person we were looking for?"

"Yes, I remember."

"Well, that's exactly what I let happen. So I'm going to go call Lloyd while you question Alice and Lodema. But starting tomorrow you'll be handling this case because I'm going to turn in my badge. And that's final."

Tommy turned and walked away before I could get another word out. I stood there for a long time running what Tommy had just told me through my head. And once again I was left scratching my head. When I walked back to talk with the ladies, I just happened to look out towards the crowd and standing right there in the middle of the people was Madison. I walked past Shadow, grabbed Madison by the hand and pulled her away from the crowd.

"Madison, how long have you been here?"

"I've been here ever since you and Ricky flew by me out on Adams."

"Oh yeah, I forgot about that."

"Junior, what is going on in Burt's house?"

"Well, actually it's Burt's mother's house," I said as she gave me a stare.

"Ok, well, I think you already know that I can't tell you." She gave me another stare. "I can tell you that nothing happened here, but something terrible has happened somewhere."

"Junior, that is the most convoluted and just plain crazy thing I've ever heard you say."

I looked down at the ground before I answered her.

"Madison, I admit that what I just said does sound crazy. So you're just going to have to trust me because I can't say any more. You should probably just go on home. I'll talk to you tomorrow, ok?"

She gave me one of those heated looks she used to give me when we were kids. Then she turned and walked away. I followed suit. As I was walking, I pulled out my notepad and walked straight back to the front porch. I wanted to ask Mrs. Silvers a few more questions. She and Mrs. Taylor were nowhere in sight. I walked in the house and I could hear 'em talking. When I walked in the front room, Mrs. Taylor was sitting right next to Mrs. Silvers on the couch. They were both crying.

"Can I get either one of you ladies something to drink or–"

"No Junior, I've already got a pot of coffee brewing," Mrs. Taylor said.

"Ok, I'm sorry Mrs. Silvers, but I need to ask you a few more questions if you don't mind." She didn't say a word. "Ok, is there anything else about last night that you haven't told me?"

"Go ahead Lodema, tell Junior what you told me," Mrs. Taylor said.

Mrs. Silvers sniffled a couple of times before she said, "Junior, all I can tell you is that after I hid in the trunk they came into my bedroom."

"There was more than one person?" I asked.

"Yes, I heard at least three different people talking, maybe four." Go on I said. "They were whispering, but one of them had a high-pitched voice. Sounded like a female to me. Anyway, they were going through my things when someone opened the trunk lid. I thought for sure I was dead. What would they want with an old Jewish woman and her son?"

"I don't know," I lied.

"Then the person stopped because someone else said, 'Look at what we've got here.' And whoever had opened the trunk let the lid slam back shut. Then they were gone. I waited an hour, maybe two, and was going to get out of the trunk when I heard them come back. They came upstairs but didn't come into my bedroom. That's the last I heard of them before I fell asleep again. I woke up when I heard you police officers walking around. I didn't know who you were, so I stayed in the trunk. You understand don't you?" she asked.

"Yes ma'am, I understand completely. I think maybe we should go up and see if there's anything missing in your bedroom," I said.

"We don't have to because I've already gone back up. Young man, they stole one of my very best wigs and my diamond bracelet. My late husband had the bracelet custom made at Saks Fifth Avenue, in Manhattan. It's platinum and has a birthstone for each of my four children and there are twenty-five exquisite diamonds throughout. It's extremely valuable. But I don't care about that. I just want to know where Bertrand is. I won't rest 'til you find him. Please find him," she begged as the tears began to flow again.

"Mrs. Silvers, we're going to dust the entire house and garage for fingerprints. We'll do everything we can to find Burt." I hesitated for a moment before I said, "Mrs. Silvers, is there anything else you remember hearing last night that might lead us to Burt?" I asked.

"I can't think of anything else right now," she said as she buried her face in her hands.

"Mrs. Silvers, do you have a receipt for the bracelet that was stolen?" I asked.

Then Mrs. Taylor said, "She can do better than that. She has the receipt and a picture of the bracelet. You stay here, Lodema, I'll go get them," she said.

"Mrs. Taylor, could you wait just a minute, please. Look, I have to ask you to do something right now that could save lives, even your own."

She immediately gasped. I'd mentioned her life to make sure I had her full attention.

"Mrs. Taylor, you've heard some incredibly private information tonight. People's lives are at stake. You cannot say a word to anyone about what you've heard. Do you understand why?"

"Well, no - I guess I don't. Why?"

"Because if the people that were here last night hear about a neighbor telling the world what happened. Well, they might decide to come back. And I don't think you want that. Do you?" I asked with an ominous overtone.

"No young man, I truly don't," she said as her right eye began to tick shut

"I'm counting on both of you to not say a word to anyone. Ok?" I said as they both nodded yes. "All right Alice, you can go get the picture and receipt now."

I sat there with Mrs. Silvers and she didn't look up at me when she said, "Young man, you've been very nice, and I want to thank you for that. But the truth is, I know that Bertrand is not ever coming home. I hope he didn't suffer."

I didn't know what to say at that point, so I just sat and wondered. I wondered how all of these terrible things could have happened in a place full of so many good people, Crestfield that is. Eventually, Mrs. Taylor brought down the picture and the receipt for the bracelet. As she was coming down the stairs, Tommy and Lloyd Brown were going up. Mrs. Taylor asked why the coroner was here. I told her that it was routine for the coroner to help look for clues in a case like this. I lied again and felt horrible inside for doing it. I did dust for prints and spent nearly the entire night going through the house and garage looking for anything that might lead us to Burt. There was just nothing there. Mrs. Taylor watched everything I did from her house. Mrs. Silvers left me alone. I think she had given up the ship. When I drove home that morning, I wasn't just exhausted, I was mentally and physically paralyzed.

I crawled into bed and the moment my head hit the pillow, I was smack dab in the middle of one of my mean dreams. Halloween was just around the corner and a witch came to visit me. She was a beautiful but very wicked witch.

Junior/**I woke up at noon** the next day in a fit. Even though it was very cold in my bedroom, I was sweating like a horse. I got up and dragged around the apartment. I was trying to get over the awful dream I'd had and the undeniable fact that Burt Silvers was probably dead. I just knew I couldn't feel any worse about the world around me. I was wrong. My phone rang and when I picked up the phone, Uncle Ajax was screaming at me.

"Junior! What is wrong with Tommy? He just came over to my office and handed me his resignation. I tried to get him to tell me why, but all he said was ask Junior. What in tarnation is going on?" he asked at high volume.

"Uncle Ajax, please stop yelling at me. I asked Tommy the exact same thing last night. And he told me he feels responsible for what has happened to Burt."

"Burt? What has happened to Burt? Junior, tell me right now," he demanded.

"I don't know what has happened to Burt. But those feet that were left in his room are probably his," I said.

"Feet! What goddamned feet?" he screamed.

"Ok, obviously nobody told you. There was a pair of feet in Burt's bedroom. There was no blood or anything, just the feet. They'd been cut off right above the ankle. Those feet are one of the most dreadful things I've ever seen. Anyway, I'd say all things considered there can be little doubt that they're Burt Silvers' feet."

I immediately heard Ajax say, "Good lord."

"Now as far as Tommy goes, he thinks that the letter of apology he made Burt write to Ricky pissed off the murderer we're looking for. If you remember, Burt did say the guy was a soulless jackal, among other things. Anyway, that is why Tommy feels responsible."

"Now I'm beginning to understand. Yes, Tommy has always, for whatever reason, felt that he is not allowed to make mistakes. And he is tormented beyond reason when he does. I'm going to talk to him, but I'd say this is going to take some time. Tommy will brood for a while, but I think eventually he'll come to the realization that this person we're looking for is just plain evil and this isn't his fault."

"That's something else I should tell you, Uncle Ajax."

"Oh good gracious, don't tell me it gets worse," he said in a funk.

"I don't know if it gets worse, but I do know that it gets more complicated. Lodema Silvers told me last night that there were several people that came to her house. She said one of them might be a female."

"Junior, if this gets out, we're in a world of trouble. We have got to do some damage control and I mean today. I'm going to call an emergency meeting. I'd say about five this evening. I want everyone there. We need to suppress this information."

"Ok Uncle Ajax, but it could be too late. You see, Mrs. Taylor also knows about all of this. And even though I warned her of the consequences, there's every chance that she will spill the proverbial beans."

"Not if I can help it. Listen, I'm going to take care of Alice Taylor and Lodema Silvers. You just make sure you have everybody in my office this evening at five sharp, Rita Streams too. Got it?"

"Yeah, I got it," I said as Ajax hung up.

The first thing I did was call the station. Randi answered after the first ring.

"Hello, Crestfield police –."

"Randi, it's me, Junior. Listen, I know its short notice, but will you please call everybody, Rita too. The mayor wants us all to meet in his office tonight at five."

"Did you say in his office?"

"Yes, that's what I said. Listen, if you need help, let me know and I'll do what I can. Is Ricky there?"

"No, after you guys left Mrs. Silvers' house, he came into work. He's been out on patrol ever since."

"Wow, that's unbelievable. Now I feel guilty for sleeping in."

"Don't feel guilty, Ricky wanted to work today. Tommy told him last night to keep an eye on the Thornton farm."

"That's interesting. Ok, well, thanks sis - I'll see you tonight."

I sat down at my kitchen table and opened up my notebook, but I couldn't see even one word. I was thinking about Ricky watching Billy, and for some reason that bothered me. So I called Randi back.

"Hello, Crestfield police department. How can I–"

"Randi, it's me again. Can you do me a favor and get in touch with Ricky?"

"Sure, is there something you want me to tell him or ask him?" she asked.

"No, just tell him I said to keep a lookout in his rearview mirror. Ok?"

"Junior, is there something you're not telling me?" she asked.

"No, and try not to alarm him. I'm just a little concerned since we don't know where the creeps, Perry Smith and David Daniels, are. Oh never mind, guess I'm just a little on the edgy side. Did you get a hold of anybody yet?"

"Junior, you just talked to me a minute ago. What's up?"

"Oh nothing, just call Ricky and make sure to tell him about the meeting. Ok, I'll see ya this evening. Bye," I said.

I waited for her to say goodbye, but the line went dead. Five o'clock rolled around in a hurry and everyone was there, except Uncle Ajax. So we waited and fidgeted and waited some more. Finally, at about half past the hour the mayor came strolling into his office. He had a smile on his face and his holster, gun, and little Jax were back.

"Ok people, I believe we may have narrowly escaped a catastrophe."

"Ajax, why do you say that?" Matt asked before anybody else could get the words out.

"I say that because Alice Taylor is now on the train to Chicago. And before you start asking a thousand questions, just listen. I paid for Alice to go visit her sister for a week - maybe two. And the Prescott police found Lodema's car. It was parked behind a filling station. They went all through the car and it's clean as a whistle. So Lodema is now in her car and on her way up to Fargo to stay with her daughter. I convinced her that when Burt heard the people in the back of the house, he probably tried to confuse them and went out the front. And if I know Burt, that might be exactly what he did."

"What? You can't do that. Sooner or later she's going to find out that Burt is dead. This is unbelievable. What about the feet?" I asked.

"Well, I guess you noticed that I was smiling when I came in. And the reason for that is those feet we found are not Burt's feet," Ajax said with a smile.

"This is insane. They have to be Burt's feet. How do you know they're not his feet?" I asked.

"I know that because the coroner just told me so," Ajax said with a smile.

Then Ricky said, "Ajax, I saw the feet. And I get sick just thinking about them. How does Lloyd know they're not Burt's feet?"

"He knows because Burt Silvers wears a size nine shoe and the feet he has at the morgue are a size thirteen. They belong to a much, much bigger man," Ajax said.

"Holy smoke," was all Ricky could say.

"Holy smoke is right. Ajax, you're saying that Burt took off and left his mother there with some crazys. That's nuts. And have you forgotten that we're still stuck with the fact that Burt is missing and now we have the ghoulish task of finding the guy that is missing his feet - and has probably been murdered," I said in disgust.

"Yes, but... Look, my gut tells me that Burt is still alive," Ajax said as Rita began to cry.

We all looked at Rita and Randi asked her why she was crying.

"I'm crying because I never liked Burt, but I don't want him to be dead," was all she said.

"Rita, please don't cry. Trust me, Burt will show up pretty soon," Ajax said.

"Hey, what about Tommy? He still thinks he's responsible. We have to let him know the feet aren't Burt's," I said.

"I called Tommy several times and I drove out to his house, but he's not home. As soon as I find him, I'll let him know. Junior, we have to go about this one thing at a time. Which is exactly why I called this meeting," Ajax said.

"Why did you call this meeting?" I asked.

"I called this meeting because we have to start over with this entire investigation. And before anybody says anything, just hear me out. To begin with, who is this big guy? I was gonna suggest we make a list of names of big men that live in or near Crestfield. But after I thought about it, that wouldn't have made any sense either. I mean, if he's from around here, why didn't Wally or Shadow recognize him when they saw him at the hospital? They didn't recognize him because he's obviously not from around here. But he knows his way around. And why is that?" Ajax asked.

I didn't let Ajax finish because I knew what the answer was. At least I thought I knew.

"Ajax, there's not just the big guy. There's someone else that's very familiar with Crestfield leading this guy around. So who is not the question? The question is why?" I said.

"Junior, thank you. That's exactly why I think we need to start over again. We need to figure out why, not who. What is the motive? Anybody have any ideas?" Ajax asked.

Once again we were stumped, but at least we were thinking along the right lines.

"I suggest we make a list of the people that have been hurt or worse. Then after we have the list, maybe the why will pop out. Ok, I have the people listed in my notes and I'm going to write them down so we all start thinking of a group instead of just one person.

1. Miller

2. Jack

3. Marjorie

4. Burt

Ok, what is the common denominator between these people? I mean, other than the fact that they all live in or are from Crestfield," I said.

"Well, for starters Miller and your dad grew up together. And Marjorie has at one time or another probably taken care of all three. And the first three can't stand Burt. And they all like pie," Ricky said.

"What? Ricky, what does liking pie have to do with any of this?" I asked.

"Didn't you just ask us what the common denominator was between these people? Well, I'll betchya they all like pie," he said as the rest of us snickered and looked at each other.

"You know what, guys? Ricky is right, maybe not with the pie, but he's on the right track. There must be a group or organization that all four have been in at one time," Ajax said.

"Maybe they all belonged to the four H club," Shadow said.

"No, Dad likes eating what the four H club is raising, but he wouldn't like all the work that comes along with it," Randi said.

"How about the city council or maybe the planning committee for the fourth of July? You know something like that?" Matt said.

"No, Miller never comes into town enough to get involved in that kind of stuff," Rita said.

"Maybe it's something that happened when they were going to school?" Ricky said.

"No, Burt is from Fargo. He's heard stories about school, but it wasn't there," I said.

"Maybe they're in a secret society. You know like the Masons, or maybe the Communist Party, something like that," Ricky said as we all stared at him.

"Ricky, they don't let women in the Masons. And Communists! How in the world do you come up with this stuff?" Shadow asked.

"Oh, I don't know. I guess it just comes natural," Ricky answered with a smile.

"You're a nut," Randi said with a shake of the head.

"Ok, we've got to stay focused. I want all of you to think about this. And when you come up with an idea, I want you to write it down. Junior, since you're the detective around here, I want you to ask your dad and Miller if there's anything they can think of that connects all four people. We're going to meet this coming Monday and every other day after that 'til we come up with the answer and catch these maniacs. Now I have a meeting to go to over in Afton. I'll see all of you here in my office this coming Monday at five sharp. Randi, make sure you stay by the phone. I've got a feeling old Burt is going to be calling, and sooner than later. Ok, bye," he said.

"Not so fast. Uncle Ajax, why did you start carrying your gun and little Jax again?" I asked.

"Because I had a talk with Tommy," he said as he picked up little Jax and ran out of the room.

I left the meeting with a glimmer of hope and hungry as all get out. I asked, but nobody there wanted to go eat at the diner or anywhere else for that matter. So I went to Dad's.

He threw some Pillsbury biscuits in the oven and then whipped up some homemade cream-corn. Meanwhile, I fried some ham and onions for our sandwiches.

I decided to have a beer with dinner, but when I looked in the fridge, there weren't any.

"Dad, do you have any beer?"

"Sure I do. They're down with the vegetables. Ricky says they stay colder that way."

I just had to smile after hearing that. And of course, I smiled real big when I popped the top off a frosty Falstaff. Things were looking a lot better than they were last night, except for the fact that Burt was still missing. But I made up my mind on the way over to dads that I was gonna do my best to accent the positive and eliminate the negative. I made a sandwich for Maggie and the three of us sat down at Dad's little dining table and ate in peace.

After dinner Dad didn't wait for me to clear the table. He just jumped up and turned the TV on.

"Uh, you're welcome, Dad."

"Sorry Junior, but you know Maggie and I never miss the Smothers Brothers show."

"Don't you mean the three of us?"

"I suppose, but I guarantee you I know exactly what's going on. You just fill in the finer points. Now can you get over here and start with the fillin' in."

"Sure, can you give me a minute, so I can put the dishes in the sink? Maggie, he sure is pushy." She barked a yep back to me.

After the show, I got up to do the dishes and it seemed like a good time to ask Dad if he knew of any organization or committee etc. that he might have been a part of with Miller, Marjorie, and Burt. I think the question annoyed him.

"Junior, you know how I feel about Burt, so the answer is no. However, I do remember seeing Marjorie and Burt together in the newspaper, but I don't recall why. As far as all four of us goes, I'd say we've never even been in the same room together. Why do you ask?"

"Oh, no particular reason other than... never mind."

"Junior, is this about Miller's cow?"

"Yes Dad, I suppose it is. We never did catch the person responsible."

"I'd say the persons you're looking for are a couple of spurious knot-heads. They'll make a mistake somewhere down the line and then you'll catch 'em for sure."

"I hope you're right... Wait, Dad how did you know there were two of them?"

"I know because one guy couldn't have got that cow loaded onto a truck. I think you'd need one guy to push and one to pull."

"Yeah, I suppose you're right."

I was hoping he'd say something about the day he was attacked, but no such luck. I had just finished putting the dishes away when the phone rang.

"Hello, oh hi Ricky. What's up?"

"What? Are you sure? Where? Oh gosh, I was hoping to have a quiet night. Yes, I'll get over there as soon as I can. Yeah, bye."

"Dad, we've got a little bit of a problem going on."

"What's that, Junior? You don't sound so good. Can I help with something?"

"I don't think so, well, maybe."

"Junior, what is it? Just tell me."

"I guess Uncle Tommy has fallen off the wagon. Ricky says Tommy is pretty darn drunk."

"What bar did he choose to rid himself of the demons in his head?"

"He's in the Alibi."

"Junior, bring me my shoes."

"Dad, you don't have to go."

"I do if you want to get Tommy out of the bar. Cuz I'm the only person that knows how to do it."

"Ok Dad, where are your shoes?"

"Well, they're not on my feet. So they're probably on the floor in my bedroom. That is if Maggie hasn't taken 'em out back. She sure does like to chew on my doggone shoes."

I looked in the bedroom and no shoes. So I walked out and turned on the back-porch light. His shoes were there, all chewed up and soggy.

"Dad, are you sure you wanna wear these shoes? They're so chewed up they don't even look like shoes."

"Of course I wanna wear 'em. Junior, we're going in a doggone bar. When was the last time you went in a bar and

221

stared at people's shoes? Yeah, that's just what I thought. Now give me the damn shoes."

"Dad, do you want a sweater or a jacket?"

"Nope, I'm gonna be awful hot pretty soon."

"Why's that?"

"Stick around for a while and you'll see."

"Oh boy, this does not sound good at all."

"Junior, do they still have a band playing in the Alibi?"

"Yeah, they just got some band in from Sioux City."

"Damn city slickers?"

"Um, I suppose you could say that."

"Ok, my shoes're on. Maggie, let's go have a listen to this band from the big city."

The minute I got Dad and Maggie in the patrol car he said, "Junior, first you need to stop by the 66 station and get me a pack of Viceroys. Oh, and make sure you say hey to Jump for me." I drove up to the Phillips station, ran in and grabbed a pack of smokes for Dad. I waved to Jump as I ran out and got back in the patrol car.

"Did you say hello to Jump for me?"

"Yes Dad, I did. Now where do you want to go?"

"Head across the tracks to the corner of south Vine and east Monroe. I'll tell ya which house when we get there."

"Which house? Dad, it's against the law for the public to sell liquor. We need to go to the ABD store on Adams."

"The state store is closed. And I get a better deal from my person."

"Dad, I'll be breaking one of the laws I'm supposed to be protecting."

"No you won't. There's not going to be any money involved. Listen, John Q Public has to make a living too. So just tell the lady what I want and then get back in the car."

"Dad, what are you getting me into?"

"I'm not getting you into anything. Now do what I told you to do. Just drive Junior, Please."

As I pulled away from the gas station Dad asked me if the farmers had brought the corn in.

"Yeah they have Dad, harvested most of it by the last week or two of September. I drove over to Osceola a while back and there wasn't an ear of corn in sight. Why do you ask?"

"Oh no reason other than I can smell the difference in the air. Haven't you ever noticed that when the corn's still out, the air tastes sweeter and heavier. You know how the smell inside a barn is different than the smell outside? Well, now it smells like I'm outside the barn and not on the inside."

"You know I think you're right, Dad. Although I don't have as good a sniffer as you do, I can tell that the air is as you said, not as sweet?"

"Junior, what does the sky look like tonight?"

"What do you mean?"

"Just look out the window and tell me what you see."

"Well, it's always a little darker on this side of town. But there's a little bit of light or glow around us because the stars are for some reason especially bright tonight."

"That usually means we're in for a cold spell. Don't know why that is, but it is. Junior, can you see Polaris?"

"No Dad, remember we're heading due south, but maybe we'll see it on the way home."

"That'll be great. Can you try to remember to look for it?"

"Sure Dad, I'll look for it."

"Thanks."

I drove for all of about five minutes before I stopped and told him we were there.

"Ok, well, you know Marylou. Go in there and buy me a half-pint of Old Crow."

"What? You can't take liquor into a bar."

"Boy, you sure have led a sheltered life. I've been bringing liquor into bars since I was... Well, ever since when."

"Ok, but don't blame me when Dolly throws you out of the bar."

Dolly is the rock-jawed, no nonsense owner of the Alibi.

"Oh hell, Dolly knows we do it. She brings in her own bottle too. Junior, there's a whole lot of stuff about people and things they didn't teach at that fine college of yours. Oh, and get me a plug of Bloodhound chewing tobacco."

"I'll be right back, Dad."

"Yeah, ok take your time."

As I got out of the car, I told Maggie to keep an eye on Dad. She barked an ok back to me. I knocked on the door and Marylou opened it so fast I was startled. She looked me up and down and then she looked up and down the street before she said, "Junior, how's things?"

"Hi Marylou, things are fine. Why?"

She looked me up and down again and then smiled like there was no tomorrow. I thought, *she's awful pretty, but she's also the sassiest little brunette in this entire town. So be careful.*

"Oh, everything is just fine, thanks. How'd you know to come here, Junior?"

"Dad told me, is that ok?"

"Why certainly. What can I do for you?"

"Can you get me a half-pint of Old Crow and a plug of Bloodhound, please?"

Marylou did a double take and then just stood there and stared at me like I was a juvenile delinquent or something.

"Marylou, are you ok?"

She laughed but didn't say a word.

"Oh, I understand. Look, it's not for me, it's for my dad." She giggled. "Really," I said.

"Yeah right, and I'm giving the same stuff to my mom tonight." Her giggle turned into a full-blown riotous laugh.

"Marylou please, I'm kind of in a hurry."

"Yeah, I'll bet you are. You've probably got some little stuffed bra high school chick waiting out in the car. You know young girls usually like Bali Hai or Peppermint Schnapps or something like that. They want to pretend that they're not actually drinking alcohol."

"Marylou, it's not for a high school girl."

She didn't hear a word I said.

"Don't go gettin' her that rot gut Old Crow. You won't even get past first base. That is unless of course you don't mind them being knocked out. Junior, you wouldn't dare take advantage of a young girl, would you?" She smacked her gum real loud. "Junior, I get off in about an hour."

"Oh, that's nice to know Marylou, but I really do have to get going."

"What's wrong, Junior? Are your pants on fire? The little Philly you have in the car can wait," she said as she laughed right in my face.

"Marylou, I'm in a hurry and I don't have a young girl or a little Philly in my car."

224

She walked out and looked through the front window at my patrol car and kind of lost her breath.

"Gee-whiz, Junior. You can do better than that. She's kind of a dog face isn't she?"

I walked over and looked out the window and all I could see was Maggie staring back at me. It took me a few seconds to realize what had just happened.

"Hey, she's better than nothin'."

Marylou hauled-A into a back room and then back out with the half-pint of Old Crow. "We're all out of Bloodhound, will Red Man be ok?" she said as she stuck them in a bag.

"Sure Marylou, I'll come back when you get off work. I think my girlfriend Maggie would like it if you joined us. If you know what I mean?"

"Oh thanks Junior, but I just remembered my mom's sick, so I gotta stay home."

I grabbed the liquor and as I walked out, I said, "I'm sorry about your mom Marylou, if you ever get the hankerin' give me a call."

She smiled as she waved, but the whole time her eyes were saying, *go away*.

I was thinking I was pretty darn clever and started to swagger back out to the car when Marylou said, "Junior, your fly is down."

I looked down and didn't feel so clever when I zipped myself up. I turned around and bolted out to the car. And the moment I got in Dad says, "Did she tell you your fly was down?"

"What? How the heck did you know that?"

"I know because she pulls it on everybody."

"Oh," was all I could come up with to say.

"Sounds like maybe your fly really was down."

I didn't say anything.

"It was, wasn't it?" Dad said before he choked from laughing so hard.

"Gosh darn it, Dad. Do you have any idea what I just went through to get this stuff for you?"

"Yeah, I do. Marylou gave you a hard time - did she? Poor guy, listen pee-pants, you're a great kid and all, but do the world and yourself a favor and stop your belly aching. And then give me that bottle."

I handed him the bag and told him he'd have to get by with the Red Man, he didn't say a word back to me. He just cracked the top off the bottle of Old Crow and took a long pull.

"Whoopee!" Was all he said as his head violently shook from side to side.

"Gosh you're funny sometimes Dad. Hey! Keep the bottle down so nobody sees what you're doing."

"Junior, just drive would ya. On second thought why don't you let me drive?"

I didn't answer him.

"Ok I won't drive, but I changed my mind about the jacket. I forgot that I'm gonna need a place to hide my bottle. You need to go back by the house and get me that brown work jacket I wear all the time."

"Dad, we need to get to the bar. And at this rate we're never gonna get there. Ok, is there anything else you want me to do?"

He couldn't answer me because he was taking another long drink. When I pulled up in front of the house, I whipped a U-turn and had the car pointing due south and towards the bar. That way once I got the jacket, we could make a fast getaway.

"Ok Dad, where exactly is the jacket?"

"Uh, give me a minute to think. Junior, are there any cars parked on the street?"

"No Dad, there's not. Where's the jacket?"

"Oh yeah, it's in the back of my closet. You can't miss it."

I ran in the house and went straight to his closet, which was a mess. I looked in the back and the front and then on the floor, but there was no brown jacket. I was getting a little more frustrated by the second. So I ran back out and told him the jacket wasn't there and he says, "You know, I think I made a mistake. The jacket is hanging up in the garage. You can't miss it."

I ran out back to the garage and turned on the light and took a good look around. There was no jacket. Boy I was getting frustrated. So I ran back out to the car and Dad was sitting behind the steering wheel. The motor was running.

I walked up and started to say don't do anything foolish, but it was no use. He heard me and threw the car in drive and pressed hard on the accelerator. He took off speeding down the street. I was running and screaming at the top of my lungs for him to stop. After about a half-a-block he came to a screeching halt. I ran up, reached in the window, put the car in park, and then I turned off the motor. Dad was laughing so hard he could barely breathe. I yanked the keys out of the ignition and yelled, "Are you crazy? What if there had been another car parked in the street?"

He stopped laughing just long enough to say, "Junior, have you forgotten that I have lived here for a long time. There's no cars parked on this street, ever. You even said so yourself."

I walked back to the trunk as Dad continued laughing like a jackal. I opened up the trunk and got out my old fishing jacket. It didn't smell so great and I didn't care. I opened the driver side door and shoved Dad over to the passenger side. I started down the street when Dad rolls down his window and chucks the empty bottle of whisky out on old man Hopkins front yard. And then he slurred, "Junior, you gotta go back and get me another bottle of whiskey."

"No way Dad, you're already drunk."

"I ain't goin' in the bar without a bottle, and that's final. Except this time I'd like a pint of Fleischmann's. I need a variety of whiskey when I'm drinkin'."

"Oh Dad, do you know how awful you're gonna feel tomorrow?" He didn't answer. "Ok, but don't say I didn't warn you."

I got out of the car and picked up the bottle Dad had thrown out the window and then I drove back to Marylou's.

I made sure to take the keys out of the car before I walked up to her door. Marylou was standing there looking at me like I was the devil incarnate. I asked her to give me a pint of Fleischmann's. She just stared at me some more.

"Please Marylou; I really am in a hurry."

"Yeah, I can see that. Can you do me a favor, Junior?"

"Uh yeah I guess so. What can I do for you?"

"You can stop that hoppin' around? You look like some little boy that has to take a leak."

I stopped hopping and thought to myself, *how'd she know?*

She grabbed the pint of whiskey and threw it in a paper bag. And as I was walking out she said, "Hey Junior."

I turned around, "Yeah?"

"Your zipper's down."

I looked down and then I looked back at her and she just busted up laughing at me. I ran back out to the car and when I got in, Dad started laughing too.

"Now what's so funny?"

"She told you your zipper was down again, didn't she."

"Yes she did."

"And you fell for it again didn't you."

"Dad, have I ever told you that you're a smart aleck?"

"Many times - what about it?"

"Oh nothin' I guess."

"Junior, were you hoppin' around in front of Marylou?"

"Yes, how'd you know?"

"I know because you're the only person I've ever known that can hop around while you're sitting down."

We were only a block or so from the Alibi. Dad laughed all the way there. The moment I parked the car he got out and put the smelly jacket on. He put the whiskey in his right front pocket and the cigarettes in the left front pocket. Then he got the Red Man out of the bag, opened the pouch, and put a huge wad in his mouth.

"Dad, I hope you know what you're doing."

And of course, he immediately spit and said, "Mmm, that's good. Junior, did you let Maggie out?"

"Yes, why?"

"Come here girl." Maggie was next to Dad in nothing flat. "Ok, here's the plan. You're gonna let Maggie walk me right past Tommy, he'll be sitting around the corner to the right when we walk in. Just keep on walking me up to a table in front of the dance floor. Then go back and get us a pitcher of draft beer. I think they have Pabst and Bud on tap, either one will be just fine. Then bring me the glass of beer so's I can make myself a boilermaker. Oh and don't converse with Tommy. In fact, kinda ignore him if you can. You got it?"

"Yes Dad, I got it, but I don't understand it."

"You'll have to trust me and be patient. Oh and one other thing. Ask Dolly where the spittoon is? She used to keep it over on the floor at the far end of the bar. Anywho, make a show of it while you're carrying the spittoon. Got it?"

228

"I'll do better than that. I'll have Ricky carry it. He's a show all by himself."

"Good thinking. Now help me into the bar, cuz I'm getting a little tipsy."

I grabbed him by the arm and told Maggie to go slow. She understood I had to really work hard at keeping Dad steady as he walked. He was further into drunkenness than I had realized. We did as he had instructed. And sure enough Tommy was sitting at his usual spot right inside the door and back a ways. I think he likes it there because he can see the whole bar.

And it would be impossible for someone to sneak up on him. When we walked by, Tommy started an involuntary wave which I ignored. I took Dad straight to the front of the dance floor and parked him at an empty table. Then we heard Ricky yell from the back of the bar.

"Jack, what the heck are you doin' in here?"

That was all we heard Ricky say before he rushed up to us and started petting Maggie. Dad and I both said hello to Ricky and then I pulled him aside for a minute.

"Ricky, I'm gonna need your help here. I've got to get Dad and me a pitcher of beer. He'd like for you to go get the spittoon and bring it to him. Ok?"

"I didn't know your Dad chewed tobacco."

"He doesn't, this is just for show."

"What?" Was all Ricky said.

"Ricky, just go get the spittoon and bring your beer over here. Please?"

"Ok, I gotchya."

Ricky took off and so did I. I ran straight to the bathroom. When I got done, I walked up to the bar to order the pitcher of beer and Dolly smiled real big and said, "Hello Junior."

"Hello Dolly, how's things?"

"Well, other than Tommy bein' here in a drunken stupor, things couldn't be better. You know I haven't seen your dad in here since, well, not since the accident. It sure is good to see the two of you. Can you tell Jack I said hello?"

"I'm gonna tell him for sure. He told me the same thing, that is to say hello to you. Dolly, can I please have a pitcher of beer, doesn't really matter what kind."

"Sure thing, Hamm's is on sale, would that be ok?"

229

"Yes ma'am, that'd do just fine. And I'll need two glasses if you don't mind."

"Junior, you've always been so polite. I sure do like that in a man. Somebody taught you right."

"Thank you."

I was standing there watching Dolly fill the pitcher of beer when I heard somebody hit a snare drum. Then all everybody in the bar could hear was Dad yell, "It's about damned time you guys started playing. You little knot-heads are half-an-hour late. If you'd stop playing grab-ass with each other, you'd be on time."

"Test, test, uh listen we're sorry about that. We'll be ready to go in a minute," the guitar player said into the microphone.

Dad yelled, "Ok, I'll let you off the hook this time, but don't let it happen again."

It was kinda quiet in the bar after Dad yelled, and then I heard the crash and bang of Ricky's beer and the spittoon hitting the floor. Thankfully the spittoon was empty. I walked over and picked it up while Ricky kicked at the broken glass on the floor.

Dolly yelled, "Ricky, leave the glass alone. Roland will sweep it up. Now come over here and get another glass."

Ricky walked over with a hangdog look on his face and apologized to Dolly so many times I was gonna tell him to shut up. Dolly said it for me. I just happened to look over my shoulder and Tommy was doing his best to pretend that he didn't notice, but he had his eye on us.

Roland was almost done cleaning up the broken glass when Dad pounded on the table in front of him and spit across the dance floor.

"Where's my damn spittoon. Roland, where are you?" Dad yelled.

Dolly yelled, "Jack, you mean son of a gun. You spit on my floor again and I'm gonna pick you up and throw you out myself, blind or not."

"I'd like to see you try, you big old whiskey drinkin', mangy varmint."

"Jack McCool, don't you dare make me come around this bar," Dolly warned.

I guess Roland didn't want any part of what Dad was selling so he grabbed his bucket real fast and mopped up the chewing tobacco that Dad had deposited all over the floor.

"Junior, take this beer over to your dad and tell him I said he's doin' a good job," Dolly said as she winked at me.

By that point I was tired of trying to figure out my dad and the dark little world he lives in. So I just walked back to the table and told Dad that Dolly said he was doing a good job. He smiled as he lit up a cigarette. Then he fumbled around on the table for his glass of beer. I handed it to him and he immediately poured a little whiskey in and took a big old drink. And then he yelled, "Why don't I hear any music?"

About five seconds later the band started playing a bad version of the song, "Proud Mary". Dad sat still for a minute or so puffing on his cigarette before he suddenly jumped up from the table and began thrashing about like the wild man from Borneo. I stood there stunned and a bit worried. That said, I must admit he was fun to watch.

A moment later Ricky start screaming, "Go Jack, go!"

I sat back down, pet Maggie, and drank my beer. Dad suddenly ran to me and said, "Junior, can you go get about eight or nine bottle caps for me?"

"Dad - what do you want bottle caps for?"

"Junior, just go ask Dolly or Roland - ok."

I asked Roland if he had any bottle caps and he said, "Sure, I know what those are for. I'll bring 'em over to your table in a minute or two."

"Thanks Roland, I sure do appreciate it."

I went back and told Dad his bottle caps were on the way. He put one of those smiles on his face that scare me. Roland brought the caps over and helped Dad wedge 'em into the soles of his shoes. The moment they were secure Dad jumped up and started tap dancing like he was in a movie or something. He danced all by himself for a few minutes before he came back and sat down. He was huffing and puffing and smiling as he took the bottle of whiskey out of his jacket and poured some in his beer. I thought to myself, *uh oh*. About midway through the first set and Dad's second pitcher of beer people started crowding into the bar. By the end of the second set, the place was nearly full.

And the fuller the place got, the louder Dad became. He was outrageously drunk. He tap danced with every girl in the bar. That is until one guy took exception.

A wrestling match ensued that soon turned into an all-out fist fight. The band stopped playing and the entire bar stood and watched as Dad threw one haymaker after the other. For a blind guy Dad held his own. The scrap ended when Maggie and I backed Dad's rival off the dance floor. And after a long and heated argument, the girlfriend finally talked her beau into leaving. The band had stopped playing and the bar was relatively quiet. Well, Dad was not going to miss an opportunity like that. And he staggered out to the middle of the dance floor and screamed, "Hey you! - guitar player!"

Dad got no response, so he yelled again.

"Guitar player, answer me!"

The guitar player walked to the microphone and angrily said, "What do you want!"

Dad said, "You need to tune up. I think one of your strings is too tight. I think it might be the G string."

The guitar player strummed his guitar a few times and then asked, "Are you a musician?"

And Dad yelled, "No, I'm not."

And the guitar player yelled, "You don't know what the hell you're talking about. The G string on my guitar is not too tight. It's perfectly in tune."

And Dad bellowed, "That's not the G string I was talking about."

The entire bar erupted in lawless laughter as the guitar player jumped off the stage and ran towards Dad. He made it about halfway before he was flattened by Ricky, Roland, Dolly, and me. And as he lay on the ground, Tommy walked over and slurred, "If you don't take a break right now, I'm gonna wipe the dance floor with your face. So what's it gonna be?"

The guitar player put his hands up and said, "If you people will let go of me, I'll take that break."

We let go of him and he got up and then he and his bandmates strolled out the back door. Once they were gone, Tommy walked over and sat down with Dad.

"Jack, don't you think you've caused enough trouble for one night?"

"No Tommy, I haven't. In fact, I'm just gettin' warmed up."

Tommy shook his head a couple of times before he said, "Come on Jack, you're making a fool out of yourself."

Dad quickly replied, "And wha-da-ya think you're doin', Tommy?"

Tommy clutched his Cutty and water and stared at the floor. I don't know much about the demons an alcoholic faces, but there must be times when the sense of failure and desolation are unbearable. Dolly stepped over and softly put her hand on Tommy's shoulder and said, "Look, I don't like seeing family members at odds like this. Jack, I think you've had enough fun for one night. And Tommy you have too. So I'm gonna do everyone a favor and eighty-six both of you. You can stay here 'til the band comes back in, but then you have to leave. And don't ask for anything more to drink because you're not getting it. And one more thing - Jack, give me that damn bottle you've got in your jacket."

Dad handed Dolly the empty bottle and in a drunken slur I think he said sorry. Dolly didn't respond to Dad's feeble attempt at an apology - she just walked away. I thought it might be a good time to explain to Tommy about Burt. I did my best, but he didn't buy any of it. He didn't buy it because Burt was still missing. I had pretty much given up on the whole idea when I heard a few people in the bar start laughing. So I turned to see what was so funny.

I couldn't see because there were way too many people in my way. So I stood on my chair and when I did I saw something straight out of a Roy Roger's movie. Walking across the dance floor towards us was some nut wearing a glittering red rhinestone cowboy shirt, boots, leather chaps, and a big black Stetson hat. And, of course, he was wearing his holster and gun. Little Jax was slung over his shoulder and was dressed just like the nut he traveled on.

"Howdy family, looks like everybody here is getting along famously," Ajax said with a smile.

There have been times in my life when just looking at uncle Ajax made me smile. And this was definitely one of those times. The smile on my face was short-lived. Without a warning Ajax erupted into a heated rant.

"You know I can't recall a time when I have been more disappointed in my own family. And in particular I'm talking about you, Tommy. Our parents didn't raise us to be quitters. I don't know what's gotten into you, but it's time you stopped acting like a baby. You need to cowboy up and get yourself back to work," Ajax said as he turned and edged over to Dad. "And you're no better, Jack. I haven't seen you this far in the bag since the night you got drunk and ate that paper plate. Well, your antics may have been funny then, but they're far from it now."

Dad started slurring something under his breath and Ajax hollered, "Ah - shut up, Jack."

Dad did shut up and it got quiet, but not for long. Ajax wasn't quite finished.

"Now, I'm gonna take Tommy home. Junior, you take your dad home. Got it," he said as I nodded my head. "But before you go, I want to tell all of you something that may ease tomorrow's throbbing heads. I just got through talking on the phone with Burt Silvers. And other than the fact that he's a no-good coward, he's very much alive," Ajax said with force.

I couldn't contain my excitement and I'd say the others must have felt the same way.

"Ajax, tell us what happened with Burt. I mean, what made him leave his mom like that? And did he see anyone?" I asked.

"It happened exactly as I thought. Burt said he was hoping to lead the people he heard away from his mom. And in a weird way it worked. And it turns out Burt was the other person that called the station. And no, he didn't see anyone," Ajax said.

"Where was Burt when he called the station?" I asked.

"Burt had run down to Widow Jackson's house to use her phone."

The moment Ajax finished the sentence Dad lifted his head up and slurred, "Ajax, when did you start talking like Elmer Fudd?"

"Jack, what the hell are you talking about?"

"You just said he ran down to witto Jackson's house, didn't you?"

"No, you numbskull, I said widow, as in a woman whose husband has died."

"Oh," Dad said as he laughed and then fell off his chair onto the floor.

I looked down at Dad and he was out cold. Maggie licked him on the face a few times, but he didn't move.

"Leave him there Junior," Ajax said. Then he mouthed witto Jackson to himself and grinned.

"Where is Burt?" Tommy asked.

"Burt's up in Fargo with his mom. And he says he and his mom are never coming back. They're going to sell the Canon and their house. And if you think about this whole situation for just a moment and you're honest with yourself, well, I think you'd do the same darned thing. Things could've turned out worse, a whole lot worse," he said with conviction.

We still didn't know whose feet we'd found, but I had a feeling that eventually we would. Dolly walked up right when Ajax finished telling Tommy about Burt and said, "Ok, time for you guys to go home. And I mean right now."

If you've ever tried to pick up an unconscious person, you know that it's darn near impossible. First Ajax took little Jax off of his shoulder and gently laid him on Tommy's lap. Button-eyed little Jax and blurry-eyed Tommy just stared at each other. Then I pulled Dad up by the arms into a sitting position and Ajax grabbed him around the waist and put him over his shoulder like a fireman would. Ajax huffed and puffed, but he managed to carry Dad all the way out to our car. I think I heard Dad laugh a couple of times along the way.

When I got Dad home, I used the same technique Ajax had and carried him into the house and laid him on his bed. I left him there, clothes and all. I was absolutely dead-dog tired when I staggered from Dad's bedroom into the spare room and collapsed on the rollaway bed. A moment later I realized I'd forgotten to look for the North Star. And as I drifted away on cloud 9, I sang, *twinkle, twinkle, little star...*

**Junior**/**I crawled out of bed that morning** and through the cobwebs decided to make some coffee for Dad. I thought a little caffeine might do him some good. When I walked in his room with the coffee, he was leaning over the edge of his bed and dry heaving into a large bowl. I guess he'd somehow managed to retrieve the bowl during the night. When he rolled to his back, I noticed that both of his eyes looked like they were bleeding. Oh, and he had a bottle cap stuck to his forehead. And to top it off his left eye was swollen shut and turning from fuchsia to a fine brawler black. He was going to be sporting one heck of a shiner.

"Morning Dad, would you like a little hair of the dog that bit you in your coffee?"

He immediately rolled back over the bowl and retched. He waved his hand at me and made it painfully clear that he didn't want any coffee. From what I could see Dad wasn't getting out of bed any time too soon. So I left him there in his misery and went out and sat on the back porch with Maggie. Dad had told me last night that we were in for a cold spell and there was definitely a winter chill in the air. But the air was crisp and clean, and the sky was clear and bright.

By the time I finished Dad's coffee, I had no complaints. I got up to get another cup of coffee and Maggie took off across the yard. I had removed the temporary fence in the backyard so that Maggie would have free range. I wanted to be darn sure she could get away if somebody meant to do her harm. I told Dad I was going to take down the fence hoping he might say something about who attacked him, but no such luck. He just said that the fence shouldn't have gone up in the first place. He reminded me of the fact that there are no fences in Crestfield.

In any case Maggie was thrilled to be able to once again explore the backyards of all the neighbors. And after what had happened to Dad, I don't think the neighbors minded one little bit. Mr. Hopkins told me he was more than happy to have a non-stop security guard watching out for him. He said nobody should ever be fenced in. _I wonder if Cole Porter was from the Midwest._

Maggie ran back to me as I sat in peace and reported no bad guys in the neighborhood. So we went on back in the house. I wanted to make sure Dad was ok so I peeked into his room. He was snoring like a crosscut saw, so I left him alone. Some wounds take more time to heal than others, and hangovers are one of those wounds.

After I made sure Maggie had plenty of food and water, I drove home and got cleaned up and went to the diner. I walked in and said hello to Mary. *Her hair was black.* I was hungry and ordered the works. When Mary walked away, I looked down at the newspaper that was sitting on my table. It was turned to the back page. In bold print the headline read: **Wild night at the Alibi.**

Under the headline there was a picture of the dance floor in the Alibi. There looked to be at least fifty people in the picture. And smack dab in the middle of the people was Dad tap dancing his legs off. I started to read the article when somebody with a hoarse voice said boo as they tapped me on the shoulder.

"Morning Ricky."

"Mornin' Junior, how's Fred Astaire doin' today?" He asked in good fun.

"Not so great. When I asked him if he wanted some coffee this morning, he puked. And he's got the makings of one heck of a black eye."

Ricky snorted and said, "Man, your dad was crazy last night. I'll bet he could have broken the world tap dancing record. How much did he have to drink?"

"He only drank a pint and a half of whiskey and three pitchers of beer."

"Only? Junior, if I drank that much I'd be out of commission for a week. Wow, your dad must feel horrible today."

"Yes, he does. But he did get Tommy out of the bar and that's what we set out to do. So all in all I'd say the mission was a success."

"I think you're right. You know I just saw Ajax over at the station and he said Tommy's going to take this week off. I guess he needs a little time to get himself right and standing up straight, if you know what I mean."

"Well, that's a funny way of putting it, but I do know what you mean. I guess we can handle things for a week or so, can't we?"

"Sure we can," Ricky said as he sat down. "Junior, did you hear about the phone call that Randi got last night?"

"No, I didn't. Don't tell me the maniac called again."

"Nope, but some guy from the state police did. And you won't believe what he told Randi."

"Ok Ricky, I can see that you're dying to tell me, so spit it out."

"Ok, this big shot captain was wondering if we'd seen or heard from officer Dumbrowski. Said the guy's been missing for a week now."

"Who's Dumbrowski?" I asked.

"Why Junior, I'm surprised at you. He's the Lieutenant Tommy told us was going to take over the investigation if we didn't start making some progress. Don't you remember?"

"Yes, now I remember. Gee-whiz, this is not good. Ricky, you don't suppose…"

"Yes Junior, I do. In fact, I'd bet my bottom dollar that the feet we found belong to this Dumbrowski guy. Maybe he was on to our perps and got a little too close. Kinda creepy isn't it."

"Yeah, it sure is. Did this captain say anything else?"

"No, Randi tried to get some more information out of the guy, but he was tight-lipped after she told him about the feet."

"She told him about the feet?"

"She sure did. What was she supposed to do?"

"I don't know. I guess she thought the state already knew about the feet. Isn't reporting stuff like that the job of the coroner or the medical examiner or… Gosh, this is awful."

"You know something, Junior? The state is bound to put two and two together. And when they do, they're gonna be breathing down our necks."

"Ricky, we need to let Ajax know about all of this. He's gonna take some heat for us not being able to find these people."

"Ajax already knows. Randi told him about it this morning. And after she told him, he ran back to his office. Can you imagine what the state is thinking about Crestfield right about now? I know one thing, it ain't good. And that's for sure."

"Ricky, for the life of me I can't figure out how the bad guys are moving around without being noticed. It's just not possible. What are they, spooks or something?"

"I don't know Junior, but now that you mentioned spooks, what are you gonna dress up as for Halloween?"

"Well, Dad said I was the Tin Man in his dream, so I guess that's what I'll be, how about you?"

"Your dad was right on about all the characters in his dream. So Randi is gonna be a witch, but a good one of course. And I guess I'll be the Scarecrow. I tried to talk Matt and Shadow into being flying monkeys, but they said they were gonna be busy Halloween night. Ajax told them he's gonna pay 'em time and a half to keep an eye out for the bad guys."

"That doesn't mean they can't dress up. Heck, I think it'd be fun if everyone in the department dressed up for Halloween."

"You're right, Junior. I'll ask them again, but it would help if you asked them too."

"Yeah, I'll talk to them today. I'll tell 'em that if they dressed up, they'd be able to move around without being noticed. It's Halloween."

"That'd be great, Junior. You know it won't take much to make Shadow look like a monkey. He's already about halfway there."

"Oh Ricky, you're so funny. How do you come up with stuff like that? Can you imagine me telling Shadow he looks like a monkey? He'd have a fit."

"That'd be two fits. He already had one when I told him he looked like a monkey."

"Geez Ricky, you're too much."

Mary walked up and politely asked Ricky what he wanted for breakfast. You could tell she was still waiting for him to get back at her for the bad things she'd said about him. Ricky was real calm and collected and told Mary what he wanted. He was exceptionally polite which I could see made Mary even more nervous. Ricky laughed when she walked away. We ate and then headed over to the station.

About noon I drove over to see how Dad was getting along. He never knew I was there. I quietly left him alone so he could sleep off his hangy. I went back to the station and rode around on patrol with Ricky. All was calm in Crestfield.

After work, I drove to Dad's house and he was finally up and moving about. That is if you can call sitting in his chair moving about.

"Hey Dad, it's good to see you're out of bed. I was getting a little worried about you. You ok?"

"I suppose I'm ok, but I'm a little confused about a couple of things."

"What are you confused about?"

"For one, how'd I get home? And two, do I have a black eye? It sure feels that way."

"I drove you home and yes you have the beginnings of a shiner. And I think it's gonna be a doozy. Hold on I'll get you some ice," I said as I walked over to the freezer.

I pulled the ice tray out and cracked it over the sink. I grabbed a dish towel and threw the ice in it. I wet it down a little and when I laid it on Dad's eye, he winced and pushed it away.

"Dad, you have to hold this on your eye."

"Ok, ouch that hurts. Junior, how'd I get the black eye?"

"Don't you remember the fist fight you got into last night?"

"No, I don't. Who was I fighting with? And what were we fighting about?"

"Well, you were dancing with this guy's girlfriend, and I think you got a little fresh with her. Anyway, her boyfriend took exception and the next thing I know the two of you were dookin' it out right in the middle of the dance floor. He was from outa town and didn't know you were blind. But don't worry, Dad, you got in a couple of good ones."

"I was dancing?"

"Yeah you were. You danced the whole night with every gal in the bar. Don't you remember?"

"Um, yeah, maybe. Junior, why did you let me drink so much?"

"Dad, I didn't let you do anything. You demanded."

"Oh yeah, did Tommy go home?"

"Yep, Ajax drove him home last night."

"Ajax was there?"

"Ok Dad, that's enough of the questions for now. Is there anything I can do for you?"

240

"Yeah, can you take the vice off of my head? It's killin' me."

"How about I get you some Alka Seltzer?"

"Would you please? Mercy my head feels like hammered baloney. I haven't felt this way since..."

Dad started crying and I figured it might do him some good to get it out, so I let him.

"Dad, if it makes you feel any better. You did a wonderful thing getting Tommy out of the bar. Thanks to you he's gonna come back to work."

Dad stopped crying, but he didn't say anything more. He just sat in his dark little world and fell asleep. His ice pack fell on the floor. So I picked it up and put it in the freezer. I was going to make something for dinner when Madison walked through the front door. She had one of those looks on her face.

"Hi Madison."

"Don't you hi me. Junior, you must be an idiot, because only an idiot would let a blind man get drunk and act like a fool in public. Why did you let Dad do that?"

"Madison, I didn't let Dad do anything, he demanded. Ricky called and told me Tommy was in the Alibi and really drunk. So Dad says I have to take him because he's the only one who knows how to get Tommy out of the bar. And if not for Dad, Tommy might still be there."

She just stared at me. I must have confused her when I brought up Tommy. She continued to stare at me so I went through the entire story from the beginning. I started with the night at Burt's house and how Tommy felt responsible for what had happened to Burt. Eventually she says, "And what about the fight last night, Junior? How could you let a blind man, a blind man that just happens to be your dad, get into a fist fight?"

I didn't say anything.

"Answer me!" she screamed.

"He did pretty good," I said in defense.

"Oh yeah, I can see by that black eye how *well* he did."

I started to ask her to leave me alone, but I didn't have to. Dad woke up and did it for me.

"Madison, for Christ's sake can you please lower your voice about a hundred decibels. And stop giving it to Junior.

241

The entire idea was mine and mine alone. So mind your own business and you won't be mindin' mine."

"Dad, I'm sorry. And I know your intentions were good and all, but you just got the stitches plucked out of your head and a new front tooth and then you go back for more. What's wrong with you?"

"There's nothing wrong with me that a good night's sleep won't cure. So please drop it."

"Ok Dad, I'm sorry for caring about you."

She huffed out to her car and Dad waved his hand for me to go get her. I chased after her and caught her as she stood next to her car.

"Madison, please don't go. I promise to never let Dad get drunk or fight again. Or at least I will try not to ever let it happen again."

"Junior, it's ok, I understand. And I wasn't leaving. I was just coming out here to get the chicken noodle soup I made for Dad."

"Oh, here let me help you."

We went back in the house and I got Dad the Alka Seltzer. Madison went straight into the kitchen and warmed up the soup for the three of us. At first Dad balked at the idea of eating, but he finally gave in. And after he got a little soup down, I'd say by his reaction that he felt better.

"Dang it, that's good soup, Madison. You know I feel like I could go another ten rounds. Junior, go get my gloves out of the garage."

Madison and I gave Dad a courtesy laugh and just shook our heads. Sometimes I wonder if it's all just an act. Nah...

Trick or treat   38

***Junior*/The big day arrived** and the whole town was ready for some fun. I had Dad dressed in some boxing shorts and a bath robe. And with his old boxing gloves on and the massive black eye he was in perfect character. Randi pieced together the costumes for Ricky and me. And I have to admit that we looked an awful lot like the Scarecrow and Tin Man. Dad handed out the candy to the screaming kids. I hid behind the door and as the kids walked up, I told Dad what they were dressed as. He complimented every little ghost, pirate, and hobo on their costumes. Maggie stood next to Dad and as each group came shouting trick or treat, she would bark. Her bark kinda cooled their jets and forced them to stick out their bags in a more orderly fashion.

The good witches, Madison and Randi, came by and helped Dad hand out candy for a while. We had a blast. But the highlight of the evening was when the flying monkeys, Matt and Shadow, stopped by. They crouched on the porch with their paper mache wings proudly displayed. And as they silently swayed from side to side, they chomped on candied popcorn balls and stared at the frightened trick or treaters.

Shadow was especially convincing and I think he resented it when a couple of excited kids ran and told their friends that they saw a real monkey at Dad's house. The evening flew by as did Matt and Shadow. They had rounds to make and I think it was a nice community touch to have them riding around town in costume. The kids continued coming by in droves. Some were on their second and third time to Dad's house. They were obviously stocking up on the Necco's, Red Hots, mini Abba-Zabas, wax teeth, and candy cigarettes that Dad was handing out.

Our last group of kids came to the front door at about nine o'clock. There was a little girl in the bunch dressed as Raggedy Anne. She had a cast on her left leg and walked on crutches. She wore an exceptionally sad painted face and when she stuck out her bag, Maggie began to growl. I put a handful of candy in her bag and told her not to be afraid. She didn't say a word and paid no attention to Maggie. She just turned and ambled out to the street. As I shut the door, her mother came into view.

She was dressed as a witch, broomstick, pointy hat, tattered ankle length black dress and all.

Maggie continued to growl as I watched them slowly amble away. I figured Maggie was growling at the witch and Raggedy Anne because she was tired of all the trick or treaters, I know I was. And when they were gone, she immediately stopped growling and started begging. Maggie knew that the kids had been given treats and I think she wanted some treats of her own. Dad keeps a box of Milk-Bones in the kitchen cupboard and I decided she had done a good job keeping the kids in line and deserved a treat or two. I gave her two.

Dad and I had both fallen asleep listening to the T.V. So when the phone rang, I jumped up in a daze. I looked at the kitchen clock on my way to answer the phone. It was three o'clock in the morning. I picked up the phone after the fourth ring and quietly said, "Hello."

"Junior! Junior! We have shots fired out at the Thornton farm."

"Young lady, stop screaming at me. Who is this?"

"It's me, Ricky."

"Oh, you sound just like a girl when you scream."

"Shut up Junior, and get yourself dressed. I'll be by to pick you up in about one minute."

I ran to the spare room and grabbed my holster and revolver. As I threw on my jacket, a thousand scenarios arced through my head. I ran outside and stopped for about five seconds. Then I ran back inside to get Maggie. When I got inside, I stopped again and said out loud, *it could be a trick to get me to leave Dad alone.* I was just about to call Tommy when I saw the lights on Ricky's roller come flashing up Dad's drive.

"Maggie, you stay here and watch over Dad."

She barked and I knew she would. I ran out to the car and jumped in.

"Ricky, did Billy or Nel call you?"

"No, Matt did. He says Shadow is pinned down behind a tree and taking fire from several places. Matt tried to get to Shadow, but when he did, he caught a bullet to his right thigh. He told me he's bleeding something awful. I called the Sheriff's office for back up and they said they'd call for an ambulance. Put your seat belt on because I'm gonna drive as fast as this damn car will allow."

As we raced west across Townline, I tried calling Matt on the CB, he wasn't answering. Ricky mashed the accelerator to the floor when we started heading north on 25. I leaned over and looked at the speedometer; the needle was pinned on the one hundred. I was going to quietly holler something but managed not to.

When we got close to the Thornton farm, I turned off the siren and tried to reach Matt one more time, still no answer. Ricky didn't slow down one little bit and drove right by the house and headed east. I knew that he was going straight out to Billy's mobile home, but we needed to be careful.

"Ricky, we can't just go barreling into Billy's carport. We need to stop before we get there and assess the situation."

"Assess my ass. We gotta get our guys out of there."

"Ricky, we won't be able to help them if we get shot along the way. Now when we get to that old watering trough, you need to stop."

"Junior, I can't stop."

"Ricky, you are going to stop and that's an order!"

He looked me in the eye and then slammed on the brakes.

"Thanks Ricky. Now listen, when we get to that clump of trees where the trough is, we'll head north and go about halfway to his mobile home. Then we'll stop and try to figure out where Matt and Shadow are. Ok?"

"Yeah, ok."

"Did Matt tell you where he was?"

"He just said he was close enough to where he could see a light on in Billy's place. That's all I remember."

"And his radio was working then?"

"Yes, of course it was."

We drove through the clump of trees and got to a point where we could just barely see Billy's place and stopped. I picked up the microphone to use our loudspeaker and Ricky says, "It's broke Junior."

"That's just great. Ok, give me the keys. I'm gonna go back and get the blow horn. Grab the rifle and be ready to cover me. Can you turn off the overhead lamp? I don't need to advertise the fact that I'm getting out."

Ricky turned off the overhead light and I slowly opened the door. I got out and ran in a crouch to the back of the car. I opened the trunk and grabbed the blow horn and when I reached up to close the trunk, a bullet pinged off it. Then Ricky let loose with a six-round volley. I left the trunk lid up and ran back and jumped in the car.

"Ricky! Stop shooting. You might hit Matt or Shadow."

"No I won't. If you look to your left about forty yards, you'll see Matt's patrol car."

I did and he was right.

"Ok, then what were you shooting at?"

"I saw the muzzle flash. It came from the right rear of Billy's truck. I know Matt's in his car and it can't be Shadow that fired, he wouldn't shoot at us. It has to be one of the bad guys."

"You're probably right. Thanks for covering me, Ricky."

"Anytime - pardner."

Just then our radio squawked. I knew it just had to be Matt. I picked it up and answered, "Crestfield police."

"Junior, it's me Sheriff Shelby. We're to the east of you guys. There's an old Chevy pickup parked here, could belong to the perps. Our car can't make it across these fields so my deputy and I are going to come in on foot, any special instructions? Over."

"Just go slow and be careful. Oh, and that truck definitely belongs to one of our bad guys. Is anybody else coming out? Over."

"Yeah, Randi and Tommy are on their way. And the ambulance is waiting at the Thornton house. They have orders not to drive into a skirmish, over."

"Ok, good deal. Listen, at least one of the two bad guys has a rifle. So stay down and be careful, over and out."

I got the blowhorn ready and rolled my window down.

"This is the police. You're surrounded. Drop your weapons and come out."

Immediately after I said come out, our car was hit several times. All was very quiet for a moment before someone yelled, "You can kiss my ass."

"Ok, Ricky it doesn't sound like they're coming out any time soon. While it's still dark, one of us needs to get over to Matt."

"I'll go Junior. I told him I'd come and get him out and I gotta keep my word."

"Ok Ricky, here's the plan. I'm gonna open my door and then jump in the back seat and open that door too. I'll have more cover that way. I'll count to three and start shooting. You take off when you hear three. Ok."

"Ok, gotchya."

I opened the passenger side door and it was immediately hit with two rounds of fire. Then I jumped in the back and opened that door, nothing happened. I figured maybe they couldn't see the door open because of the front door.

"Ok Ricky, hand me the rifle." He did. "Ok, I'm gonna count to three, you ready?"

"Yeah, I'm ready."

I stuck the barrel of the rifle out the window and counted to three and started shooting at the right side of Billy's truck. The bad guys returned fire, but they only got off a few rounds before I heard one of them yell, "I'm hit."

Then someone from behind me yelled, "Stop, stop. Don't shoot, you're hitting my truck."

I turned around ready to shoot when Billy stuck his head around the rear of the car.

"Billy, what the heck are you doing? How'd you get back there? I mean where were you? Never mind. I'm gonna count to three and fire a couple rounds. When you hear me start shooting, go around and jump in the driver side. The door is open. Are you ready?"

"Yes, just don't shoot my truck, ok?"

"Billy, just get your ass in the car when I start shooting."

I counted to three again and fired at the bad guys. This time a barrage of bullets came my way and hit the front door. I guess the bad guys weren't that hurt. Billy was now on the floor of the car on the driver's side. I looked over the seat at him and then out of the corner of my eye I saw a cloud of dust and dirt kick up. It was Matt's car. The car was rockin' and rollin' heading straight west over the bare cornfield. I don't know why, but I had a good feeling run through me at that point. The bad guys fired a couple of rounds at Ricky, but it was pointless. He'd made a great move and was out of their reach now. I just hoped that Matt was ok.

"Billy, where are your parents?"

"I woke up when I heard voices outside my workshop. I knew it was Benny and David. So I called mom and told her to get the heck out of the house. I took off running and they started shooting at me. Then somebody started shooting at them. I guess it was Matt and Shadow. I've seen them watching the farm for a couple of weeks now. Why have they been here?"

"Never mind why. They saved your butt and you know it."

"Yeah, I suppose you're right. What are we gonna do now?"

"We're going to find Shadow, that's what we're gonna do."

"Shadow's over behind those two trees. He's only about forty yards from my truck."

I looked to the east and the sun was just beginning to come up. And for the first time I could see Shadow. He was slumped down behind the trees. I grabbed the blowhorn.

"This is your last warning. We have the entire farm surrounded. Drop your weapons and come out with your hands up."

"Go to hell," was all I heard.

Then Shadow yelled, "You shot me you son of a bitch. Come out and the two of us will settle this right now."

I watched Shadow stand up. He still had his paper mache wings on. He yelled, "Come out you coward, now it's just you and me."

I grabbed the blowhorn and yelled, "Shadow, get down! We have them surrounded. We can wait them out. Get down!"

"I'm not waiting for anybody, he shot me."

Then from behind Billy's truck somebody yelled, "Yeah, and I'm gonna shoot you again. I'm coming out."

Over and over I yelled for Shadow to get down, but it was no use. He came out from behind the tree and started walking towards Billy's truck. Then for the first time I saw the big guy. He stood up and started walking towards Shadow. Shadow had both hands securely on his forty-five and was pulling the trigger in rhythm with each of his steps.

The big guy had his rifle slung down at his waist like Chuck Connors as he slowly walked towards Shadow. He was cocking the rifle and pulling the trigger as he walked.

The big guy was the first to be knocked down, but he got right back up. They continued firing for another five steps or so as they walked towards each other. Then the big guy took two in succession to the upper torso and staggered. And as he collapsed, Shadow fell forward. I ran as fast as I could to Shadow and knelt down beside him and turned him over. His eyes were open, but they were just staring into space. I put my hand on his chest and felt it rise and fall, he was breathing.

I looked over at the big guy and he was reaching for his rifle. I ran over and kicked the rifle away from him. When I got down next to him, he exhaled one time and then didn't move. I felt for a pulse, there was none. Sheriff Shelby and his deputy walked up as I knelt over the big guy and the Sheriff asked if we had both men. In my haste to get to Shadow I'd forgotten about Perry Smith. I started to ask if they'd seen him on their way in, but the Sheriff answered before I could even ask the question.

"No, we didn't see anybody. And there is no way he could have gotten by us."

Sheriff Shelby and his deputy searched the mobile home for Perry Smith while I did my best to stop Shadow from bleeding to death. I could see an entry wound on his chest and one near his hip. A minute or so later the Sheriff walked back and shook his head no.

"I guess he's not here. Billy Thornton told me he heard two people talking last night. So the second person, who I believe is Perry Smith, must have taken off before we arrived," I said.

I sat there with Shadow and did my best to keep the bleeding to a minimum. When the paramedics arrived, they tore off his wings and quickly loaded him on a gurney and into the ambulance. He was still very much alive when they drove away. Tommy and Randi pulled up right after the ambulance left. Tommy told me he'd take over if I wanted to go see about Shadow. When I walked to my car, Billy was still hiding on the floor. I told him to get out and was just about to tell him he had a lot of questions to answer when Tommy grabbed him by the collar and walked him back to the carport.

I drove like Ricky all the way back to town. I parked the car on the street and ran through the front doors of the hospital to the nurses' station and asked where Shadow was.

"Officer Bose is in surgery and I don't know when he'll come out. I'm terribly sorry, but it could be hours before we know anything more. However, you can see officer Healey. He was just taken to room twenty," she said as she pointed down the hall.

I walked down the hall and into room twenty. Ricky was sitting at the side of Matt's bed. He had his hands covering his face and didn't see me come in. I put my hand on his shoulder and when he looked up, there was one tear sitting just under his left eye.

"You doin' ok, partner?"

"Yeah, I suppose so. Poor Matt, he suffered for a long time. The doctor told me losing the circulation of blood and oxygen to a limb is one of the most painful things a person can go through. Matt has already gone through enough pain in his life. You know Junior I love it during the summer when Matt wears that leopard-skin bathing suit out to the pool. It's so great when he does those swan dives, and the kids callin' him Tarzan. What would we do without Matt? Poor Matt and Shadow had no idea what they were getting into." Ricky stopped reminiscing and stared at me. "Junior, where is Shadow? Didn't he come with you?"

I really didn't know how to explain what happened to Shadow. So I just said, "He's in surgery."

"What do you mean he's in surgery? What happened?"

"Ricky, it's not a long story, but it is kinda complicated. But basically Shadow just walked straight to that big guy and shot him dead. Only problem is the big guy shot Shadow a couple of times too."

"What? Are you serious?"

"Yes Ricky, I'm dead serious."

"Why would Shadow do something like that?'

"I don't know, Ricky. But I do know that Shadow had already been shot by this guy. So I guess he was pissed and wanted to inflict some payback. The whole darn thing is just crazy."

"Junior, what about Perry? Where is he? Did you get him?"

"Nope, don't know how he got out of there or where he went. But we'll find him pretty soon. He can't have gone very far because he had no wheels. He left his truck behind. Ricky, I'm pooped and I'm sure you are too. Do you want to take a break? I'll stay here with Matt."

"No, I'm fine and I want to be here when Matt wakes up."

"Ok, well, I'm going to go sit out in that little courtyard for a while. Come get me if you hear anything about Shadow."

I walked down the hall and looked into the courtyard. I guess I was hoping to see Jenny. She wasn't there. I sat and slowly but surely became agitated. Why? I don't know. So I got up and walked out the front of the hospital and sat down on that old familiar wooden bench.

I sat there for a minute or so before I fell asleep. I was immediately in one of my mean dreams. I was back in that tunnel of light and all the trick or treaters were yelling at me. They paraded by me and as they did, they pointed and stuck their tongues out. When I tried to grab them, they jumped up in a huge tree. They were sitting side-by-side on a husky limb and staring down at me.

Then Raggedy Anne and the Witch sauntered by and stopped directly in front of the tree. The Witch waved her broomstick in the air a couple of times and it lit up in a ball of evil flames. She floated over to the tree and set it on fire. I wanted to help the kids, but the big hands held me back. Raggedy Anne walked by and her miserable frown turned upside down into a wicked smile.

The big hands finally let go of me and gathered all the children out of the tree. I was relieved until the big hands put me up in the tree. And as the fire raged closer and closer, all the children laughed harder and harder. My clothes started to burn and then someone started violently shaking the branch I was sitting on back and forth.

"Junior! Junior! Wake up, it's me, Randi. Please wake up."

I woke up flailing my arms and gasping for air.

"Junior, what in the world are you doing out here?"

"I don't know. I mean Shadow is going to be in surgery for a long time. I guess I just got flustered and decided to come out here and get some fresh air. Whoa, that was a mean dream. Randi, did you find out anything new at the Thornton farm?"

"No, we don't know where Perry went or for that matter how he got away without being seen. And Billy says he doesn't know where his parents are either. We did find two sets of footprints coming in from that old Chevy truck of Smith's. So we know which way they came into the property, but there aren't any prints leading back out. It's a mystery."

"Sis, let's walk back inside. I want to call Dad and make sure he and Maggie are ok."

"Junior, I just talked to Dad and he's fine. He said not to worry, just find those jerks that hurt him."

"What! Dad said something about the guys that hurt him?"

"He sure did. I guess the news about the shootout shook something loose in his brain. Either that or he just decided to talk about it, doesn't really matter one way or the other. Junior, guess what else Dad told me?"

"What? What did he tell you?"

"Dad just told me no more than five minutes ago that one of the guy's names is Benny. He said the big guy that attacked him never said his name but that he had a bit of a southern twang when he spoke. Dad says Benny did talk and if he can hear our Benny say a few words, he'll be able to identify him for sure."

"Oh man, we gotta find Benny or Perry or whoever the heck he is. And we gotta find him fast. Does Tommy know about all of this?"

"Yeah, I told him, but he didn't sound that convinced. I can't figure Tommy out lately."

"Well, he's never really thought it was Perry. But in any case I know he'll still want to find Perry, that's for darn sure."

Randi and I walked back in the hospital and went straight to Matt's room. Ricky was still sitting next to the bed. Randi nearly knocked Ricky over when she ran and hugged him. I decided that it'd be ok if I waited outside for a few minutes.

I grabbed one of the chairs in the room and carried it out and sat down. I was sitting there worrying about Shadow when my cousin Wally walked by.

"Hello Junior - sure is good to see you."

"Hi Wally, how you doin'?"

"Why I'm doin' just fine, thanks. Say, I heard Jack has made a full recovery. That's just wonderful. I think somebody must have been watching over him."

"You know something Wally, I think you could be right. Listen, have you seen the nurse named Jenny in the hospital lately?"

"Can't say that I have. As a matter of fact, I'm not sure I've ever met her, but there are a lot of nurses that work here. Why's that Junior?"

"Well, you said somebody must have been watching over Dad. Oh never mind."

Wally turned and looked down the hall a couple of times before he said, "Well, I'd like to stay and chat for a while Junior, but I've got a lot of work to do. So, if you'll excuse me, I'll leave you alone."

"Ok, I'll see ya, Wally."

I opened up my notebook and started writing down everything that had happened in the last twenty-four hours. I was right in the middle of the showdown between Shadow and David Daniels when somebody walked up and stood in front of me. I looked up and it was Wally.

"Wally, is something wrong?"

"No, nothing is wrong. I was just wondering if you ever caught that big guy that I saw sitting by the elevators."

"What guy is that Wally? My mind is a little fuzzy right now."

"I'm talking about the big guy that sat in the chair that made the dog bark so loud."

Then it hit me like a ton of bricks.

"Wally, you saw the guy, didn't you?"

"I sure did. Saw him a couple of times. Why, is it important?"

"Listen Wally; if I showed you a photograph of that guy, do you think you could identify him? I mean pick him out in a group of let's say six men."

"Yes, I believe so. Sure I could. I've got his face stamped right here in my mind's eye. Yep, I see a lot of folks every day. And when I see someone more than once, well, they're kinda stuck in my mind forever."

"Oh that's great, Wally. If you can identify him, this will once again be a safe and peaceful town. I'll be in touch."

"Sure thing Junior, I'd do almost anything to help out the folks here in Crestfield. Bye now," Wally said as he went back to work.

I sat there for another minute or so thinking about all of this being over with. Then suddenly I heard Ricky yell, "That's great. Are you sure, Randi?"

I went in Matt's room and asked what was going on. Then Randi explained that she'd told Ricky about Dad's memory coming back. Then I told 'em all about Wally identifying the big guy he saw that night by the elevators. We were in awfully good spirits when a doctor we didn't recognize came into the room.

"Hello, I'm Doctor Robert Kuhl," he said as he shook our hands.

"How's Shadow?" I asked.

"Officer Bose suffered one potentially life ending gunshot wound to the upper chest and one very serious wound to his abdomen. We've extricated all the slugs and have the bleeding stopped. It's really quite amazing that all of the bullets missed vital organs, but he's not out of the woods just yet. The bullet that entered through his back has caused some severe damage and will require constant care, possibly for the rest of his life. Only time will tell."

"Doctor Kuhl, did you say he was shot in the back?" I asked.

"Yes, you didn't know that?" he asked in genuine surprise.

"No, I didn't know that. I watched the whole thing happen. There was nobody behind him. This is crazy," I said.

"Well, I'm sorry, but the bullet did enter his back and it glanced off of his spine and lodged between the ninth and tenth ribs. Whether or not he has permanent damage remains to be seen. He is a fighter, that's for sure. And that may prove to be his crowning point of recovery. As things stand, I believe he has full movement of his extremities. I see no signs of paralysis, but things can change."

"Doctor, Shadow did say that he'd been shot before he received the other wounds. Is there any way for you to tell which wound or wounds occurred first?"

254

"I'm sorry, there may have been before he was closed up. But I don't believe so now. There are a few things I can check on if you'd like?"

"Well, if it's not too much trouble. I'd sure like to know when he was shot in the back."

"I'll do what I can. Officer Bose has been taken to room thirty. Bye."

He walked away, and I was so confused I couldn't stand still.

"Junior, what's wrong. Why does it matter when he was shot or where for that matter? The doctor said they've removed the bullets and stopped the bleeding. And most importantly, Shadow is still alive. Junior, please. You've got to learn to relax. Come on, let it go this time," Randi begged.

"Yeah, ok," was all I said.

I walked down to my Dad's old room and once again hoped that Jenny would be there. When I walked in the room there were a lot of nurses, but none of them was Jenny. Shadow had more tubes in more places than I thought was possible.

I stood there knowing there wasn't a thing I could do but wait and see. It was kinda like Dad all over again. I found out later that Matt was unconscious when Ricky got to him. Ricky tied his belt above the wound on Matt's leg to stop the bleeding. The theory is, lose a limb to save a life. Well, Ricky's fast thinking didn't just save Matt's leg; it probably saved Matt's life. I believe with all my heart that Matt, Ricky, and Shadow each deserve a medal for their extraordinary bravery. And I knew the one person that could make that happen.

Junior/**For the next three days** the crime scene at the Thornton farm was searched with a fine-tooth comb. Eventually we found Perry Smith's footprints leading out of the farm. He'd taken off somewhere during the night and headed straight north. In the beginning our thinking was he'd definitely head east back to his truck. So going north threw us off his trail. We reasoned that someone must have picked him up. So Tommy contacted the girlfriend in Illinois, but she had an airtight alibi as to her whereabouts on Halloween. We were stumped.

Matt was released from the hospital three days after the shootout. He was able to walk from the wooden bench to his car. Shadow regained consciousness a day after surgery and told us he'd been shot soon after he first confronted David Daniels and Perry Smith. He said he did have his back to them as he ran to the trees, but believes that he'd already taken the bullet to his hip. In the end we figured he was alive and that was all that really mattered. All three slugs removed from Shadow's body were immediately sent to the state criminal investigations lab.

We hoped that one of the slugs removed from Shadow would match one of the slugs recovered at the Reed farm after Marjorie was shot. They told us to give them a few weeks and they'd have an answer. In the meantime, Dad gave a recorded statement concerning the day he was attacked. He confirmed that there were two men that attacked him. One was very big and spoke with a southern twang. And that the smaller man named Benny had an unusually high-pitched voice.

My cousin, Wally Ramsbottom, was taken to the Liberty County Morgue to identify Daniels. Wally was emphatic that David Daniels was not the man he'd seen in the hospital. He said his hair was much too dark. That caused a mass of confusion. We were all sure we had the right guy. Then photos from prison were retrieved and when Wally looked at the photos, he made a positive identification. Turns out Daniels had dyed his hair dark brown just prior to the shootout. Remember, he and Perry Smith were on the lamb.

Shadow was released from the hospital on Thanksgiving Day. And one week later a public ceremony led by the Mayor of Crestfield was held on the steps of the courthouse. Matt, Shadow, and Ricky were honored for their bravery.

The next day a very large picture of them receiving their awards was on the front page of the Canon. Along with their picture Helen wrote an impressive editorial detailing the events of that harrowing Halloween night. Two days after the awards ceremony Tommy received news from the state criminal investigations lab confirming that one of the slugs recovered on the Reed farm did in fact match one of the slugs taken from Shadow's body. It was concluded that either Perry Smith and/or David Daniels had to have been involved in both crimes. An APB was immediately issued for the apprehension and arrest of Perry Benjamin Smith.

Madison/**After the story** about the town's three heroes was in the paper, a sense of calm filled the air in Crestfield. I think the hustle and bustle of the holidays also helped everyone forget the tragedies we'd been through. Buck and Dezi came rolling into town on the train a week before Christmas. And for the next two weeks it seemed as though we did nothing but eat, drink, and be merry. The entire police force and my family celebrated New Year's Eve at my house. It was an unusually joyous occasion. Probably due to the fact that everyone, except Tommy, started the evening with a Blue Cheer, Dezi's little blue bomb disguised as an innocent beverage.

We played every card game known to man that night. I believe it's a Midwestern tradition or something like that. Playing cards in our family is begun as soon as a child can hold a few cards in their diminutive hands. After the card games were over and done with, we all stood in front of the television and watched the ball drop in Times Square. When the clock struck twelve, fireworks and shouting could be heard from one end of town to the other. In my house hugs and well-wishes abounded and raw emotions were shared by all as we sang Auld Lang Syne. At twelve-thirty Junior and Ricky had to leave the party due to a disturbance over on the south side of town. They soon returned with a bagful of firecrackers and every person at the party proceeded to blow off each and every one of them. I participated in the fireworks with blissful abandon and blurry eyes. We have a family rule that I insist upon. That is, nobody leaves our New Year's party by themselves. So two by two I hugged my guests as they departed. I was feeling no pain and quite cheerful when my head finally hit the pillow.

The first day of the New Year came in with a gigantic bang; at least it did in my head. I had the hangover from hell and an empty punch bowl to prove it. When I got up out of bed, I shivered something awful. I turned my television on and cranked the dial to the weather channel. It was minus seven degrees out. I turned the heat up and jumped back in bed. I slept for most of the day and sometime later I dragged myself out of bed, got dressed, and went to Dad's to watch football with the guys.

Crestfield

A sad mood prevailed as Indiana lost to USC in the Rose Bowl. Some guy named OJ was named player of the game. After a hot toddy and eating enough homemade fudge and pumpkin pie for three people, I drove home and jumped back into bed. My headache was gone when I woke up the next morning, but my heart was filled with pain. It was once again time for Dezi and Buck to leave. We all met at the diner for breakfast, but this time before we finished eating, Junior went out and started his police cruiser and turned up the heat. There was no way we were going to walk to the train station in this freezing weather. We hopped in the car, three in the front and three in the back. Randi sobbed all the way to the station. And as the train pulled out of sight, I held on to Randi with all my might. Junior and Dad just stood there flapping their arms.

Junior/**The New Year,** as Madison said, came in with a bang, but soon turned very sour. Tommy was admitted to the hospital on the fifth of January for alcohol poisoning. A day later he was transferred to the Clarinda Cove chemical dependency treatment center. Tommy fought everyone that tried to help him in the treatment center and due to his denial and raw behavior, he wasn't released until the end of February. When a person struggles with alcohol addiction, their entire family usually struggles along with them. The bitterly cold weather in January along with Tommy's battle with his demons made it seem like the earth stood still.

There was one day of excitement for most of the folks living in the middle of the country. Our vastly superior Green Bay Packers beat the Oakland Raiders in Super Bowl II. But after that Sunday, the doldrums continued. Then on the last day of the month Dad and I decided to drive down to Clarinda and see Tommy and Madison. We sat in the recreation hall with Tommy for quite a while. He was in good spirits as he sat and pet Maggie. I know he wanted to come home something awful. But his doctor said no.

We talked about almost everything except Tommy getting out of the center. He just wasn't ready to admit that he was an alcoholic. I was tired of talking about the weather. And I knew the one thing Tommy never takes for granted is work. I had a question in my head about work that I wanted to ask Tommy, so I did.

"Tommy, I hate to bring up work, but there's a question that has been burning a hole in my head." He didn't say anything. "Ok, well, I know a slug taken from Shadow's body and a slug found at the Reed farm matched, they came from the same rifle. But I also know that neither of those slugs came from the rifle that Daniels used at the Thornton farm, which we found out was actually Billy's rifle. So I was wondering if you had a take on how that could happen."

"Yeah, that has bothered me too. And I believe there are only two ways of explaining that. One, Perry took the gun that does match with him. Two, there is a third person involved."

"I don't believe that's possible."

"Junior I don't either, but that's how I see it. And until we find Perry and that gun, there is still the chance that our maniac is out there somewhere planning his next move."

"I didn't want to say it, but that has crossed my mind. It's an unsettling thought and we really can't be sure 'til we find that jerk, Perry."

Dad sat there listening and didn't offer up an opinion, which is a bit unusual.

"Jack, I know you've been asked this before, but are you sure you'll be able to identify this Benny guy just by listening to his voice?" Tommy asked.

"Absolutely, he had a real nasally voice. Almost like there was something wrong with him or maybe he was sick. I don't know which one, but I could pick that voice out of a thousand voices. That's for damn sure," Dad confidently said.

"Don't worry, Junior. Perry is going to make a mistake somewhere down the line and we'll get him," Tommy said.

"Yeah, I believe you're right. Listen, Tommy, we're gonna go—"

"Junior, you don't have to explain. I know you want to see Madison while you're here. So go on, I'm fine. I'll be out of here and back to work before you know it. Thanks for coming out to visit." Tommy said as he turned to Dad.

"Jack, why didn't you come watch the Super Bowl with me?" Tommy asked.

Dad squirmed in his seat.

"I'm just kidding. I know you wanted to drink a beer or two while you watched the game. I did too, but I don't now. And that's a wonderful thing," Tommy said.

"You're right. I should have come out here, Tommy. I'm sorry, but I'm not completely at fault. I mean I couldn't have driven down here myself," Dad said as he turned to me.

"You guys go ahead and visit with Madison," Tommy said with a smile.

Dad patted Tommy on the back just before we walked away and said, "Tommy, I know you want out of here, and I believe you will be out of here very soon. But you have to fight this demon with everything you've got. You hear me, you've got to fight."

I looked back and waved to Tommy as we walked away. And I could tell he knew that he had said the exact same thing to Dad right after Dad was attacked.

Dad and I walked down the hall towards Madison's office.

"Dad, did you hear Tommy talk to you that day in the kitchen after you'd been attacked?"

"Of course I did. What do I look like? Wait, on second thought, don't answer that."

We got to Madison's office and the door was shut. I knocked and she said, "Who is it?"

"It's Maggie," I said as Maggie barked.

Madison came flying out of her office and ran straight to Maggie.

"Thanks for coming to see me, girl. I've missed you the last couple of weeks. Have you been taking good care of Dad?"

Maggie barked again.

"Madison, did you forget that we're here?" Dad asked.

"No Dad, I didn't. Come here and give me a hug."

Dad and I gave Madison a hug at the same time.

"What's new, Maddi? Are you staying busy?" I asked.

"Junior, January is the busiest time of the year for me. The holidays absolutely destroy some people. The highs they experience during the holidays are many times matched by the lows that follow. And the depression some are left with can be overwhelming. And just so you know, people in my profession are not immune to these feelings. But I'm happy right now and so I'm going to fly with it."

"That's good," Dad said as he fumbled to find a chair. "Say Madison, I heard about five seconds of something on the radio today that has me puzzled. What is an offensive tit? I mean, I've never run into a tit that wasn't nice to me."

Madison and I just looked at each other.

"I'll answer that. Dad, there's no such thing as an offensive tit," I said.

"I didn't think so," Dad answered back.

"Dad, what you heard is the Tet Offensive. Tet is New Year's in Vietnam. There's been a bunch of surprise attacks by the Viet Cong. We were supposed to be in a ceasefire, and we the public were led to believe that the communists couldn't put together such a massive force. Anyway, it's awful over there right now. Gosh, I hope Buck quits with the helicopter stuff. I don't want him going to war."

Dad didn't say anything, he didn't have to. The look on his face said it all.

"Ok, I'm not going to let that war ruin our time together. How would you guys like to go down and have a late lunch in the cafeteria? I'm buying," Madison said.

"Sounds good to me, what do you think, Dad?" I asked.

"I think I hate war and always have. That's what I think," Dad said as he began to cry.

Madison and I just looked at each other. We were caught somewhere between trying to get Dad to stop crying and letting him get it out. I didn't say anything and neither did Madison, and within a minute or so Dad stopped crying. We went ahead and ate in the cafeteria. I didn't care much for the food, but Maggie sure did. Dad and I made sure to thank Madison for the meal when we left.

I headed up highway 71 and then made the change to 34 heading east when Dad says, "Junior, we're heading east now aren't we?"

"Yeah, how'd you know that?"

"I can tell when you change directions. And if you'd take the time to listen, you'd know that 34 is noisier than 71. Anyway, that's not why I asked. I asked because heading east is what I'd like Buck to do. Not the Far East just east and home. So, I want you to promise me you'll call him after you drop Maggie and me off."

"Dad, it's real difficult to get through to him at the barracks. It's not as if he's the only guy there. I mean do you know how many soldiers there must be?"

"Junior, that's why you're gonna call from the station. You can make it sound a little more official."

"Ok Dad, I can see that you're not gonna let this go, are you?"

"Nope, I'm not."

"You tell him I said for him to get the hell out of those helicopters and that's an order!"

"Well, I'll do my best Dad, but the army doesn't let civilians give them orders."

"Damn it, just do what I asked."

"Gosh, ok I will."

I dropped Dad off at home and drove up to the station. I hadn't heard my dad use that tone of voice in a long time, maybe never. He sounded like he was frightened or something. When I walked in the station, I headed straight to Randi.

"Listen Randi, I've got to ask you to do me a favor."

"No Junior, I'm not gonna find you a date. Last time I did that—"

"Randi! Stop it. Listen, ok you don't have to do me a favor. But would you do Dad a favor?"

"Of course I would, what is it?"

"He wants you to get a hold of Buck and he means right now today."

"Junior, it's hard to get him on the phone. Last time they only let me leave a message. They said he'd call when he had a chance."

"Sis, I know it's hard, but Dad sounded so upset or well, maybe even frightened."

"Dad sounded frightened?"

"Yes Randi, he did."

"Ok, what is it you want me to tell him?"

"Nothing, just give me the phone when you reach him."

"Okie-dokie, but it could be a while."

"Thanks sis. I'll be in my office."

I went in my office so that I could go over my notebook one last time. My gut told me there was something wrong, but up to this point I had not been able to figure out what that was. I started with the Billy interview. I read it and re-read it at least three times and nothing. I was just about to go through the interview again when Randi yelled, "Junior, I've got Buck on the phone. Hurry, he just told me he's being transferred."

I raced over and picked up the phone.

"Hello Buck."

"Yeah, it's me. How in the world did you know to call right now?" he asked.

"Never mind that, Randi just said that you said you're being transferred. Is that true?"

"Yes, that's why I'm here in the main office. I just got my orders to go overseas."

"Oh no, you're going to Nam."

"No Junior, I'm going to Germany."

I put the phone down by my thigh and bent over and sighed in relief. I could hear Buck yelling, "Junior! Are you still there?"

I picked up the phone and said, "Yes I'm still here. Oh man that's great news, how'd that happen?"

"Well, when I got back after Christmas, they told me that I was going to start training as a gunner. I couldn't see any future in being a gunner. So, I said I'd like to learn how to be an air traffic controller. Long story short, that's what I'm gonna do now. And the training for that is in Germany. Junior, isn't it strange that a person can fly west to go to the east. Sure glad I'm not going west to Nam."

All I could think of at that moment was to cheer. And I yelled, "Yahoo! Oh Buck, you don't know how happy this makes me. And Dad is going to be thrilled."

"Listen Junior, I have to let you go. The commanding officer and the private that handed me the phone are giving me strange looks. I'll call you when I get to Germany, bye."

I said goodbye, but I think he'd already hung up. I held onto the phone so that I could call Dad with the good news when the phone rang. Gosh, I hate it when that happens. I lifted the phone to my ear and said, "Crestfield police, how can I help you?"

"Hello, young man. I didn't think you'd answer. Guess I got lucky."

"Hello, I'm sorry, who is this?" I asked.

"Why, it's me, Hank Bodine."

"Oh hello Hank, what can I do for you?"

"Well, something has been bothering me since I spoke to y'all that morning. And I finally decided I'd better call and explain what that is." I didn't say anything.

"Ok, well, do you remember me saying that Billy was home all three days I was there in Crestfield?"

"Yes," I said with a question mark behind it.

"Well, I wasn't exactly correct when I said that. You see, the first night I was there I called and called, but Billy never answered. When I drove out to his place the next day, he was washing down the back of his flatbed truck. Said he must have slept through my calls. Something didn't feel right. That's about it."

"Hank, what didn't feel right?"

"I can't put my finger on it, but something wasn't right. I guess you'll have to figure that part out for yourself."

"Hank, you have no idea how much I appreciate you calling. Thank you so much."

"I just thought y'all oughta know. And you're certainly welcome, young man. Ok, well, I'll talk at ya later, bye-bye."

I hung up the phone and said to myself, *that's strike one Billy*. I went back and opened up my notebook and went about searching through it with a whole new perspective. All I had to do was concentrate on Billy. I started with the day at his home and there was just nothing there. Then I read the notes I'd taken after he showed up that rainy night at my apartment, and there it was. It had been staring me in the face this whole time and I said to myself, *that's strike two Billy*. Then I picked up the Miller Hagen file and looked at what he said were rectangle footprints.

And that's strike three.

I grabbed my heavy service jacket and gloves and asked Randi where Ricky was.

"He's been out on patrol, but he's coming in right now for some hot chocolate. He says the heater isn't working in his roller."

"Ok, I can wait," I said.

Didn't have to wait for more than a half-a-minute or so before Ricky came flapping his arms and walking sideways into the station.

"Hey pardner - how's everything? Sure is cold out there. Thought I was gonna freeze. Oh boy Randi, I can't wait for that hot chocolate," Ricky said as he shivered.

"You're gonna have to drink your hot chocolate while I drive. We're on our way out to Billy's. Ricky, make sure your revolver is loaded. Come on let's go."

"Junior, what' going on?" Randi asked.

"Hopefully nothing, but Billy hasn't told me the whole truth about a couple of things. So, we're just going out there to ask him a few questions."

"Do you want some backup?"

"No, we'll be ok. And besides, I don't think Matt or Shadow ever want to go out there again," I said.

"I meant me, Junior," Randi said in disgust.

"Oh gosh Randi, I'm sorry. I didn't mean it that way. I know you can handle anything out there that we can. I'm just going to ask a few questions. Ok?" I said.

"Ok," Randi said back.

I didn't mean for it to happen, but I could tell that Randi's feelings had been hurt. Ricky and I walked out the door and headed towards my car when Ricky says, "If I had just made an ass out of myself, I'd go back in and give her a hug. Because I know if I didn't give her a hug I'd pay for it ten times over."

"Oh, so now you're an expert on women, are you?"

"Junior, getting mad at me isn't gonna help matters."

"Gosh! All right," I said before I walked back inside.

"Randi, listen - I really am sorry. I didn't mean anything by what I said."

"I know that, Junior. Why'd you come back in here?"

"Uh, I came back in to apologize."

"You didn't need to do that," she said.

I gave her a big hug and as I walked out she said, "Junior, I know how you are. Don't you dare trust that club foot Billy for even a second. He'll turn on ya."

I waved my hand and nodded ok. When I got in the car, Ricky says, "Don't you feel better now that you apologized?"

"Ricky, I made a trip in there for nothing. She wasn't even mad."

"Oh Junior, have you got a lot to learn. You don't know about the opposite rule yet, do you?"

"What opposite rule?" I asked.

"Ok, now listen carefully. When a female says something she really means just the opposite. For example, when you went in there Randi wasn't gonna admit that she got her feelings hurt. That would indicate that she is weak. And she's never gonna admit that, unless of course it's part of the opposite rule. She'd rather confuse you and let you think she was ok with everything from the very beginning."

"Maybe she was."

"Oh Junior, you don't know about the maybe rule either. Do you?"

"What?"

"Junior, there is no maybe in the female vernacular. She is or she isn't, period! Man, you gotta lot to learn. If a female says maybe we could go get a frosty after dinner, it means

267

we're gonna go get a frosty, period! And if we don't go get a frosty, you're not just gonna be sorry, you're gonna wish you were never born."

"What if the maybe is part of the opposite rule? What if she really didn't want a frosty in the first place? And she was just saying that to see what you'd say. Can't the opposite rule and the maybe rule run into each other sometimes?"

"Maybe?"

"You know what, Ricky?"

"What?"

"Just be quiet for a little bit and listen. Billy told me that rainy night he showed up at my apartment that he knew Dad had what he called a guard dog."

"Well, that would be an easy mistake to make. She is kind of a guard dog."

"Ricky, when did you, Dad, and I go pick up Maggie?"

"Oh, I'd say a little over a year ago. Why?"

"Well, the first time I went out to see Billy at his place he told me he hadn't left the farm for over two years. So how could he have known about Maggie?"

"I don't know. Maybe somebody told him about her. Crestfield is a small town."

"Yeah, well, did you tell him about Maggie?"

"No, of course not."

"Then who did?"

"Maybe his mom or Dad told him."

"Yeah, maybe, but I don't believe so."

"Junior, you can't do anything unless you know for sure."

"That's not all there is to it. I got a call today from a guy in Texas that bought a couple of saddles from Billy. And he told me there's every chance that Billy wasn't home the night Miller's cow was cut up. So, we're gonna go see what Billy says about that night."

"Don't get me wrong, Junior. There's nothing I'd rather do than put that little club foot rapist back in prison."

"Ok, I'm gonna go inside Billy's place and check on a few things. You're gonna look over the bed of his truck and see if there's anything that looks like blood. Check underneath and between the slats. Ok?"

"Sure thing, and then what?"

268

"We'll cross that bridge when we get there."

We turned off the highway and headed towards the Thornton farm. I drove in real slow and easy, I kept going right past the house. We got to the old watering trough and as I drove up the little road to Billy's, I reminded Ricky to switch the safety off on his gun. I wasn't taking any chances. We pulled up behind his truck and stopped.

"Ok Ricky, stay in the car until I go in the mobile home. Then start checking the truck."

"Gotchya."

I knocked on Billy's door, he didn't answer. So I turned the knob and went in. I hollered hello several times, still no answer. I went down into his work room. He wasn't there either. So I started searching at a fevered pace. I checked his workbench, his toolbox, I checked every inch of his closet, nothing. So I walked out back and started looking around. There was a dumpster full of cut leather. I began pulling leather out hand over fist when I happened onto Shadow's flying-monkey wings. When I picked the wings up, I saw four wooden handles worn smooth from use. They had been taken off the trowels that lay next to them. Each trowel had leather straps fashioned tight around them to secure the persons feet. I picked them up and turned to go show them to Ricky. Billy stood in my way, with one eye closed as he sighted down his Grandpa Thornton's A H Fox shotgun; the end of the barrel was inches from my nose.

"Junior, you do realize that I can't let you leave the farm with those."

"Billy, you told me that the firing-pins had been removed from that shotgun."

"Yeah, well, I lied. Sometimes you're just a little too trusting, Junior."

"Maybe, ok what now, Billy?"

"Now, you're gonna drop those trowels."

I dropped all four of them.

"Now real slow like take that 38 out of its holster and drop it on the ground."

I took out the gun and dropped it on the ground.

"Now back up," he said as he thrust the shotgun towards my face.

I backed up and he moved over and kicked the gun away from us.

"Billy, how'd you know I was coming?"

"Hank called to let me know he'd called you. Said it was the fair thing to do, and I agreed. Problem is, I didn't have enough time to get rid of the trowels, too bad for you. Ok, we need to go out and stop your idiot partner from doing something stupid. You know, like shooting me."

"No way around it, he had me. I decided to stall him for as long as I could. Maybe Ricky would come and get the jump on him.

"So tell me, Billy. The trowels were a great idea. How'd you think that up?"

"Junior, I know you're trying to stall, but I'm gonna answer the question. You know, set your mind at ease before I shoot you."

"Let me explain," I said.

"Ok, go for it."

"You didn't put the trowels on your feet to disguise the size or style of shoes you wear. You put them on to disguise the way you walk."

"Clever idea, wasn't it, Junior," he said as he puffed out his chest.

"Yeah, I suppose so. There are four trowels, so who has been helping you all this time? I mean you didn't get that cow off Miller's farm by yourself."

"Shadow killed my partner. But don't worry, after I take care of you and Ricky, I'm gonna get Shadow too. In fact, I'm gonna get all of you."

"All of who?"

"Never you mind, just keep your hands up. Now start walking and don't do anything stupid. I guarantee you this old shotgun will take your head clean off."

I started walking through the workroom and up into the living room. My mind kept telling me to take a chance and jump sideways or maybe yell. But I knew all that would probably do is make Ricky come running into a shotgun. We walked through the living room and when I walked out the front door, Ricky said, "Junior, I found what looks to be blood underneath the flatbed. Junior, why do you have your hands up like that?"

Billy was right behind me and at the top of his lungs yelled, "Ricky, you dumb son of a bitch. Take that gun off your hip and throw it under the truck."

Ricky froze.

Billy screamed at the top of his lungs, "Now! I said. Or I'm gonna blow your partner away."

Ricky still hesitated.

"Ricky, you'd better do what Billy says."

Ricky slowly took his revolver out of the holster and threw it towards the right rear tire.

"Junior, keep walking all the way over to Ricky. And when you get there, don't turn around or I'll shoot you in the back."

I started walking again and when I got to Ricky, I stopped.

"Now turn around, Ricky," Billy hollered.

The moment Ricky turned, Billy hit him on the back of the head with the butt of the rifle. Ricky crashed face-first in the dirt and didn't move. "Billy, you son of a bitch!"

"Shut up, Junior. Now I'm gonna move back a little and when I do I want you to turn Ricky over on his back."

I heard him shuffle a couple of steps away from me and then I turned Ricky over. I put my hand behind his head and held him. He was bleeding something terrible.

"Now what, you little coward!" I screamed.

"Oh, so now I'm a coward too, huh? We'll see who's a coward. Let go of him and start walking straight south towards the old tree house."

I laid Ricky's head down, got up, and walked straight south. And as I walked I said, "Billy, don't you dare shoot Ricky. You'll never get away with it. Stop and think for a minute. You'll be back in prison before you know it."

"I'm never goin' back to prison, so shut up! This is gonna be self-defense."

I turned just enough to see Billy pick up Ricky's revolver and position it in Ricky's right hand. Billy stood up and grit his teeth before he said, "Ricky, you miserable asshole. You made me spend half of my adult life in prison, and now you're gonna pay."

Billy lifted the shotgun to his chin and then I heard a boom and a loud thud. Billy's shotgun blew a hole in the ground about a foot above Ricky's head. Billy backed up a couple of steps and cocked his head sideways. He gave me the strangest look. I think he was gonna say something but decided not to.

He turned and pointed the shotgun at Ricky again. I heard the second boom as Billy flew back into the tailgate of his truck. The shotgun had been jarred from his hands. I ran and picked up the shotgun and pointed it at Billy's head. I wanted to kill him.

I sighted down the barrel when someone yelled, "Put the gun down! Junior, I said put that gun down!"

I looked behind me and watched Randi walk out from the trees by the old watering trough.

"Junior, put that gun down and take care of Ricky," she hollered as she walked towards me carrying her prized Remington M-40 rifle.

I dropped the shotgun and cradled Ricky's head. He opened his left eye a little and muttered, "What happened?"

"I'll tell ya later, pardner. Right now I gotta get somethin' on the back of that thick skull of yours."

I took out my handkerchief and pressed it to the back of his head. As I held him, I turned and yelled at Randi to call an ambulance. When she was maybe thirty yards from me, she said, "I called an ambulance about five minutes ago. I would've shot Billy then, but you were in the way."

"Sorry about that sis."

"That's ok. You know Junior, I just shot Billy twice with full length thirty-aught-six ammo. How in the world he remained standing after the first shot is one for the books."

"That is strange. Randi I'm glad you're here and all, but you said your feelings weren't hurt?"

"Junior, haven't you ever heard of the opposite rule?"

"Uh, now that you mention it, yes, I have."

Randi looked down at Ricky with a concerned eye before she walked over to Billy. She knelt down and unzipped his jacket and lifted his sweatshirt and looked up at me.

"So that's how he did it. The little shit is wearing a vest."

"What?" I asked.

"He has a bulletproof vest on. How in the heck did he get his hands on a vest? Did he know you were coming?" she asked.

I started to explain but was drowned out by a siren. I turned and watched the ambulance bounce around as it drove into the little shaded area where the old watering trough is. From that point, they turned left and raced north up the narrow path to us and slid to a stop.

Dale Benson flew out of the driver's side and Jim Keuter leaped out of the passenger side. Dale ran to Ricky and Jim ran to Billy. Randi and I got out of their way. Ricky was a little more alert by the time Jim got to him. Ricky blinked a few times before he babbled, "Hey Jim, what are you doin' here?"

"Well Ricky, I'm here to stop the blood from pouring out the back of your head."

"My head's bleeding?" Ricky asked.

"Yes, it is. Junior, can you sit him up for me? I want his head above his feet for a while, thanks," Jim said.

I was holding on to Ricky when Nel rushed by me. She let out a blood curdling scream when she saw Dale pound on Billy's chest. Then Jim told me to hold the compress he'd applied to the back of Ricky's head. He ran over and the two of them started performing CPR on Billy. Jim was doing the chest compressions and Dale was doing the breathing. And about every six breaths Dale would listen for a heartbeat. After about two minutes or so Dale exhorted, "We got him. Whoa! Great job, Jim. Get me the gurney please."

As Dale put an oxygen mask on Billy, Randi and Jim pulled the gurney out of the back of the ambulance. And in a matter of seconds Billy was rolled to the back of the ambulance and lifted in. Dale ran over to me. "Ricky can go with us, but he's gonna have to sit up front with me. Is that ok?"

Randi walked back to me and we looked at each other for a few seconds before Randi said, "Yeah, Ricky will ride with you. Junior and I have a few things to do here. Thank you."

The three of us picked Ricky up and walked him over to the ambulance and lifted him into the passenger side seat. Dale cinched the seatbelt tight around Ricky and then ran around to the driver's side and jumped in. Nel immediately screamed, "I'm going with you!"

"I'm sorry Mrs. Thornton, but you can't go. Jim has to have room to work on your son."

I shut Ricky's door and said, "Go."

Dale whipped the ambulance around a tight half-circle and sped away. I watched the ambulance drive down the little path and then disappear through the trees. I heard the siren start up as they headed out to the highway.

When I turned around, Nel was peering at me with the eyes of an angry tigress. She catapulted over and got in my face and shrieked, "Junior! What happened here? What have you done?"

"Mrs. Thornton, I didn't do anything. Billy was going to kill us. He said so himself. He was only seconds away from shooting Ricky. I'm sorry, but I don't know what else to say."

"Junior, you don't have to say anything, at least not to her," Randi said as the two women's eyes locked onto each other. "Mrs. Thornton, you're going to have to leave the area."

Nel responded by shouting at the top of her lungs, "Leave the area, I own the area!"

"Your son attempted to murder a police officer. This is now a crime scene. I suggest you get a good lawyer," Randi said.

"That's what you say," Nel Thornton said in English just before she began an angry tirade in her native tongue.

"Mrs. Thornton, I don't know what you just said, but you're lucky Billy didn't shoot Ricky. Cuz if he had, I'd of aimed right between his eyes. And I would not have missed," Randi said as she moved towards Nel Thornton.

I stepped between the two of them and then Nel started crying. I reached for my handkerchief, but I'd used it on Ricky. Randi gave me her handkerchief and I handed it to Nel. She stared at Randi before she threw the handkerchief on the ground and walked away.

"Randi, did you have to be so blunt?"

"Look Junior, this was between two women, which is something I doubt you could ever understand. Anyway, I don't believe the acorn fell too far from the tree. There's a witch inside of that woman. You just can't see it through your rose-colored glasses."

I started to walk away when Randi said, "Junior, do you need some help?"

"Yeah, I guess so. We need to search the mobile home, the workshop, and the grounds."

"Yes we do, but first we need a search warrant. Remember the fourth amendment."

"Billy has to be a fourth amendment waiver. I want to find out as much as I can. And I want to find out right now."

274

"Junior, I called Uncle Ajax right after I called for the ambulance. He's on his way. Let's be sure and make this a righteous bust. So please sit down and relax 'til Ajax gets here."

I couldn't sit so I walked to the back of the workshop, picked up my gun, and then trudged around in circles. I felt awful and knew there was something I had to do. I walked back out to the front and gave Randi a big hug.

"Randi, I can't say thank you enough times. You saved Ricky's life and probably mine too. Anyway, thanks."

She didn't say anything. But she did smile. I guess all she needed from the beginning was a hug and a thank you. It took Ajax longer than he thought it would to get a judge to sign the search warrant. When he got to Billy's, the three of us searched high and low but found zilch.

When I say zilch, I mean nothing other than the trowels and the blood on the back of Billy's truck. But those alone were probably going to be enough to send him away for a long, long time. As it turns out, the vest Billy was wearing had Alabama State Police stenciled on it. We had no idea how Billy had gained possession of the vest. But we did know that if not for the vest, he would most certainly have been dead. Billy was to be charged with several crimes, not to mention violating his probation. I'd say a probation violation was probably the least of his worries. The day Billy was declared fit enough to travel he was hauled back to prison.

Ricky and I followed the van that carried Billy all the way to Fort Madison. From there we drove the twenty or so miles south along the Mississippi River to Keokuk.

Junior/**A while back** one of the bad guys called our police station and talked to Randi. A few of the things he said were extremely disturbing. Eventually, the phone company told us the person had called from a phone booth in Keokuk. When I drove up to the phone booth, I wasn't surprised to see it was right in front of a pawn shop. There was a very large sign on top of the building that read, Mostel's Pawn, we'll buy or sell almost anything.

I parked the car in the back of the pawn shop. I saw no reason to advertise our being there. We walked in and a razor thin young man immediately scurried away. We could hear him whispering to someone in the back of the building. A few seconds later a short, balding, middle aged man wearing a wrinkled brown suit slowly walked out to greet us. He didn't wave, Ricky and I did.

"Hello officers. I'm Harvey Mostel, the owner of the store. Is there something I can do for you?" he said with a practiced smile.

"Hi, well, I sure hope so. We've driven a long ways to get here," I said.

"I see," was all he said.

I opened the manila folder I'd brought with me and showed Mr. Mostel a few recent photos of David Daniels.

"I was wondering if you've ever seen this man before,"

He studied the photos for a bit and I could see the recognition written all over his face before he ever said a word.

"Yes, I believe so. He came into my store maybe six months ago," he stopped and scratched his head. "He needed change for the payphone outside," he said as he looked me straight in the eye.

"Six months ago?" I asked.

Mr. Mostel nodded yes.

"Six months ago kinda confuses things. Are you sure this is the same man?" I asked.

"Yes, I'm pretty sure," was all he said.

"How can you be so sure?" I asked.

"I'm sure because he has come in several times since that first time."

"Oh, well, now that makes more sense."

276

I started to ask him about the more recent times that he'd seen Daniels when Ricky interrupted me.

"Say, Mr. Mostel. Would it be ok if I asked you a crazy question?"

Mr. Mostel smiled and said, "I know what the question is young man and the answer is yes."

"Ok smarty pants, what was I going to ask?" Ricky said with a wrinkled brow.

"Young man, you were going to ask me if I am related to the actor, Zero Mostel. And I know because I've been asked that same question a thousand and one times. Yes, he is my first cousin and a very stingy man."

"Wow, you're right. I mean about the person not the stingy part. Say, is that a fake limp or is Zero really crippled or something?" Ricky asked.

"No, it is definitely not a fake limp. Samuel's leg was crushed by a bus. That limp caused him to become very rich and very poor."

"I don't understand. Can you explain?" Ricky asked.

"He is wealthy when it comes to money and very poor when it comes to friends."

"Oh, I think I understand," Ricky said with a scratch of the head.

"Ricky, are you all done interrupting me?" I asked.

"Uh, sure I am. Just pretend I'm not here," Ricky said.

"That's easier said than done," I said as I took out my notebook and turned to Mr. Mostel.

"You were saying that Daniels has come in several times. Do you remember the last time he came in?" I asked.

"Yes, he came in with a little guy just before Halloween."

"Are you sure?" I asked.

"Absolutely, he sold me a beautiful diamond bracelet."

"Can I see this bracelet? If it's the bracelet I'm thinking it is - it's definitely stolen property."

"Young man, I never buy stolen property. He had a receipt and a copy of his great aunt's will. The bracelet was bequeathed to him. I can assure you it's all very legal."

"Ok, well, can I see the bracelet?" I asked.

"I'm sorry, but I sold the bracelet the day after I bought it. I could give you a physical description of the bracelet if you'd like."

"What? Ok, I guess that'll work."

Harvey Mostel walked over to a file cabinet and quickly walked back with a sales receipt. He began reading the receipt, "The bracelet is pure platinum, with what I'm pretty sure are four birthstones surrounded by a sea of exquisitely cut diamonds."

"Mr. Mostel, who did you sell the bracelet to?" I asked.

"A miss Addy Haugen bought the bracelet. I can give you her address, but it's someplace in Mobile, Alabama. There's no phone number."

"Can you describe her?" I asked.

"She was tall, finely dressed, black hair tied in a bun, and she had a soft southern accent. And, I might add, she had a lot of cash."

I looked at the amount she paid for the bracelet and said, *Whoa*, to myself.

"Is there anything else you can tell me about Mr. Daniels?" I asked.

"Well, he didn't go by that name. I believe the little guy with him called him Kaleb. Yes, I'm sure of it. Kaleb is a name you don't often hear."

"What did this little guy look like? I'm sorry, I mean can you describe him for me?"

"Oh, sure I can. He was tiny like a boy but a man. He had fiery-red hair and a little attitude to go with it. And, of course, he had a strange way of walking. He walked with a skip and a hop."

I looked at Ricky right after Mr. Mostel said skip and a hop.

"Well Ricky, I guess our little trip down here was worth it. There can be no doubt now that Billy is the little guy Mr. Mostel is talking about."

Ricky nodded and said, "Yes-siree-bob."

"So Billy wasn't afraid of Perry or Daniels. He was working in concert with them. Um, listen Mr. Mostel, I should tell you that the bracelet was definitely stolen." I showed him the picture of the bracelet Mrs. Silvers had given me. "It's from Saks Fifth Avenue, New York."

Mr. Mostel looked at me and sighed before he yelled, "Son, can you bring me one of the stolen property affidavits. I'm sorry to hear that the bracelet is stolen. Can you please sign the affidavit for me? It's state law."

I said sure as the young man we had seen earlier appeared. I signed the affidavit and as Ricky turned to leave, I stopped him.

"Ricky, is there anything else you'd like to ask Mr. Mostel before we go?"

"Just one thing," Ricky said.

"What's that?" Mr. Mostel asked.

"What's your son's name?"

The boy giggled and offered, "My name is Zero."

The four of us had a good chuckle before Ricky and I walked out the door. As I was driving out of the parking lot, something flashed in my head. I stopped the car right in front of the phone booth.

"Ricky, I have to make a phone call."

I jumped out, ran over to the phone booth, and then I ran straight back and opened Ricky's door.

"Ricky, have you got any change?"

"Sure do. I always carry a few dimes and quarters in my coin purse."

"In what?"

"My coin purse."

He reached in his pocket and pulled out one of those little red football shaped rubber things that elderly people keep their change in.

"Ricky, where did you get that thing?"

"Grandma had an extra one, why?"

"Never mind why. Just give me a couple dimes and quarters, please."

I grabbed the coins out of his hand and hollered thanks as I ran back to the phone booth. I put a dime in and dialed the operator.

"Hello operator. Can you dial Crestfield for me?"

"Yes, that'll be an additional thirty-five cents," she said.

"Ok, thanks."

I put the money in the coin slot and then I gave her the number and waited. It rang about six times and then Dad said, "Hello."

"Hey Dad, it's me, Junior. Listen, I wanted to say I'm sorry about not getting back to you after I talked to Buck. He's–"

"I know what he is, Junior. He called me from Germany. You have no idea how happy and relieved I was when he told me he was not going to be a helicopter pilot. Good thing I didn't hold my thumb to my butt when I was waitin' on you for an answer. It might have grown there."

I heard Dad and Randi laughing.

"It's not that funny, Dad."

"Oh yes it is. Say, where the heck are you? You sound like you're in a damn phone booth."

The operator broke in and said, "You have one minute."

"Dad, I am in a phone booth. I'm in Keokuk, I'll explain later. Are you and Maggie ok?"

"Yes, we're fine. Randi's here and she brought a big gun with her. And Madison will be here any minute. We're gonna call Dezi, it's her birthday. Did you forget?"

"No Dad, that's one of the reasons I called. Can you tell her I said happy birthday."

"I suppose so, but first chance you get you'd better call her yourself."

"Ok Dad, I will. Thanks, tell the girls I said hey. I'll talk at you later. Yeah, ok. Bye."

Ricky and I had at least a five hour drive ahead of us. So I handed him my notebook and asked him to write down whatever we talked about. We started at the very beginning with Miller's farm.

"Ricky, write down the number 1. Ok, we know for sure that Perry Smith was still in prison, so he couldn't've been involved at Miller's farm. And the trowels Billy wore on his feet tell us he was there. And I'd say David Daniels helped him. 2, Dad said there was a big guy and a little guy that attacked him. I was with Billy when Dad was attacked so that leaves Daniels and Perry Smith. 3, Marjorie and Shadow were both shot with the same gun. Billy was with me during the shootout. That means Daniels and/or Smith is responsible. 4, we know that Daniels and Billy were at Burt's house. We know that because Mr. Mostel identified them as the persons who sold him the stolen bracelet. 5, David Daniels sometimes goes by the name Kaleb. And if you put the initials DKD together it fits the 4, 11, 4 that was signed on the note you found on the windshield of your roller. 6, gosh I'm hungry. I think maybe we'll stop in Fairfield. I'd really like a slice or two of pepperoni pizza."

"Junior."

"Yeah, what is it, Ricky?"

"How do you spell pepperoni?"

"Ricky you can stop writing now. Does pizza sound good to you?"

"Um, I think I'd rather have a well-done hamburger."

"Ok, here's what we'll do. Whichever sign we see first, pizza or hamburger, is where we'll go."

"Junior."

"Yeah, what is it?"

"About a mile back I saw a sign for a hamburger joint in Mount Pleasant. Can we stop there?"

"Yeah, I suppose since you saw that one first we can stop there."

"Junior."

"Yeah, what now?"

I looked over at Ricky and he had an unusually serious look on his face.

"Junior, we really gotta find Perry or Benny or whoever the heck he is and that rifle."

Funny, just when I think Ricky's mind is somewhere in outer space, he says something serious and meaningful.

"Yes we do, pardner. Yes we do."

***Junior*/February hung around like a sore toe**. The snow that once covered our little town had all turned to brown sludge and the sky was a mean shade of gray. Most of the folks in Crestfield had decided they'd stay inside 'til spring arrived. I was sitting in my office freezing my rear end off on the morning of February 29th when the phone rang. Randi and Ricky were on patrol, I think. So I answered the phone.

"Crestfield police, how can I help you?"

"You can help me by coming down here and picking me up."

"Tommy, is that you?"

"Sure is, and they're setting me free today."

"Oh, that's great! I'll leave soon as we get off the phone."

"Hold your horses there, Junior. First the doctor wants to talk to you."

"Ok, put him on."

I heard the phone rattle around and then someone with a real husky voice says, "Hello, this is Doctor Essie Davison, to whom am I speaking?"

"Uh, this is officer McCool with the Crestfield police. How can I help you?"

"Officer McCool, you can help by giving me your word that when Tommy leaves here, he will be driven straight home."

"Yes ma'am, of course I will or he will. Yes, we'll go straight home."

"Young man, this is a very serious matter. The first 72 hours after an alcoholic is released are the most critical. He will try to browbeat you into allowing him to drink. He'll come up with every excuse in the world why it's ok. Don't you dare give in. You will in essence have the devil riding in your car. Do you understand me?"

"Yes, I won't let the devil out of the car. And besides it's about ten degrees out right now. Who'd want to get out in this cold?"

"The devil would that's who," the doctor said before the line went dead.

I sat there wondering if I had just dreamt talking to Tommy and his doctor when the phone rang again.

"Uh, hello, Crestfield police, how can I help you?"

282

"Junior, please get down here as fast as you can. I think the doctor is about to do an exorcism on me."

"Ok Tommy, I'll be there as fast as I can."

I threw on my heavy service jacket and grabbed my gloves. I didn't want to go out in this cold, but for Tommy there was nothing that could have stopped me. I was freezing for the first five miles or so. Finally, the heater in the car thawed me out. The drive down to Clarinda Cove usually takes about an hour. But the weather and the traffic were not cooperating. It took nearly half-again as long to make the trip. When I pulled up in front of the main entrance, Tommy was frantically waving to me. He was still wearing his robe, pajamas, and slippers. I drove up and rolled down the window and Tommy ran out the door and yelled, "Get me out of here."

I parked the car and started walking back to the entrance. I'd made it about halfway when I saw two very large male orderlies holding on to Tommy. One looked like Brutus and the other one looked like Bluto. When I walked up to them, Bluto says, "You have to go in and sign before the patient can be released."

"Ok, sure," I complied.

I went in and signed the release form and grabbed the small gym bag Tommy brought with him to Clarinda. We braved our way through a sudden blue northern to the car and the moment Tommy got in he said, "Drive fast."

I got out of there as fast as the car would allow. And as soon as we got onto highway 71, Tommy hollered yahoo.

"Tommy, why do you still have your pajamas on?"

"They take your clothes from you when you get there. And don't give 'em back 'til you're leaving. I guess they've had a couple patients' get dressed and just walk out the front door."

"That wouldn't be good," I agreed.

The roads were slick and the wind and weather were brutally cold. We were coming up to the exchange onto highway 34 when I saw two young men huddled next to the road. I pulled the car over and before I jumped out I said, "Tommy, I promised the doctor that you would not get out of the car. So stay here."

I ran back to the two kids.

"What the heck are you two doing out here? You know you could freeze to death."

The younger looking of the two says, "Our car broke down a mile or so back and my brother is too drunk and sick to walk."

"Come on, help me get him to his feet."

We picked up the brother and pretty much carried him back to the car. I opened the door and we lifted the drunken brother in and shoved him across the seat. He immediately slumped over. His head was jammed tight against the door knob. The other brother jumped in after him and I ran around and got in the car. It was miserably cold out, but the car was toasty. I took off down the highway heading east for Crestfield. I was lookin' in the rearview mirror at the brother that was sitting up and he says, "Thanks officer, I sure was getting worried. We were gonna hitchhike once we got to 34, but my brother just couldn't make it."

"You know the two of you are lucky you didn't turn into popsicles," I said.

"Oh no, we've got enough antifreeze in us to last for a couple days. Would you like a drink?"

Then he pulls a bottle of shine out of his coat pocket and holds it up right in front of Tommy's nose. Tommy started to reach for the bottle, but I grabbed it before he could. I put the brakes on and pulled off the side of the road. I got out and walked to the back of the car and emptied the bottle onto the icy dirt. I was gonna chuck the bottle, but decided I'd better just put it in my pocket. I got back in the car.

"You know that stuff is illegal. Where the heck did you get that liquor?" I asked.

The younger of the two started to answer me when his eyes rolled back. He passed out and slumped against the rear-passenger-side door. When we pulled up to the station, Tommy threw the older brother over his shoulder and carried him in and laid him on one of the beds in our jail. We were about to carry the younger brother in when he woke up and took a swing at me and says, "I can walk my own damn-self inside. Thank you very little."

That did not sit well with Tommy. So he followed the kid all the way to the cell door. Once there, he gave the kid a swift kick to the rear-end and shut the cell door.

284

"Young man, you need a lesson or two on manners."

The kid looks at Tommy and slurs, "You know what you can do with your manners?"

And Tommy says, "No, why don't you tell me."

As the kid lies down on the floor he says, "You can shove 'em…"

Before he could finish the sentence, he put his hands up to his mouth and puked all over the place. Tommy walked back to me and said, "I'm not cleaning that up."

I thought to myself, *neither am I.* I left him there in all his glory. An hour later Randi and Ricky came bopping into the station.

Randi immediately hollered, "What's that smell!"

She walked back to the cell and looked in at our two hoodlums and then she gave me a couple of dirty looks just before she says, "Junior, what is going on?"

Tommy was in his office and I don't think he was coming out any time too soon. So I explained to Ricky and Randi what happened. Randi immediately grabbed a mop and bucket and went in and cleaned the place up. Then she and Ricky dragged a mattress off of the other bed in the cell and put it on the floor. They rolled the younger brother onto the mattress. She grabbed a couple of spare blankets out of our storage closet and threw them over our two drunken delinquents. Then she and Ricky walked into Tommy's office and gave him a hug and told him how nice it was to have him back. Tommy smiled a little, but mostly he just turned red. He was understandably embarrassed.

I asked Tommy if he'd like to go home.

"Yeah, I suppose you'd better drive me home. I'd like to take a long hot shower and get a good night's sleep in my own bed. And before you ask me Junior, no there isn't any alcohol in my house."

"I wasn't going to ask you that. At least I don't think I was. Ok, are you ready to go?"

"Yeah," was all Tommy said.

We walked through the station and just before we stepped outside, Randi asked what she was supposed to do with the two kids when they woke up.

"Nothing, and don't let them leave. I've got a few questions for them, but they can wait 'til morning," Tommy said as we walked out the door.

285

I went home that night and made myself a ham and onion sandwich. I sat in my little kitchen, ate my sandwich, and drank a beer. After I finished eating, I turned the TV on just in time to catch the beginning of Daniel Boone, but I made the mistake of lying down on the divan and before I knew it, I was asleep. When I woke up, Dragnet was on. I'm not crazy about cop shows so I switched the channels and watched Peyton Place for all of about ten minutes. I woke up in the middle of the night, cold and dreary. I turned the TV off and sleep walked to bed.

I woke up bright and early the next day. For whatever reason I didn't have any of my mean dreams that night. I took that as a good omen. I got myself ready for work knowing it was Friday. I thought with Tommy being back I might get the weekend off. I whistled my way through the cold all the way to the diner and had myself a big breakfast. I finished eating and crossed the street to the station with a smile on my face. When I walked in, Tommy was already in his office. I said good morning to Tommy and then someone said, "Good morning, cowgirl. Why don't you let my brother and me out of this cell?"

I'd forgotten about the two kids and I guess Tommy was ignoring them. I walked back to have a look at the younger smart alec brother. He had a grin on his face that made me want to slug him. I looked over at his older brother and he was still sawing logs.

"Don't you ever get tired of trying to be clever?" I asked.

"Heck no, it comes easy for me. Now you, well, I can see that you're wrapped up just a little too tight to be clever. You need to chill. Maybe stick your head in a bucket of ice water for an hour or two."

He got a good laugh out of that one. I walked over and got right up next to the bars. I was going to tell him to shut up, but when I got there, the fresh smell of alcohol hit me right in the face.

"Hey, you've got another bottle in there, don't you?"

And the kid says, "Yeah, what of it, cowgirl."

"Hand it over, and right now!" I demanded.

"Why don't you come in here and get it."

I got the keys and started to open the door when Tommy took the keys out of my hand and says, "Kid, when I come in there, you're gonna be sorry you woke up today."

Tommy unlocked the door and when he opened it, the kid jumped back. And Tommy says, "This is your last chance to give me the liquor. If you don't hand it over, there's a better than average chance that you're going to be needing a dentist. And I mean real soon."

The kid thought about it for a second or two and then reached in his jacket pocket and hands over the bottle of hooch. Tommy looked at the bottle for a long time. I don't think he knew what he was doing, but we sure did. He was licking his lips and shaking. I walked in and slowly took the bottle out of Tommy's hand.

The kid started laughing and says, "We got ourselves a full-blown alcoholic here. Now I know where you two were coming from. That's why you had your pajamas on. You were down at the Looney Bin in Clarinda Cove, weren't you?"

He no sooner got the words out when I took a swing at him. He ducked the punch, stepped back, and started dancing around on his toes like Cassius Clay and says, "You're gonna have to be quicker than that, I'm a bad man."

He took a step towards me when his brother stood up and slugged him hard on the shoulder and says, "Shut up, Greg."

Then the older brother put his hands up, squeezed his temples, and groaned. I thought he was gonna get sick again, but he just lay back down. The smart alec younger brother didn't say a word after that. Tommy stood in the middle of the cell shaking. I thanked the older brother, walked Tommy out, and slammed the cell door shut. Tommy didn't say anything. He just walked back and sat down at his desk. About an hour later Tommy walks in my office and says, "Thanks Junior."

I was going to tell him he didn't have to thank me when he says, "We need to find out who these kids are, where they got that liquor, and then get them home."

"Yeah, you're right. Somebody is going to be out there looking for them. And that somebody is probably worried sick," I said, happy that Tommy had answered the bell.

We walked over and stood in front of the cell door and looked in at the two brothers. They had both nodded off again.

"Ok, time for the two of you to step up and stop acting like a couple of ten-year old's," Tommy said as he raked a tin coffee cup back and forth across the cell door.

The older of the two sat up and said, "Thanks for getting us out of that cold yesterday. I thought we were gonna freeze for sure. If it's ok, I'd like to get word to our mom so she doesn't worry herself sick."

"That's more like it," Tommy said before he turned to me. "Junior, I'll ask the questions. You take a couple notes."

Then Tommy said, "Ok, you can start by telling us what your names are."

"I'm Terry Snyder, and this wisenheimer is my younger brother, Greg Snyder."

"Snyder, *Snyder*... wait a second. Aren't you related to our officer Healey?"

They looked at each other for a second and then Terry says, "Yeah, Matt's our cousin."

"Does Matt know about any of this?"

They looked at each other again and Greg says, "No, can you please not tell him. He'll kick our asses for sure."

"Well maybe you deserve it. Now I know who you are. You live in Albia, don't you?"

"Yeah, you want the address?" Terry asked.

"No, but in a little bit you're gonna give your mother a call so she can come pick you up. Now what in the world were you doing all the way over here?"

"We heard about this gal named Birdie Yashak that sells liquor down in Diagonal. I gave her a call and she says come on down and call me again when you get here. So I find a phone booth and call her. Some guy answers the phone and tells me to go to the water tower at the north end of town and then head south 'til I come to a Schlitz sign. So I drive down to the sign, park the car, and get out and sit on the bench right there on the sidewalk. Then the gal and this guy pull up. The guy gets out and asks me what my name is. I tell him and then he walks back to the car and gets the two bottles of shine. Then the jerk doubled the price on us."

"What was his name?"

"He didn't say, but when Greg heard that the guy doubled the price he got out of our car and went over to tell the guy off. Well, the guy gets out like he's gonna fight Greg and then the girl yells, 'Benny - get back in the car!'"

"What did this Benny look like? Can you describe him?"

"Yeah, he was on the small side. He had bushy brown hair, needs a haircut. He acted real tough too," Terry said.

Then the younger brother Greg says, "The guy kept looking over his shoulder all the time, like somebody was after him or something."

"What were they driving?" Tommy asked with renewed energy.

"She was driving. It was an older model Plymouth or maybe a Dodge. The car was black and really big," Greg said.

"Ok, listen, we need to get the two of you home. So I'm gonna let you call your mom, but before I let you guys out of here, you're gonna call this Birdie gal and ask for some more hooch. Can you do that for us?"

The two brothers looked at each other and in unison nodded their heads yes.

"Good deal. Now, I want to know what you two plan on doing for the rest of your lives. Because if you continue drinking and screwing around, you're gonna be sorry. Trust me I know."

Then the younger brother Greg says, "Terry goes to college and I plan on going to college too."

"You can't get there from here," Tommy said.

"And here I thought I was the only smart alec in the room," Greg said with a cheeky grin.

"Ok, you two follow me into my office so we can call your mom and then Birdie. By the way, what were you doing all the way over on highway 71?"

Greg says, "We couldn't go home drunk. So we decided to drive around and have some fun."

Tommy just sighed. I think he'd done the same thing, and many times. Terry called home and we heard him say hi mom and then we saw him cringe. She was probably giving him heck, and for good reason. She was also probably very happy to hear that the two of them were safe. Terry told her about his car breaking down and assured his mother they were ok. Then he suddenly had a gigantic frown on his face and said bye.

"What happened?" I asked.

"Mom says if we can't fix my car, our Uncle Vertis will have to come get us. He'll kick the crap out of both of us," Terry said.

"Maybe not, I think with some help we can get your car up and running," I said.

"You think so?" Greg asked.

"Sure. And if all goes well, you might end up having a good reason for being here," I said.

Tommy had been standing watching us this whole time and finally he says, "Ok Terry, time to make that call. I want you to sound as relaxed as you can. Don't make any demands. Let them decide when and where you can pick up the liquor. Got it?"

"Yeah, I got it," Terry said as he dialed the number. He sat there hammering his fingers on Tommy's desk and then suddenly he said, "Hello, Birdie. Yeah, hi this is Terry. Ah ha. Yeah, we did. That's some good stuff. No, we feel fine. That's why I called. We'd like to buy some more. Yes, today. No, whenever it's good for you. Sure, anytime. Ok, same place two o'clock. Yep. All right I'll see you then. Ok, bye," he said with a smile as he hung up the phone.

"Well, you heard. Is two ok?" Terry asked.

"That'll work out fine. Thanks Terry, you did a good job." Tommy said as he turned to me.

"Junior, we need to round up a couple of cars that don't have police written on the doors. I'm gonna use your phone to call Ajax. Junior, when Randi comes in, tell her to go back home and change into some civilian clothes. We're gonna need her. She'll be perfect. Benny wouldn't know her from Adam."

Then Greg asked the obvious.

"Say, why do you want this Benny guy so much. I mean you're all frothing at the mouth. What'd he do, steal your mom's panties?"

I looked at Tommy and he shook his head.

"Greg, the truth is we want him because he has the answers to more questions than Carter has pills. And right now that's all I can tell you," I said as Greg looked back at me with the only smiling frown I've ever seen. I turned to Terry.

"Terry, he's you're brother. What does that look on his face mean?" I asked.

"Beats me, but you'd better get used to it. Because he wakes up and goes to sleep with it," Terry said as the smiling frown on Greg's face warped into a smirk.

"Ok, you two listen up. We have to get your car back out on the road. If you drive up in a different car, Birdie and Benny just might take off. So what was wrong with the car?" I asked.

Greg said, "It's your car, Terry. You tell 'em."

"It has needed a new battery and maybe a solenoid and generator for a long time now. When we stopped to take a leak, the doggone car died on us. For the short term I think a jump will do," Terry said as Greg's face bent back to the smiling frown.

"Ok, well, you won't believe this, but I have an uncle named Jump. He works here at the 66 station. I'll give him a call and see if he can't help the city out and get your car back on the road."

Greg shook his head a couple of times and says, "An uncle named Jump, huh? This sure is a strange little town you've got here."

"Not really, but if not for this strange little town, by now the two of you would probably be ice cubes," I said.

Terry said, "He's got a point there, Greg. So do the world a favor and keep your big mouth shut for a while."

"Ok, I'll be quiet right after I get something to eat. I'm starving," Greg said in a rehearsed deadpan voice.

I gave the two of them enough money to go over to the diner and get a good breakfast. Then I called the 66 station and made arrangements with Jump to get Terry's car up and running. When Randi came in, she was delighted that she was gonna get to help grab Perry Benjamin Smith. She raced home and changed into her street clothes. And then she raced back. We ended up driving Ajax's Imperial and Randi's Skylark down to Diagonal.

We met up with Terry and Greg two miles north of town. Terry was driving a faded brown 58 Impala. We all piled in the Imperial to go over the plans. We wanted no mistakes made in capturing our fugitive. Terry and Greg were given strict orders not to get out of the car for any reason. We didn't want 'em getting hurt. And we decided that Ajax's Imperial and little Jax might look out of place in Diagonal. So, against his will, Ajax was told to go home.

Ricky and I hid in the back seat of Terry's Impala. And Tommy drove Randi in her car down to the tavern where the Schlitz sign was and dropped her off. Then he turned around and headed back towards the water tower. When he got to the end of the street, he turned the car around and parked facing the Schlitz sign and waited. At two o'clock Terry drove down the street and parked in the same spot he had the day before. We all sat and waited and waited.

We kept the car running with the heater on. It was bitterly cold out. Two-thirty arrived and still no Benny. We had decided before we came into town that we'd wait 'til three o'clock and if they didn't show, then we'd try to find out where this Birdie gal lived. She wasn't listed in the phone book and when we called the phone company, there was no listing for anyone with the last name of Yashak. At three o'clock I told Terry to go ahead and drive back to Tommy. Just as he was going to pull away from the curb, he looked in the side mirror and says, "Hey, her car is coming down the street right now."

The big black Plymouth drove right in front of us and parked, but nobody got out.

"Terry, what are they doing?" I asked.

"They're not doing anything because there is no they. It's just her. Hey, if she gets out and walks over here, she's gonna see you two back there. What should I do?" he asked.

I didn't get one word out when Greg jumps out of the car and walks over to her.

"Terry, what's he doing?" I asked.

"He's standing there talking to her. Wait a second. Now he's pointing at something? He's pointing at the tavern. Why would he do that?"

Terry watched his brother walk around the car and sit down on the bench.

I said, "What's he doing now?"

"He's sitting on the bench and pointing at the tavern. Benny must be in the tavern."

I started to get up when somebody rapped hard on the passenger side window. Ricky and I looked up at Benny. He was grinning at us. He took off running north towards the water tower. And before we could get out of the car, I heard a gun go pop, pop, and then Randi yelled, "Stop! Police! Stop where you are!"

292

By this time Ricky and I are out of the car and we start to take off up the street when Greg runs into us. Benny kept running and looking back over his shoulder. He was halfway up the street when we watched him run into Tommy's fist. He wilted like a dead flower right there in the middle of the sidewalk. The next thing you know every person in the little town of Diagonal was hovering in a circle around Benny. Ricky, Randi, and I hurried up and pushed through the crowd of people and helped Tommy pick up his handcuffed fugitive. I happened to look back for Terry and his car was gone. We stood in the cold waiting for Terry for a long time, but he was nowhere in sight. As we looked down the road, Perry Smith started screaming, "Let go of me! You piece of crap cop, let go of me!"

He was drowned out by a siren coming full speed from the south towards us. I looked down the street and the Ringgold County Sheriff, Shane Ahrens, was driving hard at us. He came to a screeching halt, jumped out of his car, and turned a full circle while pointing his gun at the crowd and yelled, "Move back, I said move it!"

Tommy ran over waving his hands in the air.

"Hold up there, Shane. You can put your gun away. Everything's under control."

"Yeah, well, it sure as hell doesn't look like it. Tommy, what in the world are you doin' down here anyway? We got several calls saying there had been shots fired in Diagonal."

"I can explain Sheriff, please put the gun away."

Finally, Sheriff Ahrens put the gun back in its holster. And everyone there exhaled. Tommy explained and when he mentioned the APB on Perry Benjamin Smith, the Sheriff understood.

"Tommy, why didn't you let me know you were coming? I could have helped," the Sheriff said out of frustration.

"Shane, I didn't let you know because I couldn't take the chance of Perry seeing you. He would have run for sure."

"Yeah, maybe he would have at that," the Sheriff acknowledged.

I walked over to the Sheriff. "Hi Sheriff, listen do you know where a gal named Birdie Yashak lives?"

He gave me a strange look before he says, "Do you mean Belinda Yashak?"

"Yeah, I guess. We heard that she goes by Birdie," I said.

"Well, matter of fact she just drove by me as I was coming in," he said.

"Where?" I asked?

"Right there," he said as he pointed south down old Route 66.

"Oh no," I said.

"No worries, Junior. She must be heading home. And I know exactly where she lives. Come on - you and Ricky can ride with me," he said as he ran to his car.

"Ok, Randi you drive and I'll keep Mr. Smith quiet," Tommy said.

Before you know it, we were all speeding south down the old highway. We went about five miles when the Sheriff took a hard right down an old gravel road. I looked back and Randi was right on our tail. I thought, *she's gonna be pissed if she has rock dings on her car. Oh well.*

We drove about a quarter of a mile in before we saw Terry's car. He and Greg weren't there. Tommy stayed in the car with Perry while Randi got her sniper rifle out of the trunk.

"Randi, you stay hidden behind the car and if Perry gives you any trouble, shoot him."

Perry looked at Randi, his eyes wide open. "You hear me, Perry?" Tommy said as Perry frantically nodded his head yes. "Ok Randi, keep your eyes on the house. If it looks like we're in trouble and you have a shot, go ahead and take it. Can you do that?" Randi just nodded yes.

The four of us crept up to the house and stormed in through the front door with our guns raised - the house was empty. Sheriff Ahrens quietly said, "Follow me."

We walked out back to an old barn and looked inside. I peered inside and my eyes immediately met Greg's. He was frantically jerking his head towards the back of the barn. We walked around to the rear doors not knowing who or what to expect. There was no one there.

We slowly walked in the barn. Greg and Terry had been tied back to back to the center support post and Terry says, "Man, am I glad to see you guys."

Greg had a huge knot swelling over his right eye. He was frantically trying to tell us something. We couldn't understand a word he said because somebody had covered his mouth with duct tape. I yanked the duct tape off his mouth and he yelled, "Ouch! They went that a'way."

"What do you mean, they?" I asked.

"There are two more guys with the gal. We didn't see 'em when we ran in the house and they got the jump on us," Terry said as he wriggled side to side trying to free himself.

"They got the jump on us my ass. They clubbed me a good one across the eye is what they did!" Greg yelled.

"Imagine that," Tommy said.

When we got them untied, Sheriff Ahrens asked what their attackers were driving.

"They're in a white, four-wheel drive truck. I think it's a Dodge. They headed straight west through that field," Terry said.

"Well, we can't follow them on foot. And our cars will never make it through that field," Sheriff Ahrens said.

"Terry, did either of the guys or the gal have a rifle with them?" Tommy asked.

"No, but they had a pistol. That's what the guy hit Greg with," Terry said.

Tommy turned to Greg and says, "I thought I made it perfectly clear that you were not to get out of the car." Greg started to say something, but Tommy told him to shut up. Then he turned to Terry.

"Terry, why'd you follow that gal? You could have both been killed. How would I have explained that to your mother?" Tommy asked.

Terry didn't answer, but he did turn and stare at Greg. And Greg says, "Ok, I'm the one that drove after the girl. Terry didn't want to."

Visibly frustrated Tommy said, "Greg, do you know what you are?"

And Greg says, "No, but I think you're about to tell me."

And Tommy says, "You are an irresponsible, royal pain in the ass."

And Greg says, "You didn't mean that, you just wanted to say something."

Tommy closed his eyes for a moment and then started mumbling as he walked out of the barn.

We went back to Randi's car and dragged Perry inside the house. We tried everything to get him tell us who the guys with the gal were, but he wasn't talking.

Sheriff Ahrens got on his radio and let the local law enforcement know about the white Dodge truck.

We knew it could be days before we heard anything back on the truck. We searched that house inside and out and found absolutely nothing. No rifle, no liquor, no nothing, but we had Perry, and that was a good thing. Now all we had to do was get Dad to identify Perry as one of his attackers; sounded easy at the time. We said a tension filled goodbye to the Snyder brothers and headed home.

When we got back to the station, we put Perry behind bars and notified the state authorities. Terry and Greg should have been halfway home by this time. So we were a bit surprised when they walked in the station and asked if they could talk to Tommy. I took them into his office and Terry started to say something when Greg says, "Terry, most of this was my fault. So it would probably be a good idea if you let me explain."

Then he moved in front of Tommy's desk and says, "Chief, I want to apologize for all the dumb stuff I said and did. I'm really sorry, and I mean it. I just wanted to help. If there's ever anything my brother and I can do for you guys, just let us know." He hesitated for a moment. I was positive that he was thinking of something clever to say. He sure fooled me.

"This may sound a bit strange, but the funny thing is... I mean the thing is... well, after what we've been through, it kinda feels like we're family now. Anyway, thanks."

Tommy walked around his desk and shook their hands, one at a time of course. I followed suit. Tommy and I walked 'em out to their car and as we waved goodbye, Tommy said, "Junior, does Greg remind you of anybody?"

I thought about it for a second or two.

"Well, now that you mention it he is an awful lot like a combination of Ajax and Dad."

Tommy let loose with one of his rare big smiles and walked back inside. I stood there and smiled because I'd put a finger smack dab on the answer Tommy was looking for.

I stared into the distance and said to myself, *what are the chances of there being anyone else in this world like my uncle and my dad? No really, what are the chances?*

296

Dad identifies our man   44

__Junior__/**Perry Benjamin Smith** made his first smart move as soon as we got him in our cell. He lawyered up. We knew then that it was going to come down to whether or not Dad was given the chance to listen to Perry speak and then positively identify him as being one of the two men that had brutally attacked him. Marcia Wallace, our assistant district attorney got together with Perry Smith's attorney and explained the situation to him. Perry's attorney then made it perfectly clear to Perry that he could prove his innocence just by saying a few words to Dad. And after a couple hours of pondering the situation, Perry Smith finally agreed to say a few words in front of Dad, but only a few.

We brought Dad and Maggie in the station at ten o'clock on Monday morning. And under the scrutiny of Perry's attorney, Miss Wallace, and the entire Crestfield police force, Perry was given a note card with instructions as to what Dad wanted to hear him say. Dad and Maggie were seated right in front of the cell door as Perry prepared to read from his cue card. Miss Wallace gave Perry some preliminary instructions.

And when Perry said he understood, the game was on. Then Miss Wallace said, "Ok, now please read the first line in what you believe to be your everyday true speaking voice."

And Perry said, "My name is Benny."

Dad cocked his head to the side and then he said, "Can he read the line one more time?"

Perry's attorney nodded his head yes to his client and Perry said, "My name is Benny."

Dad cocked his head again. I can only think he wanted to be dead sure about his recollection and the decision he was about to make. Then Perry's attorney asked Dad if he'd like his client to read the next line. Dad said yes. Then Perry said, "Shut up."

Dad immediately requested that Perry yell the two words at the top of his lungs. And then Perry screamed, "Shut up!"

And Dad said, "Yep, I've heard enough. I don't like this guy. Can you get me out of here?"

We walked Dad into Tommy's office and then Perry's attorney came in and says, "This isn't fair. My client tells me he's never seen your dad in his life. And he's never been to his house."

And Marcia Wallace says, "Well, he can say what he likes, but the fact is Mr. McCool has identified him."

Then Dad says, "Yes, I did identify him as someone that I don't especially like. But that's only due to the rotten feeling I get in my gut when he speaks. And that's all there is to it. I did not identify him as one of my attackers, because he's not. I'm sorry for all of your time and trouble, but you have the wrong guy."

Dumbfounded looks filled the room.

"Dad, are you sure? I mean absolutely positive?" I asked.

"Yes Junior, I am. In fact, I have never been surer of anything in my life. He's not the guy. But you didn't need me to tell you that."

"What do you mean?" I asked.

"Maggie pretty much told all of us he wasn't the guy the moment we walked into the building. She will never forget who attacked us. And I can guarantee you if he was one of the guys, she would have done everything possible to get at him. I'm sorry Junior, but he's not the guy."

Perry's attorney walked out of the room and went straight back to his client. We all heard a forceful 'I told you so' screamed from Perry's cell. During the days and weeks leading up to that day we were fairly convinced Perry was our man. Now, well, we were back to square one and there was no hiding our disappointment.

That evening Perry agreed to help us out and answer a few more questions, mind you, under the condition of immunity.

"Perry we know you were still in prison when Miller's cow was killed. Do you know anything about that day or night?" I asked.

"No, I absolutely do not. And why someone would do such a thing is beyond me. I may be many things, but a butcher of animals I'm not!"

"Ok, let's go back to the day my dad was attacked. Where were you that day?" I asked.

"I was in Illinois with my girlfriend. We went to a matinee and watched Cool Hand Luke. I'll bet Peggy still has the tickets."

"Peggy is your girlfriend?" I asked.

"Was my girlfriend, we broke up the day before I was thrown in jail in Osceola. She's the reason I got so drunk."

Tommy looked at me and shrugged his shoulders.

"Perry, we know you were at Billy's the day your friend David Daniels was killed. Why'd you leave?" Tommy asked.

"We were just supposed to give Billy a taste of his own medicine, you know, pay him back for cuttin' off my damn ear. But when David shot those policemen, I decided I didn't want any part of that. So I went in Billy's place and called Birdie. I told her exactly where to pick me up. I walked out the back of his workshop going north and then we headed south to Diagonal. Threw you guys off course, didn't I?"

"Yeah, I guess you did, for a little while anyway," Tommy said as he stopped and thought about his next question. "Ok, who are the two guys that were at Birdie's house?" Tommy asked.

"They're just two locals that were there to buy some liquor. Older one's name is Robert and the younger one is Gene. Not sure about their last name. They're not bad guys. And I'm sure they wouldn't have done anything if they hadn't been spooked by those two crazy kids."

"Who's Birdie?" Tommy asked.

"Just a gal I met. Her dad died recently, and she was broke so we started selling the liquor."

"Who makes the shine?" I asked.

"It's not really shine. We buy some cheap whiskey and soak the labels off. Then we add a little rubbing alcohol and antifreeze. We nearly double our volume and it turns out to be some great hooch."

"Gosh! No wonder those kids got sick. You let 'em drink antifreeze! You should be ashamed of yourself." He didn't bat an eye. "You said we, who exactly is we?" I demanded.

"Hey! You said I didn't have to incriminate anybody. I'm not gonna tell you any more about it."

Perry's attorney gave us a hard look. So I let up on that.

"Ok, I only have a couple more questions. Do you think David Daniels shot and killed the nurse, Marjorie Jessen?"

"No, I know he didn't because he was in jail in Illinois that week."

"There's no middle name on his birth certificate, have you ever heard anybody call him Kaleb?" I asked.

"No, that's crazy. We weren't friends in the joint, but I know everyone called him dirty Dave. Why would anyone call him Kaleb?"

"Just asking that's all. I don't think I have any more questions, how about you, Tommy?"

"Yeah, I do. Perry, have you ever owned a rifle that uses thirty-aught-six ammo?"

"No, as a boy I had an old sixteen-gauge shot gun and a twenty-two rifle. And that's it. Why?" Perry asked.

"No reason, I'm just asking is all. I guess I don't have anything else right now, but if I do, I want your word that you'll help us out," Tommy said as he gave Perry a hard, hard look.

"I said I would, so I will. Are we done here?" Perry said with attitude.

"Hold on for a sec. When did you start using Benny as your first name?" I asked.

"Right after I got sent to the joint." Perry hesitated for a second. "I got tired of everybody calling me Perry-winkle. Ok?" he said with even more attitude.

Tommy looked at me.

"Junior, do you have anything else you want to ask Perry?"

I shook my head no. We were done and we knew it. We were both dead certain now that Perry didn't do any of the things we thought he might have. As far as David Daniels was concerned, we just didn't know.

A picture is worth... **45**

Madison/ The day after Perry Smith was taken back to prison Junior went back to the drawing board, his notebook of course. He read and reread 'til he couldn't see straight. And all he came up with was a great big zero. So he sat with Dad one evening and went over the entire case with him. And after they were done Dad, thought to himself, out loud.

"Junior, you're just plain worn out on this whole thing. You need a fresh start. So I'm gonna suggest that you let someone you trust take a look at your notes. I hear about people in law enforcement hiring consultants all the time. There must be somebody you trust that could just read what you've got and then tell you what they see." Enter me.

I heard the knock on my office door closely followed by the bark that I love.

"Come in, Maggie. And I guess you two enlightened rogues can come with her."

Maggie ran in my office followed closely by Junior and Dad. They tried to hide the mischievous look on their faces.

"Ok, out with it. And I mean right now," I demanded.

"Sis, I was wondering if you would do me a big favor," Junior asked in his little boy voice.

"Maybe, depends on the favor," I said.

"I'd like you to read over my notes and see if you find anything there that I might be missing."

"What notes?"

"The notes I've taken concerning all that's gone on since Miller's cow."

"Junior, are you talking about Dad and Marjorie?"

"Well, yes I suppose. And everything else."

"Those are privileged notes."

"Madison, Junior is just asking you to take a look at his notes, that's all," Dad said.

"I would never let anyone look at my notes," I said.

"Madison, just take a look. Do it for Junior. If you don't say anything to anyone, then nobody has anything to worry about," Dad said.

"Dad, now you're talking in circles," I said.

"Circles? Ok, Junior, let's go," Dad said.

Maggie didn't move a muscle. That is until dad hollered, "Maggie, come here."

Maggie put her head down as she walked away from me. Dad grabbed hold of the harness and started walking at twice his usual speed.

"Ok, tomorrow I have the day off. I'll take a look then, but I'm not making any promises. Now bring Maggie back here right now," I said.

Junior smiled as I watched him relax.

"Junior, I told ya Madison would do almost anything for Maggie and me," Dad boasted.

"Dad, I'm doing this for Junior. And like I said, I'm not making any promises."

"Thanks sis," was all Junior said as he handed me his notebook.

The two of them hung around for the requisite length of time. And then they took off for greener pastures. I was fine with them leaving. It's just that I always want Maggie to stay with me. I love that dog. At twelve o'clock sharp I went to our cafeteria and bought a salad and brought it back to my office. And while I ate, I skimmed over the notes beginning with Miller's cow. That was awful to read. Junior was very detailed in his description of what had been done to that poor little cow.

As I read I noticed Junior used a system of stars and check marks. He'd make a check mark next to things he needed to work on and then after he'd done his research he'd put a star over the check. It seemed like it worked for him, but I'm not sure that's how I'd have gone about it.

Some of Junior's notes were so detailed it was a wonder he had any room left in the little notebook. And then at times it was obvious that he was simply too tired to write. He'd written a lot of cryptic notes about his dreams. They were by far the most interesting, at least to me. The problem was they had little to do with the case itself. And I didn't have time for what were probably just inconsequential utterings. I put the notebook down when I finished eating my salad. I decided that when I got home that evening I'd have another go 'round.

When I finally made it home, I was for whatever reason too tired to make dinner. So I had leftovers. Then I sat down on my sofa, turned on the floor lamp, and started in on Junior's notes. It didn't take long for me to fall asleep at the wheel.

302

I'm sure I would have slept through the night if not for the phone ringing. I got up to answer the phone, but the line was dead. Hearing a phone ring when you're asleep is an unsettling thing for most people, including me. I sat back down and figured since I was wide awake I'd try going over the notes again. This time I went in reverse order. And about ten pages back I found an entry with neither a check nor a star.

I read the entry about three times and decided to give Helen a call at the newspaper. She answered on the first ring.

"Hello Helen, it's me, Madison McCool."

"Hello Madison, how've you been?"

"I'm just fine thanks. Listen Helen, I have something I'd like to find out about, but I can't do it without your help. Do you think you could research something for me?"

"Why sure, if I can that is. How can I help you?"

"My dad thinks he remembers seeing a photo of Burt Silvers and Marjorie Jessen in the paper. Is there any way you can go back and find something like that?"

"Yes, of course there is. We keep everything on microfiche, but it would sure help if you could give me a date range."

"Well, that's going to be a problem, because I have no idea when this could have taken place. But we might be able to narrow things down a bit. When did Burt move to Crestfield?"

"Gosh Madison, I think he'd just graduated from high school when he and his mom moved here. That would be nearly twenty years ago."

"Ok, well, let's narrow it down a little more. When did he take control of the paper?"

"His mother bought the paper for him right after he graduated from Drake. Can you hold on a minute, Madison? I think he left a copy of his degree in his desk. I'll go take a look. Hang on, I'll be right back."

I sat and twiddled as the anticipation was building. I thought to myself, *detective work is actually kinda fun.* Then Helen came back to the phone.

"Sorry Madison, he must have taken it with him that last time he came by. Listen, I'll go back as far as it takes. I know a couple different ways to do this. Maybe I'll get lucky and find the picture right away. That is if there is one."

"Helen you're going to think I'm a dolt, but I just realized that my dad said he saw the picture. So it had to be sometime before he lost his sight."

"Gosh Madison, I'm really sorry. This must bring up some bad memories for you. When did your dad lose his eyesight?"

"He lost his sight early October 57."

"Well, that will certainly narrow things down. If there's a picture, I can almost guarantee you I'll find it. Madison, I'll start looking right now."

"That'd be great. Please give me a call if and when you find it. Ok, thanks. Goodbye."

Helen also said goodbye and I hung up the phone and thought *it's nearly time for bed. I should have said goodnight.* I sat back down and opened Junior's notebook. But I didn't read because I now realized why Junior hadn't done anything about the picture Dad said he saw. He knew that it was so long ago it couldn't possibly have any bearing on the here and now.

I sat staring into space. I was just too tired to continue. I set the notebook down on the arm of the couch and got myself ready for bed. The moment my head hit the pillow I was catapulted into a dream about a witch and a tree full of mean little children. And the witch was going to light the tree on fire. There was no way I was going to let her harm those children. I took off running towards the witch when Junior grabbed me by the arm and yelled, "Madison, what are you doing in my dream? I can take care of myself. Get out!"

The dream took a big turn at that point. Junior and I were now stuck up in the tree and looking down at the children, and the witch of course. She lit the tree on fire and as the smoke billowed up in my face, I screamed for help.

No one came. Then Junior grabbed my hand and said, "Sis, get ready to jump."

We hit the ground with a loud bang and then another. The second bang woke me. I lay in bed for a few moments before I realized the banging was someone at my front door. I threw on my robe, jumped into my slippers, and hurried out to the living room.

I looked through the window. It was my best friend from high school, Jan Hughes. I opened the door.

"Jan, is everything ok?"

"Yes, I'm sorry I knocked so loud. I thought maybe you were in the shower or something."

"No, but I was just about to make some coffee. I lied. Would you like some?"

"Oh yes, that'd be nice. Listen Maddi, I can come back another time if you'd like."

"No, please sit down. When I saw you outside the store, I told you to come by any time. And I'm off today so... Jan it's ok, let me get the coffee started."

I got a pot of coffee started and went back and sat down with Jan.

"Jan, I don't want to hurry you or dissuade you from whatever it is you have to say. So why don't we just get started?"

"Madison, you always were one to get right to the point. Ok, then that's what I'll do. I haven't spoken to you for all these years because Ray asked me not to."

"Your husband Ray?" I asked in surprise.

"Yes, my Ray. Or I should say my soon to be ex-Ray. That's kind of funny. I never thought about how that'd sound, you know ex-Ray."

"Jan, why didn't Ray want you to talk to me?"

"He didn't want me to talk to you because he didn't want me to tell you the ugly truth."

"Jan please, what is the ugly truth?"

"When you and Ray were going out in high school, he was also seeing me."

Jan stopped talking and began to cry. I walked out to the kitchen and grabbed a napkin; it was all I had at the moment. When I gave it to her, she looked at me and cried even harder. I was about to go get her a tissue from the bathroom when the phone rang.

"Excuse me Jan - I need to get the phone."

She just waved at me to go ahead. I answered the phone and the coffee pot started whistling and Jan cried harder.

"Hello. Oh, hi Helen. Can you hold on a second? I've got to get the coffee off the stove."

"Ouch. Helen, I didn't expect to hear from you so soon."

"Madison, are you home alone?"

"No, Jan Hughes is here. Why?"

"Never mind, Madison I found the picture. And it's not a good thing. The picture is Burt taking a statement from Marjorie and Becky."

"About what?" I asked.

"About Billy Thornton."

"Oh no - Helen you said Becky, Becky who?"

"Miller's wife Becky," she said.

"Oh no."

"Oh yes. The picture was taken a week after Billy Thornton was sent to prison for attempting to rape Jolene Meadows. Anyway, Marjorie said some awful things about Billy and his family."

"Helen, what did Becky say?" I asked.

"That's the tragic part, Madison. Becky didn't say one word."

I stood there silent for a few moments digesting what Helen had just told me.

"You mean to tell me that Miller's cow was killed just because his wife was in a picture with Marjorie?"

"Yes, it looks that way; guilt by association. Madison, there's more and it has to do with your dad. Might be the reason for..."

"What? Why would Marjorie talking to Burt have anything to do with my dad?"

"It has to do with your dad because during the interview Marjorie quoted your dad."

"Oh no - What'd she say that my dad said?"

"Marjorie said that your dad was speaking about Billy Thornton when he said, 'Only a worm from hell would do something so heinous and cowardly.' "

"Oh dear god," I said.

"Madison, Billy Thornton was in prison, but someone close to him must have run your mom and dad off the road that night."

"Helen, it would destroy my dad if he found out. We can never say a word about any of this. Now promise me you won't reveal any of what we've discussed to anyone - ever!"

Helen didn't respond.

"Helen, you won't like what I do if you don't promise me right this very second. Helen, tell me you will keep your mouth shut. Now promise!"

"Ok Madison, I promise. But this would be the biggest story I've ever had to write about."

"Helen, you won't be able to write or tell anyone anything when I get through with you. Do you understand that people's lives may be at stake?"

"Yes, I'm sorry Madison, but there's more to what I've already told you. There's a man in the background of the picture. And he has the most evil look on his face."

"Helen, can you describe this man?"

"That part of the picture is blurry. The man is way in the background and hunched over, he's leaning on a cane. I'm sorry I can't accurately describe him, but I can tell you he's wearing a slanted John Deere hat. Madison, David Daniels was not responsible for Shadow or Marjorie, was he?"

"Helen, don't you dare go jumping to conclusions. Listen, I'm going to let you go because I need to call Junior right now. Helen remember, not one word."

"Madison, I'm sorry, but I've already said a word. I was frightened, so I called Junior about the picture. Please don't be angry with me."

"It's ok, Helen. Just get off the phone and for now on keep your mouth shut! Bye."

I ran into the front room to take another look at the notebook.

"Madison, is something wrong?" Jan asked.

"I'm sorry Jan, I forgot you were here. Yes, something is very wrong. Please, you'll have to excuse me."

I went to pick up Junior's notebook, but it wasn't where I'd left it.

"Jan, this is very important. Did you see or pick up a small notebook off of the couch?"

"No, of course not," was all she said.

I frantically picked up the cushions and then I searched the floor under the couch. I ran into my bedroom thinking that maybe I'd taken it with me to bed. No notebook. I ran in the front room and turned a full three hundred and sixty degrees at least four times. No notebook.

"Madison, does this have something to do with that plumber I saw in your driveway."

"What plumber!" I screamed.

"That big guy that said he had been working on your plumbing."

"Jan, this is extremely important. Where did you see this plumber?"

"He was getting into his car. Don't worry Madison - he was leaving."

I ran into the kitchen and dialed the police station.

"Hello, Crestfield police, how can I help you?"

"Randi, is that you?"

"Yes, Madison, is that you?"

"Yes, where's Junior?"

"He and Dad are eating at the diner. Then they're heading over to your house. Why?"

"Never mind why. Is Tommy or Ricky there?"

"No, they're out on 34. Do you want me to call them?"

"No, I want you to run across the street and tell Junior to get here as fast as he can."

"What should I tell him is wrong?"

"Nothing, just tell him to get here. And I mean right now! Do you understand me?"

"Yes, ok."

I hung up and went back out to the front room to tell Jan she'd better go home. She was crying again.

"Madison, I didn't get to apologize for sneaking around behind your back with Ray. I'm sorry. Can you ever forgive me?"

"Yes Jan, I forgive you. Fact is, I knew about the two of you all along. It didn't bother me that much," I lied. "Jan please, I think you should go home right now. Ok, please go."

She gave me one of those, I don't believe you looks. Then she picked up her purse and started marching towards the door. I was going to open it for her, but she beat me to it. She only took one step out the door when I heard the crack of what sounded like a bat hitting a ball. Jan stumbled and fell backwards into my living room. Her eyes blinked up at me as the blood from her forehead zigzagged its way across her face. I kicked my door shut and locked it just before the glass window above my door shattered. Someone was doing all they could to kick my door down; I knew I had to go get help. I ran through the kitchen and slammed out the back door. I leaped off my porch and in an instant was running at full speed. I was confident I'd make it to my neighbor's house when everything went black.

To wit   46

"Benny, pull the car around the back. We're gonna have another passenger with us."

"Oh no, why'd you go and do that? You must have some kind of death wish or something."

"Just do what I told you before I crack open that little head of yours."

"Maybe I should just leave you here and drive home. Big guy, why do you have to hurt people all the time?"

"That's funny coming from you. I've told you a thousand times you're the meanest little cuss in the world. Look Benny, if you don't move it and right now you're going to be staying the night in a hotel that has bars and mean people with badges that stare through the bars at you. Now get moving."

"All right, stop yelling at me."

"Benny, help me get her in the back. That's good, yeah right there."

"What about the other one?" Benny asked.

"Don't worry, she won't bother us now. Her heads cracked open."

"She saw me. We can't leave her here."

"Benny, its go time. So make up your itty-bitty mind. Are you coming or not?"

"Ok, I'll come with you, big guy. But at the first sign of trouble you're on your own."

"Fair enough, now get in the car."

"Mat it big guy."

"Benny, what does mat it mean?"

"It means put your foot to the floor."

"I can do that. Only thing is where are we going?"

"Home big guy, we're going home."

***Junior*/Randi came charging in the diner**, she didn't have to say a word. The look on her face said it all.

"Junior, Madison was screaming at me. She wants you to get to her house, and right now!"

"Let's go, Dad. Randi, did you call Tommy and Ricky?"

"Yes, they're on their way to Madison's. It's going to take them a while. They're several miles east on the highway. A tractor has overturned."

"Stay in touch," was all I said to Randi as Dad, Maggie, and I hurried across the street and jumped in my cruiser.

I floored it heading west on Adams Avenue. I got off on Jarvis and headed for Madison's house. That's when I spotted the tan 57 Ford heading south on Sumner and moving fast. I yelled, "Dad, it's the guys that attacked you. They're heading for the highway. Don't know if they're going to go east or west?"

He turned right on Taylor and headed west. I was gaining on him and he knew it. I was still a city block or so behind him when Dad yelled, "Shoot him, shoot the son of a bitch – shot him, right now!"

I took out my revolver, aimed it out the window, and fired once at his rear tire. I missed.

"Keep shooting, Junior. You're bound to hit something!" Dad yelled in a high-pitched scream.

"That's the problem Dad. What if I hit somebody else?"

"Do you see somebody else?" Dad hollered.

"Not right now, but there could be. What the heck? He just turned onto Monroe. He's heading into Cromwell."

He headed for Marjorie's driveway. He raced around her garage and kept going across the field behind her house.

"He's heading for that old farm house behind Marjorie's. He'll never make it across that field and neither will we."

"Junior, don't you dare stop. You keep this car going. If he can make it, so can you."

He had a fifty-yard lead on me as we bounced across the field. I was straining to see how many were in the car. All I could see was the driver. He flew right by the old house and headed for the barn. He swung around the right side of the barn and I lost sight of him.

310

To wit   48

"Benny, Benny! What should I do?"

"Let me out! That's what you should do. They won't see me. I'll get behind them."

"You're gonna hide in the barn like before aren't you."

"No I won't, Kaleb. I'll follow and sneak up behind them. I'll drop Maxwell's silver hammer on 'em."

"You promise?"

"I promise, just let me out."

"Ok, get out."

"I can't get out, you haven't stopped yet."

"Alright we're stopped. You better come and get me."

"I will, see ya. Now go!"

The car sped around the barn and the driver whispered,

"Drizzle drazzle druzzle drome, time for zis one to come home. Be vhat you is, not vhat you is not. Folks vhat does zis are ze happiest lot."

Junior/**I was going to follow him** around the barn, but I didn't want to drive into a trap. So I had nearly come to a stop when the tan Ford came around the opposite side of the barn, heading straight at me. Everything seemed to move in slow motion at that point. And then for just an instant the other driver and I stared at each other. He was wearing a slanted John Deere hat. I turned hard right but not hard enough. He hit the left rear fender of my car and Dad flew against the passenger side window and Maggie yelped. My car had stalled so I jumped out and aimed my 38 at the back of the Ford. I pulled the trigger five times as fast as I could. His rear window exploded, but he kept on going.

"Dad! Are you ok?"

"I'm fine. Get back in this car. He's gonna get away. Junior, catch that son of a bitch."

I turned the key and the motor sputtered for a long time before it finally turned over. I whipped a U-turn and floored it. He had a pretty good lead on me, but I knew I could catch him. I heard the fender rubbing against the rear tire on my cruiser. I couldn't straighten the fender out so there was no point in stopping.

I flew by Marjorie's house and headed north on Monroe. I figured he'd take Cromwell road and head for highway 34. I couldn't see the Ford yet, but I knew I was close. His car was leaving a trail of smoke behind. He must have damaged the radiator when he hit my car. I was at full speed and finally caught a glimpse of him as he slowed to make the turn onto Sumner. He was heading back into Crestfield. I didn't have a clue as to why, but it didn't matter because I'd caught up to him. He was coming up to Adams and I thought for sure he'd head towards the center of town. But he turned west and away from town. We were going in circles.

I was right on his tail and then for the first time I could see that there was someone in the back seat. The person in back was hitting the driver with what looked to be a shiny hammer. The person in the back suddenly turned and, in a panic, started waving at me. It was Madison. Then a light from my rearview mirror bolted through my eyes. I turned my head around to take a look.

312

There was a car with a row of flashing lights on its roof coming hard behind me. When I turned my head back to see in front of me, the Ford was gone. He'd turned onto Lake Shore Drive, the road that goes around the lake.

I braked hard and barely made the turn. The Ford was still nowhere in sight. I floored it and was flying at top speed 'til I got close to the southern end of the lake. The trail of smoke suddenly ended. I slowed down thinking maybe he'd doubled back when I saw him in my side mirror. He pulled up next to me and smiled just before he violently jerked his steering wheel to the right and rammed my side of the car. My car lurched to the edge of the road. He moved away and then came back at me again. I slammed both feet on the brake pedal. He hit the front of my car as he flew by me. His car slid sideways, tumbled over the spillway, and sailed nose first into the lake.

I skidded to an abrupt stop and jumped out. Dad was right behind me. I watched as the Ford slowly sank below the water's surface. Before my mind could even process what was happening, I had my shoes off and was swimming out for Madison. The water was so cold just breathing was painful. I was about halfway out to where the car had sunk when Maggie swam past me.

"Maggie! Go get Madison."

She didn't slow down and was soon over the spot where the car had sunk. She swam in circles barking the entire time. Then I saw a head pop up through the surface of the water.

It was the driver of the other car. He looked at me and then frantically started swimming away. Even in water I could see that he was a huge man. I wanted to go after him, but first I had to find Madison.

"Maggie! Go get him. Go get him."

Maggie headed his way and when the big guy saw her, he screamed. I dove down just far enough to where I could see the sunken car. Madison was nowhere in sight. I came back up and gasped for air. My heart was pounding in my ears. It was nearly impossible to get any air in my lungs, but I took the biggest breath I could and headed back down to the sunken car. Somehow I made it and swam straight in through where the back window had been. Madison was not in the car. I swam back to the surface and gasped for air.

That's when I heard the big guy yelling for help. Maggie had caught him and was gnawing on his neck. He turned for shore and dipped under the water. I watched Maggie follow him and when he surfaced, she was on him again. He screamed for help. Then I heard Dad holler, "Junior! Junior! I have Madison. She's here with me."

I saw Tommy and Ricky run down to help Dad. Dad yelled, "Go get that son of a bitch!"

I made it to dry land and looked down the shore line. The big guy got out of the water and tried to run. He made it all of about three steps before Maggie was on him. He was obviously too tired to fight her off. She was letting him know just how much she enjoyed being poisoned. I reached for my gun, but it was gone. I must have lost it when I dove down after Madison.

I lay on the shore too cold and winded to move even one muscle. I watched as Ricky tried to pull Maggie off of the big guy. Maggie would not stop. Ricky finally had a good grip on her harness and was able to pull her away. The big guy was trying to get to his feet when Tommy jumped on him. I wanted to help, but I just couldn't move. My teeth chattered and my body shivered. And as I inched towards Dad, I watched Tommy cuff the big guy. I was close enough now to see that Madison was also cold and shivering but safe in Dad's arms. She was very much alive and that's all that mattered to me.

I watched Madison being loaded into an ambulance, but after that everything was a blur. One thing I do remember is hearing Ricky say, "Junior, can you please stop your teeth from chattering like that. You're making me cold."

Healing   50

___*Junior*/**I woke several times that night shivering** from a
slight case of hypothermia but no worse for wear. I looked
around the room and Dad was standing there looking at me.
At least it felt as though he was looking at me.

"Dad, how long have you been here?"

"Not long. I was in Madison's room up until about ten
minutes ago."

"How's Madison doing?"

"She caught a little shattered glass to the face and
neck." I thought, *no thanks to me.* "She's bruised from head
to toe and turning black and blue to prove it. And the blow
she received to the side of her head was a nasty one. But all
things considered I'd say she's lucky to be alive. She's
resting comfortably now and the Madison I know is a
fighter. So I'd say she will be up and running before you
know it."

"Dad, did you swim out and get her?"

"No, I waded out in the water and yelled her name.
Didn't you hear me?"

"Uh, no I didn't hear you."

"Anyway, after I yelled a couple of times, Madison swam
straight to me."

"Wow," was all I could say.

I looked around and something wasn't quite right. Then
it came to me.

"Dad, where's Maggie?"

"I left her to stand guard over Madison. Somebody needs
to be on the lookout for Benny. The day I was attacked the
big guy didn't do anything until Benny showed up. That son
of a bitch Benny is the mean one. And I guarantee you it's
only a matter of time 'til he tries to get to Madison."

I dozed off thinking about what Dad had said about
Benny. The moment I fell asleep the mean dreams began.
The witch, the naughty children, and a little hunchback
named Benny had me trapped in the tree again. The witch
lit the tree on fire and the flames raged upward. I crawled
out on a limb, but the flames followed. First my shoes lit up
and my toes sizzled. They looked like little burnt gherkins.
The fire climbed up my legs and body and then yoked
around my neck. The pain was unbearable and I cried out

for help. Then a gentle hand pulled me away from the flames. It was Jenny.

"Junior, go to the tree house."

I crawled into the tree house and the pain subsided. When I turned to thank Jenny, she was gone.

I woke up drenched in sweat and panting like an injured animal. I looked around hoping Jenny would be there waiting for me, but the room was dark and empty. A nurse hurried into the darkness.

"Officer McCool, are you alright?" I was breathing so hard I couldn't answer her. "You were yelling for help," she said.

"I'm fine. Just had a bad dream is all."

"Must have been a doozy, we could hear you clear down to the nurses' station."

"What time is it?"

"It's half-past 8. Would you like your breakfast now?"

"Um, I suppose so. Thanks."

After I ate my breakfast, I was checked over by a young female doctor. She said I was fine and that I could go home. I got myself dressed and went straight to Madison's room. She had a bandage wrapped around her head and her face was swollen and discolored. I couldn't help but notice that she looked like Dad did after he'd been attacked. She was sleeping so I just sat and watched her. As I sat there, I wondered how they had got the jump on her. Madison would not be easy prey for anyone, which probably explains her head wound.

I was going to get up and call the station when I heard a familiar voice coming my way. He was by himself, but Ajax was still talking up a storm. I believe he was talking to little Jax. He bum-rushed me the moment he came into the room. Teary-eyed and smiling from ear to ear he picked me up and squeezed me 'til I thought my head was gonna pop off.

"Junior, I can't begin to tell you how proud I am right now. My doggone nephew caught the stinking no good bad guy. Oh, and he saved the damsel in distress at the same time. This will be a story for all the papers. I can't wait to see the little town of Crestfield spread across the news. Junior, how the hell are you?"

316

"I guess I'm ok. Listen, Uncle Ajax, can you tell me what is going on. Where is everybody?"

"Ok in a minute. But first how is Madison doing?"

"I just got here so I don't really know. But she looks comfortable to me."

"Yes, she does. Boy you ought to see Jan. She's got a purple lump on her forehead the size of a goose egg. Man, she got hit hard."

"Jan Freeberg? How'd she get involved in all of this?" I asked.

"She says she just went over to visit with Madison. Said she was walking out the door when someone turned all the lights off, if you know what I mean. You must have just missed her when you started after Mr. Jones."

"Who is Mr. Jones?" I asked totally confused by the name.

"The bad guy you just caught. He told us his name is Jones. Says he's from Mobile, Alabama. He sounds like somebody from the south. I've got people checking on all of this as we speak."

"Wait a second. This guy attacks and maybe murders people and you believe him when he tells you his name is Jones? Uncle Ajax I think there's something wrong with all of this."

"You sound like Tommy. Look, I don't really care what his name is. But for now it's Jones. That's my story and I'm..." Uncle Ajax stopped and began mumbling something. Then he looked at me. "Oh phooey, maybe you're right. Ok, we'll wait 'til we find out who he really is before we give him a name."

"Ajax, where is this Mr. Jones?"

"We've got him locked up in the jail. Matt and Ricky are there watching him. He's not going anywhere. The funny thing is I don't think he wants to go anywhere."

"What do you mean?"

"He acts like a frightened little boy. I'm telling you the guy is afraid of his own shadow. And he mumbles all the time. He keeps saying the same nursery rhymes over and over. There's definitely something wrong with that boy."

"Yeah, well, I'd still be very careful. Uncle Ajax, where's Tommy?"

"Tommy and Shadow were with the guys that came over from Corning to get that old Ford out of the lake."

"You said were. Where are they now?"

"They went out to that farm house in Cromwell you raced around. Tommy figured the guy was trying to go home. And, of course, they're looking for Benny."

"Oh yeah, I forgot about Benny."

"That reminds me, they found your gun in the Ford and I've got something else for you," Ajax said with an inquisitive look on his face.

He reached in his coat pocket and pulled out my notebook and handed it to me.

"Where'd you find this?" I asked.

"It washed up to shore when they were pulling the Ford out of the lake."

I tried to open my notebook, but the pages were all stuck together. When I finally got it open, the ink had run all over the pages. I couldn't make out a single word.

"Ajax, how in the world did this get in the lake?"

"Junior, I was hoping you could tell me."

"Well, all I can tell you is that Madison was going over the notes in an effort to find anything that I might have missed. Maybe she had it with her when she was taken hostage."

"I wasn't taken hostage you knucklehead. I was clubbed over the head," Madison said with the same old spirit I know so well.

Ajax and I turned at the same time and looked over at Madison. She was trying to sit up in bed. She had a fractured smile on her face.

"Madison - oh am I glad to hear your voice. How're you feeling?" I asked as I attempted to hug her.

"Ouch! Junior, stop that." I backed away to a safe distance. "How do I feel? Well, except for this headache from hell I feel ok. Junior, how did you find me?"

"First Helen called me about a picture she wanted me to look at. Then Randi came storming into the diner and told me to get to your house as fast as I could. So Dad, Maggie, and I took off. When we got close to your house I saw the tan Ford heading west on Taylor and the chase was on. Do you remember any of that?"

"No, all I remember is waking up when the car stopped. I heard two guys talking to each other. That's when one of the guys got out of the car. Then there was a collision and I was thrown off the back seat onto the floor. I landed on the meat tenderizer I used to hit the driver with. Say, that reminds me. Junior, were you the one shooting?"

"Yeah, why?"

"You could have killed me, that's why."

"Madison, I didn't know you were in the car. I had to try and stop him, lucky thing too. If I hadn't shot out that back window you might not have made it out of the car when it sank in the lake. Madison did you say meat tenderizer?"

"Yes. I'll bet it's the same tenderizer that went missing after Dad was attacked," she said.

"Yes, I'll bet you're right. I mean it has to be. Gosh, what a strange twist of fate. Were you scared when you woke up?" I asked.

"No, I wasn't scared, I was pissed off. Imagine being clubbed over the head and possibly on your way to being murdered, but you wake up. I was pissed off and instead of being clubbed; now I was the one doing the clubbing."

"Madison, did you have my notebook with you?" I asked.

"No, I left the notebook on the couch the night before. But when I looked around the front room the next day, I realized it was gone. That's when I became alarmed and told Jan she'd better leave. One of those guys or maybe both of them were in my house at some point and took the darn notebook. Geez, just the thought of that gives me the creeps. Wait a second, how's Jan?"

"She's down the hall from you. She's going to be ok, but she's got a lump on her head that matches the one you've got," Ajax said.

"Madison, did you ever get a look at the other guy?" I asked.

"No, the only thing I saw was the back of the driver's head. You know when I was hitting him he screamed like a girl. He didn't sound much like a tough guy at all."

"See Junior, I told you so," Ajax said as he puffed out his chest.

"Hey, if I remember right, Maggie was really doing a number on him. Mr. Smith must have bites covering his entire body," I said to Ajax.

"Yep, it took Doc Mayland over an hour to sew him up. The guy acted like he felt no pain. Maybe he is a tough guy," Ajax said.

"Ok, tough guy or not, Ajax, please stop right there and listen to me, you too Madison. I know you're excited and all, but I want you to know the truth. And the truth is I didn't catch your Mr. Jones - Maggie and Tommy did. Madison, I didn't pull you out of the water either - Dad did. So Uncle Ajax, if anyone comes to me for a story I'm not saying a word. And that's all there is to it. I'm tired of all this. I want it all to go away."

"Junior, please don't make your mind up just yet. We can cross that bridge when the time comes," Ajax said.

"No, I've been back and forth across that bridge so many times I'm sick of it. All I want to do now is go see this Mr. Jones for myself. Then I want him out of our lives for good. For now I'm gonna stay here with Madison."

"Junior, I'm ok - you can go. As long as Maggie is here nobody, is going to harm me," Madison said with a ton of conviction.

Upon hearing her name, Maggie barked with her own style of conviction.

"Madison, I believe Maggie will protect you, but we're not taking any chances. So, as soon as Tommy and Shadow come back, Shadow will be stationed in front of your room," Ajax informed.

I was still suffering from the remnants of being in the freezing water. And as confused as ever about how the pieces to this jigsaw fit together. But hearing that someone would be guarding Madison helped thaw my misgivings. Ajax, Madison, Maggie, and I regurgitated all that had happened 'til I was sick of hearing about it. Finally, Shadow showed up with news about what he and Tommy had found in that old farmhouse.

"Hey Shadow," we all said in unison.

"Hey, how you doin'?" Shadow said as he waved hello.

"Thanks for asking, I'm doin' fine," Ajax said with a smile.

"Not you mayor, I was talking to the other two," Shadow said with a smile.

I looked at Madison and she said, "I think we're fine, but thanks for asking."

"Shadow, that's enough with the small talk. What'd you and Tommy find out?" I asked.

"Well, we found out that the cupboards are bare and there's no furniture to speak of in that old house. And we found out that two people live there," Shadow said with a twinkle in his eye.

"Shadow, why do I get the feeling you're stalling," Madison asked.

"Um, I don't know," Shadow said.

"Ok, out with it," I said.

"Ok, there's an old man and his nephew that live there. Old man's name is Merle Haugen. Says he's lived there for over twenty years now," Shadow said.

"Hold it right there. Did you say his last name is Haugen?" I asked.

"Yeah, his last name is Haugen. Is that important?" Shadow asked.

"I don't know? It could be. The lady that bought the bracelet stolen from the Silvers' house has the same last name. And she's from Mobile, Alabama, has to be a connection there somewhere. Say, what's the nephew's name?" I asked.

"The old man wouldn't tell us his nephew's name," Shadow said.

"Ok Madison, you should be safe with Shadow and Maggie watching over you. I've got to get to the station and see what else Tommy found out," I said.

"Wait Junior, there's more," Shadow said.

"I can't wait. I'll find out the rest from Tommy," I said with renewed excitement.

"Junior, wait a second. I'll give you a ride," Ajax said.

"No thanks, I want to walk. I'll see you guys later," I said as I hurried out of Madison's room.

I wanted to run but held myself to a fast walk. My mind was racing a thousand miles an hour. I thought to myself, *there must be a lot more to this old guy's story. And I want to hear it firsthand.* When I got to the station, I ran through the back door all the way to the holding cell. Tommy was standing there staring in at the big guy. He was curled up in the far corner, on the floor. The guy was wearing a green plaid shirt, overalls, and huge hobnailed boots.

Tommy looked over at me with a keen eye and said, "You feeling ok, Junior?"

"Yeah, good as new." I said as I turned and stared at the prisoner again. "Tommy, tell me what you found out?"

"For starters, the old guy that lives in the house knows a lot more than he's letting on."

"Hey, where is the old guy?" I asked.

"He's in my office."

"Aren't you worried he'll take off?" I asked.

"Trust me he's not going anywhere. He's crippled. Says he got polio when he was a young boy. That part of what he says must be true, but I'm not so sure about anything else he says. Just doesn't feel right."

"Tommy, could he be the Benny we're all looking for?"

"Junior, I wondered the same thing. So I brought your dad down here to listen to the old man talk. The moment he and Maggie walked in the door, she made a beeline towards my office. The old man shut the door just in time. But Maggie sure did want a piece of him. Anyway, after listening to the old guy talk from inside my office, your dad said that he's not Benny."

I started to ask Tommy about the house and barn when the big guy lifted his head up and mumbled, "Ricker racker firecracker - Benny got away. He'll come back and get me - just ask Uncle Ray."

Then the big guy cradled his head back between his hands and closed his eyes.

"Tommy, who do you suppose is Uncle Ray?"

"I don't know, but he's mentioned Uncle Ray about three times now. Boy Junior, we sure do have a strange one here. You know when I jumped on him he could have fought me off. I mean look at the size of him. But he just gave in. He reminds me of Lennie Small from the story of mice and men. And that scares me. I have no doubt that if he wanted to, he could put a serious hurtin' on somebody," Tommy said with attitude.

Tommy hesitated for a second or two before he said, "As we speak there's a man and a woman driving over from the prison for the criminally insane in Oakdale. Maybe when they get here we'll find out a little more about this guy. But until they get here, I don't want you or anybody else going in that cell alone."

322

"Uh Tommy, you don't have to worry about me going in there. That's for darn sure."

"Junior, let's go talk to Uncle Merle."

We started to walk away when the big guy lifted his head up and said, "I sure am parched. Could I please have a drink of water?"

"I'll give you some water in a little bit. You rest easy 'til I get back," Tommy said.

We stared at the prisoner and then Tommy motioned me to follow him. We walked into his office and the old man waved to me and said, "Hello, young man."

Then he pulled his crutches under his arms and stood from the wooden chair that sits next to Tommy's desk. The metal braces on his legs grinded and clanked something awful as he moved to shake my hand.

"I'm Merle, sure is nice to meet you."

I didn't know what to say in return and fumbled a bit trying to get a word out.

"Young man, it's ok. I truly understand your being tongue-tied. This is an awful situation we're all in."

I was finally able to blurt out a hello, but that's where the dialogue ended. Tommy could see I was having a problem and came to the rescue.

"Mr. Haugen, you can go ahead and sit back down. I want to keep everything kinda casual if that's ok with you."

"Sure thing, Chief. I ain't gonna argue with any man that treats me with kindness, as you have done. Can you please call me Merle?"

"Ok, Merle it is. First things first, your nephew says he's thirsty. Would you like to give him a drink of water?" Tommy softly said.

"No Chief, if he sees me, he'll begin to cry. And I don't think we need to go through that right now. Do we?"

"No Merle, we don't. My brother Jack does the same thing now and then. Ok, I'll go give him a cup of water. Be right back."

Tommy walked out and went straight to the water cooler and filled a paper cup. I looked over at the old man and he looked back at me and flicked his blue eyes towards Tommy.

"Young man, I can see that yer itchin' to go have a look. I understand, go right ahead if you want."

"Thanks, and my name is Jack, but you can call me Junior if you like," I said.

"Jack, I like that name. You must be the blind man's son."

"Yes, I am."

I hurried out to have another look at the prisoner. I followed Tommy down the hall to the jail cell and we both stopped in our tracks. The big guy was standing up and had his face smushed between the bars. His hands were cuffed, but he had them extended a couple of feet through the opening in the bars. He was a giant of a man, much bigger and broader at the shoulders than David Daniels was. I guess we mistook the two because we really had no point of reference. Tommy handed the big guy the cup of water and he pulled the cup to his nose and smelled it. Then he stuck his tongue in the water for a second or two and said, "You didn't put no medication in this water, did you?"

Tommy looked at me and then back at the prisoner and said, "No, of course not. You don't have to worry. We don't have any medicine here."

"Oh goody, I don't like medicine. Makes me sad," he said just before he tipped the cup back. He downed the entire cupful in one big gulp. "Can I have another, please?" he immediately asked.

"Sure thing, I'll be right back," Tommy said as he hurried back to the water cooler.

"Say mister, you forgot the cup," the big guy hollered.

Tommy didn't answer. He just filled another cup of water and hurried back.

"Say, do you like games?" Tommy asked.

"Oh boy - do I. What game you wanna play?" the big guy asked.

"How about we start by you letting me guess what your name is," Tommy said.

"Now you sound like Doctor Cook. I don't like those kinda games so much. Can we play later?" the big guy said.

"We could play later, but then you wouldn't have any water," Tommy said.

The big guy pulled his hands back through the bars and clinched his jaws. His eyes squinted and then he turned his back to us and violently pounded on the bed he chose not to sleep on. Tommy and I took a couple of steps back and then

324

we heard Mr. Haugen's crutches pounding the tiles on the floor.

"Chief, chief, there's no need for games. You will upset him," Merle said as he skipped up towards the bars in the cell. "Kaleb, the men don't want to play any more games right now. You can turn around and have your water. Come on, it's ok now, everything is going to be ok," Mr. Haugen softly said.

The big guy turned and reached his hands through the bars again.

"May I?" Mr. Haugen asked Tommy.

Tommy handed him the cup of water. And he gently handed the cup to the big guy.

"Chief, if you need to know something about either of us - please, just ask. Kaleb is his name. And he can become extremely violent if he thinks someone is trying to use or abuse him. I'm sorry, but that's just the way things are since he stopped taking his meds," Mr. Haugen said.

"Do you have the medication he needs?" Tommy asked.

"No, he's been off his meds now for about a week. And you can readily see the results. He would never have attacked those women or tried to run from you if he had been medicated. I'm truly sorry for that, but I've run out of medication. And I haven't had time to get down to Clarinda Cove to get some more," Mr. Haugen informed.

"Wait a second. You take Kaleb to Clarinda?" I asked.

"No, of course not - why they'd put him away for life if I took him there," Mr. Haugen said.

"Then how do you get the medication?" Tommy asked.

"Well, long and the short of it. The medicine is for me, but that's only because I fooled them into believing I need to be medicated," he said with a sheepish grin.

"And how did you accomplish that?" I asked.

"My sister Addy made those arraingments years ago in Mobile," Mr. Haugen said.

"Addy Haugen is your sister?" I asked.

"Was my sister, she has since passed away. How do you know her name?" he asked.

"This last fall somebody using the same name bought a stolen bracelet from a pawn shop in Keokuk. Can you describe your sister for me?" I asked.

"Addy was very tall, she had blue eyes and long blonde hair. She usually kept her hair in braids of one fashion or another. She was a very typical looking Norwegian woman," he said.

I started to tell him about the woman that the pawn broker had described to me, but she had black hair and was more importantly - alive.

"Doesn't sound like the same woman?"

I started to ask Mr. Haugen how his sister died when Kaleb stuck his empty cup back thru the bars.

"Thank you. I'm famished. Can I eat now?"

"Yes, you can eat. The owner of the diner is bringing over a lunch for you. She'll be here any minute now," Tommy said.

"Chief, can I go now?" Mr. Haugen asked.

"No, I'm sorry, but we have many more questions to ask you. For the time being your nephew Kaleb has been charged with reckless driving and evading a police officer. Those are the lesser crimes. The more serious charges are assault and battery, adult kidnapping, and possibly murder. And Merle you may be charged with aiding and abetting a known criminal," Tommy said with a stern look.

"Why that's ridiculous. I've never done any such thing, least not knowingly," Merle said.

Tommy was just about to ask Mr. Haugen something else when we heard Mary from the diner holler, "Anybody home?"

I walked out to the front desk to pick up the tray of food. *Mary's hair was pot roast brown.*

"Hi Mary - how you doin' today?"

"I'm fine. Do you want me to take the food back to the prisoner?"

"No Mary, you're not going back there."

"Oh come on, Junior. Please let me take the food back. I want to see what this guy looks like. The whole town is depending on me to give them a description of this 'Wildman' you have in that cell."

"No, and that's final. Now go on back to the diner. You'll know all about the 'Wildman' in a day or two."

"You know what, Junior?"

"What Mary?"

"Never mind. You owe me a dollar and forty cents."

326

"Put it on our tab."

She gave me one of those, 'I'd like to slap you' looks and huffed out the front door. As I carried the food back to the cell I realized that Randi, Ricky, and Matt weren't in the station.

"Tommy, where is everybody?"

"Randi is waiting for a search warrant to be signed. Ricky and Matt drove over to Cromwell. They're waiting to search Mr. Haugen's house and barn."

"Chief, I've already told you there's nothing there for you to find. But I guess you're just gonna have to see for yourself," Mr. Haugen said.

"Yes Merle, I have to see for myself. And while Kaleb eats I'm going ask you a few more questions."

I took the tray of food over and held it next to the opening in the cell bars.

"Kaleb, put your hands through the opening. I'm gonna takes the cuffs off, but if you try anything, anything at all, I'm going to shoot you. Do you understand me?" Tommy asked.

"I understand," was all Kaleb said.

Tommy unlocked the cuffs and then I handed him the tray of food. Kaleb rubbed his wrists for a bit and then gently grabbed hold of the tray with his gigantic hands and walked back to the corner and sat on the floor to eat. There was something so childlike and peaceful about the big guy that you couldn't help but wonder how he could hurt anyone. The three of us left Kaleb to eat and walked back to Tommy's office.

"Ok Merle, I've already told you that you can have an attorney here with you if you want. Are you still willing to answer our questions?" Tommy asked.

"Sure thing, I have nothing to hide," was all Mr. Haugen said at that point.

"Ok Merle, for now I'll be asking all the questions. Think through your answers before you speak. First question. Who is Uncle Ray?"

"I don't know any Uncle Ray, but if you're connecting this person to Kaleb, he has many imaginary friends and a few imaginary relatives too."

"Fair enough, second question. Who is Benny?"

"There is no Benny, least none I've ever heard of. Why do you ask?" Merle said with what seemed like genuine concern.

"I asked you about Benny because when Kaleb attacked my brother last fall, he had an accomplice named Benny. Now I'm going to ask you again, who is Benny?"

"Chief, Kaleb wouldn't attack anyone and if I knew of a person named Benny, I'd tell you. One thing I can tell you is Kaleb suffers from an extreme form of schizophrenia. He hears voices, especially when he doesn't take his meds. The voices tell him to do things, awful things. I'm truly sorry about your brother, but I can't help you because I don't know anybody by the name of Benny."

"Ok, next question. Who owns the Ford Fairlane that Kaleb was driving?"

"I bought that car for Kaleb. It came right off the showroom floor at a dealership in Mobile. Kaleb got in an accident driving here from there. As far as I know, the car hasn't been driven in over ten years. Least not 'til it went into the lake yesterday."

"What color was the car when it was new?"

"The car was originally black, but after the accident, Kaleb painted the car tan. Painted it right there in the barn at home."

"Merle, what if I told you we have statements from reliable people that say they've seen the car on the road before yesterday."

"Well, like I said. I don't know anything about the car being driven before yesterday."

"Next question, does Kaleb know of or is he related to Billy Thornton?"

"Who is Billy Thornton?" Mr. Haugen asked.

"Never mind who he is. Just answer the question," Tommy insisted.

"Why, that's ridiculous. How or why would Kaleb know this Billy Thornton?"

"I don't know. That's why I asked you."

"No, Kaleb does not know Billy Thornton."

"Merle, do you own any guns?"

"Yes, I have a German Lugar I brought back from the war. Nobody is supposed to know about that."

"So, it's not registered?"

328

"Why, of course not."

"Ok, do you own any registered guns?"

"Other than the Lugar I told ya about, I have three guns that are registered. A Browning twelve gauge, a Winchester rifle, usually referred to as the Rifleman's rifle. And a twenty-two pistol I've had since I was a boy."

"Your rifle is the Winchester model 70?"

"Yes, best rifle ever made."

"What caliber ammo do you use?"

"Three-oh-eight, why do you ask?"

"I think you must know why."

"I hope you're not referring to Marjorie. Cuz if you are, that's an awful thing to insinuate. Marjorie and I were neighbors. We were friends."

"I'm not insinuating anything, but I'll tell you something right now. If I find out that your nephew's car was the one that forced my brother off the road and killed his wife." Tommy stopped for a moment and looked over at me. His eyes raged with passion. "If I find out that his car was used in the commission of that crime, I'm gonna make sure the two of you rot in hell."

Tommy stopped and stared at Mr. Haugen. And Mr. Haugen stared right back before he said, "Sounds like you need a drink, Chief."

Tommy stepped close to Merle Haugen and raised his fist.

"Tommy! Tommy! Don't do it. He's just trying to get under your skin. Don't you dare hit that man!" Randi screamed.

Mr. Haugen and I turned and watched her run and grab hold of Tommy. She threw her arms around his chest pinning both of his arms to his sides. Tommy didn't resist.

"Mr. Haugen, I have the signed search warrant with me and the law says you have to be made aware of the warrant before we can search. It states what we are looking for and where we will be looking. Please come with me. I'll give you a ride out to your farm," Randi said in a businesslike voice.

Tommy and I watched as Mr. Haugen clinked away. When they walked out the back door, we both immediately turned to see what the strange noise was coming from behind us. We turned just in time to jump out of the reach of Kaleb. He was moaning and groaning as he tried to reach out and grab Tommy. He looked at us with wild eyes just before he said, "You wanted to hurt Uncle Ray. Benny will stop you, you'll see. Fee-fi-fo-fum, I smell the blood of a policeman. Be he live, or be he dead, I'll grind his bones to make my bread."

"Kaleb, I didn't want to hurt anyone. Now go sit down!" Tommy ordered.

The giant slowly withdrew his hands and slinked back to the corner of the cell and sat down. "Now finish your lunch. It's bad manners to waste good food."

Kaleb lowered his head and proceeded to devour the food left on his tray. Tommy turned to me and nudged me away from the cell.

"He's a lot like having a naughty child. If you give them room, they'll find any and every way possible to get into mischief. But if you keep the leash tight enough, they can be managed," Tommy said.

"Yeah, well I'm gonna stay a safe distance from that kid. He gives me the creeps," I professed.

Tommy nodded in agreement and walked away. He was obviously troubled by all of this. And I'm sure the comment made by Mr. Haugen about Tommy needing a drink didn't help matters. I stood there and watched the giant finish his meal. When he was done, he wiped his face with his shirt sleeve and walked the tray back over to me. He passed the tray thru the opening in the bars, smiled, and said, "Sure was good. Thank you."

I stayed as far away from him as I could and then quickly grabbed the tray. As I backed away, he smiled at me and said, "Ain't no need for you to be afeared. I ain't gonna hurt you. Ok if I use your bathroom now? I gotta go number one."

I didn't know what to say. Probably because the thought of him walking anywhere in this police station gave me the willies. I turned to take the tray back out to the front desk and ran right into Tommy.

"Whoops, sorry Junior. Listen, somebody has to stay here with Kaleb. So if you want to go out and help with the search, I'll stay here," Tommy said.

"Yes, I'd like to have a look at the farm. But first we have a problem." Tommy tilted his head a little and leaned an ear my way. "He says he has to go number one. What should we do?" I asked.

Tommy raised an eyebrow and walked away. I stood there thinking, *ok what's he gonna do now?* I looked at Kaleb and he shrugged his shoulders as if he was asking himself the same question. Then he hopped a couple of times the way little boys do when they really gotta go. About twenty seconds later Tommy walked back with a small plastic waste basket and tried to fit it thru the opening in the bars, but it wouldn't fit. Tommy walked away and about a minute later came back holding a mason jar that had been full of pickles. He set the jar in the opening in the bars. Then he stepped back and pulled his gun out of its holster. Kaleb hopped a few more times as he backed away.

"Chief, I'm afraid of guns and knives, swords too. Could you put that gun away, please? Kaleb said with a convincing sulk covering his face.

"Kaleb, my brother told me that you threatened to gut him like a fish when you were in his house. Do you remember being in Jack's house?" Tommy asked.

"I remember Jack. Benny hurt him, not me. Benny likes guns and knives, but I don't. Please I'll behave, I promise."

"Kaleb, where is Benny?"

"He's hiding."

"Where does he hide?"

"He hides in the barn, but sometimes he hides in trees. And sometimes he hides in plain-sight."

"Does Benny know where you are?"

"Yes, he'll be here pretty soon. He's gonna save Uncle Ray and me. You'll see."

"Kaleb, is Merle your Uncle Ray?"

"No, Ray is my bad uncle."

Tommy shook his head before he said, "Ok Kaleb, I'll put the gun away, but if you make a move at me, you'll have to be punished. Do you understand?" Kaleb nodded yes. "Now take the jar over to your corner and go number one."

Kaleb did as he was told. And then he looked back at us. His eyes were saying can you turn your backs, please? Tommy and I did and then we heard what sounded like a broken pipe let loose. I tried not to smile, but it was such an awkward thing to experience, I just couldn't help myself.

It took a long time before Kaleb walked back to us and held out the nearly full jar.

"Tommy, you know Dad and I are very squeamish when it comes to stuff like this. So you're gonna have to empty the jar," I said with a grin.

Tommy walked over and quickly grabbed the jar out of Kaleb's hand. He didn't waste any time and in a matter of seconds was in the bathroom emptying the jar. I walked to my office and grabbed my coat when the phone rang. I heard Tommy pick up the receiver in his office and say hello. A few mumbles were exchanged before Tommy said goodbye.

"Junior."

"Yeah."

"That was Ricky. He says they started the search a little early. He found butcher paper and lots of it. I think you'd better get out there and find out exactly where the butcher paper came from and what Merle uses it for."

"Ok, I'm on my way." I paused for a moment. "Tommy, did you believe Kaleb when he said he was afraid of guns and knives?"

"Junior, I did believe him. And that causes me a lot of grief. You know he just doesn't seem capable of committing most of these crimes." Tommy stopped talking for a moment and scratched his forehead. "Junior, I also believe there's a connection between Billy and Kaleb. But for the life of me I can't figure out what that might be." Tommy stopped and stared into space for a second or two before he spoke again.

"Getting back to Kaleb, it has crossed my mind that maybe we have the wrong guy. But it's more likely that we just don't have all the guys. I don't think Kaleb could have planned all of this by himself. I think someone has been helping him from day one."

"Tommy, I agree, but let's not forget that he did try to run me off the road. And there's no telling what he had planned for Madison. Was someone else with him? Maybe, but at this point we really don't know."

Tommy nodded in silent agreement before he walked back to his office.

Skeletons in the closet   51

Junior/I jumped in the remaining squad car and headed west for Cromwell and Merle Haugen's farm house. As I drove, I asked myself, *if Kaleb didn't commit these crimes, then who did? We know that Billy was responsible for Miller's cow. And he was definitely at the pawn shop when the stolen bracelet was pawned. And that probably puts him in Burt's house when the bracelet was stolen. But he couldn't have attacked Dad because he was at home. I know that because I was there with him. And he couldn't have shot Shadow or Matt because he was in the back seat of my squad car. Did he shoot Marjorie? Maybe.*

I stopped thinking about all of that stuff for a moment and shook my head. I shook my head because I knew I was back to square one. Square one being, we have no murder weapon. Then I said to myself, *maybe we'll get lucky and find it today?* I pulled onto the gravel drive that I'd sped over when I was chasing Kaleb. Somehow the place felt bigger and more desolate than I remember. As I was pulling up next to the house, Ricky came walking down the front porch steps. He was holding a bunch of butcher paper in his hands.

"Junior, that son of a gun Merle is lying about everything. I can feel it in my bones. He comes off as this simple old crippled farmer, but there's something rotten about that guy."

"Ricky, where'd he say he got the butcher paper?"

Ricky looked down at his hands.

"Oh yeah, the paper, well, you can ask him yourself. He's coming out right now. Then we're gonna go out to that damn barn and find out if he's telling the truth about a few things."

I was gonna ask Ricky about the barn, but when I heard the grinding of Merle's braces coming my way, I turned and watched him maneuver his way down the porch steps. He had his shirtsleeves rolled up and the muscles in his arms chorded up and danced. It was easy to see that at one time Merle was one strong son of a gun. Then I thought, *maybe he still is?*

"Hello, officer McCool. I sure am glad to see you. Mr. Reed here sure is bein' difficult about things. I can't seem to convince him of the truth no matter what I do. Maybe you can talk some sense into him for me," Merle said.

I was just about to ask Ricky why he didn't believe Mr. Haugen when Randi came walking out of the house carrying a busted up rifle.

"Hi Junior, we found the guns Mr. Haugen told us about. The problem is he failed to tell us at the station that his Winchester model 70 is broken and so rusted it couldn't shoot a BB. Mr. Haugen, tell us again how and when this gun was broken," Randi demanded.

Merle Haugen turned to me and rested on his crutches a bit before he said, "Officer McCool, the gun was broken by Kaleb many years ago. I was goin' on a hunting trip. I put my rifle and supplies in a duffle bag and carried it out and set it next to my truck. Kaleb is deathly afraid of firearms. Anywho, he got in my old truck and ran over the duffle bag. Nearly broke the gun in half. Smushed the lunch I had prepared too. Boy was I peeved."

"When did this happen?" I asked.

"Happened eight, maybe nine years ago."

"Merle, why didn't you tell Tommy about the gun being broken when he asked you about it at the station?"

"I figured you'd still want to see for yourself."

"Ok, well, I guess that makes sense. Randi, are you sure this gun hasn't been fired in the past six months or so."

"Yes Junior, the firing pin is bent so far sideways it wouldn't get anywhere near the primer or the rim of a cartridge. And it would take a long time for any gun to build up this kind of rust and corrosion. I can guarantee you that this gun has not been fired in years." Randi said with confidence.

"Ok, I trust your judgment." I thought to myself, *shoot I was hoping this was the gun we've been looking for.* "Ok Merle, that explains the gun. Can you explain the butcher paper for me?"

"Is it ok if I address you as Junior?"

"Sure."

"Junior, the butcher paper is for wrapping meats. I go over to Omaha every year and buy a side of beef, some pork, and poultry. They could wrap it up nice and neat for me, but I would have to pay for the service. So I just bring the meat home and do it myself."

"That makes sense to me. Merle, where do you keep all the packaged meat?"

"Out in the freezer. I think that's where Officer Reed was headed in the first place."

I looked over at Ricky and he said, "Yep, let's go see this freezer."

Ricky, in his typical sideways gait, lead the way as the four of us headed for the barn. We marched at a very fast pace. Merle's braces and crutches were grinding, clanking, and clattering something fierce, but he kept right up with us.

When we got to the huge barn doors that face east and towards the front porch of the house, I stopped and told Randi and Ricky to take out their guns. I did the same.

"Why Junior, there's nothing to be alarmed about," Merle said.

"Listen, Kaleb told Tommy and me that Benny hides in the barn. So I'm not taking any chances. Merle, please open one of the doors."

He said something under his breath, shrugged his shoulders, and then rolled the left door open. It was obvious that he'd done this many times before. It was dark inside and I for one wasn't going in there 'til I could see. Merle could feel the anxiety dripping off of Randi, Ricky, and me. So he walked inside for a ways and then a bright overhead light came on in the middle of the barn.

We slowly walked in, our guns still at the ready. Merle walked away from us over to the east wall of the barn. There was a freezer there that was about five feet long and four feet high. He opened the lid on the old horizontal chest freezer and backed away. Then the three of us looked in. The freezer was filled to the brim with what looked to be packages of meat. Each of the packages was neatly labeled as to its contents.

I pulled out nearly two dozen packages and Randi and Ricky began opening them. Each time they opened one of the packages the meat inside matched exactly what was written on the paper. There were pork chops, ribs, and porterhouse steaks just to name a few. There was just about every cut of meat you can imagine. I took out a few more that were marked giblets, breasts, and legs.

I opened all three, looked inside and then told Randi to close the packages so we could put them back. I put the packages back in the freezer as close to the same place they had been. I closed the lid on the freezer and then turned and asked Merle to show us around the barn. He said, "Follow me," and walked us to the very back of the barn and then pointed to his left. We all looked in a stable. There was a small night stand and lamp next to a very large single bed. A giant pair of pajamas and a robe were neatly folded and lying on top of the pillow.

"Kaleb spends most of his days and nights out here. He loves sleeping in the barn. Says he feels free that way. There's not much to it, but he doesn't need much."

There was an old immigrant's trunk at the foot of the bed. A large pair of slippers sat next to the trunk. I walked over and opened the lid. It was full of children's books, comic books, coloring books, a small dictionary, and a box of crayons. There was also one of those kits for making pot holders out of different colors of yarn. I felt someone breathing on my neck and turned just enough to see Ricky's head leaning over my shoulder.

Ricky blurted out, "Doesn't the big guy get cold out here?"

"Kaleb doesn't seem to mind the cold so much. I've tried to get him to sleep in the house, but he just won't do it. Says he's afraid of monsters with swords that hide in closets. You have to do your best to remember that Kaleb is a tormented child in a man's body."

"Yeah, well, he's the biggest child I've ever seen," Ricky said followed by a snort.

A moment after Ricky laughed, Randi smacked him hard on the arm.

"There's nothing funny about any of this, Ricky. If I hear you laugh at Kaleb again, you're gonna be sorry," Randi said with attitude.

"There's no need for squabbling. All of these reactions are quite normal. I've heard them all, and many, many times before," Merle said.

I walked away from the chaos and climbed a ladder up into the loft. I took my flashlight out of my jacket pocket and clicked it on. Nothing happened. So I shook it a couple of times and the light came on.

I searched from one end of the loft to the other with my light bouncing off the planked flooring. And other than some mouse droppings and a few bales of hay, the loft was empty. We had looked through every inch of the barn and there was just nothing there to raise any suspicions. I hollered down to the others, "Ok you guys, we're out of here."

I came down the ladder and when my right foot hit the floor of the barn, someone hollered, "Anybody home?"

I looked over to the open barn door and Matt was standing there holding a shot gun and what looked like a small caliber pistol.

"I've gone through every room in the house, every closet, and every cupboard and there's just nothing there," Matt said in a tired voice.

"Yeah, it's the same in here." I looked over at Merle. "Merle, are there any more outbuildings or sheds on this property?"

"Nope, at one time there was a corn dryer straight north of here, but that was destroyed by the tornado that touched down in 63."

"Merle, do you have any wells or outhouses?" I asked.

"The well dried up about fifteen years ago. There is an outhouse that Kaleb uses when the weather allows. Come on, I'll show you."

We all walked around the house and maybe fifty feet out from the back porch there was a rickety outhouse under a small clump of trees. It was leaning so hard to the left it was a miracle that it was still standing. I opened the door and a huge wasp flew out and buzzed my head. I let the door fly shut and ran as fast as I could while swatting my hands in the air. I didn't hear any buzzing so I stopped and watched the wasp slip back inside the outhouse. The others were standing with their hands covering their mouths so as not to laugh too hard. I smiled.

"Ok, you guys can laugh all you want, but it wasn't that funny to me."

I started to walk back to the outhouse when I noticed a worn trail leading straight south. I followed the trail with my eyes. The trail led right up to the back door of Marjorie's now vacant home. The others had their backs to me when I said, "Merle, who has been walking this path to Marjorie's house?"

Merle stopped his clanking and turned to me and quietly said, "Now and then I walked over to visit with Marjorie. I sure do miss her."

I had a chill run through me. I don't know why, but I didn't say a word after that and neither did anyone else.

A song to sooth the beast   52

Junior/**When we got back to the station,** we walked in the back door and stopped dead in our tracks. We stopped because we could all hear Tommy singing. He sang, "Oh lord, you delivered Daniel from the lion's den, Delivered Jonah from the belly of the whale and then, The Hebrew children from the fiery furnace, Oh the good book do declare, Well Lord, Lord if you can't help me, for goodness sakes don't you help that bear, Oh Lord, Lord if you can't help me, for goodness sakes don't you help that bear."

The moment Tommy was done singing, Kaleb clapped his hands and hollered, "Oh goody."

And then he asked for more. Tommy proceeded to tell the rest of the story about the preacher and the bear. And when he was finished telling the story, Randi, Ricky, Matt, and I all clapped right along with Kaleb.

When we rounded the corner and looked into the hallway, Tommy was sitting on a stool in front of the cell. Tommy had his old black Martin guitar resting on his lap. The giant was sitting with his legs crossed Indian style facing Tommy, on the other side of the bars of course.

Tommy is extremely shy about playing and singing in front of people, so it was a rare treat that we all got to enjoy.

"Hey Tommy, doesn't look like you had any problems with the prisoner?" I said.

"You don't know the half of it. But the fact is he's been remarkably calm and attentive," Tommy said a little red faced and without looking at me.

"How'd you keep him so calm?" I asked.

"I sang him every song I know. But when I sang the story about the preacher and the bear, well, he was spellbound. He said he'd never heard that one before."

"Why don't you tell the story again? I'd sure like to hear it. And I know everyone else would too. Do you want to hear the story again, Kaleb?" I asked.

"I sure would. I like Mr. Tommy and I like his songs too," Kaleb said with a childlike smile.

"Junior, that was the third time I told Kaleb the story and as far as I'm concerned, that was enough, at least for now. Walk with me to my office and tell me what you found out at the farm," Tommy said, still a little red faced.

"Will you come back, Mr. Tommy?" Kaleb asked.

"Yes Kaleb, I'll be back," Tommy answered.

When we got to Tommy's office, I told him everything we found, which was a bunch of nothing. While I was talking, his face changed from curious and attentive to brooding and kinda sad.

"Tommy, what's wrong?" I asked.

Tommy looked down at the floor before he said, "Well, one of the two people that were supposed to come and get Kaleb and take him back to Oakdale called and said they can't make it. He said they've been called out to a more critical situation. He wouldn't say what that was. Anyway, tomorrow we're supposed to take Kaleb down to Clarinda. And that will not be an easy task. Right after you left, Kaleb told me he had to go number two. So I told him if he behaved himself, I'd sing him some songs. He said ok and I put the waist restraint on him and secured his left hand to it. He didn't fight me at all, but he quivered and shook like a frightened animal. This time it was just to the bathroom, but taking him in a car all the way down to Clarinda will be a whole different story. I talked to Madison about it and she's going to conduct a few sessions with him. She wants to find out all she can about why Kaleb is Kaleb."

"Tommy, we can't let her do that. It's too dangerous. And besides, she's still in the hospital and might be there for a while," I said with a worried mind.

"Junior, we don't have any choice in the matter. And I guess you couldn't have known, but Madison is home now. She demanded to be let out of the hospital and Doc Mayland gave in. Madison and your dad can be very stubborn at times, if you know what I mean?" Tommy said with an edgy smile.

"Yes, yes they can," I agreed.

I stood there with my mind racing at the speed of light, well, as close to that as my mind can go. And then it came to me.

"Tommy, I know how we can get him down there without too much of a fuss," I said.

"And how's that Junior?" Tommy asked.

"Simple, we give him something to knock him out. Just like Billy did with that poor cow," I said thinking I was pretty clever.

340

"That's sounds like a good idea, Junior. And you're just the guy to give it to him. I'll open up the doors and you can go in there and pin him down and shove the pills or whatever down his throat. Shouldn't be that difficult," Tommy said with half-a-smile.

"Ok, ok, you don't have to rub it in, Tommy." I said as my shoulders slumped.

"Junior, I was just ribbin' you. That's actually a good idea. And it's probably the only way it can be done. I'll call Madison and ask her to bring something to the station that will knock him out. He'll be a heavy load, but at least he won't fight us," Tommy said with a smile.

"Now all we have to do is figure out how to get him to take whatever Madison brings," I said.

"I think I know exactly how to get that done. We could put the drug in his food, but he's pretty savvy to that kinda stuff. And other than darting him like some animal, I think the safest way is for someone that he trusts to give him the medicine. And that person is his Uncle Merle. I'll bring Merle into town and explain to him what's going on. I don't trust him much, but what harm could there be if he helps us medicate Kaleb?"

"Ok, I agree with all of that except for the fact that now I think Kaleb trusts you too Tommy. If all else fails maybe you could talk him into it. Maybe you could sing to him, you know like the Pied Piper," I said.

"Junior, are you trying to be funny?"

"No Tommy, I'm serious."

"Ok, well thanks, but I think I'll reserve that option as a last resort," Tommy said as he picked up the phone and dialed Madison's house.

**Junior**/**Madison and Tommy** debated on which medication would be best for Kaleb. They finally agreed on the sedative, Nembutal; known on the streets as "Yellow Submarine." At the time I thought, _so what is the Beatles song really about?_

Merle agreed to help us, but only if I would come and get him. Said he didn't much care for Tommy. I understood. We all agreed that the best time to medicate Kaleb would be the next evening just before he ate. Late in the afternoon the next day I drove over to Cromwell to get Merle. He smiled and waved hello as he ambled down his porch steps. He was wearing overalls, brown boots, an old denim jacket, and a green John Deere hat, which he wore slanted to the left. I loaded his crutches in the back seat and he held onto my arm as I helped him into the front. His grip was strong and steady. I figured he'd done this many times before.

I held the back door to the station open for Merle when we got there, and he clicked and grinded his way straight to the jail cell. He knew his way around. Kaleb immediately popped up from the floor and reached thru the bars so he could hold on to his uncle's hand.

"Uncle Merle - have you come to take me for a walk?" Kaleb asked.

"Well, not exactly. But they are going to let you out of here this evening."

"Oh goody," Kaleb said as he let go of his uncle's hand and clapped.

"These nice folks want to take you to a place that's very neat and clean. In fact, it's so clean that nearly everyone there wears white clothes all the time."

"Why, I couldn't wear white clothes in the barn. I'd soil 'em for sure," Kaleb said with a guilty smile.

Merle Haugen turned to me.

"Junior, I'd like to get this over with. Is your sister here with the sedative?" he said with a scowl.

"I'm sorry she's not here yet, but I know she will be, and very soon. Have you thought on how you want to get Kaleb to cooperate?" I asked.

"Yes, thought about it all night. I will not trick or mislead him. I'm just gonna tell him the truth. He may fuss a bit at first, but he's always obeyed me in the past. And I see no reason why now would be any different," he said without any hesitation.

As we were talking, Tommy and Madison came walking into the station.

"Junior, will you and Mr. Haugen please come out here for a minute?" Tommy asked.

"Hi Mr. Tommy, are you coming with me to the white clothes place?" Kaleb asked.

"Yes Kaleb, I will go with you. We're gonna go right after you eat your supper. Ok?"

"Oh goody, yes right after I eat," Kaleb said.

Merle and I walked out by the front desk and both said hello to Madison. She looked at me for a moment before saying, "Mr. Haugen, I can grind up the pills, so you can put them in his food or in a drink if you prefer."

"No, I believe I'll just tell him to take the pills, so he can go with the Chief down to Clarinda. For whatever reason he seems to have taken a shine to your uncle," Merle said with a trailing note of sarcasm.

Madison pulled a small envelope out of her pocket and slowly tore one end open.

"Please, just give me the pills, I'll do the rest. You all should stay here whilst I talk to him. That is everyone but the Chief. I think Kaleb will be a little more agreeable if his Mr. Tommy comes with me," he said not hiding his jealousy.

Madison handed Merle Haugen the pills.

"Please make sure that he swallows both pills," Madison warned.

"I know what I'm doing. Just make sure you all stay out of sight," Merle said.

Tommy filled a cup of water and followed Mr. Haugen into the hallway and stood behind him. I continued to watch from a point where I knew Kaleb could not see me.

"I don't trust that Mr. Haugen. Junior, make sure you keep an eye on him," Madison said as she peered over my shoulder.

"Kaleb, now if you really want to go with the Chief here, you have got to take these pills," uncle Merle said.

"But I don't like pills. They make me sad," Kaleb replied.

"Kaleb, these are happy pills. And they are your ticket out of here. Please don't make me go get Uncle Ray. He won't be happy at all," Uncle Merle warned.

"No, I don't want Uncle Ray to come here. Ok, I'll take the pills."

Merle Haugen turned and Tommy handed him the cup of water. He then turned back to Kaleb and handed him the pills and said, "Now put them in your mouth. When I see your hand is empty, I'll give you the water."

Kaleb did as he was told and then Uncle Merle handed him the cup of water and watched him swallow the pills as he drank the entire cupful of water.

"Kaleb, now open your mouth and stick out your tongue so I can be sure that you swallowed the pills."

Kaleb opened his mouth and both pills were sitting atop his tongue.

"Ok, I guess I'm going to have to go get Uncle Ray," Uncle Merle once again warned.

"No, no, please don't. Give me some more water and I'll swallow the pills," Kaleb begged.

Tommy ran back to the water cooler and filled the cup again. He returned to the jail cell and handed the cup to Kaleb. Mr. Haugen moved back behind Tommy and they watched Kaleb tip the cup back and then swallow in an exaggerated manner. Then he opened his mouth and showed Tommy that he had indeed swallowed the pills.

"Now can we go, Mr. Tommy?" Kaleb asked.

"Sure we can. Right after you eat your supper," Tommy said with a smile.

I turned back to Madison and we both relaxed a bit. That was just before we heard a couple of loud clanks in the hallway.

I turned around and looked back at Tommy and Kaleb as they looked at Merle Haugen. He was standing tall, without his crutches. He was a much bigger man than we had thought. He had a small hand gun pointed at Tommy.

"Ok you drunk sum-bitch, move back over there and away from this here cell," Mr. Haugen ordered with a pronounced southern twang.

The two of them slowly switched places and Kaleb cried out, "No Uncle Ray."

Merle Haugen backed over to the cell door making sure to face Tommy. He had his gun pointed at Tommy's chest.

"Kaleb, everything will be ok. This man and these people have lied to you. They want to hurt you and then take you far, far away. Uncle Ray will not let them hurt you." He stopped for a second and yelled, "Junior, you get the keys to this cell right now. And remember, if you make one wrong move, I will shoot your damn uncle. That goes for you too Ms. Madison."

I felt as though I was paralyzed. I just couldn't move.

"Junior, do as Mr. Haugen told you and go get the keys. They're on my desk," Tommy said.

"Why now, that's the first intelligent thing I've ever heard you say Chief," Mr. Haugen twanged.

I ran by Madison into Tommy's office and grabbed the keys off of his desk. I ran back to the hallway.

"Stop right there, Junior. Now slide them keys over here," Mr. Haugen ordered.

I slid the keys over to him.

"Uncle Ray, please don't hurt Mr. Tommy. Please, please," Kaleb pleaded.

"So you're the Uncle Ray that Kaleb has been talking about. He says you're the bad uncle. Why would he say that?" Tommy asked.

"Yes, I'm Uncle Ray. Raymond Merle Haugen at your service. And right after I get Kaleb out of here, I'll be the good uncle again. My nephew and I will be taking your niece as collateral. And if you follow us, then I'll be forced to kill her. Junior, I know what y'all are thinkin' and if you make one wrong move, I'm gonna have to shoot your good uncle Tommy."

"You've thought this all through, haven't you, Uncle Ray," Tommy said.

"Yes, and the next time you serve a search warrant on somebody, you oughta remember to search that person too. I had the gun on me the whole damn time. Good thing your dummies didn't find what they was looking fer. Cuz I'd have shot ever last one of 'em."

"So you were the one driving the car that night my brother and his wife were run off the road, weren't you!" Tommy alleged, his jaw clinched tight as a drum.

"You're a smart-alec, you know that, Chief. Yes, I was the one driving. I was just gonna have a little fun with the pretty lady, but your stupid brother had to come along and spoil things for me," Merle Haugen said with a menacing smile"So Billy didn't drug Jolene Meadows for himself. She was going to be a present for you, wasn't she," Tommy said in a demanding tone.

"You know smart guy, I'm tired a talking ta you. Now it's time for me and Kaleb to get out a here. And it's definitely time fer you ta die."

"No Uncle Ray. Don't hurt Mr. Tommy," Kaleb once again pleaded.

"Shut up, you big dummy!" Uncle Ray yelled.

"I'm not a dummy. You and Benny shouldn't call me a dummy. It's not nice!" Kaleb yelled.

"Screw Benny! I told you a thousand times he's a dummy too!" Uncle Ray screamed.

"The medicine you get at Clarinda isn't for Kaleb at all, is it. It's for you. And you haven't been taking your meds, have you Uncle Ray," Tommy said in a threatening tone.

Merle Haugen's face contorted and then quick as a cat he pounced forward and hit Tommy across the face with the butt of the gun. Tommy staggered back a step, and then fell to the floor. I ran to Tommy and pressed my hand over his eye. Blood began to seep through my fingers.

"I need a towel or a rag or something to stop this bleeding!" I hollered.

"No, no! Uncle Ray, you hurt Tommy!" Kaleb screamed.

"Both of you shut up! He's gonna die anyway. So what's a little blood gonna hurt!" Uncle Ray hollered.

I looked back at Tommy; his face was now a harlequin's mask of blood. I heard a gurgling sound. I turned to look at Uncle Ray and his feet were kicking wildly, about six inches above the floor. His braces began clanking against the cell bars in a desperate rhythm. He was trying to speak, but Kaleb's arm was far too tight around his neck. And the more Uncle Ray wriggled, the harder Kaleb squeezed. Then two shots rang out from the gun Uncle Ray held in his right hand. Both slugs ricocheted off the floor. Then he slowly raised the gun and pointed it at Tommy.

Two more shots in close succession rang out just before Uncle Ray's gun fell to the floor. I peered over my shoulder and Madison was standing there with her arms extended. She had Tommy's revolver held tightly in both hands. It was kinda like watching a black and white movie while standing on a sidewalk and looking through a storefront window.

As I continued to watch the movie Madison ran over to Kaleb and ordered him to let go of his Uncle Ray. Kaleb did as he was told, and Raymond Merle Haugen's limp body clanked hard to the floor. Madison felt for a pulse. Then she felt all over Uncle Ray's upper body and peered at her hand, no blood. Even from behind the storefront window I knew what had happened. She had missed with both shots. We looked over at Kaleb.

He was lying face down on the bed. A trail of bright red blood was splattered on the floor between us and him. Madison tore the cell door keys out of Uncle Ray's clinched left fist. She worked the key hard in the lock and then slung the door back. She ran to Kaleb and somehow managed to turn him over. He was bleeding profusely from the left side of his chest. She yanked the pillow from under Kaleb's head and pressed it tight to the wound.

"Junior! - Junior! Get over to a phone and call for an ambulance," she said as tears of rage began to fall.

It was right about that time when Randi and Ricky came waltzing through the back door. And as Ricky whistled his way over to his desk, Randi ran back to us. I don't know how women do it, but it seems to me that at times they have senses that us guys just don't have.

Randi looked at me, then she looked at Merle Haugen, and then her eyes locked onto Madison's. Didn't say a word. She just ran to her phone and called for an ambulance. Well, actually she said we needed two ambulances. Right after she called for the ambulances, Tommy moved my hand away from his eye and jumped to his feet.

"Tommy, what are you doing?" I said.

"Junior, go get Ricky. Then the two of you get back in here. Do it now! " Tommy screamed.

I ran towards Ricky's desk and he ran towards me. We nearly collided. Then we ran back to the cell. Tommy was inside and had the blankets on the bed wrapped around Kaleb like a hammock. He started sliding Kaleb across the floor and had him out near the back door before Ricky or I could help.

"Ricky! We don't have time to wait for the ambulance. Get your roller over here so we can load Kaleb on it." Ricky moved fast and had the car as close to the back of the building as he could and when he got out of the car, he said, "Tommy, did you say on it?"

"Yes I did. Now stop standing around and grab hold of the blanket."

Tommy grabbed the blanket near Kaleb's head. And Ricky and I grabbed hold at his feet. Tommy counted to three and we lifted him onto the hood of the car. Then Tommy yelled, "Ok Junior, just drive the way you usually do. Ricky and I will hold onto Kaleb."

By this time Madison and Randi were huddled together staring at us.

"I'll call and tell them to have a gurney waiting outside for you!" Randi hollered.

I took off going about five miles an hour. Oak Street and the hospital are only two blocks away and safety was more important than trying to go fast. Three young orderlies were waiting for us in front of the hospital. They did a double take when they saw Kaleb on the hood of the car. But they didn't let that get in their way and quickly loaded him onto the gurney and whisked him into the hospital.

Ricky parked the car and the three of us sat down on that bench in front of the hospital and listened to the ambulance scream out the back on its way to pick up Uncle Ray. Ricky couldn't sit still and got up and went inside the hospital. Tommy and I sat there for only another minute or so when we heard footsteps coming our way. It was our cousin Wally Ramsbottom.

"Hello Junior, hello Tommy. Listen, Ricky told me to come out and get you, Tommy. He said you need to have your eye looked at." Wally stopped talking and actually looked at Tommy's eye. "Gee-whiz Tommy, you really do need to have that eye looked at. Please come with me."

Tommy didn't move.

"Please Tommy," Wally quietly repeated.

"Tommy, they're gonna have to sew that eye up some time. And now's as good a time as any," I said.

Tommy looked at me and then he looked at Wally for a moment just before he stood up and walked inside the hospital. Wally waved goodbye and went back inside. Ricky came back out and sat down next to me. We sat for another twenty minutes or so before we watched the ambulance slowly drive into the parking lot.

When the ambulance driver finally came to a stop, the gurney carrying Merle Haugen's body was rolled to the back of the hospital. Eventually the girls walked up and quietly squeezed in next to us. Not a word was spoken by anyone until it dawned on me that the police station must be empty.

"Hey, did you lock up the station, Randi?"

"No."

"Why not?" I asked.

Randi didn't even look at me when she said, "I didn't lock it because Matt and Shadow are there."

"Oh," was all I could come up with from my side of the storefront window.

Madison/I fought pent-up emotions and tears as I waited for a report from Doc Mayland. The loathing I once held for Kaleb was now mixed with an agonizing regret. Over and over I asked myself, *how could I have missed with both bullets from such a short distance?* The bare-knuckled truth is that I hate guns and don't want anything to do with them. And I guess that, in and of itself, is what has caused the riff, no it's actually more like the great divide. Anyway, that's what has always come between my sister, Randi, and I. Guns!

Yet, there I was in a situation where a gun was controlling the very lives of every person in that darn police station. Guns! I was just about to go through another round of confusion when a nurse walked up and told me I had a phone call. I walked from the waiting room to the front desk and picked up the phone, "Hello."

"Hello Madison, this is Jenny. I've just heard about what happened and I am so sorry. How are you doing?" Jenny softly asked.

"I guess I'm ok, thanks. It's just that I, I–"

"I know. You're trying to figure out how it happened. And at the same time you're beating yourself up. Madison, you have set some very high standards for yourself. And at times they're impossible to achieve. Please try to remember that you're only human."

"Jenny, how did you know?"

"News travels very fast between nurses and caregivers," Jenny softly said.

"But–"

"Madison, Kaleb is going to be fine. And above all else you have to remember that none of this was your fault. Now I'd like you to please listen to me for a second. You are a trained listener, and I might add, a very good one. But there's one thing that you and all people sometimes forget. And that is when you're dealing with matters of the heart, you in turn must listen with your heart. Madison, I have to go now, but could you please pass on a message to Junior for me?" she asked.

"Of course," I said.

"Just tell Junior I said hello. And to solve this mystery he needs to stop being a professional for a moment or two and listen with his heart."

"Jenny, will you–"

"Yes I will and goodbye now."

The line went dead, and I stood there for a long time holding the phone to my ear.

"Madison, Madison! Are you ok?" Doc Mayland asked.

"Oh, yes, I'm ok. How is–"

"Kaleb is going to be fine. I'm really not sure how or why he didn't bleed to death. Maybe, just maybe it was the Nembutal that he'd taken. It might have slowed his physical and emotional being down just enough so that he didn't panic. Any more movement and stress at all and he might have bled out. I guess we'll really never know. If I didn't know better, I'd say there was an angel looking over him."

"Doc, did you examine Kaleb's uncle Ray?"

"Yes, I did."

"How'd he die? I mean what was the cause?"

"Well, for starters his windpipe was crushed, but I believe the cause of death was probably his broken neck. The final determination will be up to the coroner. Madison, I know you want to see Kaleb. He's in room thirty. After you see him, I suggest that you go home and get some rest. Goodbye," Doc Mayland said as he turned and walked away.

I stood there numb to the world around me.

"Madison, what are you smiling about?"

I turned around after hearing Junior's voice. He and Tommy were staring at me. I reached up and touched my face.

"I'm smiling because Doc Mayland just told me that Kaleb made it and he's going to be fine."

Junior whooped like an Indian and Tommy smiled as he clapped his hands."

"Junior, you won't believe this, but Jenny called."

"When?" Junior excitedly asked.

"Just about five minutes ago."

"What'd she say?"

"Junior, calm down. She told me that Kaleb was going to be fine and that she wanted me to give you a message." Junior started to blurt something out, but I put my hand up in the universal stop position to make him listen.

"Jenny wants you to slow down. And she said you can solve this entire thing if you'll just listen with your heart."

Junior mouthed what I'd just said to him and started to say something. I put my finger to my mouth again and softly shushed him. The three of us walked down to room thirty and stood and watched the giant sleep. From where I was standing Kaleb looked like a very large child. I looked over at Tommy and for a moment, just a moment, he did too.

Heart of hearts   55

***Junior*/That night I went to bed** a little more informed about the who's and the what's. But there was still a tremor rumbling through me. I expected to have some of my mean dreams, but I didn't expect having all of them in one night, and in brilliant 3D Technicolor. I finally came to the end of my dreams and once again I was looking through the storefront window. Jenny was on the other side. Over and over she said, "Junior, listen with your heart."

I woke up the next day and I knew what had to be done. I got dressed and ran to the diner. Ricky was sitting there just like my heart told me he would be.

"Ricky, I sure am glad to see you. Stop eating, we need to go someplace and right now."

"Ok, well good morning to you too, Junior."

Mary walked up and gave me a suspicious look. *Her hair looked like it was on fire - again.*

"Junior, are you just gonna stand there or are you going to order something?"

"Yes Mary, I am. I'd like one black coffee to go please."

"What? You've never ordered a coffee to go in your life. Ricky, is this some kind of trick you thought up? I go get the coffee and then the two of you skedaddle on out of here," she asked.

"No Mary," was all Ricky said.

She looked at the two of us with a stern eye.

"Mary, it's not a trick. Please hurry, this is important," I said.

She brought the coffee back in a Styrofoam cup and I set fifty cents on the table. Then Ricky stared at me.

"What?" he kept staring. "Ok Mary, how much was Ricky's breakfast?"

"Eighty-five cents," she said.

I put two dollars down on the table. Ricky picked up the fifty cents that was supposed to pay for my coffee and walked away. I followed him for just a second and when I looked back at Mary, she had her tongue sticking out. We jumped in Ricky's roller and headed north on highway 25 towards the little town of Orient.

"Junior, are we going to Orient?" Ricky asked.

"No, we're going back to the Thornton farm to look in that tree house."

"Why? We looked all through that tree house and there was nothing there," he said with authority.

"Yes, I know that. But I had a dream a while back and in that dream Jenny told me to go to the tree house. Ricky, you gotta make hay while the sun shines. And that's what we're gonna do."

"What the heck? Make hay? Junior, have you lost your mind?" he asked with a credible amount of sincerity.

"Ricky, sometimes a person needs to listen with their heart. And that's what I'm doing. You should give it a try some time."

He shook his head a couple of times just before we turned off the highway and headed east to the Thornton farm. Ricky then turned left onto the gravel drive that leads up to the house. We drove right by the house and headed out to Billy's mobile home and the tree house. We both got out of the car, but Ricky just stood there. So I left him staring into space and climbed up into the tree house. I walked from one end to the other with my eyes glued to the floor. Then I walked around the perimeter and looked at the walls. There was nothing there and I began to doubt the entire idea.

"Junior, you're not moving. Do you need some help?" Ricky shouted.

"Yes, I suppose I do. Ricky, please help me for about ten minutes. If we don't find anything, then we'll go," I said disregarding my heart.

Ricky climbed up and began crawling on his hands and knees around the edges where the floor and the walls come together. I thought *that was a good idea* and followed suit. He was heading west along the north wall and I headed east along the south wall. When I got to the far southeast corner, I saw it shining in the new day sun. It was stuck in an open crack in the wall. I put a glove on and picked it out with my pocket knife and said, "Eureka, we can go now, Ricky."

He stood up and slowly walked over to me and peered into my open hand.

"I'll be a blue-nosed gopher. I don't believe it, Junior. That has to be–"

354

"Yep, it has to be the thirty aught six shell casing from the bullet someone used to shoot Shadow in the back. Now all we have to do is figure out whom the shooter was. Ricky, I think we're on the right trail. Let's get out of here."

"Yeah let's, I don't like '*whom*' we might meet. This place gives me the creeps," Ricky said.

We drove back along the path to the house and Nel was standing out in the middle of their drive waving at me. I rolled my window down.

"Hello Junior, what are you doing out here?" she asked.

"We were just looking around, but we didn't find what we were looking for. I think we're looking in the wrong place. Tomorrow morning Tommy, Ricky, and I are gonna go back out to that old man's farm in Cromwell and have another look see. I'm confident that this time we'll find what we're looking for."

"I heard all about that giant you arrested. And I heard you had a shootout or something like that. Too bad about the old man," she said.

"Yes, it is. Well, I'd like to talk some more, but we have to get back. We'll be seeing you," I said as Ricky pressed hard on the accelerator.

I looked back. Nel Thornton was not waving.

"Junior, did you notice that she didn't say hello to me? She's nothing but an old witch."

"You could be right about her being a witch. And yes, I did notice that she didn't say hello to you. I also noticed that she knew about the old man. How'd she know that?"

Ricky put his finger to his forehead like the Scarecrow in the Wizard of Oz and said, "Yeah, how did she know that?"

Junior/**It was a cold, cold night** so I dressed especially warm. I shivered as I peered down at the lights that were heading towards us. I watched as someone got out of a pickup truck that had stopped just below me.

"Junior, do you think it's Benny?" Ricky asked.

"Maybe," I whispered.

I heard the door to the barn open and then whoever it was walked straight to the old freezer and lifted the lid. The stranger began taking the packages of meat out that I had carefully put back a few days ago. The individual stopped for a moment, looked around and reached deep down and pulled out a long package. I shined my flashlight down on the person. It was a woman with long black hair wearing a heavy overcoat. She looked up at the light shining in her face and started running for the open door. She might have made it back to her truck if not for the fact that Tommy was standing in her way. The woman stopped in her tracks and hung her head. She didn't say a word when Tommy turned her around. And as he fastened his handcuffs on her, he firmly proclaimed, "You're under arrest for the murder of Marjorie Lynn Jessen."

Ricky and I backed down the steps as fast as we could. I ran over to where Tommy and the woman were standing and shined my light into the hostile face of a raven haired Nel Thornton.

"Hello Nel, I thought we might find you out here," I said in disgust.

And in a soft southern drawl she answered, "My name is Addy, Addy Haugen. And I have every right to be here. This is my brother Raymond's farm."

I shook my head a couple of times and looked over at Tommy.

"Junior, it looks like we have an entire family of people that have more than one name and personality. Whoever you are, do you have any weapons on you?" Tommy asked.

"No, and these are the last words I will speak to you, you trespassers! I want my lawyer," she said with a snooty debutante attitude.

"Junior, hold on to her while I pat her down," Tommy said.

First, Tommy pulled up her left sleeve. She was wearing the bracelet that had been stolen from Mrs. Silvers. He took it off of her wrist. He opened her coat and there was a large inner pocket on the right side. He reached in and pulled out a shiny black revolver.

"I thought you said you didn't have any weapons," Tommy mimicked with contempt.

He continued to pat her down and then said, "I guess that's it. Ricky, can you hold on to her while Junior and I go through the freezer?"

Ricky walked over to Nel Thornton.

"Tommy, I don't like her. Do I have to hold on to her?"

She spit in Ricky's face and then immediately bawled, "This is all your fault. You sent Billy to prison for something he didn't do. I hate you!"

Ricky wiped his face and then grabbed hold of her arm and shouted, "The feeling's mutual, you wig wearin' witch!"

Tommy and I walked over to the long package she'd dropped knowing full well that it was the rifle we'd been looking for. I tore the butcher paper off a thick cardboard box made to transport rifles. I opened the box, but there was no rifle inside.

First, I pulled out a pair of small wooden crutches and a bright red Raggedy Anne wig and matching outfit. Then I pulled out a broomstick, a tattered black witch's dress, and a pointy black witch's hat. The stuff I pulled out of the box was creepy. I stopped what I was doing for a moment and looked over at Nel Thornton.

"So that was you and Billy that came trick or treating on Halloween. What were the two of you up to?" I asked.

She didn't respond. She just stood there stone-faced.

"Never mind, I guess it doesn't really matter anymore," I said as I looked back in the freezer.

I was to the bottom of the freezer now; at least I thought I was. The more I looked, the more something wasn't right. I stepped back and looked at the freezer from a distance and realized what was wrong.

"Tommy, there's what looks like the bottom of the freezer, but I think it's just a piece of plywood painted white so as to look like the bottom."

I reached back inside and tried to pull the false bottom up, but it wouldn't budge. Tommy said, "Let me try."

357

He reached down and rather than pull he pushed on one end and the other end popped up. He pulled the plywood off, looked in, stepped back, and gasped, "Good lord."

I looked inside and immediately gagged.

Ricky asked, "What's wrong, Junior?"

"There's a man in the freezer, that's what's wrong," I said as I shuddered.

And Ricky said, "Well, help him out."

"I would Ricky except for the fact that he's frozen stiff as a board!"

Ricky let go of Nel and ran over and peered into the freezer. And when the visual hit home, he ran to a shadowy corner and vomited. Tommy and I both took a breath and then looked back in the freezer. There was a badge sitting on the frozen man's stomach. Tommy turned to Nel and grit his teeth before he roared, "You cut off his feet just so he'd fit in the freezer, didn't you!"

She flinched hard but didn't say a word.

"Is it?" I started to ask.

"Yes, it has to be Dumbrowski," Tommy said in disgust. Then he turned to Nel and hollered, "Where's the damn rifle you murdering-witch?"

Nel didn't say a word.

"Tommy, I think I know where the rifle is," I said with some confidence. "Where'd you park the cruiser?"

"I parked it out in that clump of trees by the outhouse."

"Perfect, we can put Mrs. Thornton in the back of the car while we look for the gun. Let's go," I said.

Tommy closed the freezer lid and grabbed Mrs. Thornton by the arm. The four of us walked out to the clump of trees and Tommy deposited Nel Thornton in the back seat of the car. Then I motioned Ricky and Tommy to follow me. I walked straight over to the outhouse, opened the door, and shined my flashlight in. The same wasp I'd encountered a few days ago flew out at me. But this time he had a couple of friends with him. And once again I ran swatting my hands in the air. When I thought I was a safe distance away I watched Tommy brave the wasps and go into the outhouse. I heard him say, "Christ, it smells awful in here."

He rummaged around for a bit and then said, "Junior, I think you're right."

Ricky and I shined our flashlights in and watched Tommy begin pulling a braided rope up that was attached beneath the makeshift toilet seat. Tommy pulled maybe five feet of rope up. There was a long object wrapped in butcher paper attached. Tommy unfastened the rope and carried the package out in the fresh air.

"Ok you guys, I believe this has to be the rifle we've been looking for. But I don't want to touch it out here. I think we should wait and open it in the light back at the station."

Ricky and I looked at each other. We were impatient as all get out. But we knew Tommy was right.

"Ok, we can do that. That way we can have a witness or two there with us," I said.

"Yeah, and we can put that bitch in a jail cell where she belongs," Ricky said.

"Ricky, I think you meant to say witch, didn't you?" Tommy said more than asked.

"No, I meant to say bitch," Ricky said with a snort.

Before we headed back to the police station, we put the rifle in the trunk of the car and just to be on the safe side we chained and locked the doors to the barn. Ricky drove while I sat in the front seat, and Tommy rode in the back with our scornful detainee. As soon as we got back to the station, Nelbjorn Adel Thornton lawyered up. She ended up calling Stanley Corbett, the same attorney Burt Silvers called after he was caught breaking into the Crestfield police station.

Junior/**The first thing we did** when we got back to the station was call Ajax. We wanted him there when we took off the butcher paper. We knew it was a rifle, but we didn't know if it was the one we'd been looking for. Tommy carefully removed the butcher paper and it turned out to be a shining, fully loaded, Winchester model 70. The shell casings in the gun were an exact match to the shell casing I found in the tree house. And there were fingerprints all over the rifle. We were confident that between the fingerprints found on the rifle and the matching shell casings, the state could ultimately prove that it was without question Nel, her brother Ray, and possibly clubfoot Billy, that had murdered Marjorie. And that Nel was probably the person that hid in the tree house and shot Shadow in the back.

Tommy immediately called the state police and was told to leave everything as it was and wait for their investigators. Everyone went home to get some sleep, everyone that is, except Tommy. Somebody had to stay with the prisoner. Tommy called me at nine in the morning and told me three guys from the state were already there at the station.

I got dressed as fast as I could and walked into the station at the same time Uncle Ajax did. You should have seen the looks on the state investigators' faces when they saw Ajax. I should say when they saw Ajax's holster and toy gun, and of course, little Jax. After some headshakes and handshakes, their ranking Lieutenant, a tallish, dark guy, named Timmons politely told us that they were taking over everything.

"Lieutenant Timmons, we've been through more than you'll ever know during the course of this matter. So I think the fair thing for you to do is to give me a little time so that I might speak with my people," Tommy firmly said.

"Yes, I suppose you have been through a lot. Go ahead and talk to your people if you want," Timmons said.

I called Randi. I knew she could get everyone here in a hurry. Within thirty minutes everyone was in Tommy's office.

"Ok, nothing like what we've been through this last year has ever happened in Crestfield. And I hope to heaven nothing like this ever happens again. We've all been to hell and back. So I say we let the state take over. It's time for us to get back to normal, whatever that is. And the sooner the better," Tommy softly said.

Everyone in the room looked at each other a couple of times and not one person objected. Tommy was right. We needed to get back to the slow steady pace of life we were accustomed to. So as a unit we all walked out of Tommy's office.

"Ok officer Timmons, the case is all yours," Tommy said.

"Thank you. Chief, I have to tell you that right now our main concern is to take officer Dumbrowski back to his family so that he might have a proper burial. You're sure it's him?" Timmons asked.

"Yes, positive. You'll find his badge there with him. There is something else you should be aware of before you go out there," Tommy said.

"And what's that?" Timmons asked.

"There's a dangerous person still out there somewhere who played a major role in all of this. We were told that he sometimes hides in that barn. But my gut tells me he's miles away from here by now. We know little about this person other than his name is Benny," Tommy said.

"Do you have a description of this Benny person?" Timmons asked.

"He's small in stature and has a high-pitched voice is all we really know. But make no mistake, he's very dangerous," Tommy said.

"Well, if this Benny is out there, we'll get him. Listen, thanks for all your hard work. You solved a very tough case," he said in earnest.

"Well, when it comes right down to it, Junior here is the one that solved the case," Tommy said as he pointed to me.

I turned a little red and then something in me couldn't let it go at that.

"Actually, well, I mean, the truth is Jenny's the one that solved the case," I said.

Everyone there looked at me just before officer Timmons asked who Jenny was.

"She's the nurse that took care of my dad after he was attacked," I said.

Officer Timmons looked at me then he looked at the others for an explanation, but none were offered.

"Ok, a nurse solved the case," he shook his head for a second. "Listen Chief, we've made arrangements to have Butch taken home and–"

"Who is Butch?" Tommy quickly asked.

"Well, his name is Burl Dumbrowski, but everyone called him Butch," Timmons explained.

"Oh, I see," Tommy said.

"And in a week or so we'll have someone here to pick up this Kaleb character. I will–"

Uncle Ajax cut him off at the pass.

"That is one thing that we will not allow you to do. Kaleb will stay here until he is physically well enough to be moved. And when he is able to be moved, he will be transferred to Clarinda Cove to be evaluated by one of our professionals. And this matter is not open for discussion. Now, if you want to fight us on this, you'll have to go through about ten doctors. And that's after you go through little Jax and me," Ajax said as he snatched little Jax off his shoulder and shook him at Timmons.

Lieutenant Timmons looked over at Tommy. I think he was gonna laugh but decided not to.

"The Mayor and I discussed this long before you got here. We knew you'd want to take over, and that's ok, but we won't let you take Kaleb. Not yet anyway," Tommy said with his heart.

Timmons looked over at the bookends that had come with him. And they in turn looked back at Timmons and shrugged their shoulders. Timmons looked at Tommy and said, "Chief, I know you wouldn't do anything that could be considered obstructing justice. So I'm going to give you a little professional leeway on this one. But sure as you're born there's going to come a time when that man you have in your hospital is gonna have to answer some questions."

We all looked at each other and a couple of us smiled. That is, we smiled on the inside at the thought of Kaleb answering questions.

Kaleb   58

***Junior*/We helped the state investigators** when we could, but for the most part we pretty much told them we were going fishing. Matter of fact Ricky, Dad, and I did head out to Green Valley Lake. Fished all day and caught a few bullheads and about a dozen crappie and bluegill. Didn't really matter what we caught. I think the three of us were just there to clear our heads. Dad was unusually quiet the entire day. I think finding out part of the mystery connected to mom caused him more grief than relief.

Nel Thornton, AKA Addy Haugen was to be transferred to Union County. Her lawyer had fought for and won a change of venue. He argued that his client could never receive a fair trial anywhere in Liberty County. The day after she was transferred, her husband, Jeb Thornton, came in the station. Jeb slowly hobbled through the front door and wasted no time with formalities. He asked Randi if he could speak with Tommy and me.

"Mr. Thornton, let me go tell them you're here. I'll be, or I guess, they'll be back in a minute."

"Thank you, young lady," Jeb answered.

Randi nearly ran to Tommy's office.

"Tommy, Jeb Thornton is here, and he wants to speak with you and Junior. What should I tell him?"

"You don't have to tell him anything; I'll do it myself. Right now you go get Junior and tell him to meet us here in my office."

"Gotchya," was all she said.

Tommy walked out to meet Mr. Thornton and was met with a smile. Tommy wasn't sure what to think.

"Hello Jeb. I have to tell you I wasn't expecting to see you here in the station, especially with what looks like a smile on your face."

From a distance I watched Jeb shake Tommy's hand.

"Well Tommy, this smile is here because the sheer meanness and misery this town and its people have been through has got to stop. Tommy, would it be ok if we talked privately in your office?"

"Sure, but I want you to know right up front that there are many things I can't discuss with you. So, if you came here for answers, you're probably going to leave a little disappointed."

"Thanks for being honest with me, Tommy. But you have it all wrong. I didn't come here to ask any questions. I came here to give you some answers."

By this time I was standing next to Tommy and heard what Jeb Thornton had just said.

"How you doin', Junior," Jeb said as he extended his hand to me.

"I'm fine thanks and you?"

"I think I'll be doin' a might better once we have a little pow-wow of sorts."

We slowly walked to Tommy's office. It was easy to see that walking caused Jeb more pain than he would probably ever let on. The three of us sat down and before Tommy or I could say a word, Jeb began.

"You have probably wondered who Kaleb is. Well, I'm gonna do my best to tell you. He is Nel's deceased sister, Adel Dardanelle's, son. Kaleb has always been a bit on the special side. Some might even say he's retarded and they'd be right. But once you get to know him, he is a wonderful soul. The joy he wants to share is as genuine and true as the morning sun. Now I don't know what Ray may have said about Kaleb, but I'd say he lied about most of it. Ray was a dirty old man and I don't miss him one little bit. In fact, I think the earth is definitely a better place without him on it."

"Jeb, I don't mean to interrupt, but would it be ok if I asked a few questions?" Tommy asked.

"Of course, that's why I came to see you."

"Well, for one, did you know about any of this when it was going on?"

"No, I've known for years that Nel and her family were a bit on the shaky side, if you know what I mean. But I had no idea they were capable of such violent behavior. I just thought Nel was protecting Billy from what she considered to be a mean old world. Tommy, I really didn't know," Jeb said with heart.

"Ok, I have another question. Not including the strait in Turkey I've heard the name Dardanelle before today, but I can't figure out where or why I've heard it."

"Oh, I see. Well, I can explain that too. You've probably heard of the former world fencing champion, Dirksland Dardanelle."

"Yes, that's it. Is he connected in some way to all of this?" Tommy asked.

"Well, since he is Kaleb's father, I'd say he's very connected."

"Excuse me Jeb, but is Kaleb named after his father?" Tommy asked.

"Why yes, of course he is."

Tommy and I looked at each other. The reason for the 4114 had just become very clear. And I whispered to myself, "*Dirksland Kaleb Dardanelle*. Jeb, what happened to Kaleb's father?"

"I guess you don't remember, but he was sent to prison in Switzerland. He's probably at the heart of why all of this happened. I only know what I've been told, but I guess he was quite the womanizer. Well, one thing led to another and Nel's sister Adel had had enough. She attacked her husband late one night with one of his own swords, which he promptly took from her. A short fight ensued and he ended up killing her. It was tragic and devastating news for poor Nel. She and her sister were very close. Dirk, as they called him, was given a life sentence. I suppose he's still there."

"Good lord, no wonder Kaleb is so frightened of knives and so on," Tommy said.

"That's not the half of it. Kaleb was a bit on the slow side to begin with. And that was difficult for Dirk to live with. So naturally he wanted another son. You see the greater tragedy in all of this is that Nel's sister was with child when she was murdered. Poor Kaleb went into a tailspin after that day. He'd not only lost his mother and father but a younger brother too. That's when it was decided Kaleb would move to Mobile to live with his Uncle Ray, but soon after Kaleb arrived in Mobile, Ray lost his job."

"What job was that?" Tommy asked.

"Until he got caught stealing, Ray worked as a custodian for the Alabama State Police."

Tommy stared at me and I thought, *that explains the bullet-proof vest Billy was wearing.*

"Ray getting fired is the reason we bought that wicked broken-down property outside of Cromwell."

"Wait a minute, Jeb. Ray Haugen told us he brought back a German Lugar after the war. Did he serve in our military?" Tommy asked.

"No – never! Ray moved to Mobile before the war ended, not after. I believe he had to get out of Europe for fear of being hanged. I don't know this for certain, but I believe Ray may have been a Nazi sympathizer. So it's no wonder he brought back a German gun. I warned him several times about saying or doing anything negative towards this country. He always swore to me that he was pro-America in every regard. And because he never did anything to show me otherwise, I believed him."

I thought to myself, *Burt Silvers and his mother are Jewish. I wonder if...*

"Jeb, did Billy and Kaleb hang out or anything like that?" Tommy asked.

"No, Billy thought Kaleb was an idiot. That said, Billy did like going over to see his Uncle Ray from time to time. But that's been many years ago," Jeb softly said before he abruptly stopped.

He took his handkerchief out and pressed it to his right eye before he continued.

"That's one of the reasons I came here today. I wanted to explain some things about Billy. The poor kid never did have a chance. His mother and I were hoping for a healthy baby boy. But from the day he was born, it was one hill to climb after the other. His physical deformity was only the tip of the iceberg. His emotional frailties were much, much worse. And I might add, tougher to deal with."

Jeb stopped again and I thought maybe a little change in direction might help.

"Jeb, have you been to see Billy?" I asked.

He sobbed and wrenched his handkerchief.

"I was gonna go see him before he went to court this afternoon, but that won't be necessary now. The warden called me yesterday." Jeb swiped at a tear. "They found Billy hanging in his cell." Jeb said as he stared off into space.

"I'm so sorry Jeb. Was anyone else involved?" I asked.

"They don't believe there was any foul play, if that's what you're asking. From what they found, it appears Billy just couldn't put up with the demons in his head for even one more day."

366

"From what they found?" Tommy asked.

"Yes, Billy left a suicide note. Of course, I haven't read it yet, but it's there."

Jeb stopped talking and stared at the floor, but it was obvious that he had something else to say. Then he looked up at us.

"I just wanted you to know how sorry I am for all the trouble my family has caused you good people. I'm so sorry," Jeb said as he covered his face with his hands.

I looked at Tommy because I wanted to say or do something to ease the heartache poor Jeb was going through. Tommy shook his head no. Some wounds take longer to heal than others. And I guess some things are better left unsaid. So the three of us sat together, in silence.

When Jeb walked out of the station that day, a part of me went with him. I don't know if it was the angry part or the sad part, but I know he took it with him.

***Madison*/Jeb Thornton** had filled in many of the blanks for Tommy and Junior. And I guess that goes for the rest of us. But the fact remained that we still had no idea where this Benny character was. I believe Benny knew that if caught, he would be sent on the fast track to prison. So as most cowards do, he left poor Kaleb to fend for himself.

Kaleb recovered from his injuries in a hurry. He wasn't just big, he was also strong and healthy. Least that's what Doc Mayland said was the reason for his quick recovery. It took some doing, but we finally talked Kaleb into going down to Clarinda Cove. Actually, it was Tommy that explained to him that he had a choice to make. Go to Clarinda or the alternative. Kaleb was savvier than most people understood and decided he didn't want to go sit in a jail cell.

Once there, I tried every technique I knew of and a few that were foreign to me to get Kaleb to open up about his past. He was reticent to let me in and was even more guarded about the immediate future. He did not want to play along. This went on for a couple of weeks. So out of my own frustration I decided a shock to his system was in order. Enter Dad and Maggie.

I called Junior that night and he answered on the first ring.

"Hello Junior, it's me Madison."

"Geez, I hate when that happens."

"When what happens?"

"When I'm holding on to the phone and it rings. I was just going to call you. Madison, have you had any luck with Kaleb?"

"No, I haven't. And it's becoming very frustrating. Why do you ask?"

"I'm asking because that investigator from the state called today. He told Tommy that they can't wait any longer. I guess time has run out. He said come rain or shine, people from Oakdale are coming on Tuesday to pick up Kaleb. That gives you all of about four days. And, of course, you know Tommy is adamant in his belief that Kaleb is incapable of hurting a person or for that matter an animal. So I think you should just count on letting him go. Madison, what's the point in all this?"

"The point is I have an idea as to why Kaleb is who he is, but in order to find out, I have to jar something loose in his head. And that could be risky. I need you, Tommy, Dad, and Maggie to be here. Please Junior, I need all of you here tomorrow. Can you get down here before lunch?"

"I suppose so, but why before lunch? I mean, I don't work so great on an empty stomach."

"I want you here before lunch because Kaleb is easier to work with when he knows there could be a reward for his talking with me. And tomorrow I'm going to need every advantage I can get."

"Don't you mean we?" Junior asked.

"Well, no not exactly. You see, I want to stir up some good memories along with some bad ones. Maybe if Kaleb sees Tommy and you along with Maggie and Dad, it'll bring something out of him that he hasn't yet let go of. Junior, I know in my heart that I'm close to a breakthrough. I just need to somehow light a fuse."

"Oh that's great, Madison. You want to light a fuse in a guy that's as big as a house and probably nuts to boot."

"Junior, up to now he's been calm, maybe too calm. So to hasten a reaction, I've taken him off his meds, but he'll be restrained. Do you want to help Kaleb and me or not?"

"Yes, of course I do. Ok, we'll be there tomorrow before noon. Anything else?"

"No, just make sure all four of you are here. Thank, Junior. I'll see you tomorrow, bye."

I woke up the next day excited and hurried into work. I spent the morning making sure everything was in place. I wanted no mistakes. Although all of my previous meetings with Kaleb had been calm, I thought it best to be safe rather than sorry. So that morning I had two of our biggest and most physical orderlies transfer him to our session room. I asked the orderlies to stay there in the room. I was taking no chances. I brought a small tape recorder with me as usual. I hoped I'd get something on tape this time that would shed some light on my patient. I heard the back door to the session room open; then Kaleb came in the room - with an orderly on each arm. They pushed him through the room - Kaleb was smiling.

"Hi, Miss Madison. Can I go eat after we talk? I'm famished.

"Yes, of course you can. But Kaleb, I need you to be extra special honest with me today."

"Ok, I will, but no talking about my mommy or daddy. That makes me sad."

"No, we won't talk about them. Kaleb, what do you think about seeing the dog that bit you when you were swimming in the lake?"

"I like dogs. Can I pet the dog?" he asked.

"Well, I suppose that will be up to Maggie."

"Who is Maggie?" he asked.

"Maggie is the female dog I just told you about. Don't you remember seeing her when you went to Jack's house?"

"No, I don't remember her. I could ask Benny. Maybe he remembers her."

When Kaleb mentioned Benny, my heart skipped a beat. Benny was our proverbial key to the highway. I looked at the tape recorder to make sure it was on and working. It was rolling and I hoped that soon I would be too. Then I saw the blue light come on behind Kaleb. That light meant that Junior and the rest were in the observation room. I knew they were watching from behind the one-way mirror. I felt comfortable and a little empowered and decided to give it heck. I asked a question that Kaleb had ignored from day one.

"Kaleb, do you know where Benny is?"

"He's hiding, but I know he'll come back. He told me so last night."

My heart skipped another beat and a chill ran down my spine. We all know that Benny is a very dangerous man.

"Kaleb, you spoke to Benny last night?"

"Yes, he snuck in the same way he did at the hospital."

"How did he sneak into the hospital?"

"He dressed in his pajamas and slippers. Just like everyone else."

I was breaking ground that had up to now not even been raked.

"Oh, that is clever. Benny must be a very smart man."

"Yes, he's smarter than me, but sometimes I hate him. He tells me I'm stupid. I'm not stupid!" Kaleb said as the muscles in his neck jerked and corded up like new rope.

370

One of the orderlies immediately came over and stood next to Kaleb. Kaleb looked up at him, grit his teeth, and said, "Benny won't like you standing there like that. He will hurt you."

The orderly looked at me and, without saying a word, let me know he was more than a little concerned. I was going to tell Kaleb that everything was ok when Tommy walked into the session room. Kaleb's eyes lit up and he immediately forgot the orderly was there. Tommy told the orderly to move away and then he put his hand on Kaleb's shoulder.

"Hello, Kaleb."

"Hi Tommy. Oh, I'm so happy you came to see me. Can you sing me a song? Let's sing some songs."

"Yes, we'll sing some songs, but not right now. Kaleb, you can't be angry when you're talking with Miss Madison. Ok?"

"Ok Tommy, I'm sorry. Now can we sing?"

"Maybe in a little bit, but first I think Miss Madison has something she wants to ask you."

Tommy looked at me, but I'd forgotten what I was going to ask Kaleb.

"Kaleb, I think Madison wants to know if you'd like to pet Maggie. Would it be ok if I brought Maggie in to see you?" Tommy asked in his fatherly voice.

"Yes, I like dogs. I want to pet her, but I don't want Benny to find out. He doesn't like Maggie."

"Um, well, Benny won't know because we won't tell him," I said.

"No, Benny won't know," Tommy repeated.

"Well ok, but Benny is smart. What if he finds out?"

Tommy let go of Kaleb's shoulder and said, "Kaleb, I won't let Benny find out. Now are you going to behave and be nice to Maggie or not?"

"Yes Tommy, I will be nice. But I can't pet her with these on." He pointed at his restraints. "Tommy, please take them off of me. Please, I'll be good," Kaleb pleaded.

Tommy looked at me before he said, "Madison, if you want to continue, you're going to have to take the restraints off Kaleb. I'm here and of course so are your goons." Bluto and Brutus both stared at Tommy.

"Ok Harry, you can remove the restraints," I said to the nearest of the two orderlies.

"Dick, you should probably help him," Tommy said to the other orderly.

The orderly stared Tommy down before he moved to help his co-worker. The restraints were removed, and Kaleb stretched just like a little boy would right after getting out of bed in the morning.

"Thank you Tommy, now can we sing?" Kaleb asked.

"We can sing after you are nice and pet the dog," Tommy said.

"Ok Tommy, I'll be nice," was all Kaleb said.

"Wait here Kaleb. I'll be right back with the dog," Tommy said as he walked out of the room.

Kaleb and I waited for a minute or so before Dad slowly walked Maggie in the room. Maggie had a low rumble in her throat and I expected her to charge, but Dad held tight to her harness. Kaleb smiled and reached out to Maggie. And Maggie walked straight to him.

"Hi nice doggy, you sure are pretty," Kaleb said as he stroked the top of Maggie's head.

"As I said before, that is not the voice of the man that attacked me. Madison, we have the wrong person," Dad said in a desperate tone.

The sound of dad's voice did not deter Kaleb one little bit as he knelt down in front of Maggie. She licked his face and he laughed in approval. "I always wanted a dog, but Benny and Uncle Ray told me I wasn't responsible enough to have a pet. I can be responsible. It's not fair. I want a dog like Maggie to take care of. Tommy, I would be very nice. Can I have a dog? Please," Kaleb asked in the manner of a child.

"Kaleb, is Benny always mean to you?" I asked.

"No, just sometimes," Kaleb said as he continued to pet Maggie.

"Why is Benny mean to you?" I asked.

"He's mean because I'm so big and he's so little. And I have friends and he doesn't," Kaleb said as he continued to pet Maggie.

"Why doesn't Benny have any friends?" I asked.

"Benny says I'm the reason he doesn't have any friends. But that's not true."

"Kaleb, where is Benny right now?"

"He's close by, but he's too smart to ever let you catch him. Benny will sneak in again, you'll see. He gets mad at me when I talk too much." Kaleb abruptly stopped petting Maggie. "Miss Madison, I'm famished. I want to go eat now! Remember, you promised me. Benny says it's not nice to break a promise."

"Yes, Benny is right. And I did promise you we'd eat if you were honest with me. And I think you have been very honest. Kaleb, can we talk about Benny again?" I asked.

"Maybe, but first I have to eat. When Benny comes back tonight, I'll ask him. But he was awfully mad at you when we went to your house. He said we should get rid of you. I'm glad we didn't get rid of you, Miss Madison. I like you and I like the dog too. Oh, and I can't forget Tommy. He's my friend. Is Tommy going to eat lunch with me?" Kaleb asked.

"I think he will, yes, I think he will. Kaleb, I'm going to take the dog back outside and then I'll talk to Tommy about staying for lunch. Would you like that?" I asked.

"Yes, yes I'd like that a lot," he said.

"Ok, promise me you'll sit and behave yourself," I said in an assertive tone.

"Yes, I promise. Bye doggy, maybe you can come back again," Kaleb said.

Dad, Maggie, and I walked out of the session room. Then we went the short distance to the observation room and the moment we walked in Junior said, "Boy Madison, it was beginning to get kinda spooky in there. I think we'd better be ready tonight. If Benny shows up, we'll grab him for sure."

"Junior, Benny has avoided us from the very beginning. We can wait here all night, but I doubt he'll show up," Tommy said.

"Tommy is right. Benny is definitely not going to come here tonight," Madison said with confidence.

"Madison, why are you so sure Benny won't come here tonight?" I asked.

The moment I finished my question, a high-pitched voice rang out from inside the session room.

"Kaleb, you're so stupid! I told you a thousand times she was going to lie to you. Now look at what you've done. They'll find me for sure, and it's all your fault!"

Dad immediately yelled, "Its Benny, he's here. Junior, go get that son of a bitch!"

Dad's yelling made Maggie bark and then Junior yelled, "How'd Benny get in there?"

The yelling stopped and for a moment all was quiet as Junior, Tommy, and I stared into the session room. The back door to the session room was wide open and Kaleb was gone. In his place was a repulsive little man bent over with his hands on his knees. His eyes raged with the faraway countenance of a beast. And in a barmy high-pitched voice he screamed across the room. "Knife! knife! he has a knife!"

We all turned and looked at the orderly named Harry. He was standing there with this thunderstruck look on his face. He had been cleaning his fingernails with a small file. Benny ran and knocked Harry down with one great blow to the head. Benny knelt down and raised both fists to finish the job when Tommy yelled, "Stop! Benny! Stop!

Benny hesitated and snarled up at Tommy before he turned back to the orderly and once again raised his fists. Tommy ran and tackled Benny and pulled him away from Harry. Tommy roared, "Stop! You hear me? Stop!"

Tommy held tight to Benny's arms but was thrown about like a small boat on a violent sea. Tommy would not, did not, let go. And as the struggle raged, Benny twisted, jerked, and spun across the floor like a gator in a death roll.

Tommy held tight, but he was clearly losing the battle. Junior leaped into the fray. He wrapped his arms and legs around Benny's legs. Junior looked exactly like children do when they hold tight to their father's leg and go for a ride. I was spellbound as I stood watching.

Junior held firm and rigid as Tommy slid behind Benny and slipped his left arm under Benny's left arm. Then Tommy followed with his right arm and locked his hands in a full-nelson tight over the back of Benny's neck. Firmly tethered by Tommy and Junior, Benny violently wriggled and quaked in a last-ditch effort to free himself, but to no avail. Now still and in a near catatonic state, Benny's eyes seemed to be transfixed on a memory deep inside his past. He was staring at a distant thought, far, far away. Not a word was spoken as I quietly knelt down and reached out to stroke Benny's furrowed brow. Without warning, he lurched and nipped at my hand. I quickly pulled back. I waited a moment and then once again reached out. This time Benny allowed me to trespass, if you will.

And as the guys held firm and I stroked his brow, Benny slowly morphed back to the innocent man-child we had come to know. I nodded to Tommy.

"It's ok, it's all over now. Kaleb, Kaleb! Junior and I are going to let you up. Will you behave if we let go of you?" Tommy softly asked.

"Yes Tommy, I'll behave."

Tommy nodded to Junior and he let go of Kaleb. Tommy slowly removed one arm then the other before he stood up.

"Ok Kaleb, you can go sit down now."

Tommy followed Kaleb as he cowered back to the chair he'd been sitting on. Then we all turned and watched the other orderly help Harry get to his feet. Tommy gently put his hand on Kaleb's shoulder before he said, "It's all over now. Benny can't hurt you or anyone else while I'm here."

"Thank you, Tommy. You saved me. Benny was going to do something wicked again. And then I would have to live in a jail."

Junior and I slowly walked out of the session room and back to Dad. Maggie barked and Dad screamed, "Did you get Benny?"

"Yes Dad, we got Benny. Everything's ok. But I think Madison should be the one to explain what happened. Dad, hang on for a minute," Junior said as he turned to me.

"Madison, is that why you said Benny wasn't coming here tonight?"

"Yes, Junior. I didn't know for sure, but I had a strong suspicion that Benny only existed in Kaleb's mind. Dad, Kaleb is Benny and I suppose I should say vice versa. Sadly, there can be no doubt now that Kaleb and Benny were when you were attacked."

"Kaleb and Benny are one in the same," Dad exclaimed in utter disbelief. "Good gracious, try to imagine the torment that poor soul has been through. Poor Kaleb."

"Madison, what now?" Junior asked.

"Well, up to now Benny has probably been doing most of the thinking and talking for the two of them. And Kaleb has been on an E ticket ride from hell. What now you ask? I don't know. I just don't know."

*Junior/***Tommy stayed and ate lunch with Kaleb** that day. He knew full-well that Kaleb was probably going to spend the rest of his life in a place where loneliness and confusion would eventually destroy most of the good that existed in his heart. Dad, Maggie, and I headed for home. And along the way, Dad made a very strange request.

"Junior, can you stop by Merle Haugen's home?"

"I suppose so, but why?"

"I want you to go in and look for something. I think Maggie will be able to help you."

"What? Dad, this is very strange. Where do you want me to look? I mean, we've been all through the house and the barn. There's nothing there that we haven't already found."

"I want you to look in the house, and in particular, Mr. Haugen's bedroom."

What do you want me to look for?"

"A pair of leather gloves," was all he said.

I stopped the patrol car in front of the house. There was already a 'for sale' sign up. I guess Jeb had decided to get rid of the place and all the bad memories that came with it.

Fortunately, Jeb had not changed the locks. In fact, the place wasn't locked up at all. Maggie and I walked in and with every step I took, the echo of footsteps followed me. I did as Dad asked and went in Ray Haugen's bedroom and began searching. I looked under the bed and mattress, nothing. I went through his old chest of drawers, nothing there of any consequence. I spent a lot of energy going through the closet, still nothing. I think I'd given up the search when I eased over and gazed out the window at Marjorie's house. I was tugged out of a trance when I heard Maggie scratching on the floorboards inside the closet. I knelt next to her to have a look-see. "What is it, girl?"

I took out my pocket knife and pried up one of the boards. There beneath the floor was a coffee can full of U. S. and German paper money and coins. There weren't a lot coins but enough to make the can a bit on the heavy side. There was also an old dome top tin lunch box. I opened it hoping to find a pair of gloves inside but no such luck. It was chock-full of aged family photos.

I was glancing through the photos when Maggie barked in my face. I set the lunch box down.

"What is it girl?" I asked, knowing full well that she couldn't answer me.

I was wrong. She answered by sticking her nose in the empty space and pulling out an old, roughly treated leather glove. I got down and reached in as far as I could and grabbed the other one. I wondered what a pair of old gloves could have to do with any of this. Maggie did not stop barking as we walked back out to the car.

"Dad, I found the gloves. What do you want me to do with them?" I asked.

"Hand them to me is what I want you to do with them."

Dad pressed the gloves against his face and neck. Then he put the gloves to his nose and immediately pushed them away.

"Maggie, come here girl," Dad said.

Maggie walked over and stuck her head inside the car. Dad put the gloves to her nose and she answered him with a loud bark.

"Here Junior, you can have the gloves. I don't need them anymore."

"Dad, are you going to tell me why the gloves are so important or not?"

"Junior, put the gloves up to your nose and take a whiff," was all he said.

I did and they had a faint smell to them that I could not identify.

"Dad, what is that smell?"

"It's hamburger. And the man that tried to poison Maggie and then dragged me across my front room was wearing those gloves, which by the way, can mean only one thing. It wasn't Kaleb that came into my home with evil intentions. It was his Uncle Ray Haugen."

"Yes, I suppose so. But we now know that Kaleb, or I should say Benny, was there too."

"Yes, but I believe Ray Haugen knew that Kaleb was not capable of initiating something so evil. He also knew that Benny was."

"Dad, I think you're right, but, the fact is, we'll probably never know the whole truth."

"Yes, and maybe that's the way it should remain. Junior, can you hand me the gloves again?" I did, and Dad threw them on the ground and said, "Let's go home."

I went back in the house and grabbed the coffee can and lunch box and put them in the trunk of the car. Then we drove back to Dad's house. I went straight in the kitchen, picked up the phone, and dialed. After ringing and ringing, Jeb Thornton finally answered.

"Hello."

"Hello Jeb, it's Junior. How you doin'?"

"Hello, Junior. I suppose I've been better, but thanks for asking. What can I do for you?"

"Well, I was wondering if you might know what Kaleb's brother's name was. Or, I guess I should say, what was his name going to be?"

"No, I don't know, Junior. But if you'll give me a minute or two I might be able to find out. I have some pictures and family keepsakes that Nel put in a photo album. Hang on."

Jeb was away from the phone when Dad asked me what I was doing.

"I'm talking with Jeb Thornton. There's something I just have to know."

"Oh," was all Dad said.

Jeb came back on the line.

"Junior, you still there?"

"Yes, I'm here."

Jeb went into a long story about photos of the grave site where Nel's sister was buried. After he was finished with the story, I told him about the coffee can and lunch box. He said he didn't want 'em. When I hung up the phone, Dad asked if I'd found out what I'd wanted to know.

"Yes Dad, I did. Kaleb's younger brother was going to be named Benjamin."

"Oh my," Dad quietly said as I watched grief grab him by the bootstraps. "Now what?" he muttered.

"Now I think I should call Madison and let her know. Dad, please don't cry."

I was too late. Dad's body shook with a pain that no one could ever really understand. And this time the cry was real and so were the tears. I guess knowing the truth about Mom and then finding out about Kaleb and the gloves was just too much for him.

378

I was fighting back my own tears and holding on to the phone when it rang. I thought, *I really don't feel like talking right now.*

"Hello."

"Hello Junior, this is Jenny."

"Jenny, oh it's so good to hear your voice." I made sure to say Jenny loud enough to get Dad's attention. "How have you been?"

"I'm fine, thanks. Listen, I know you've had a lot to deal with lately, but there's something I was hoping you could do for me."

"Yes, anything, what can I do for you?"

"Well, my friends, Traci and Uncle Tommy, were just by the train station and they told me there's a young Asian lady sitting there all alone and crying. If it's not too much trouble, I was hoping that maybe you could go help her."

"Um, well, I suppose so. But you see, my dad is here and he's not doing so great. I hate to leave him here alone right now."

"Junior, may I please speak with your dad."

I turned to tell Dad Jenny was on the phone. He was standing right next to me.

"I don't know where it is you're supposed to go, Junior, but go."

I handed Dad the phone and as he said hello, a great big smile spread across his face. And then he waved me away. I thought to myself, *what a turnaround.*

"Dad, I'm taking Maggie for a ride. I'll see ya later."

He didn't hear a word I said. So Maggie and I jumped in the car and headed uptown to the train station. I walked in with Maggie and there all alone in the corner sat a young Asian lady. I walked up and when she looked at me, I just couldn't help but saying, *oh my, she's pretty.* Of course, I was talking to myself.

"Hello ma'am, my name is Junior. Is there something I can help you with?"

She looked at me and started to say something but stopped. I stood not knowing what to do next when Maggie sidled up and nudged the young lady with her nose. She had no choice but to pet Maggie.

Then I think she said, "Nice dog."

I couldn't be sure what she'd said because her English was difficult to understand. The lightbulb finally turned on in my head. I understood why she didn't want to talk. She wasn't comfortable speaking English.

"Listen, I'm here to help you. Do you understand me?"

She nodded her head yes a couple of times and I sighed a little in relief.

"Oh good. Ok, were you supposed to meet someone here today?"

She nodded her head yes again and then reached in a large carry bag that was sitting next to her. She fumbled around a little bit and then handed me a folded piece of paper. I unfolded the paper and read to myself the name of the person she was supposed to meet. I tried not to frown. She saw right thru me and began to sob.

"Ma'am, I don't know how to tell you this, but Billy Thornton will not be able to meet you here today or, for that matter, any day. I'm very sorry."

She sobbed even harder.

"Ma'am, please don't cry. I've already had a lot of tears thrown at me today and..."

She looked up at me with a confused look on her face and stopped crying.

"Are you hungry?" was all I could think to say.

And in a very clear voice she said, "Yes."

I carried her little suitcase and she picked up her great big bag. When we got outside, she saw the police cruiser and glanced up at me. I think she was thinking about running away.

"Ma'am, please don't be afraid. We are not going to the police station."

She had this look on her face that asked the question, *why are you talking like that*. And I realized that I was talking very slow and saying each word as though she was from outer space.

"I'm sorry. I guess you understand English just fine."

"She smiled and said, "Yes, I do. Thank you for be nice."

"Um, you're welcome."

We got her situated in the car and then I made a critical mistake. I took her to the diner. It was past supper time so there were only a couple of people still eating. That part was just fine. The problem was Mary was still there.

The moment she walked up, I realized my mistake. *Mary's hair was the color of a chalkboard.*

"Hello Junior, is this your girlfriend?"

"Mary, I just met her. So don't start."

"Yeah right, you just happened to pick up a pretty Asian girl wandering down the street."

"Yes, something like that. And she's not a girl - she's a lady."

"That may be true Junior, but I still think you're a horny little you know what."

"Mary, if you don't stop, we're going to leave. And when we do I'm going to call Ricky and tell him to come down here and do something you won't like."

"Ok, truce for now. What would you like to eat?"

I ordered a hamburger and fries for each of us. And from the way she dug in and attacked the hamburger, I realized a couple of things. One, she'd eaten a hamburger before. And two, she was very hungry. While we were eating, I thought of something that made me so embarrassed I couldn't stand it. I had not even asked what her name was.

"Do you like the food?"

She smiled and said, "I like."

"Oh, that's good. Listen, I'm very sorry, but I didn't ask you what your name was?"

She laughed and said, "Name was? No name still is."

Then she said something in her native language that I knew I would never be able to repeat.

She smiled again and said, "It ok, many American not able to say name. It mean flower, but ok to call me Lily."

"Lily?"

She smiled again and nodded yes.

"Oh, I like that. Ok, Lily it is."

She smiled again. In fact, she never stopped smiling all the way to my apartment. I had no idea what to do with her. Or I guess I should say where to take her. She seemed very happy. Once inside the apartment, I told her she could sleep in my bed and I would sleep on the divan. I got her settled in and then told her I had to take Maggie home, but I would be right back. She smiled and said, "Ok, I here when come back."

I drove Maggie over to Dad's and we both smiled the entire way. I think Maggie knew I was happy. When we went in the house, Dad was sleeping in his chair. The radio was on and he had a smile on his face. He must have enjoyed talking to Jenny. I made sure Maggie had plenty of food and water and I left her sleeping next to Dad. I drove home hoping to find out a little more about my unexpected guest.

When I walked in the apartment, it was dark and very quiet. I just knew Lily had changed her mind or she'd become frightened and took off.

I was so relieved and happy when I looked in my bedroom. Lily was there in my bed. The covers were pulled up to her chin and she was fast asleep. I think she might have been smiling. I know I was.

I didn't have one mean dream that night. In fact, I had several very nice dreams. And right in the middle of the best dream of all, I heard a teapot whistle. I opened one eye and looked across my front room. Lily was sitting in my kitchen with a coffee cup in her hand and one sitting next to her on the table. She smiled and said, "Good morning, Junior. I make for you."

"Good morning, Lily. Excuse me," was all I said.

She giggled as I stood up in my underwear. I grabbed my pants and headed for the bathroom. I washed up, got dressed, and walked out to my little kitchen table and picked up a toasty warm cup of Postum. I hate Postum.

"Thank you. This is very nice," I lied.

When I sat down, I couldn't help but notice how her jet-black hair glistened in the morning light. And as I stared I thought to myself, *you don't even know what language she speaks or where she's from. How are you gonna find out?* Then I had a great idea pop into my head.

"Lily, what city are you from?"

"Cu Chi," was all she said.

"Oh, that's nice," I said as the anxiety grew.

I still had no idea where she was from. I thought to myself, *Billy told me and I wrote it down, but the notebook is of no use now.* She could see my confusion and gave me a break. And with a perceptive grin on her face she said, "My home close to Saigon."

"Oh yes, South Vietnam," I said in relief.

She smiled and nodded her head yes. I was just going to ask her if she was hungry when the phone rang. I picked up the phone.

"Hello."

"Good morning, you Casanova you."

"Ricky, is that you?"

"Yeah, I heard all about the little lady you picked up last night. Bring her down to the diner. We're all waiting to meet her."

"What do you mean by all?"

"Well, I think Mary told the whole town. Randi, Madison, Tommy, Ajax. Oh yeah, your dad and Maggie are here too."

"How'd my dad and Maggie get there?"

"Randi and I went and picked 'em up."

"Ricky, can you hang on a minute."

"Sure thing, pardner."

"Lily, would you like to go have breakfast at the diner?"

She nodded her head yes.

"All right Ricky, we'll be there in a little bit. Ok, yeah, bye."

I put the phone down and turned to Lily. I thought I should warn her about the crowd.

"Lily, I hope you don't mind, but the diner is going to be very crowded when we get there. You see, everybody wants to meet you. Ricky, I mean my friend, told me that the whole town is there waiting for us."

Lily gave me a puzzled look.

"Whole town?"

"Yes, maybe," I said.

"Is possible?" she asked.

"Well, I guess you could say it's possible, that is, in a manner of speaking." I said as we headed out the door.

As we walked out into the morning sun, I did my best to explain.

"Lily, because our town is so small, news travels very fast. Crestfield is a small town. Matter of fact, it has always been a small town. And I suppose it always will be. And that's just the way I like it."

Epilogue

***Junior*/You may have noticed** Randi and Ricky didn't get married in the spring. They decided things were just fine the way they were. And I believe they were both a little afraid of losing their independence. Summer came gleaming in on the twenty-first of June. It was a gorgeous sunny day. And with the temperature hovering in the eighties, the pool out at the park was full of screaming, happy children. I think everyone in Crestfield was pleased summer had finally arrived.

The entire family was at the train station to greet Buck and Dezi when they rolled in a few days before the 4th of July. When the train finally came to a stop, we gave them a small-town cheer. Buck had on his full-dress uniform. And before he stepped down from the train, he feigned a salute and then gave everyone a joyous wave. Dezi giggled and waved hello as she jumped off the train. She was wearing purple bell-bottoms, Jesus sandals, and a tie-dyed halter top. Her hair was up and she had a bright yellow flower neatly placed behind her left ear. She squealed with joy as Dad hugged the two of them. I think Dad was a little extra special excited to have his family all together again.

We didn't tell Dad about the peace sign Dezi had tattooed on her right wrist. Or for that matter, the tattoo of the 'keep on truckin' dude' she had on her left ankle. Dad says tattoos are for drunken sailors and convicts.

Madison played the dramatic recording of Kaleb to so many professionals so many times she got to the point where she wished she hadn't recorded at all. Eventually, she made it clear that the tape was off limits. And after working tirelessly for weeks on end, she pieced together a stunning examination on the dysfunctional psyche of the Haugen and Thornton families. A condensed version of her work was scheduled to be in the October issue of the new magazine, *Psychology Today*.

Near the end of July, Tommy told little Jax he was taking a vacation. He packed up his guitar and drove over to Oakdale to visit Kaleb. He told me that he planned on making the journey several times each year. Lily and I made a trip down to Maryville in August, and she enrolled in the little college there for the fall semester. She'd tested so high in math and science that I, for one, was simply amazed.

Crestfield

Lily was to major in Biology and she was thrilled beyond words at the opportunity this country was giving her. The idea of Lily going away to college was tough for me to handle. You see, I had fallen head over heels in love. And I think Lily had done the same. But for the time being, Crestfield would be our home. And that was ok by me.

www.ingramcontent.com/pod-product-compliance
Lightning Source LLC
Chambersburg PA
CBHW020322180626
46812CB00001B/11